Also by Jonathan Miles

Want Not
Dear American Airlines

Anatomy
of a
Miracle

The True* Story of a Paralyzed Veteran, a Mississippi
Convenience Store, a Vatican Investigation, and the
Spectacular Perils of Grace

*a novel

Jonathan Miles

Hogarth
London / New York

Copyright © 2018 by Jonathan Miles
Reading Group Guide copyright © 2019 by Penguin Random House LLC

All rights reserved.
Published in the United States by Hogarth, an imprint of the Crown Publishing
Group, a division of Penguin Random House LLC, New York.
crownpublishing.com

HOGARTH is a trademark of the Random House Group Limited, and
the H colophon is a trademark of Penguin Random House LLC.

EXTRA LIBRIS and colophon are trademarks of Penguin Random House LLC.

Originally published in hardcover in the United States
by Hogarth, an imprint of the Crown Publishing Group,
a division of Penguin Random House LLC, New York, in 2018.

"How I Got This Story" by Jonathan Miles first published on Powells.com
on March 21, 2018. http://www.powells.com/post/original-essays/how-i-got-this-story

Library of Congress Cataloging-in-Publication Data is available upon request.

ISBN 978-0-553-44760-6
Ebook ISBN 978-0-553-44759-0

Printed in the United States of America

Book design by Lauren Dong
Cover design by Darren Haggar
Cover photograph by Steven Mullen

10 9 8 7 6 5 4 3 2 1

First Paperback Edition

this is for

JOHN H. TIDYMAN

who made smoking Camel straights while

cursing at a typewriter look like fun, even if it isn't

(sometimes it is)

and also for

MARK RICHARD

the good Reverend Blotoad

A Note on Methodology

ALL THE SCENES AND DIALOGUE contained herein were reconstructed from the recollections of participants and observers and further supported, whenever possible, by audio recordings, video footage, diaries, notes, court transcripts, and other corroborating materials. In scattered instances where there remains a dispute in recollection, this discrepancy is parenthetically noted.

One who believes all these tales is a fool;

but one who denies them is a heretic.

HASIDIC SAYING
CREDITED TO RAV SHLOMO OF RADOMSK

what happened

*and his flesh came again, like unto the flesh
of a child, and he was clean*

one

O N THE AFTERNOON OF AUGUST 23, 2014, TANYA HARRIS
wheeled her younger brother, Cameron, to the Biz-E-Bee store on
the corner of Reconfort Avenue and Division Street in Biloxi, Mississippi.
Nothing about the afternoon or about Cameron or about Tanya herself
suggested this would be her final time doing so; she was merely out of
cigarettes, and her brother, slack-faced and sulky on a day that felt lethally
humid, short on beer.

Tanya Harris is a squat, wide-hipped woman of twenty-nine whose
gently popped eyes lend her face an expression of perpetual surprise or
amazement, and whose flat-footed manner of walking appears consciously
orchestrated, as though she's never outgrown the fear of stepping on a
crack thereby breaking her mother's back. She'd recently dip-dyed one
side of her hair, which is naturally a dingy shade of blond faintly slashed
with premature gray, and on this afternoon streaks of a vividly chemical
pink spilled down one side of a white T-shirt on which was printed HAP-
PAY HAP-PAY HAP-PAY. Some of her many tattoos were already ridging
from the heat, their edges swelling as though the ink was approaching a
simmer. Pushing her brother's wheelchair down the center of Reconfort
Avenue, to avoid the uneven jags of the sidewalk and the mini-dunes of
sand swept there, she maintained the freewheeling stream of humming,
commentary, rhetorical questioning, and singing that is her hallmark to
family and friends. ("She does *not* shut up," grumbles her brother, with
acerbic affection. "Not ever.") The chorus to Jay Z's song "99 Problems"
came flitting between observations about the "swampy-ass" August heat
and her sharp denunciation of a neighbor whose neglected laundry,

drooping on a mildewed clothesline, had already weathered, by Tanya's reckoning, its third rainstorm. "Gonna need to re-wash every one of those shirts," she muttered, over the *fwap fwap fwap* of her flip-flops spanking the asphalt. The sight of a chow mix, chained to a ginkgo tree in another neighbor's front yard, elicited the same cluck of pity it had been eliciting from her for almost a decade.

Her brother, Cameron, wasn't listening; or, if he was, he doesn't remember it. As he explains: "She repeats things two or three times if you're supposed to answer." But Cameron was also, by his own admission, "a little out of it." He'd popped his first can of Bud Light at noon, to wash down the Klonopin and Concerta he was taking for anxiety and memory loss, and he'd followed that beer with three, maybe five more. "Thermal angel blood," he calls it, a reference to a blood and intravenous fluid warmer he'd seen medics use during his combat tour in Afghanistan.

Afghanistan was the last place Cameron ever walked—more precisely, on a ridge outside the mountain village of Sar-Dasair, in the Darah Khujz District of Zabul Province, where, in the early hours of March 22, 2010, Private First Class Harris and a fellow soldier wandered off-course during a foot patrol. Cameron was roughly twelve yards away when the soldier, a staff sergeant, stepped on a PMN-2 land mine—a buried remnant from the former Soviet occupation. The explosion sheared off the staff sergeant's legs, genitals, and right forearm and blasted seventy-nine pieces of shrapnel, along with bone shards from the sergeant's legs, into Cameron's body. One or more of those fragments severed the nerves of his lower vertebrae, instantly paralyzing him below the waist. Two doctors at the Landstuhl Regional Medical Center in Germany divulged the permanence of his condition to him on the evening of his twenty-second birthday, bookending the news with brief and awkward apologies for the poor timing.

Cameron's most prominent physical feature, paralysis aside, might be the long alabaster scar that runs down the side of his face, from just below his left temple almost to his jawline. It's a squiggly, sinuous scar, evoking a river's course on a map, but it's not, as one might reasonably presume, collateral residuum from Afghanistan. The scar dates to his early childhood, when he slipped while running on a slick fishing pier and snagged his face on a nail. The scar only adds to the rugged, almost harsh cast of his face, which is further amplified by his high cliffside cheekbones, sharp-cornered jaw, the military-specs trim of his blond hair, and an angry vein in his neck that pulses and squirms from even the mildest aggravation. His eyes, however, cast a different spell: They're wide and large like his sister's, with a peculiar boyishness to them, as though his eyes retired their development at puberty while the rest of his features forged ahead. They impart a dissonance to his expressions that can sometimes be jarring; his temper, when it flares, can seem both fearsome and puerile. Most of all, however, those eyes highlight the gross tragedy of what happened to him in Afghanistan—that he had yet to fully graduate from boyhood when he was struck down in the Darah Khujz.

On this particular August afternoon, Cameron was dressed in his usual way: a T-shirt, this one advertising the Mississippi Deep Sea Fishing Rodeo, atop a pair of baggy black knee-length nylon shorts, and on his sockless feet a pair of red Nike tennis shoes that he sometimes called his "front bumpers." The home that he and Tanya share is a narrow, half-century-old shotgun-style house that wasn't designed with a wheelchair in mind, and, without shoes, his insensate feet often bore bruises from colliding with sheetrock and doorframes.

Their hometown of Biloxi occupies a skinny, six-mile-long peninsula that juts eastward into the Gulf. For most of its history Biloxi was a fishing village, with canneries lining the water and shrimp boats and oyster luggers docked in its harbor. Immigrants drawn by jobs in this seafood industry—Slavs and Italians especially—lent the city an idiosyncratic seasoning, tilting its spirit more toward south Louisiana than to the rest of Mississippi lying north of the salt line. "Most were Catholic," as the former Biloxian Jack Nelson explained in *Scoop: The Evolution of a Southern Reporter*, "and they brought with them a more relaxed attitude toward drinking, sex, gambling, and other human frailties." In the 1950s, when the state dumped leftover dredging sand on the coastline to create an artificial beach, Biloxi began advertising itself as "the Poor Man's Riviera," a Deep South analog to Coney Island. Elvis Presley vacationed here. Jayne Mansfield had just left a Biloxi supper club, in 1967, when she died in a car wreck on U.S. 90. Casinos arrived in the 1990s, adding another layer of sheen, and yet, for all its synthetic, tropical-print ease and its tolerance for frailties, Biloxi has never comported itself like a resort town. It bears no illusions of itself as a paradise. It doesn't mind the smell of fish guts. Its hands are cracked and calloused and it sweats a lot.

The Harris house, near the end of Reconfort Avenue, where the street dead-ends at the CSX railroad tracks, is the only house Cameron and his sister have ever known. Their parents bought it in 1985, just after Tanya was born. After their father left for an oilfield job in Texas when Cameron was three, and failed to return, the children remained in the house with their mother. They remained in it, too, after their mother was killed in a car accident on I-10 when Cameron was sixteen. And they remained in it as well—if more accurately beside it for a time, during the year they spent living in a FEMA trailer—after the storm surge from Hurricane Katrina devastated their East Biloxi neighborhood, their house included, just fourteen months after their mother's death. "The back bay kinda swallowed up the whole street, and flooded us up to the ceiling pretty much," Tanya explains, with a detachment that seems oddly clinical until you consider that Katrina, following so closely their mother's death, was, for them, less disaster than aftershock, loss tailing loss.

The hurricane also explains why the house—which a group of volunteers from an Indiana church, with Cameron's help, put back together—is so starkly devoid of family history. The living room, once a shrine to their mother's porcelain collectibles, contained on this day a black vinyl couch, purchased at a Rent-A-Center closeout; a television propped on cinder blocks; a blue plastic coffee table upon which an Xbox video game console sat nestled amid its black burrow of cords; and nothing else. The walls, like those of every other room in the house, were unadorned and painted the blunt white shade of mold-resistant primer. The only photographs of Cameron and Tanya on display were the sole images, predating Katrina, that they know to exist: a half-dozen snapshots, taped to the refrigerator door, that came in the mail from an aunt in Alabama whom the Harrises visited twice as children. Every one of them is a group shot, with Cameron and Tanya posed beside cousins whose names they don't remember. "That's all we got," Tanya says, pressing a fingertip to one of the photos— the only image of their mother they possess—as if to sponge a nano-droplet more memory from it. She hums, grunts, smiles. "Poor Cameron's gotta take my word for it that he was such an ugly little kid."

The outside shows minor neglect—curls of peeling paint, a cracked windowpane, knee-high weeds poking through the concrete—but no more than some of the other surviving houses on the street. At least half didn't survive the storm surge: Nine years later, Reconfort Avenue remains pocked with empty lots. Forgotten-looking FOR SALE signs stand wiltingly in a few of these sand-and-scrub parcels, occasionally joined by newer-looking signs advertising, in English and Vietnamese, legal counsel for OIL SPILL CLAIMS resulting from the Deepwater Horizon disaster in the spring of 2010. The effects of that spill greeted Cameron's return home from Brooke Army Medical Center in Texas, adding insult to very literal injury—or loss tailing loss tailing loss tailing loss, an interminable freight train of misfortune. "I remember Tanya bringing home a sack of oysters, for this 'Welcome Home' deal she did for me, and saying, 'Well, Tippo says these might be the last Gulf oysters we eat in our lifetimes,'" Cameron recalls. "And I'm thinking, well, *shit*. A lotta fucked-up shit's happened to me, right? I mean, I could go down the list, you know. But no more oysters? Goddamn, man. I was just like: Maybe life's *really* over now." It's unclear how earnest he is when he credits the oysters' comeback for his endurance of a six-month murk of depression, though oysters—invariably cornmealed, fried, and slathered with ketchup—do comprise a notable share of his diet.

Of the street's pre-Katrina residents, only two other households remain. One is a large Vietnamese fishing family known to Cameron and Tanya as "the Ducks" (a mangling of their surname), who keep sharply to themselves. The other is Mrs. Dooley.

Eulalie Dooley is a ninety-one-year-old African-American woman who's lived on the corner of Reconfort and Division, directly across from the Biz-E-Bee, since 1965, when her late husband, Bobby, took a job with a local seafood processor. While working as a housekeeper and later as a home-health aide, she raised four children in that house, and later three grandchildren as well. She was the only resident of Reconfort Avenue who refused to evacuate for Katrina, which she survived—just barely, and, when one considers her age and frailty, rather magnificently—by climbing into her floating refrigerator. As the water rose, she punched out ceiling tiles using the sponge mop with which she'd armed herself for the storm. (The only chore Hurricane Camille had required of her, in 1969, was swabbing the floors; she'd expected similarly light duty for Katrina.) That feat of survival, reported on CNN, drew the Indiana church group to her home. A surplus of its volunteers moved down the block until they found the Harris house, teeter-tottering amid a sunbaked slosh of debris and yellowy mud, which they set upon with reciprocating saws and hammers and Midwestern Methodist cheer.

To longtime residents of Reconfort Avenue, Mrs. Dooley has always been known, fondly, as "Neighborhood Watch." This is owing to her omnipresent vigils on her compact front porch, which, by her request, was the first thing the church volunteers rebuilt on her house. It's not uncommon to see Mrs. Dooley on her porch at sunrise, quilting or crocheting while rocking in a chair that a charitable CNN viewer shipped to her "all the way from Florida," nor is it unusual to see her there after dark, beneath the bluesy glow of a bug zapper, needles still flashing in her ever-kinetic hands. Despite the intricate demands of her stitch work, every passing car, whether familiar or not, is accorded a generous salute, her left arm fully raised, her arthritic wrist avidly swishing. As Cameron says: "It's like our street's got its own Walmart greeter."

To him and Tanya, making their daily and sometimes twice- or thrice-daily walks to the Biz-E-Bee, Mrs. Dooley tended to offer more than a wave. "How y'all babies doing?" she'd call out, leaning forward in her chair, or, "What you babies out shopping for today?" From Cameron in his wheelchair she'd usually get a wan thumbs-up, or a meek and uncomfortable-looking shrug. He's never quite outgrown his fear of Mrs. Dooley, dating back to when she caught him, at the age of ten, setting off fireworks beneath cars, after which she ordered him onto her porch and slapped him three times hard on his backside then told him to head straight home and have his mama slap him there another three times. For years thereafter, up until Cameron's mother died, instead of waving Mrs. Dooley would point a stern and crooked finger at Cameron as he'd pass by on foot or on his bicycle, denoting her surveillance. "That boy was never really *trouble*," she says of the young Cameron. "More like he was always *almost* trouble."

From Tanya, on the other hand, Mrs. Dooley's greetings yielded reams of small talk, the kind of blithe sentiments you holler across a front yard, and oftentimes requests for Mrs. Dooley to hold up her latest stitching project for Tanya to see. On the afternoon of August 23, Mrs. Dooley was halfway through a lighthouse-themed quilt, which she was proud to exhibit. Tanya, whose mother collected porcelain lighthouses ("pretty much porcelain everythings"), told her it was looking beautiful. As artists are prone to do, Mrs. Dooley challenged the compliment by inventorying all the mistakes she'd made, forcing Tanya to pause the wheelchair in the street in order to acknowledge them all and politely object to some.

Cameron, Mrs. Dooley recalls, never glanced up. His expression looked dazed and bleary to her, but she didn't think much of it; she knew he took painkillers, and chalked his torpor up to their effects. She didn't know, or didn't remember knowing, exactly what'd happened to Cameron or where it'd happened—just that he'd walked off to war, the same way her husband had back in 1942, but, unlike Bobby, Cameron hadn't come walking back, he'd come rolling. Roughly twenty years before that she'd watched Cameron totter around the Harrises' front yard in his diapers, his little pale legs fat like stacks of donuts, Tanya always shuffling alongside him with her arms splayed wide like a basketballer guarding against the fast break, Cameron's high-pitched giggles audible even from the corner. Mrs. Dooley preferred, however, not to think about that hard trajectory, the jinxed there-to-here. The world, like her quilts, was riddled with imperfections, but the reasons for these were known only to its creator. You just had to trust that the intentions were good. She sank back into her rocker and watched Tanya push Cameron's wheelchair into the parking lot of the Biz-E-Bee. His elbows darted out, momentarily, as Tanya jostled the chair over a crumbled curb, reminding Mrs. Dooley of someone startled from a particularly vivid dream.

Smokes, beer, Cap'n Crunch, a half-gallon jug of milk: This was Tanya's shopping list that afternoon. For other staples, she sometimes drove her red Kia to the Winn-Dixie on Pass Road or to the Walmart Supercenter down by the beach, but because she was ten months into a one-year driver's license suspension, owing to a DUI conviction, driving anywhere was a sizable risk. She tried to limit herself to shuttling Cameron back and forth to the VA medical center in Biloxi, which was not only necessary but seemed less likely to result in her arrest or at least in her conviction. For day-to-day shopping, however, it was safer to load up at the Biz-E-Bee, which stocks most of what you want if you don't want much. Moreover, she figured the sunlight and salt air were good for her brother, whose moods tended to blacken in the late afternoon before the beer and the pills got to fermenting in his bloodstream. Sometimes during those hours, when he'd be playing the video game "Halo," she'd notice that neck-vein of his seething, and a violent froth of drool bubbling at the corner of his mouth, and think: *Time to make some groceries.*

Today, however, wasn't one of those days. Today wasn't about "distraction therapy," the clinical term that she'd later hear applied to her Biz-E-Bee excursions. Today was listless, hot, unremarkable. And, at around three thirty p.m., with none of the guests on that day's episode of *Dr. Phil* tugging a single one of her heartstrings, Tanya Harris had stubbed out the last of her cigarettes. Her brother, down to a single beer in the fridge, shrugged his lukewarm consent.

Like the afternoon in question, the Biz-E-Bee store can seem, at a passing glance, unremarkable. It sits low-slung and slabbish on the corner, with steel bars shielding a random few front windows and neon beer signs and cigarette posters and local flyers crowding the remaining windows with a look of equal impenetrability. On some afternoons, this one included, shrink-wrapped pallets of soft drinks and cases of beer are parked out front. Most often it falls to a fifty-four-year-old semi-employee named Ollie Morgan to unpack the pallets and haul their contents into the store. Ollie is more or less homeless—if you ask him where he lives, he'll point west; ask him again, the next day, and that same finger points east—and the Biz-E-Bee's owners, a Vietnamese immigrant couple named Lê Nhu Quỳnh and Lê Thị Hat, pay him in cash or merchandise, depending on his wants. Sometimes it's a twenty- or fifty-dollar bill; other times, a pickled egg and a Yoo-hoo. In exchange for this fluctuant compensation Ollie also scoops up parking-lot litter and hauls the trash out to the dumpster, and occasionally babysits the Lês' three-year-old daughter, Kim, who spent much of the first two years of her life confined to a playpen in a back corner of the store, by the mop closet, where her favorite activity was rolling a cold unopened can of Red Bull around the playpen. (Once the can warmed she'd lose interest, at which point her parents or Ollie would replace it in the cooler and fetch her a fresh one, cycling through a dozen or more cans a day.) More than anything else, however, Ollie appears to merely hang out, smoking cigarettes or chewing toothpicks outside by the front door, looking half security guard and half loiterer, his gaze sweeping the parking lot like that of a convenience-store Argos. Newcomers to the store sometimes mistake his silence for surliness, but Ollie is mute. When he tries to speak, a bass monotone bleat emerges, like a foghorn. Little Kim sometimes imitates him, though the effect is more goatish—to her parents' delight, and, to judge by his exuberant clapping, to Ollie's delight as well.

Ollie was inside the store when Tanya entered that afternoon. The broil of the slanted sunlight looked to be defeating him; he was clinging to the front counter with a Yoo-hoo in one hand, his complexion liquid with sweat. She'd parked Cameron outside by the newspaper machine, beneath a window on which was hand-painted—not quite legibly, owing to the bars striating the words—WE ACCEPT EBT. The brightness level of Cameron's mood tended to dictate whether Tanya wheeled him in or left him outside, and today's mood, while not overly dark, was lethargic enough to dissuade her from bringing him in. It didn't seem worth the trouble. She asked if he'd be okay out there, to which he nodded vacantly—a groggy and almost pained-looking single nod. This brought a frown to her face, because while Cameron often seemed to "hole up inside of himself" in this way, as Tanya describes it, he usually did so in private—in their living room, or in the backyard by the grill where on breezier days he often retreated with a six-pack and some cigs with his ears plugged with Patsy Cline songs. That she was over-vigilant with his moods was established fact, but the six months that followed Cameron's release from Brooke Army Medical Center—when the phrase "suicidal ideation" entered her life, hanging there like a spiral of storm clouds banked out in the Gulf— had left her with an acute fearfulness that felt as permanent as her tattoos. Even four years later, she couldn't help but interpret sustained moping as the potential prelude to self-annihilation. A case of indigestion had once been enough to spark panic in her; it had taken Cameron half an hour to convince the VA social worker Tanya'd called that it was diarrhea, not suicide, currently threatening his existence.

She asked him again, with her hands on his forearms: "Cam, you sure you okay? You want something besides beer?"

"Naw," he said, and without looking up flicked his left hand to dismiss her. "I'm all good." *All good:* To her that's what he'd always been, her all-good little brother. People hadn't always *gotten* Cameron, who'd been a little too "sensitive"—her word—to fully connect with his high-school football teammates but not quite sensitive enough to click with softer-minded guys, the guitar players and tattooists Tanya favored. She'd never seen anyone fight harder than she'd seen Cameron fight one awful night after their mother died when he put Tommy Landry into the emergency room with what even the doctors called a "broken face," but she'd never seen anyone cry harder than him, either: When their mother died he wept for twenty-four hours straight, came out of his room to smoke half a cigarette, then went back in and cried for twelve hours more. At the age of eight, he spent three days and nights camped beside the backyard grave of his run-over dog, to assist in case of the dog's resurrection; for the entirety of that time his cheeks remained so wet and streaky that their mother fretted about mold developing. Their mother always said Cameron had a "low boiling point," as well as "skin thinner than an onion's," and, as opposed to the Grinch on that Christmas show, a "heart one size too big." People didn't tend to see the bulge of that XXL heart much anymore, Tanya thought, probably because Cameron was so quiet—and he'd only grown more taciturn since coming back from Afghanistan, his quietude sometimes competing with Ollie's. And those who did see it, like some of his nurses and therapists, seemed to ascribe it to his injury, because every veteran confined to a wheelchair gets awarded a heart one size too big. Tanya figured that was why the Purple Heart was a heart.

She turned to soak up one more look at him before entering the store. In retrospect, she says, he looked so bleak out there, slumped in his wheelchair, his T-shirt already splotched with sweat stains, his chin drooping toward his chest, his shoulders slumped inward, his expression betraying not a single forward thought—just the same backward thoughts he constantly recycled through his head, the *what-if-I'd* . . . questions with which he quizzed himself daily. But she doesn't believe she considered all that then, in those few seconds before she slipped into the air-conditioning. Maybe some of it; Tanya's mind tends to dart, like a bullfrog navigating lily pads. If anything, she was double-checking to make sure she'd parked him in the shade.

She was inside the store, by her own estimate, for five, maybe six minutes. A more precise measurement of the time, however, comes from the

Biz-E-Bee's co-owner, Lê Thị Hat, known as Hat, who received a call from the store's tobacco distributor at nearabout the same moment Tanya entered. A billing dispute kept her on the phone, according to her call history, for seven minutes and forty-seven seconds. She ended the call almost immediately after Tanya's first scream.

During those seven minutes and forty-seven seconds, Tanya gathered up the milk and beer and Cap'n Crunch. Another customer was in the store at the time, a middle-aged man unfamiliar to Tanya and the owners. He purchased a pack of cigarettes and a Slim Jim and was out of the store by the time Tanya arrived with her arms full at the register. Ollie, she recalls, was standing a little too close to the register, appearing to be analyzing the nutrition label of his drained bottle of Yoo-hoo. If she hadn't known Ollie was Ollie, she might've lined up behind him, but instead she squeezed herself into the aromatic space beside him and dumped her groceries onto the counter. Behind the counter, back toward the office door, Hat was scowling hard at whatever she was hearing over the phone or possibly from the way Little Kim was yanking her leg and pleading for something in Vietnamese, possibly both. After waving to Tanya, Hat's descending hand morphed into a single-fingered *wait* gesture that she aimed at her daughter, who ignored it. Quỳnh, hunching on a swivel stool behind the counter, tallied Tanya's purchase while half-listening to his wife's conversation, at one point snapping, "Tell him I say bullshit," which Hat ignored just as thoroughly as Kim had ignored her. Then, with a sudden whipcrack of a smile, Quỳnh focused on Tanya and her request for two packs of Bonus Value Lights, which he had to stand up to fetch from the overhead cigarette bays, emitting a wheezy but accommodating groan as he did so.

For the remaining four minutes, they talked. Neither Tanya nor Quỳnh can recall precisely what they talked about, which isn't unusual when Tanya is involved: almost certainly the heat, they say; probably the amount of that week's Powerball lottery, for which Quỳnh planned to drive to Louisiana the next day, as lottery tickets are illegal to purchase in Mississippi; and perhaps Little Kim, whom Quỳnh, by his own admission, relentlessly brags about. Kim's had been a perilous birth, owing to underdeveloped lungs that landed her in a neonatal intensive care unit for her first three weeks, so for Quỳnh every benchmark of growth—first steps, first words, first Coca-Cola—feels doubly momentous, a strike against fate that he savors trumpeting. At some point, they agree, Quỳnh must surely have asked about Tanya's brother; whatever answer she gave, however, is lost to their memories. The unpaid total—$31.94, in blocky red numerals—shone on the register display as they kept talking, and as Ollie, beside her, gave up assessing his Yoo-hoo and turned his attention out the window.

Outside in his wheelchair, Cameron's head lolled from a sudden burst of nausea—or rather, from some unfamiliar subspecies of nausea-like feeling—that rolled through him from the bottom up, from his gut northward to his head. But then, just as quickly and mysteriously as it struck him, the sensation disappeared. Maybe a weird spurt of heatstroke, he thought, or a late-blooming pharmaceutical side effect; or more likely some kind of gas bubble, a common hazard with Tanya's cooking; or maybe it wasn't anything worth diagnosing at all, because he seemed fine again. He fished out a cigarette and lit it. The parking lot was empty now, the dude who'd been in the store having left in a Ford F150 bearing Hancock County plates. From the truck window the dude had chucked an empty sixteen-ounce Coke bottle on his way out. Below a vibrant yellow billboard for Taaka vodka across Division Street, traffic coursed east and west, all those cars and pickups glinting drearily in the shimmy-shimmy heat. Someone pulled into the sno-ball stand across Division and hopped out of the car fast, as though to remedy a bona fide case of heatstroke.

With the second or third drag Cameron sucked from the cigarette, the nausea returned, striking so hard and so fast that as if with singed fingers he tossed away the cigarette. He heard himself groan, and, as he'd taught himself to do with pain during his long convalescence, he clamped shut his eyelids to shove blackness into his mind. This blackness had always helped, for reasons he suspected were uniquely personal and maybe a little weird: Without it, the juxtaposition of the pain and the visible world compounded everything, because that visible world as he'd always known it had never included the varieties of pain he'd experienced. Plus the world, peopled or unpeopled, staring back at him in those moments added a layer of anxiety, left him feeling vulnerable, intruded upon, and in some peculiar way ashamed. Closing his eyes, he'd found, allowed him to meet the pain on a more neutral field—by taking the fight inside, rather than out, and away from prying eyes.

Except that it wasn't pain, or really even related to nausea—not exactly, anyway. The sensation was more like an interior lightness or ethereality, as though helium were being slowly released inside him, or as though his bodily fluids were transforming into a buoyant vapor—a yeasty, floaty feeling. To try to extinguish it he produced a vigorous belch, but this had no effect. The not-nausea wasn't exactly uncomfortable, he realized, yet it was alien and powerful, and wanted alleviating. A sudden gush of saliva swirled around and beneath his tongue as he felt himself beset with dizziness or faintness—again, something airy. Leaning forward in his wheelchair yielded some incremental relief, Cameron found. Leaning farther forward granted him another fraction of ease. He rocked himself forward to magnify this effect, swinging his head between his knees and feeling a slick rope of drool slap his chin.

And then. God, then.

Cameron Harris has gone over what happened next a thousand-plus times in his mind, in thunderstruck variations of his *what-if-I'd* quiz, and then hundreds more times to doctors, nurses, friends, strangers, reporters, television producers, to his parish priest, to the investigator from Rome, to the people who wrote him emails and letters and to the people who telephoned him in the darkest hours of the night from places like Malaysia and Albania plus the ones who showed up unannounced and trembling on his doorstep, but still, to this day, he cannot say if there was a signal, a command, a moment of purpose or clarity, or even an awareness of what he was doing. The closest comparison, he says, is a mindset that can sometimes develop during combat, when, flooded with the effects of adrenaline, the brain shifts into a state he likens to autopilot, and you find you're obeying your body rather than directing it, that your hands and arms and legs are doing things you didn't wittingly instruct them to, and you feel like a passenger in your own body, swept along by the force of action and some bone-marrow urge to stay alive.

What Cameron did, then, wasn't conscious. He didn't decide to do it. He says he didn't even know he was doing it until after he'd done it.

Where his memory kicks in is the Taaka vodka billboard. Whether or not his eyes were open before then, his first visual recollection is the bill-board, and his first sensation was the bizarre instability he felt staring at it, because the billboard was moving—was shifting within his frame of vision as though tilting from the collapse of its support structure, as though sliding off its struts. He was simultaneously aware of a strange and very close sound: the faint scritch of something on the asphalt beneath him. The tilting billboard above, the scrape-sound below: Neither made sense to him until he glanced down, but what he saw there didn't make sense to him either, because those were his own red Nikes on the asphalt, which meant he was out of his chair.

Which meant he was asleep, and dreaming. Except that he wasn't. He was awake, and he was standing. And what's more—he was walking. He watched his left foot rise and then descend back to the asphalt a few inches ahead of its former position: That was walking, yes, that was its very definition. He matched that step with his right foot—by now he was consciously controlling his feet, his heart flopping in his chest like a mullet in a bucket. Cameron Harris, whose spine had been severed in Afghanistan, who'd been assured and reassured by brigades of medical authorities that he would never walk again, was walking slowly but steadily across the Biz-E-Bee parking lot, his chest so frenzied with fear and disbelief and incipient exultation that he felt himself gasping for oxygen.

At that very moment, just across Reconfort Avenue, Mrs. Dooley glanced up from her quilting for no other reason than that Mrs. Dooley was always glancing up. What she spotted across the street caused her hands to bunch and shake, her quilting needle drawing a speckle of blood from a fingertip. For a moment she sat frozen, suspicious of hallucinations; in his final dementia-wracked years her husband, Bobby, had claimed to have seen his mother roaming their house, all the more remarkable and disturbing because as an orphan Bobby had never met his mother. She adjusted her glasses as a further guard, this time against a trick of the eye—but no, there he was, little almost-trouble Cameron Harris, his bottom half rendered useless by war, taking another fragile step forward like someone negotiating a high ledge or the thin ice of a frozen pond, each step cautious and consequential. "Holy Jesus," she whispered, rising from her chair and shuffling in her house slippers to her porch rail. And then, when he managed another step, this one longer and more confident and all but graceful save the buckling of his bony out-of-practice legs, she raised her head and with the same strength on which she'd drawn to survive four hours in a floating refrigerator she bellowed across Reconfort Avenue: *"HOLY JESUS PRAISE YOUR NAME."*

Inside the Biz-E-Bee, Ollie was first to notice. Without removing his eyes from the window he let out a violent-sounding moan and grabbed Tanya's left arm, wrenching her toward him. Horrified, Quỳnh reached across the counter and with a hard yank on Ollie's big arm shouted, "Stop, why you crazy?" and, with that, the three of them struggled to bust apart their triangle of armholds. All Quỳnh could think was that Ollie's brain, the fitness of which no one had ever affirmed, had somehow snapped, thereby confirming the apprehensions about Ollie his wife had spent years expressing and sentencing Quỳnh to a pecked eternity of I-told-you-sos. Ollie was bleating, and with his free hand motioning out the window, while Tanya, deploying the box of Cap'n Crunch, was bashing his shoulder and from her mouth firing blue flames of curses. Quỳnh had surrendered his grip in order to come around the corner for a more significant rescue effort when he heard Tanya scream. With both her hands she slapped her own mouth as Ollie, his point finally made, relaxed his grip on her arm and moved her toward the door. "What?" shouted Quỳnh, who as a shopkeeper of sixteen years couldn't restrain himself from picking the squashed box of Cap'n Crunch off the floor. "What's out there?" When he saw, the Cap'n Crunch plopped straight back to the floor.

Tanya remembers the sound of the bell on the door ringing as she exited the Biz-E-Bee, three trebly toy-like chimes, and she remembers the light: the great white-yellow-blue blast of it smashing into her eyes as she stepped outside, a chilled breeze on her back as the air-conditioning fled the store after her. She must've spoken her brother's name, she thinks, because at that moment Cameron turned. Somewhere in her peripheral vision, too, she caught sight of Mrs. Dooley, hightailing it across the parking lot with feebly wizened steps not so unlike her brother's, wagging her head with church-pew jubilance, her mouth wide open as though to sing. Then her brother, his head still hanging, turned fully Tanya's way and launched a step toward her. His slight stumble drew Quỳnh a few feet forward from Tanya's side, to help, but Cameron recovered, and with another step toward his sister lifted his head to reveal a look of pure astonishment—a look unlike any she'd seen on his face or anyone else's. As the bell announced Hat and Kim joining them outside, Kim pleading, "Nó là cái gì? Nó là cái gì?," *what is it?, what is it?*, Tanya raised a hand to the sky to shield her eyes from the sun or perhaps from some other raw and wondrous sky-power her retinas were unequipped to withstand. No one said a word save Mrs. Dooley, who was indeed singing now, as perhaps she'd been singing the entire time: an ancient country hymn about just such an occasion, an occasion that she—and everyone else gathered in that parking lot that afternoon—had neither expected nor even hoped to ever witness.

after, pt. 1

how precious did that grace appear,
the hour I first believed

two

C AMERON HARRIS DIDN'T CALL HIS PRIMARY CARE PHYSICIAN at the Gulf Coast Veterans Health Care System that afternoon, nor did he call her that evening. He didn't call her the next day, either, or even the next day. In fact he never called her; she called him. Dr. Janice Lorimar-Cuevas learned about Cameron's recovery from a front-page article in the Tuesday, August 26 edition of the Biloxi *Sun Herald*, which her husband, Nap, in accordance with daily routine, had laid on the counter for her that morning beside a mug of chicory coffee and a pint glass of the kale-banana-flaxseed smoothie he'd made.

"That's—that's my patient," she blurted, before even sitting down. Standing side by side at the counter, they read the article and studied the accompanying photograph, which showed Cameron posed beside his empty wheelchair in front of the house on Reconfort Avenue, Nap punctuating his reading with the same intermittent grunts of skepticism he accords news reports of insurance company benevolence or supposed regulatory crackdowns on the oil industry. Nap Cuevas—the Nap is short for Napoleon, a hereditary flourish he's never quite appreciated—is an attorney specializing in personal injury litigation. He was already late for a pretrial hearing in Gulfport, so he and Janice exchanged just a few words about the article before he left the house. She doesn't remember precisely what words, except that "miracle" was not among them.

The origins of the word, like its liturgical evocations, are Latin: It derives from the noun *miraculum,* meaning an object of wonder, which itself sprouted from the verb *mirari,* meaning to marvel, or to be astonished. And Janice *was* astonished that morning—astonished most of all that

Cameron, whose leg muscles after four years of disuse were in a severely atrophied state, had summoned the power to stand upright and walk. Slightly less astonishing was his spontaneous recovery from paralysis, which she felt certain would prove clinically explicable, though at the moment, as she marveled at the photograph, she was bankrupt of any theories. But the word *miracle* in its current, divinity-soaked usage, defined with elegant concision by the British novelist and theologian C. S. Lewis as "an interference with Nature by supernatural power": This was not among her theories, despite the *Sun Herald*'s exuberant quotations from a local priest, nor was it a factor in her astonishment. Setting aside her belief or disbelief in any supernatural power (Janice tilts hard toward the latter), the concept of "interference" struck her as antithetical to science—a concession to the idea that the known laws of nature were not laws at all, but instead mere precedents. Subscribing to the possibility of miracles forced one to concede that scientific ordinances could be warped or at least eluded. To Janice's thinking, this concession actually *negated* those ordinances, because in science the exception does not prove the rule; it disproves it. That nature still retained mysteries, she believed, was both a temporary *and* temporal condition. Whatever remained inexplicable about nature was simply waiting to be explained, like patients thumbing golf magazines before their scheduled appointment.

Not surprisingly, hers is a minority opinion in Mississippi, which the polling organization Gallup in 2012 deemed the most religious state in the United States. "Religion exerts more than mere influence in Mississippi," says the historian Reagan C. Jones, who's written extensively about faith in the South. "It is a primary force in the state's politics, in its culture, in the particulars of its residents' daily lives. It's a crucial component of the state's very atmosphere." Perhaps more surprisingly, however, Janice's is also a minority opinion among physicians nationwide. Polls commissioned by the Jewish Theological Seminary in New York City reveal that roughly three quarters of doctors believe in miracles; in one poll, more than half of the 1,100 physicians surveyed claimed to have witnessed treatment results in their patients that they deemed "miraculous." Allowing for semantic imprecision—*miraculous* is often used as a hyperbolic synonym for *extraordinary*—this remains a remarkable finding: that even among clinicians, steeped in the rigors of empiricism, a far squishier doctrine pervades.

Nothing about Dr. Janice Lorimar-Cuevas, mentally or otherwise, is squishy—almost. Her physical diligence, for instance, mirrors her mental assiduity: A devout runner (she tries to clock at least fifty miles a week), she maintains a marathon time hovering around two hours and fifty-five minutes, and in 2013 she competed in a fifty-mile trail run near Laurel, Mississippi, finishing in nine hours and forty minutes, fourth among the female racers. This exercise regimen—which she appends with Pilates classes and yoga sessions—announces itself in her appearance: in her taut, sun-polished skin, its deep tan subject to constant refreshment during her runs along the beach; in the way she keeps her licorice-colored hair almost always ponytailed, lest the opportunity for an impromptu jog arise; and in her tight, brisk, erect carriage, which suggests an asceticism at odds with the Margaritaville vibe of the Mississippi Coast, where residents tend to approach life with much the same laissez-faire attitude one finds a short ride down the interstate in New Orleans. At thirty-three, she exudes the discipline and glowy vigor of a young Olympian. But she also exudes something else: a hardened prosecutor's aura of certitude, a density of conviction that seems bricked, mortared, and immaculately leveled. One finds a clue to this mindset in a quotation from Václav Havel that's framed above the desk in her home office: "Hope is not the conviction that something will turn out well, but the certainty that something makes sense, regardless of how it turns out." She is the antithesis of squish.

The exception to that—and perhaps the explanation for it, though she waves off this line of conversational inquiry—is her family background. Janice is the eldest child and only daughter of Winston Lorimar, whose name might ignite sparks of recognition among readers of Southern literature in the 1970s. Born into a mildly prosperous but socially negligible family in Greenwood, Mississippi (his father did the accounting for a cotton broker), Winston Lorimar failed out of the University of the South in Sewanee before bouncing his way through a sequence of colorful jobs of the sort that used to pepper "About the Author" bios: circus hand, clam digger, piano player, gameshow contestant, ballroom dance instructor. In 1974, at the age of twenty-seven, he moved to Manhattan on a quixotic, bourbonized mission to rescue *Esquire* magazine—"by force if necessary," he later wrote—from what he saw as the craven overseers who'd forced out the legendary editor Harold Hayes. The mission fizzled—Lorimar never even made it as far as *Esquire*'s offices on Madison Avenue—but he funneled that same quixotic zeal (with bourbon chaser) into another endeavor: writing fiction. In this he was egged on by the author Truman Capote, whom he met through a mutual friend. For the next three years, Capote—often baroquely intoxicated during that era—served as a sporadic and oblique mentor to Lorimar. The novel that emerged, in 1978, was *Lieutenant Lucius & the Tristate Crematory Band,* the story of a Confederate cavalryman reincarnated as a psychedelic rock guitarist whose discovery of the aphrodisiacal effects of kudzu inspires him to resurrect the ancestral plantation as a kind of viny, carnal, Southern-fried commune. Critical reception was lukewarm at best, and snide at worst (the critic Eliot Fremont-Smith, in the *Village Voice,* wrote that the effect was of "Hermann Hesse reincarnated as a pork rind"), yet, commercially, the novel proved a minor sensation. Perhaps owing to a fascination with the New South that bloomed during the early years of the Carter administration, or possibly to the notoriety of a seven-page, three-sentence description of a kudzu-turbocharged orgasm, *Lieutenant Lucius & the Tristate Crematory Band* was a Book-of-the-Month Club main selection, spent twenty-seven weeks on the *New York Times* bestseller list, and was eventually adapted into a network television movie starring Bruce Boxleitner in a somewhat tragic-looking rainbow wig. In the three years following its publication, Winston Lorimar rode high: When he married his publicist, Jacqueline Hernnstein, the reception was held at Elaine's—a gift from Elaine Kaufman herself. When Jacqueline gave birth to a daughter they named Janice, the former *Harper's* editor (and fellow Mississippi Delta native) Willie Morris sprawled beside Winston in the waiting room with a cigar clamped between his teeth. Less than a year later, however, Winston Lorimar had all but disappeared.

"I just wanted to come on home," is the way Lorimar explained it back then, and it's how he still explains his retreat—not only from Manhattan, but also from writing and publishing. His courteously firm refusal to expand upon this statement, however, plus its over-rehearsed luster and the syrupy smile with which he concludes it, conveys an aspect of deception, or at least evasion. But it's an oddly avowed deception. The smile doesn't pretend to correspond to the cornpone simplicity of the words; it's a flagrant overlay of facial irony, a wink of the mouth, a silent admission of something—but of what? Friends from his New York days received much the same unsatisfactory explanation at the time, and each of them nurtured his or her own pet theories: that the pressures of writing a follow-up novel crushed him; that he'd fallen in love with another woman at life's most inopportune moment and, hewing to some *Ivanhoe*-inspired code of decency, fled south to escape her; or that Capote had secretly written *Lieutenant Lucius & the Tristate Crematory Band*, and stoked by its success was threatening to unmask himself as its author. "He left without so much as goodbye, so long," says Brock Meadows, a retired *60 Minutes* producer who frequently occupied a barstool next to Lorimar's at Elaine's. "The theory we all settled on was gambling debts with the mob. It made as much sense as anything else. Or as little sense, as the case may be. Whatever *did* happen, anyway?"

What happened—on a skeletal level, at least—is this: Winston Lorimar whisked his family from the Upper West Side to the outskirts of Greenwood. He bought a tumbledown farm and went about town in expensive Scottish bird-hunting attire. He drove rural backroads in a Chevrolet convertible while wearing antique leather aviator goggles. For ten years he zealously maintained the high score on the pinball machine at a Leflore County juke joint known as Como's. He drank prodigiously and entertainingly, though, for the era and for the Mississippi Delta, rarely to notable extremes. In immodest moments, which were many, he likened himself to Shakespeare gone silent after *The Tempest*, nestled into his retirement at Stratford.

To literary New Yorkers—fewer and fewer of whom remained curious about Lorimar, as *Lieutenant Lucius & the Tristate Crematory Band* faded from bookstore shelves—he might've appeared a recluse, a trippier version of Harper Lee, but down in Greenwood he cut a voluble, boisterous figure. He gave readings to luncheon groups, judged high-school writing contests, and edited a collection of mawkish vignettes about the Delta for a local publisher. When asked if he was working on anything new, however, Lorimar would contort his face into an expression of horror, according to one resident, and exclaim, "Work? Why ever would I want to *work*?"

Despite being a Long Island Jewess, Jacqueline alighted gracefully in the Delta. By all accounts, she was a fluent and decorous hostess, an attentive and agile mother (three boys trailed Janice into the family), and a benevolent sort of nursemaid to her husband, whose literary chops seemed to exonerate him from the standard strictures of husbandhood. That those chops went unexercised never appeared to bother her. In fact, nothing her husband did or didn't do seemed to bother her: Her friends and children recall far more complaints about the lack of decent pizza in the Delta than any marital laments. But then, in 1991, when Janice was ten and her youngest brother was three, Jacqueline Lorimar commenced a swift and sudden decline. Day after day, in perceptible measures, she weakened. After a while, fatigue gripped her so tightly that even her eyelids couldn't muster the strength to stay open. The cause, finally established via neuroimaging in Jackson after a fumbly string of misdiagnoses by local physicians, was brainstem glioma, a catastrophically cancerous brain tumor. Her life expectancy forecast, even with chemotherapy, was twelve months; she managed to eke out only five.

It was years before Winston Lorimar divulged the bare facts of their mother's illness and death to his children. For a time he blamed gremlins that he said were creeping into his and Jacqueline's bedroom at night and sucking her energy out through little cocktail straws ("but don't worry," one of Janice's brothers, Randy, recalls him saying, "kids' energy tastes like raw liver to them"). In lighter moments, he ascribed her fatigue to hours of strenuous dancing that she did after the children went to sleep, mock-scolding her for overdoing it with the Lindy hop. Her hair loss, he told them, was an avant-garde fashion statement that was currently all the rage back in New York, which was also where he said she'd gone when she died. "It took me years to shake the idea that New York City was literally a ghost town," says Randy Lorimar. One might conclude, sympathetically, that Winston Lorimar, however clumsily, was trying to shield his children from an abominable truth that he himself couldn't quite accept—if a pattern wasn't already in place.

Because while Lorimar might've abandoned writing, he has never forsaken fiction. The sign at the entrance to the family home reads LORIMAR PLANTATION, CIRCA 1848, which is about as bald as a lie can be shaved: Donovan Lorimar, Winston's grandfather, arrived in the Delta from Ireland in 1907 to work on the railroad, and the farm itself dates back only to the Great Depression. (A clue to Lorimar's career withdrawal might lurk inside a comment he once made to a friend in Greenwood: "As an Irishman and a Southerner, I ravenously suckle defeat.") The farm's history, much like his daily life appears to be, is an act of imagination. After writing a novel, he began living one. His fictions can be small ("If you see him at the diner," says one local, "he'll tell you how fine the chicken that he just ate was, with a big steak bone sitting right there on the plate") or large (to get out of a dinner engagement, he once left a friend a voicemail saying he'd been stabbed in the neck by an intruder). They can also be strikingly self-aware, even meta: He's claimed himself the inspiration for Edward Bloom, the tall tale–spouting protagonist of Daniel Wallace's 1998 novel *Big Fish.* (Wallace, who's never met Lorimar, denies this, though he regards *Lieutenant Lucius & the Tristate Crematory Band* as an "unfairly forgotten classic.") Even before her death, and more so afterward, Jacqueline provided a steady canvas for exaggerations: "You know he was married to a former Miss America, right?" asks an impressed young clerk at a downtown boutique, when Lorimar's name arises. By the turn of the century, wearier and more skeptical residents were placing his claims to have once authored a book somewhere alongside his assertions that he'd been second-in-command of New York City's branch of the Irish Republican Army and that he'd once shot an irregular thirty-one-point buck through the kitchen window of a trailer whilst having tabletop intercourse with a Choctaw woman: filed, that is, under bullshit. "Oh, every word that comes out of his mouth is a whopper," says Junie Taylor, the town's longtime librarian. "And we *adore* him for it."

It's easy to get carried away with Lorimar lore—invoke his name at the bar at Greenwood's Alluvian Hotel, and the room is instantly transformed into a trading floor for ever more outrageous stories—but of more immediate interest is Winston Lorimar's effect on his daughter, Janice. "My father is a"—she drums her fingers through a long pause—"complicated man," is how she wades into the subject, with much the same wincing one does when entering chilly surf. She speaks fondly of him, but with an almost constant rolling of her eyes. Pride and embarrassment, teamed respectively with affection and resentment, seem to wrestle inside her, yielding such ambivalences as, "He's a genius of self-destruction." She can sometimes seem riven by a wish to avoid talking about him and a competing impulse, fitfully suppressed, to talk of nothing but.

Discussing her mother's cancer and the direct link it must've had to her medical career, for instance, she quickly pivots to her father and all his dissembling about it. "I think that's where my limited tolerance for metaphor might have come from," she says. "Dressing up a fact doesn't change it, or benefit it in any way. It just obscures it." On this point she is strictly and astringently Sontagian: Metaphor and symbolic language do a disservice to our thinking about illness and suffering. Injury and disease are not imaginative; neither should our approach to them be. The extended implication is that her father's masquerades did a disservice to her, as a confused and grief-stricken ten-year-old child, though this is where the aforementioned dismissive wave comes in. "I also have a limited tolerance for that kind of pinpoint psychological causation," she says. "There's no doubt that my mother's illness and the way my father handled it were correlative factors in my going into medicine, and in the way I think about medicine and practice it. But I don't think it's accurate to suggest that if Mom hadn't gotten cancer, or if the doctors in Greenwood hadn't screwed up her diagnosis, or if my father hadn't pulled all that wool over our eyes—that if all that hadn't happened, I wouldn't be who I am today. I don't believe her cancer somehow rewired me."

For proof, she cites the tensions that often arose—before her mother's death—during walks in the woods with her father. "There's a cypress swamp on the farm," she explains, "down toward the river bottom, and I can remember—gosh, I must've been seven, maybe eight—trying to figure out why cypress trees have all those stumpy knees around their trunks. Which is something plant physiologists still haven't been able to answer, by the way—I was a pretty nerdy little girl. But there's my father spinning this elaborate explanation about swamp fairies that go about binding young trees like—this is him talking—'like chinawomen's little feets.' I can still conjure up the exasperation I felt. It was almost—livid. I was just like, *please,* Daddy, can't you just play it *straight* once in a while? Or another time, up in the dogwoods. Maybe a little bit later, a year or two. Springtime. The dogwoods' trunks are all soaking wet, and when I taste the liquid it's super sweet, so I get this idea—probably not a great one—to try to make dogwood syrup. Like, for pancakes. But my father says, 'That's not sap, it's tears.' Dogwoods start weeping every year right before Easter, he says, because they're ashamed that wood from dogwoods was what they used to make Jesus's cross. Which he said is also the reason dogwoods grow slender and twisted, so they can't ever be used for another cross. I must've been nine years old and I swear I wanted to *shake* him. I just wanted to know if the sap might make good pancake syrup, and there he is going off about the goddamn crucifixion."

Inside the family, however, this frustration of hers was a solitary one. Her three brothers all reveled in their father's magical, fib-spangled thinking, willfully and delightedly gullible. (Randy recalls drawing derisive hoots when, in first grade, he quoted his father's claim that hot dogs grow on trees, but also recalls being unbothered, because the idea of sausage orchards struck him as preferable to the gruesome reality.) As early as grade school, Janice was already recognizing herself as the family outlier. She'd been born in New York City, for starters, and not the Mississippi Delta; with her black hair and dusky Semitic complexion and string-bean frame, she *looked* different than her brothers, who all bore the sandy-colored hair and pink-splotched skin and ungovernable belly of their father; and, with her analytical bent, she was the left brain to her brothers' more intuitive right brains (though Janice would no doubt object not only to this metaphor but to the misconception of brain-function lateralization underlying it). Her grades were uniformly superb, she breezed through high school without drawing so much as a single period of detention, she steered clear of drunkenness until the third night of her freshman year at Tulane University and then never got drunk again, she graduated cum laude from the University of Pittsburgh School of Medicine, where she was elected to the Alpha Omega Alpha Honor Medical Society, and then (for the financial incentives, ever the pragmatist) she completed a Family Medicine residency with the U.S. Army in Washington, D.C., where she found a deep and stable satisfaction working within the strictures of the military system, and where she also met a Mississippi congressional aide named Nap whom she married in an elaborate outdoor ceremony at the Lorimar Plantation—all this, and she's still somehow the black sheep of the Lorimar family. The one nobody quite understands.

It's not precisely true—and in one way it's cruel—to say her brothers followed in their father's footsteps. But most would agree they've canted his direction. The oldest, Tay, is a fine art photographer, currently living in Spain, who's best known for a series of eroticized, tungsten-lit portraits of elderly nudes. The middle brother, Randy, is a studio percussionist in Nashville. The youngest, Johnny, set out to be a writer, but suffered a near-fatal heroin overdose just three months after entering the master of fine arts program at Columbia University in New York. Several relapses, and a withdrawal from Columbia, have followed; since his last relapse, he's more or less cut himself off from family contact. Talking about Johnny's addiction seems verboten in the Lorimar family. Talking about Janice's life, on the other hand, is family sport. "General Janny, yeah, I guess we give it to her pretty good," says Randy. "She's always been sort of the resident authority figure in a house full of antiauthoritarian dudes."

"My father says I'm incorrigibly square," says Janice, imitating his fustian Delta drawl ("in-CAW-gibly SKWAIR-uh"). "That I'm all data and no dreams. But that's okay with me. I *like* data. My father would run screaming if he heard me say this, but there's magic in data. I'm serious: *magic*. And the best part is—it's magic you can *see*."

Which leads us back to August 26, 2014, when Dr. Janice Lorimar-Cuevas, following her morning rounds at the Gulf Coast Veterans Health Care System, plus a tiresome meeting of a medical direction committee she was regretting having joined, ducked into her office and cracked open her laptop. The office is small, spartan, and over-bright with a light that feels unnatural. "Government drab" is how she describes it, in fair summation. She tapped in the passcode to access the Department of Veterans Affairs VistA electronic health records database. Needing to see a very specific variety of magic, she typed in a name.

HARRIS, CAMERON TIMOTHY. Her gaze hopscotched across the same standardized category windows at which she glanced twenty, thirty times daily: ALLERGIES/ADVERSE REACTIONS; ACTIVE MEDICATIONS; ACTIVE PROBLEMS (one of these could apparently be subtracted now, she thought, and it's a doozy); CLINICAL REMINDERS; RECENT LAB RESULTS; VITALS. Janice had never had cause to analyze Cameron's injury. He'd been assigned to her for outpatient rehabilitation and care continuum after his treatment at Brooke Army Medical Center, as something of a closed case. VA SCI STATUS: PARAPLEGIA-

TRAUMATIC. CAUSE OF SCD (ETIOLOGY): ACT OF VIOLENCE. His paralysis wasn't the result of transverse myelitis or some other elastic cause; from what she understood, he'd been struck by shrapnel from an IED. She surely must've scanned his records to determine any eligibility for new rehab therapies—GCVHCS was one of a dozen VA hospitals experimenting with exoskeleton suits that granted paralyzed patients the ability to walk with robotic assistance—but she didn't recall doing so. That in itself wasn't troubling; she had hundreds and hundreds of patients under her care, and, as she sometimes joked to Nap, memory enough for barely a quarter of them.

But Cameron she remembered, and liked. In a way he reminded her of her brother Randy: all bark, no bite. As a VA physician, she'd already seen more tattoos than most doctors see in a lifetime, but Cameron's stood out in her memory: an illustration of a soldier wielding an M4 carbine, but with feathered angel wings on his back, that extends down Cameron's torso from his right breast to his waistline. She'd never read the accompanying text, running across the left side of his torso, in capital letters justified to the contours of the wing, except for the top line—ST. MICHAEL THE ARCHANGEL, DEFEND US IN BATTLE—and the bottom line: AMEN. But something about the tattoo struck her as incongruous, as she got to know Cameron. It reminded her of the wispy mustaches boys tried growing back in high school—mustaches intended to project manhood, but that more often called attention to a lack thereof. On Cameron, the tattoo seemed like more of the brittle shell with which he tried masking a gooey, sensitive center. She'd found an endearing vulnerability to him, once you dug past that shell—or got past his sister, for whom Janice felt considerably less affection. One of Janice's earliest encounters with Cameron concerned pressure ulcers he'd developed from sitting in his wheelchair. He kept apologizing for the sores as though he'd disobeyed an instruction, despite Janice's patient reassurances that they were a normal condition. His sister, however, showed much less patience: "Stop apologizing for your damn *ass,*" she scolded him, something Janice quoted later to Nap for a dinnertime chuckle. Tanya Harris was a mynah bird during consultations, repeating everything Janice said—at times she'd repeat one of Janice's questions, consider it for a spell, and then answer for her brother, Cameron shrugging in mute-buttoned agreement. Janice's own brothers, she thought, would never tolerate that degree of big-sistering; within minutes she'd be wearing a stripe of duct tape over her mouth.

Finding nothing to snag her interest in the general records, she clicked to access VistA's Spinal Cord Dysfunction package, or SCD. Here were more detailed transcripts of Cameron's immediate post-injury treatment and rehab, and also, more important, his imaging reports. This was the raw data she was after: the X-rays, CT scans, myelograms, and MRIs. She fetched a protein bar from a desk drawer and gnawed it absently while examining image after image, until a deep frown buckled her forehead and her mouth stopped in mid-chew. She expanded one image window to study it, and then expanded another. Then she sized them to appear side-by-side on the screen, the neglected gob of protein bar in her open mouth beginning to dissolve. Barely shifting her eyes from the screen, she dialed a number on her cellphone. "Got a second to look at something strange?" she asked.

While waiting, she wandered deeper into Cameron's records. She looked at his Neurolevel-Sensory and Neurolevel-Motor scores, finding nothing out of the ordinary there. She made some comparative glances between his Inpatient Rehabilitation Outcomes (which charted the levels of assistance he required for basic life tasks such as eating, grooming, toileting) and Cameron's Self Report of Function records. GET TO PLACES OUTSIDE, SHOPPING, DOING HOUSEWORK: WITH HELP, was his answer. HANDLING MONEY: WITHOUT HELP. (Hardly anyone ever copped to needing help handling money.) EMOTIONAL STATUS: NEEDS SUPERVISION. His Satisfaction with Life score, she noted, was particularly low, but this came as no surprise. Some of these guys charge back hard against their injuries—they're the ones playing wheelchair basketball or sit-skiing down some icy slope, the ones roaring and sweating through their physical therapy sessions, the ones brandishing a thumbs-up in every snapshot taken. Others, like Cameron, just crumple. Now that Janice considered it, he seemed as afflicted by something like heartbreak as much as by paralysis—as if he'd lost something even more precious than his mobility over in Afghanistan.

A knock followed by her office door swinging open cut off this thought. Dr. Vishwesh "Jimmy" Patel, the center's chief of radiology, was responding to her phone call with his typical brusqueness. Dr. Patel is a short, gangly man with conspicuously long arms, and their wingspan, along with the prominence of his large beakish nose on a narrow face that looks incapable of expressing amusement, gives him the impression of a raptor, albeit one dressed in a lab coat. The quick and concentrated way he analyzes imagery only augments this impression: His focus evokes that of a falcon canvassing a field from five hundred feet in the air. Without greetings or pleasantries he went straight to Janice's laptop, as though swooping down on a rodent. "What am I looking at?"

"So check out this MRI, from back in twenty-ten," Janice said. "And then this one, from oh-twelve. Patient is a T9 complete."

Patel toggled his gaze from one to the other. "Oh-ten, oh-twelve." Then he wagged his head. "No way. You're sure these are from the same patient?"

"Yep."

He blew air from his cheeks. "Huh."

"So you're seeing what I am."

"Well, I don't know what you're seeing, but I'm seeing something"—he pursed his lips and paused, clicking to expand an image—"very not right."

"Then you are seeing what I am."

He shook his head again. "The image dates have to be wrong, that's all. Because, look, if you flip the dates, we're just looking at axonal retraction."

"The more recent one is ours," Janice said. "And the other one came from Brooke. Patient went from Landstuhl to Brooke before coming here."

"No, we're looking at a mix-up of some sort. The dates are wrong, or the scans are from different patients."

"Let's say they're not."

"Is this a game?" Annoyance darkened his face. "Okay, I'll drop into sci-fi mode. If the scans are correct, then what I'm looking at is movement of integrin vesicles inside an axon growth cone."

She nodded. "Cord regrowth over and around the glial scar."

"Right," he said, "yes, but that's not—obviously that doesn't happen. It's—not possible."

Again Janice nodded, more crisply, as though he'd just confirmed her own interpretation. "Exactly."

Patel unbent himself from studying the screen on her desk to face Janice. "I'm a little confused here," he said. "If you're asking me what I see, I see an enormous probability of incorrect labeling. Either one of the image dates or the patient ID is wrong. Explain to me why we're playing this game."

"What if I told you the patient supposedly walked a few days ago?"

He stood silently for a moment, the slow expansion of his eyes suggesting the digestion his brain was struggling to accomplish. Then he leaned back down for another look at the MRIs, emitting a chilly, nervous laugh. "This oh-twelve, is this the most recent scan?"

"It is," Janice answered.

"Is there a DTI scan?"

"Was never done."

"We should get one," he said quietly. Then he waggled his head again, as though to revive himself from a trance. "The labeling has to be wrong. There's no other—you said supposedly. How do you know the patient walked?"

Ten minutes later she was on the phone with Cameron.

"I saw the newspaper," she told him. "Wow. How're you feeling?"

"Honestly, doc?" She could hear loud music in the background, and in Cameron's voice she thought she heard a trace of slurring; she imagined a party, now into its fourth day. "Motherfucking *fantastic*."

"That's great. I mean: *wow*, right? Will you tell me what happened?"

So he did: I just stood up, he said. "My belly felt funny, I got all queasy and shit, and then, I dunno, I stood up and walked. I *walked*. Like I am fucking *walking* right now." She quizzed him on the details, asked him to retell it all to her more slowly, but every time he rushed to that same final crescendo: "I walked, I'm walking. It's almost like—like nothing ever happened. End of story, right?"

She exhaled into the phone. "Not exactly, no," she told him, staring at the MRI images on her screen, all those rainbows of data. "Cameron, how soon can you be in my office?"

three

WHAT DOES ONE DO AFTER EXPERIENCING A MIRACLE? THE Gospels of the New Testament, to examine the most conspicuous source, are stingy with details about the aftermaths of Jesus's purported healings. Those who were crippled, blind, paralyzed, deaf, hemorrhaging, mute, dropsied, fevered, withered, or lepered: After recounting their healings, the Gospels' authors tended to hustle these beneficiaries off the page, for the most part dispatching them, as in Matthew 9:31, to "spread about [Jesus's] name in all that country." Even the posthumous fate of Lazarus, whom the Gospel of John alleges Jesus resurrected after Lazarus had lain dead in a tomb for four days, is left open, the Gospels turning aside their attention to let Lazarus wander dazed into the sunset. "And he that was dead came forth, bound hand and foot with graveclothes, and his face was bound about with a napkin," goes the King James version of events. "Loose him," Jesus commanded Lazarus's sisters, "and let him go." But go where—and do *what,* exactly? In a later chapter he's seen having dinner with Jesus in Bethany—one hopes Lazarus thought to pick up the check—but this fleeting cameo is all the scriptures provide. It seems too much to ask that a man raised from the dead could merely resume life as it was, to *go,* as Jesus ordered, after such a full-tilt cosmic *stop:* to complete the fencing for the livestock pen he was building before his illness struck, for example; or to curse the sandal that falls apart just two weeks after its purchase; or to sleep restfully in the same bed where just days or weeks before he lay dead. Or is it too much? What else could Lazarus do?

Cameron Harris drank a beer. "Probably the best damn beer," he says, "I ever had." After Quỳnh and Tanya lowered him back into his wheelchair—no one really wanted him to sit back down for fear that doing so might break whatever spell he was under, Cameron least of all, but his buckling legs clearly couldn't carry him back home—Tanya went back inside the Biz-E-Bee to retrieve their groceries. Quỳnh followed her in, and a few moments later Tanya came back out to ask Cameron if he had any money. "I'm short a buck ninety-four," she said, but Cameron told her his wallet was back home, and after a pause, Tanya biting her lip in the doorway with a hand on her hip, Mrs. Dooley offered to fetch her change-purse from across the street. Tanya praised the offer as sweet but waved it away. By excluding the Cap'n Crunch, which was anyway squashed from bashing Ollie, Tanya found she had enough money, and when she came back out she dropped the two plastic sacks on Cameron's lap, the same way she usually did.

"Damn," he said after a minute. "That shit's *cold*."

His paralysis, until then, had rendered him immune to the sensation of an ice-cold six-pack parked upon his lap, and recognizing that chill brought the first smile to his face since sitting back down. He dug a Bud Light from one of the bags, twisting it out of its plastic yoke, and held it up. "Y'all want one?" Ollie stepped forward, but a sharp glance from Hat halted him. They all watched Cameron pop the top and take an eager foamy swig.

Alone in frowning, Hat felt unsettled by Cameron's celebratory Bud Light—and not only because it ran afoul of store policy (NO DRINKING OF ALCOHOL IN STORE OR PARKING LOT!!, reads a magic-markered sign on the door). She's been selling beer across the Biz-E-Bee counter for sixteen years, and from what she can gather, as a teetotaler, it doesn't seem to make people happier or better; it just makes them come back the next day to buy more of it. Unlike her husband, who maintains a vague allegiance to the Buddhism of his youth in Vietnam, Hat is a devout Catholic who serves as a layperson at Biloxi's Vietnamese Martyrs Church and until Kim's birth was a leading member of the church's choir. Punctuating an obvious miracle by guzzling a Bud Light wasn't quite blasphemous, she decided—but disrespectful for sure. She was surprised to see Mrs. Dooley, whom she understood to be a churchgoer, seeming to condone Cameron's impudence, chuckling as she swabbed a dribble of beer that was running down Cameron's chin onto his T-shirt.

"Should I call an ambulance or something?" Hat asked, but no one could see any point in that. What could EMTs do besides verify, with the authority conferred by flashing lights and sirens, what was already so obvious? "No one calls an ambulance because they got *better*," said Tanya. Nor could they see any point in lingering any longer in the Biz-E-Bee parking lot, with dirt motes rising into the thickening heat and beads of sweat replacing the teardrops that just a short time earlier had dampened Mrs. Dooley's face, especially after a car pulled in and commerce—and with it, life—seemed poised to resume. So they issued ungainly goodbyes, with none of them quite sure how to close such an occasion: Quỳnh darting out of the store to shake Cameron's hand, in much the same effusive way he thanks distributor drivers who leave him a little extra, or "lagniappe," at the end of their delivery runs; Ollie and Cameron high-fiving; and Hat embracing Tanya and then Cameron, making the sign of the cross after touching him. From inside the doorway Little Kim waved, though with a knotty expression, Cameron recalls, as though still trying to puzzle together why this most basic of actions—rising from a chair—had been cause for such commotion. Not so long removed from accomplishing her own first steps, and having drawn from her parents a similar fuss of clapping and cheering, she might've alternately been wondering why walking had come so late to this full-grown man.

With Mrs. Dooley at their side, Tanya wheeled Cameron across Reconfort Avenue, Mrs. Dooley clutching Tanya's wrist for support along the way and announcing, "Lookee there," or, "Praise Jesus," whenever Cameron kicked out his legs. Her voice was still warbly and wonderstruck but also, to Tanya's ear, tired, as if the enormity of what she'd witnessed had caught up with her. Tanya asked if she wanted help getting up onto her porch but Mrs. Dooley declined, or more precisely ignored Tanya's offer, instead bending low to speak to Cameron in the wheelchair. When he made to take another swig of beer, Mrs. Dooley lowered his arm. "I'ma tell you something now," she said.

Cameron said, "Yes ma'am."

Mrs. Dooley raised herself back upright. She brought a hand to the collar of her floral-print duster then placed that same hand on Cameron's shoulder, as if to transfer something from her heart to him. "See here," she began. "I wasn't but seven years old when my daddy brung a radio into our house. Most amazing thing I'd ever seen or heard. I remember just looking all behind it, you know, trying to figure where that *man* was I heard talking on it." She deepened her voice to mimic the announcer's call signal—"'WGCM Mississippi City'"—and patted Cameron's shoulder as she laughed either at her imitation or at the little-girl naïveté of her 1930 self. "Turn that knob and here come the Boswell Sisters over from New Orleans, singing with Bing Crosby. Most beautiful angel voices you ever heard. And there's little me, now, asking my daddy how they all *fit* in there, how all them people could be squeezed inside that radio. And you know what he told me?"

Cameron shook his head.

"That it was just some kind of *miracle*."

Cameron nodded through the prolonged silence that followed.

Mrs. Dooley said, "But that wasn't no miracle, was it?"

"No ma'am," he said.

"It was a radio," said Tanya.

She took a deep breath through her nose, her gaze bypassing Cameron as she scanned the length of the street, before continuing: "And when the sun came back out, after Katrina. There I was, in that old fridge. Soaked straight to the bone and whimpering worse than a beat-down dog. Climbing out and seeing all that terrible mess. Them trees and boats and busted-up houses and a baby carriage hung up on someone's roof antenna. Eighty-two years old that day, and no way I could figure for me still being alive. And you know what I said?"

Cameron shook his head.

"I said it's a miracle, you hear? I said it's a *miracle*."

Again Cameron nodded through the silence. After a while he felt Mrs. Dooley's grip tightening on his shoulder as she bent back down.

"But that wasn't no miracle, was it?" she said.

"Maybe . . . ," Cameron began, because to him it *had* seemed a miracle—and not only to him, but also to the church group members that'd rehabbed their house and hers, and to the CNN reporter who'd broadcast the story of her survival. That was the very word they'd all used: *miracle*. But Mrs. Dooley shushed Cameron with a raised hand.

"Oh, Lord Jesus now, he was looking out for me that day," she said, a smile swerving onto her face. "He *told* me to climb on into that fridge, I know he did. But that don't make it a miracle. Nossir." The smile disappeared. "That's something different."

She leaned in closer, dropping her voice to just above a whisper. "What happened today, now," she said. "What just happened over yonder. Jesus worked a wonder in you, you understand?"

"Yes ma'am."

"That wasn't nothing *but* a miracle."

"Straight up," said Tanya.

"I don't know why Jesus chose you, little Harris boy. But he did. And I got to witness. Praise Jesus for letting me witness, *praise* his holy name."

"That's right," Tanya said.

"But I need you to do something for me, you hear?"

For the first time since she'd started talking—and possibly for the first time since she'd spanked his bottom sixteen years earlier—Cameron looked into her eyes, which were wet and cloudy, with tears rimming the bottom edges and her corneas fogged and gray—eyes stricken with squally weather.

"I need you to pray for me tonight," she said, her voice crackling with a level of emotion that Cameron felt unprepared or unfit to receive. "I need Jesus to hear you say my name. Eula Dooley. Can you do that for me? I want you to tell him I'm in pain. That I got a grandchild in pain. You tell him Antwain needs watching over, you tell Jesus he got to keep Antwain safe. You tell him, now, you tell him there's more of us need what he just give you. I need you to pray for us, I do. I need you to tell me—you tell me you're gonna do that."

"I will," Cameron said, and from above he heard Tanya say, "I'll make sure he does."

Closing her eyes and sighing, Mrs. Dooley gave Cameron's shoulder a hard squeeze and with her other hand touched his leg above the knee. "Praise Jesus," she said, gently rubbing his kneecap. "Praise his name."

"Amen," said Tanya.

Cameron felt Mrs. Dooley's full weight on his shoulder as she used him to lift herself back upright. Her face, as she stared down at him, was drained of expression, and Cameron couldn't help but feel that some sort of transaction had just taken place—one he didn't fully understand. Requests for prayer are a common element in Mississippi conversations (*say a prayer for Mama; keep Pawpaw in your prayers*), and they're almost always met with complaisant pledges, even by those—like Cameron at the time—who don't pray.

This felt different to him, however; this felt like a promise he was expected to keep. It would be the first of many such promises he'd feel obligated to make—more, ultimately, than he could ever possibly fulfill.

The weariness Tanya heard in Mrs. Dooley's voice was also infecting her brother's, she noticed, as she delivered him to the back patio per his request. There she set him up in the same way she usually did: with his little blue Igloo cooler beside him, stocked with beer and ice, and with a three-foot-diameter industrial fan blowing his direction from atop its cinder-block base beside the back door.

"You all right?" she asked him. "How come you keep kicking like that?"

"I guess because I can," he said, craning his neck for a better angle on the rising and falling of his red Nikes. "Mind grabbing my smokes for me? Think you left them on the kitchen table."

Tanya had her cellphone cradled between her ear and shoulder when she came back out. "You are *not* gonna believe this shit," Cameron heard her saying as she dumped the pack of cigarettes into his lap then turned back inside. He could hear some indeterminate Tanya-squealing through the screen door as he lit one of the cigarettes while continuing to survey the ascending and descending of his calves, one after the other, in a slow-motion approximation of a swimmer's kick. The clacking of the screen door announced Tanya's return, her phone still pressed to her ear.

"Shannon don't believe me," she told him. (To her phone she said: "Oh shut up, bitch. I can tell you think I'm lying.") To Cameron: "Reckon you can stand back up again?"

"Maybe," he said, having been mulling the same question himself. "Probably rather be in that other chair anyhow. No frickin' wheels."

"You hear that?" Tanya said to the phone.

Easing himself out of his wheelchair, Cameron shook his head and muttered, "Hell of a thing to accuse someone of lying about."

"You need any help?" Tanya asked.

"Think I'm okay," he said, though not convincingly. Standing felt far more difficult than it had been in the Biz-E-Bee parking lot, and for a moment, with a prick of worry, he wondered why this might be, until remembering that before the Biz-E-Bee parking lot standing had been flat-out impossible. The way his leg muscles ached reminded him of the day after his first five-mile run during boot camp at Fort Benning, a day of nonstop moaning. Up he went, however—gruntingly, unsteadily, and with spastic wincing, but up.

"Hold just like that," Tanya told him. "Shannon wants a picture." She pulled the phone from her ear and frowned at its screen. "Can I take a picture and talk at the same time?"

"I gotta sit back down," Cameron protested.

"Just hang loose," she said, raising her phone up and out toward her brother. "I got it figured now. (He's *standing,* Shannon. Can you still hear me? Honest to fucking God.) Go on and smile, baby bro."

He didn't, but she clicked the camera button anyway.

"Maybe need to find me some crutches or something," he said, dropping himself into a green plastic lawn chair, but Tanya wasn't listening. "I'm sending it to you now," she was saying to her phone. He took a long drag from his cigarette as Tanya headed back inside, and when he blew the smoke from his lungs he could hear her shrieking in the kitchen: "I *told* you! I *told* you, bitch! Yeah, it's a total fucking miracle! Hundred percent."

Was it? Cameron punched himself in the thigh, just to feel it throb. That throb said yes, just as Tanya was hollering yes, and as Mrs. Dooley had said yes, as Hat had said yes. But the questions entering Cameron's mind, as he lit another Bonus Value Light off the orange nub of his last one, revolved around just what *kind* of miracle it was. "I knew something amazing had just happened to me," he explains. "I mean, I'd had zero expectation of ever walking again. It wasn't like any doctor'd ever said, well, if this happens, and then this, and maybe this other thing, then maybe there's a slim chance—no. There'd never been anything for me to even *hope* for. So I got that this was miraculous. The thing I didn't know, sitting there, was what that *meant.*"

Because a miracle, to Cameron, was like a Coke. In Mississippi, as in much of the Deep South, one uses the word *Coke* to denote any soft drink, regardless of variety. Be it a Dr Pepper, Mountain Dew, Pepsi, or Coca-Cola—it's still a Coke. So too with miracles. A miracle could denote some wildly improbable occurrence, as when Cameron's Biloxi High School Indians football team scored a game-winning eighty-seven-yard

touchdown in the final seconds against arch-rival Gulfport High (what elevated this to miracle-slash-*SportsCenter* status was the manner in which
the play unfurled: Gulfport intercepted a Hail Mary pass by the Biloxi
quarterback, but after recovering the ball on a fumble Biloxi employed
nine lateral passes to get into the end zone); or it could denote some super-
human feat of strength or endurance, as when Mrs. Dooley captained that
refrigerator of hers through Katrina's surge; or, in its highest and most
rarefied usage, harking back to C. S. Lewis's formulation, it could denote
God (or some other supernatural entity) stepping in to grant a favor so
divine that it flouted natural law, as when Jesus called Lazarus from the
dead, or when Moses parted the sea, or as in any of the other spectacles
Cameron recalled from Sunday school.

Cameron initially discounted that last variety, owing mostly, he says,
to a mushy sense of faith, but also to the weight of its ramifications.
That sort of miracle—the linguistically pure version, the Coke as Coca-
Cola—struck him as almost *too* miraculous to consider. He found himself prosecuting smaller arguments against it in his head: If indeed God
existed—and Cameron believed this to be true, though his conviction, derived from his mother, was mostly secondhand—Cameron doubted God
offered personalized service. "Back when I played football," he says, "all
those guys would strike a knee after a score, or point to the sky, thanking
God for inspiring that triple option play or whatever. We had an assistant
coach like that, actually. Mr. Jernigan. He'd be like, 'If it gets gnarly out
there, y'all just listen to God. He's the *real* coach out there.' And I just
remember thinking, dude, Auburn's playing Florida on ESPN tonight.
You're telling me God's gonna be watching the Biloxi–Moss Point game
instead?"

As miracles go, then, Cameron's seemed like a Dr Pepper. His sense
of what had befallen him, as he sat chainsmoking in the droopy swelter
of that afternoon, was more of a statistical miracle—an astonishment of
chance. He'd won some kind of biological lottery that he couldn't explain
because he didn't understand it. Just how his legs had healed themselves,
he didn't know—but they *had* (he kicked his legs to verify it yet again), just
as that long slash on his face had healed itself, something that'd seemed
impossible to the small boy catching sight of his butterflied profile in an
emergency-room mirror. Jesus might've worked a wonder in him, as Mrs.

Dooley said, but the wonder was in the design. Which meant that Jesus hadn't intervened in that moment, rewiring his circuitry to bring power back to his legs, any more than Jesus was behind D'varius Johnson's decision to toss a lateral in that game against Gulfport. Jesus didn't watch high-school football games, just as Jesus didn't hang out in convenience store parking lots.

At the same time Cameron was trying to make sense of his recovery, Tanya was inside making it public. Her friend Shannon gave her the idea to post the photo of Cameron on Facebook. (Whether or not Tanya asked Cameron's permission remains a contested point. Tanya says she did; Cameron has no memory of this, though he admits that, with no foreboding of what would ensue, he probably would've said yes.)

The photograph itself, stripped of context, is manifestly ordinary: There's Cameron in his shorts and Deep Sea Fishing Rodeo T-shirt, standing between his empty wheelchair and the green lawn chair with his knees slightly bent and with his weight shifted onto his left leg; in the background is a charcoal grill, a smudge of lawn, and an arthritic-looking catalpa tree. A cigarette dangles from his lip, but the effect is far from any James Dean strut; the facial expression above it signals a mixture of discomfort and dumbfoundedness. "Like he's constipated," as Tanya would say later. Upon closer examination, however, the photograph does convey a glint of the extraordinary: Cameron's legs seem mismatched with his torso, and even more so with his barbell-honed arms, appearing too shriveled and scrawny to be supporting his body.

With context supplied, however, the photograph is beyond extraordinary—or "beyond comprehension," as one of the early commenters on Facebook noted. Within minutes of Tanya's post, the reactions began stacking:

Annistyn Baddley WTF??? is this a joke???
August 23 at 5:43pm • Like

Courtney Hollingsworth serious? ⚠️☻
August 23 at 5:43pm • Like

Tanya Harris For reals y'all. Baby's up, baby's walking.
August 23 at 5:44pm • 26

Shannon Fisseau OMG!!!! 😄😄😄😄
August 23 at 5:44pm • Like

Laura Tickle that is Awesome!!! #trulyblessed #godisgreat
August 23 at 5:45pm • 2

Tammie Floyd Grimshaw am i really seeing wht im seeing?? txt me NOW
August 23 at 5:47pm • Like

Jay Carmean Hollllllllyyyyy shit. :o)
August 23 at 5:50pm • Like

Brooke McElwrath Yay!!!
August 23 at 5:50pm • Like

Destiny Nettles How's Cam doing that?
August 23 at 5:51pm • Like

Ricky Necaise wat up
August 23 at 5:52pm • Like

Nadara Beaugez Tammie Floyd Grimshaw just called me. I cannot BELIEVE what I'm looking at and also that it happened on same day as Randy Beaugez and I's 1st anniversary!! Greatest day EVER. 😄😎😄😄😄😄😄😄
August 23 at 5:53pm • 4

Ashtyn Dugas so confused . . . how is he standing???
August 23 at 5:54pm • Like

DeAnna Sumrall 😊 #truemiracle #goarmy
August 23 at 5:56pm • 3

Joey Mauffray No way thje fucking Obummer-run VA did that shit, tell your bro call me
August 23 at 5:56pm • 1

Skyler Huey at ease private cuz YOU . . . ARE . . . HEALED!!!!
August 23 at 5:57pm • 2

Heath Quave No one ever ever doubt the power of prayer ever again. I'm crying tears of joy for you and your brother. This is a true miracle. This is beyond comprehension.
August 23 at 5:58pm • 13

Ronda Varnau girl that is so unfuckingbelievible OMG 😊
August 23 at 5:58pm • Like

Kimberly Ladner Power of GOD.
August 23 at 6:01pm • Like

Michelle Kuhn Girard so happy for you!! wow!!
August 23 at 6:03pm • Like

By the time the following comment appeared, almost eight hours later, 294 people—almost double the total number of Tanya's Facebook friends— had posted comments on the photograph:

Jesse Castanedo Dear Tanya Harris I'm a reporter for the Sun Herald and would like to speak with your brother asap if that would be ok. My number is (228) 896-2100.
August 24 at 1:32am • Like

Cameron didn't see these. Tanya read some of them aloud but rarely, she recalls, did his responses rise above grunts or snorts of semi-acknowledgment or the occasional inquiry about names churned up from the past ("Ol' Skyler, damn. He still dating that stripper chick?"). Mostly, she says, Cameron stared at his legs, with a not-unhappy frown, as he raised them, twitched them, rubbed them, squeezed them, jolted them, bent them—as though constantly subjecting them to a battery of tests designed to verify and then re-verify and then verify again the actuality of what'd occurred, as Lazarus might've kept pressing a palm to his chest to feel the impossible thumping therein.

In other ways the evening was routine. Cameron washed down his scheduled meds with Bud Light. Tanya ordered some delivery po' boys which they ate while watching an episode of *Extreme Weight Loss*. Tanya's phone kept ringing and dinging until Cameron barked at her to silence it and then it just buzzed buzzed buzzed buzzed buzzed. They watched two episodes of *Ice Road Truckers: Deadliest Roads* but not in their usual way, not with Cameron swishing his head and sounding yawps of astonishment at the crazy risks the show's drivers took. (Tanya once asked her brother how someone who'd ridden Strykers up mountain passes laced with IEDs could be so blown away by truckers navigating ice roads. Without looking over and without a second's thought he answered, "Aw, you can do anything when you ain't got the choice not to.") Instead they halfwatched it, with Tanya monitoring her phone and Cameron his legs. Then she made for her bedroom, circling back to give her brother a long embrace, and afterward Cameron felt himself alone in the blue-lit smoke of the room, alone with his legs.

"People don't understand," he'd say about this moment later, "when you're paralyzed, your legs are there but they aren't there. They're yours but they're not yours." About his restored legs, strangely, he felt similarly: that they, too, were not quite his, that what was powering them was independent from him, apart from him, that they were his to control but not quite own. With that feeling came a passing chill of something like fear. After those years of *what-if* questions blooming weed-like in his head— what if he hadn't followed Staff Sergeant Lockwood down that trail; what if he hadn't joined the Army; what if his mother hadn't died; he'd peeled these questions back toward infinity—he'd more recently decided, perhaps just to keep those thorny weeds at bay, that the *what-ifs* didn't matter because the arc of his life was fixed: It was what it was.

Until today, when it wasn't. The movement of his legs—he lifted one now, examined it in the frizzled DirecTV glow—seemed to sweep clean his future but more importantly negate his past. What did *post-traumatic* mean when the trauma no longer applied? In that dark room he felt he had neither a sense of the past nor of the future—only the mystifying, fluid present. When his hand touched his heightened leg it was as though for the first time and perhaps also for the last. What he'd thought, what he'd felt, what he'd loved, what he'd hated, what he'd done and had done to him, what he'd lost and had taken from him: All this felt erased by that touch. In equal measures these thoughts exhilarated and terrified him and to expel them he sucked down what remained of the warm can of beer and tried focusing on the television screen. Staff Sergeant Lockwood, he remembered, used to make fun of him for this kind of starry-headed thinking, used to accuse him of spending too much time sniffing the poppy fields. What would Lockwood say—what *could* he say, having more adversely survived the same blast—about what'd happened today? But this was another thought he expelled.

Sometime after two a.m. Cameron wheeled himself to his room but stopped his chair several feet from the bed. He raised himself from the chair and hobbled those last few feet, his legs as spent as if those feet had been uphill miles. He didn't pray that first night, for himself or for anyone else, because as his head weighted the pillow his eyelids fell instantly shut. The next thing he recalls is the queer spectacle of his bedding all tangled at the foot of his bed in the late-morning light, after almost half a decade of waking to the sight of undisturbed bedding at the bottom half. He'd kicked in his sleep. He'd *kicked ass* in his sleep. "Tanya!" he hollered out. "Tanya!" He could hear the clomps of her feet as she came rushing toward his room, too stricken with jubilance to register the terror in those clomps. "Tanya, check this shit out!"

four

B Y THE TIME THE *SUN HERALD*'S JESSE CASTANEDO ARRIVED
at the Harris house, early the next evening, 790 comments hung beneath Tanya's post, with 561 people having shared the photograph with
various other Facebook friends or groups. Excepting the first sixty or seventy people who left comments, most of whom Tanya knew (or knew of,
as friends of friends), these later commenters were almost all strangers—
many of them bearing names that Tanya found not just unfamiliar but
unpronounceable.

Despite the wide scree of nationalities, races, and languages represented, these later messages tended to be uniform in their sentiments. (A
significant chunk were the result of Tanya's former high-school classmate
Heath Quave, a youth minister, sharing the photo and his explanation
for it with an evangelical Facebook prayer group.) Cameron's recovery
was God's doing, they said, and stood as bedrock proof not of God's
existence—this was mostly a given—but of his grace, his magnificence,
his mercy, his sustained attention to the modern world. Some of the commenters begged for miracles of their own, as though to piggyback on what
they saw as Cameron's consecrated fortune. Others addressed Cameron
himself, unaware of or indifferent to the oblique intermediaries. Many
typed variants of hallelujah, while more than a hundred others registered
a simple "Amen." Taken together, they exude a kind of tent-revival fervor:

Loney Renzko GOD is GOOD all the time, all the time GOD is
GOOD!!!!!
August 24 at 4:03am • Like

Mysongwi Haokip I dnt worry or afraid of anythn in dis world cozs God's with me, like hs was wid dis man, and i thank God for guidn' me and gvn' me my life til nw today .praise the Lord Amem.
August 24 at 4:12am • Like

Mark Donetto That's so cool as always and for ever and ever for hour only number one and only god and jesus chirst from the bloos of the savior from heaven
August 24 at 4:17am • Like

Eva Paranhos Leuch I pray for a miracle like this for my father's recovery for his illness who is confined in the hospital for the past three weeks and I am still hoping for the Lord's healing power. Lord this I ask to please grant me this prayer petition.
August 24 at 4:34am • Like

Muhaluleh Esau Johnny Look upon his miracles and be sore afraid. Surely his salvation is near those who fear him,that his glory may dwell in us ,"may God bless you all"
August 24 at 4:37am • Like

Chianne Hudnall Please man in the picture pray for me and my two sons John and Grant for healing of diabetes Please .In the name of Jesus
August 24 at 4:59am • Like

RaeJean Spinks The Lord has lifted this wounded Warrior into his bosom and made right what was wrong! See God's power! He's in control of everything. Then Jesus said, "Come to me, all of you who are weary and carry heavy burdens, and I will give you rest. Take my yoke upon you. Let me teach you, because I am humble and gentle at heart, and you will find rest for your souls. For my yoke is easy to bear, and the burden I give you is light." (Matthew 11:28-30 NLT)
August 24 at 5:03am • Like

Debbie Barnett Rees Amen!! . . . please say a prayer for my sweet husband Mike who also served in Afghanistan. . . . he is havin medical issues & he needs Gods healin. . . . . God is the

ultimate healer. . . . God has got this!!!. . . . TIA . . . God blees all!
August 24 at 5:18am • Like

Jhazzmine Ejaz I love you jesus.
August 24 at 5:21am • Like

Snježana Vrlićlvčin Just like this miracle.. dads scans to be
clean tomorrow.. Toddler not to have more seizures and for myself
bec i am paranoid because of that
August 24 at 5:33am • Like

Nishe Massagli I need a big miracle to all my issues god knows
them so with more prayers he can work in my miracle too god
bless you all I'm the name if Jesus Christ
Amen
August 24 at 5:39am • Like

Yankle Wazzyboy Rumbidzai Sir pls I want u to pray for a
lady who has bein attack by nitmare n things of d world.she is
in a church yard rit now,bt she did lot of thins to herself in d luv
of money n fashion thins.I want u to also pray for my mom to
except dis lady back who has bein posess by demon spirit as
her daughter dan refusing her back in d hme.i need job, travel
experience n a gud luv 1 who will luv me for who i m nt bein I
don't v wealth.
August 24 at 5:47am • Like

Willy Nzepop j'ai confiance en mon dieu et je sais qu'il mettra
tout en oeuvre pour ma réussite sur cette terre
August 24 at 5:50am • Like

Hal Baker Booyah in Jesus name Let everything that has breath
Praise the Lord
August 24 at 5:57am • Like

Shirley Coffman pleasepraythat god help me get strogerwith the
strok i had in jun i I amtierd of fighting alone
August 24 at 6:02am • Like

Cameron did read some of these, at Tanya's urging, though fewer and fewer after the first hundred, and hardly any after about the five hundredth comment. The later ones were often repetitive, hammers striking a nail already pounded deep into wood—and, reading them, Cameron sometimes felt himself to be the nail, stricken with sudden force and meant to hold something larger together. Still, they exerted a not-insignificant force on him. The unanimity in their messages—that Cameron's recovery was an incontestable act of God, an authentic miracle in its purest Coca-Cola sense—cast doubt upon his own doubts. "When you don't really understand something," he says, "and there's eight or nine hundred people claiming they do, it's hard to ignore that."

Cameron's notion of what'd happened to him in the Biz-E-Bee parking lot was a void, and over the course of the twenty-four hours that followed people came rushing in to fill that void. They did this digitally, of course, but also in person, with a parade of friends and acquaintances dropping by the house the next day. They came to congratulate Cameron, to embrace him, to toast his recuperation, to deliver him gifts of beer and flowers and fried chicken and pecan pie and seven-layer dip and a new-in-the-box football, and, most of all, to watch him showboat across the back lawn (on crutches that Tanya had arranged for him to borrow). At the sight of this they wagged their heads, slapped their open mouths, applauded, knelt down and prayed, and sometimes wept.

And while God was invoked in these offline interactions as well, it was still, to Cameron, as shorthand for something that couldn't otherwise be explained. He recalls conversations related to this back in Afghanistan, during philosophical "oxygen wasting" sessions with a couple of guys from his platoon: about the way the Afghans accepted everything that happened or was going to happen as God's will, the whole *Insha'Allah* mindset, and how impossible it was for Cameron and his platoon mates to reconcile that credo with the physical world as they understood it, with the world you sank your boots into, bled on. They'd once had to inform a villager that most of his family—wife, daughter, three sons, two nephews—was dead, having been executed by Taliban gunmen during a raid on a civilian minibus. "It's God's will," the man kept saying, according to their interpreter, eventually provoking a blast of outrage from a lieutenant: "If these motherfuckers would start understanding that shit like this is the Taliban's will, and not God's, we could start checking ourselves out of this shithole."

Yet that villager's mindset didn't strike Cameron as all that different from the way the platoon's born-agains—that same lieutenant among them—often ascribed their fates to "God's plan." Will versus plan: To Cameron the difference was like four quarters versus a dollar bill. A three-Stryker convoy goes rolling down a road in Paktika Province, with Cameron in the lead vehicle. An IED detonates beneath the Stryker in the rear. Two of the soldiers inside die almost instantly; the gunner survives, but with a crushed forehead and no eyes; and five more soldiers stagger from the wreckage bearing little more than cuts and bruises. One of the dead was the married father of twin daughters, and on his wrist was a bracelet he'd made by joining together his babies' hospital identification tags; one of the survivors enjoyed hurling filled urination bottles at Afghan children pleading for water on the roadside. To Cameron it seemed capricious and cruel to suggest this event represented divine intent, that underlying all that carnage was some semblance of a moral order. God's will or God's plan: These phrases had seemed like stand-ins for "I don't know," verbal or mental disguises masking the possibility that nothing more than random chance dictated who died and who didn't. Or as one of his platoon mates put it, quoting from the movie *No Country for Old Men:* "The point is there ain't no point."

Extending this line of thought into his Biloxi backyard, Cameron found himself wondering: If it'd been God's will/plan for him to walk, then why had God paralyzed him in the first place? He knew what his old Sunday school teacher would answer: that his paralysis had been a *test,* like when God dispatched Abraham to kill his son, Isaac, atop Mount Moriah. But if it'd been a test, wouldn't he have needed to *pass* it? Nothing Cameron had done since returning from Afghanistan seemed to qualify for a passing grade, unless he counted not killing himself—but all that should've earned him was a participation trophy. It seemed an awfully low bar for a miracle.

These were thoughts Cameron kept to himself, however, as his visitors praised Jesus and asked him what it felt like to be on the receiving end of a miracle. A few pressed him for sensory details about the supernatural: Had he heard God's voice, had he seen Jesus's face? At one point the conversation shifted to Todd Burpo and Lynn Vincent's bestselling book *Heaven Is for Real* along with the movie adaptation that had been released that spring: Had Cameron read or seen it? (No.) Would he like to borrow the book? (Yeah, sure.) For Cameron, contradicting this level of certainty with doubt felt like a futile exercise, if not an insulting one. Nor did he feel capable of articulating his own vague and more secular reckoning of what type of miracle he'd experienced—the million-to-one play that his body had somehow cooked up, the nine laterals his nerve endings must've thrown to pull off this somatic victory. Because here came his fourth-grade teacher, Mrs. Lacey, having rushed to Reconfort Avenue after seeing Cameron's photo on her daughter's Facebook page—launching herself into his arms, sobbing "thank you Jesus, thank you Jesus" until Tanya had to pry her off so that an unsteady Cameron could sit back down. Moments like these felt immune to nuance.

Not until the *Sun Herald*'s Jesse Castanedo put the question to him directly, however, did Cameron realize how much this crowd-sourced interpretation of his recovery had affected him—had in some ways overwhelmed him. "Do you think God performed a miracle yesterday?" asked the reporter. Until then, the questions had been about factual matters—what happened and when—and in Castanedo's recording of the interview one hears Cameron responding with a crisp and obliging efficiency, addressing Castanedo as sir and chronicling the previous day's events with military concision. Then arrives a very long pause after the question about God: twenty-three seconds of silence, before Castanedo gently repeats the question.

Months later, after training with a media consultant and learning that you needn't answer questions directly ("answer the question you want to be asked, not the one you're actually asked"), Cameron would come to see how easily he could've evaded it, could've bent the question to his answer rather than the other way around. But this dynamic—and the cynicism underlying it—was still alien to him. Castanedo was asking him a yes or no question, thereby compelling him to answer yes or no—even if his honest answer lay somewhere in between.

Twenty-three seconds: To reject the divine nature of his recovery, by responding with even a qualified no, was out of the question. Denying

God's active hand, he felt, would betray all the well-wishers who'd been streaming in and out of his house that day (some of whom were present during the interview, discernible in the background of the audio) as well as the hundreds of people who were still, at that very moment, hosanna-ing his photo on Facebook and channeling their prayers to and through him. Doing so would also betray Mrs. Dooley and the jubilant faith she'd shown as she'd come singing her way across the parking lot. And in some convoluted way, he thought, it would also betray his own dead mother, whom he'd never known to skip Mass on Sunday and who, for all he knew, might have engineered his recovery from up in Heaven, bequeath-ing her reward for a faithful life to her doubt-ridden son on earth. To give voice to those doubts in that moment—to answer with some variation of "I don't know"—struck him as equally wrong, or maybe, for the weakness it evinced, even worse. Because though his doubts were real, they were still just doubts: clouds drifting low and heavy through his mind.

It took Castanedo repeating the question to pull an answer from Cam-eron. "Yessir," he finally said. "I do. I think God decided he had another plan for me." This last line, he later admitted, was an inversion of some-thing an Army chaplain had said to him at the hospital at Landstuhl, a few days after his injury. "God decided he had another plan in mind for you," he'd said, holding Cameron's limp hand in his. At the time he'd registered the chaplain's line in much the same insensible way he was registering the intravenous fluids entering his arm, and he was surprised, four years later, by the ease with which he retrieved it. He saw Castanedo smiling as the reporter lowered his head to jot this into his notepad.

If Tanya's Facebook post—which required personal knowledge of Cameron's former condition to appreciate, or, in the case of the later far-flung commenters, a measure of blind trust—displayed some virality, Castanedo's *Sun Herald* feature all but exploded.

The story, which ran under the headline PARAPLEGIC BILOXI VET EXPERIENCES 'MIRACULOUS' RECOVERY; 'GOD DECIDED HE HAD AN-OTHER PLAN FOR ME,' was neither long—about eighteen column inches, in newspaper-speak—nor probing. Castanedo quoted the pastor at Biloxi's largest Catholic church, who said it sure sounded like a miracle to him, as well as an orthopedic surgeon in Gulfport, who said it was impossible to issue an "armchair diagnosis" but that he was unaware of any other spontaneous, post-traumatic recovery of function like the one described to him. (Familiar with its strict policies against public comment on specific medical cases, Castanedo didn't attempt to contact the VA hospital.) But the story's nimble atmospherics—and the quiet, low-slung heroism that underlit Castanedo's portrayal of Cameron—cast a captivating glow. By August 28, two days after its publication in the *Sun Herald*'s print and online editions, hit counters on the online version had already registered more than three million page views. "If you exclude our Katrina-related coverage, it's been the most-viewed story in the history of the paper's website," says Castanedo. "It sort of boggles the mind." By week's end, the story had been picked up not only by religious websites, such as Beliefnet, GodVine, and the Christian Post, but also by more mainstream outlets such as the Drudge Report, Huffington Post, and BuzzFeed, where, for a while on BuzzFeed's "omg" feed, a rewritten version sat lodged between 14 PLACES YOU'D NEVER BELIEVE WERE IN SCOTLAND and 7 GLORIOUS PHOTOS OF IDRIS ELBA'S BULGE.

Precisely what accounts for online virality—the particular triggers that propel people to share content, be it a news story or lolcat video—remains a knotted mystery that content producers, marketers, and social scientists are working feverishly to untie. But Castanedo has a few hypotheses about why Cameron's story broke through. "It was an incredibly positive story, for one thing," he says. "People crave uplift. And it was an emotional story—an emotional *mystery*, really. Just think about the core elements: You've got a paralyzed veteran, this very solid and relatable young man, who somehow regains his ability to walk. If you're religiously orientated, it's a confirmation of your faith that you might feel driven to share. If you're a non-believer, it's kind of an out-there mystery that makes you curious. I think it just pressed a lot of different buttons."

One button left unmentioned by Castanedo is timing. Saturated with unrelentingly grim headlines, the summer of 2014 was proving "an anxious and depressing muddle," as the *New Yorker*'s George Packer characterized it. An outbreak of the Ebola virus in West Africa was threatening to become a pandemic; Israel and Hamas were engaged in a bloody tit-for-tat in Gaza; an airliner was blown out of the sky over eastern Ukraine, the bodies of its victims left strewn across wheat fields for days on end; the manically endearing actor and comedian Robin Williams hanged himself in his bedroom; an unarmed black teenager was shot and killed by police in the St. Louis suburb of Ferguson, sparking violent unrest; and with the swift and sudden rise of the militant Islamic State in Iraq and Syria, the Middle East looked to be sinking into new depths of political instability. The night before Cameron's recovery, in fact, NBC's *Tonight Show* included a skit in which actual news anchors read fanciful stories they "wished were true," rather than the genuine ones that, as host Jimmy Fallon said, kept tilting from bad to worse.

Cameron's tale must have struck some people like a glint of hope amid all that gloom and gun smoke. Its suggestion, for those open to it, was that the impossible might be possible—that our understanding of the world and its workings, which seemed so darkly shadowed that summer, could still be dwarfed, and illuminated, by the world's enigmas. Judging by the thousands of comments left on websites and forums that week, even some skeptics found themselves wanting to believe.

Cameron himself was one of these. Despite what he'd told Castanedo— a conviction he repeated a few days later for a local television reporter—he remained privately agnostic. This discrepancy in itself didn't bother him. He'd long been adept at cordoning off his private self, at negotiating the border clashes between his inner and outer states, a skill that his Army service had only bolstered. What did bother him, however, was the agnosticism itself: the limbo of not knowing.

A party broke out at the house that second night, with a half-dozen of Tanya's girlfriends pouring steady refills of blender margaritas, and Cameron discovered, a bit to his surprise, that with inebriation came clarity, that with tequila came faith. "Every time I'd get up to pee, when I'd get a minute alone," he recalls, "I could feel myself getting more and more certain about it being a miracle. I could almost see it happening in the mirror." He even got around to praying that night, after fleeing the living room sometime after one a.m. when one of Tanya's girlfriends asked, more curiously than lasciviously, if "*everything* below the waist" had been restored. (Tanya threw a hairbrush at her.)

Cameron hadn't prayed since his mother's death—not for any dramatic reasons related to it, but rather because she wasn't there to hound him about it anymore. Kneeling beside his bed the same way he'd done as a child, with the room spinning like an unlit carousel and with the cackling of Tanya and friends bleeding through the walls, he thanked God for the healing. "I don't remember exactly what I said, and I'd probably be too embarrassed to repeat it if I did," he says. "It was pretty over the top." And then, despite the elated certainty that'd been building in his bloodstream for hours, he found himself asking God for a sign—for some kind of signal that would confirm God's role in his recovery. But even as he was asking it, he says, he was imagining God's affronted rebuttal: "Healing you wasn't sign *enough*?" He woke up on the floor late the next morning, stricken both by a hangover and the resumption of doubts. He treated both, he admits, by opening a can of Bud Light.

When Dr. Janice Lorimar-Cuevas called him the following afternoon, then, her voice was a welcome one. He'd regained a significant amount of muscle stamina by then—enough to navigate his way around the house without crutches, though not without clinging to walls or furniture for support. While his legs were strengthening, however, he felt that his mind was weakening—faltering under the weight of agnosticism. Dosing himself with beer and company was lightening that load—he describes the seventy-two hours following his recovery as "a rolling party" similar to the way they celebrate the days leading up to Mardi Gras—but he recognized the clarity this yielded him as ephemeral and artificial: "distraction therapy," to crib a term from his VA social worker, for his incomprehension. Yet that weight wasn't one from which he could free himself—his media interviews, he felt, were proof of that. Someone else had to lift that weight from him. "I guess I can be there as soon as you want me," he told Dr. Lorimar-Cuevas—because if anyone could do it, he figured, she could.

Except she didn't—at least not in the way he was expecting.

His entrance into Building 30 of the Gulf Coast Veterans Health Care System—on crutches, with Tanya at his side—provided Cameron his first taste of celebrity: double-takes of recognition, unusually effusive greetings from passing staffers, elbowings, gapes, a low hiss of whispers trailing in his wake. When he took a seat in the waiting area, as Tanya checked him in for his appointment, an elderly man sitting across from him fastened him with a hard and concentrated stare.

He said, "You the one from the newspaper."

The man appeared bloated all over, as though inflated, and some sort of rosy, flaky skin condition claimed much of his big hairless scalp. A cane rested against his chair.

"Yessir," Cameron answered.

The man nodded, and then with significant effort removed his wallet from his back pocket. Tremors shook his hands as he fished out a card and offered it to Cameron. Both men strained forward for the exchange.

The card, identifying him as a plumbing contractor, was yellowed and ancient-looking. The absence of an area code in front of the phone number suggested it was older than Cameron.

"That's my business card. I was in the Navy back during the Second World War."

"Lynn Faulk," Cameron read aloud. "I know a couple of Faulks."

The man announced, "I got cancer."

Cameron swallowed. "Real sorry to hear that, sir."

"I seen you in the newspaper. I'd be grateful you taking the time to say a prayer for me. About the cancer."

"Yessir," Cameron said. "I'll do that, I sure will. But"—he paused, portioning out his words with care—"I don't reckon my prayers'll work any better than yours."

"Sure look that way," the man said, just as Tanya walked up to say they were ready for Cameron to go back. "Already?" Cameron said, accustomed to the trademark long waits of the VA system, and glancing up he saw Dr. Lorimar-Cuevas herself waiting in the doorway.

"You take good care of yourself, Mr. Faulk," Cameron said after rising.

"You gonna say that prayer, right?"

"He will, mister," said Tanya, ushering her brother forward with a hand fixed lightly to his back.

Cameron had never experienced a medical visit quite like this one, with the doctor herself, rather than a nurse, administering the preliminary checkups: height and weight, blood pressure, the standard routine. Far stranger to him, though, was the way his mobility went more or less unacknowledged; the doctor said very little, in fact, beyond what was necessary to guide Cameron through the procedures. No one said much, not even Tanya, and after a while the silence attained such a presence that, when the doctor turned her back, Cameron screwed up his face at Tanya, to note the weirdness of it, and Tanya mirrored his expression back at him with a bewildered shrug.

Not until Janice was done hammering his knees, to gauge his now-normal reflexes, did the mood finally shift. "Jesus," she whispered, wagging her head with pent-up astonishment. It wasn't the absence of clonus, the jerky contractions his legs formerly exhibited during reflex testing, that broke her composure. It was rather the nearness of his rewired legs to her, the proximal, final incontrovertibleness of them. "Jesus, Jesus."

"Something else, ain't it," Cameron said, grinning.

"Whole thing happened in like a minute," said Tanya. "I'd just gone in to get some milk."

Recovering herself, Janice had Cameron tell the entire story to her again, transcribing everything into a notepad and peppering him with random seeming questions unlike any the reporters had asked him: what he'd eaten for breakfast and lunch that day, what medicines he'd taken and when, if he ever used illegal stimulants or steroids or other drugs ("please let your brother answer," she had to instruct Tanya), whether or not he'd applied sunscreen or anything else to his legs that day, if he'd recently received an electrical shock, whether or not he'd felt anything at all different in the hours, days, or weeks leading up to that Saturday afternoon. After a while Cameron gathered there was some *aha* detail she was hunting—was there something about how many fried oysters he ate that could shed light on this?—so when the battery of questions finally ended, without any sign of an epiphany from her, he asked, half-playfully, "So was it a miracle?"

"Ah, that." She grimaced. "I don't believe in miracles, personally. So my own answer would be no."

"Then what *did* happen?" asked Tanya.

Ignoring Tanya, Janice told Cameron, "We're going to be running you through several different tests today. MRI, EMG, some others—you're basically getting the whole alphabet. And then later this week—or tomorrow if you can swing it—I'd like to get you over to Keesler for something called a DTI. That stands for Diffusion Tensor Imaging. It's not something we can do here. And then we're going to talk about getting you back into physical therapy for monitoring."

"Damn," said Cameron.

"It's going to be a long day, I know," she said. "But a heck of a lot happier than our usual consults, right?"

Cameron nodded and smiled, and then straightening himself on the examination table he asked, "So what happened to me, doc?"

"Something I can't explain at the moment," she said. This most fundamental of questions—the first one she'd expected Cameron to ask, and one she herself wanted answered—was one she'd hoped to somehow put off answering. "Definitely not until I get a look at the test results."

Janice saw a pall of disappointment darken Cameron's expression, and she heard it, too, in the long sigh he emitted. "Then can you maybe tell me what *might've* happened, because—"

"No," she said. "I can't."

Tanya slapped her thighs and muttered something unintelligible.

"You can't?" Cameron said.

Shaking her head no, Janice watched the disappointment on Cameron's face blacken into frustration. A faint growl edged his voice as he asked, "So is there *anything* you can tell me about why I'm not sitting in my damn wheelchair right now? Or if I might be back in it tomorrow? Because you already said it wasn't a miracle, so—"

"Look," she said, setting aside her notepad and softening her tone in direct proportion to how much Cameron's had hardened. "We're kind of in uncharted waters here, both of us. Wonderful waters, obviously, but uncharted. The way medicine usually works is that a patient comes in presenting symptoms, and the physician dials in a diagnosis from a range of possibilities. In your case, we're coming at it from the reverse angle, which we definitely like"—she smiled at him, drawing a gentle nod in response—"but also without that range of possibilities."

"So you got no idea," Tanya said.

"Here's everything I know," Janice told Cameron. "The imaging from prior testing suggests—and that's all it does; *suggests*—that something we call neuroregeneration might have occurred. That's when nerves repair themselves. They do that all the time in the peripheral nervous system. That's these outer nerves"—she motioned to Cameron's arms and legs—"connecting your limbs."

"But not my spine."

"Right. That's the central nervous system. And that's where neuro-regeneration *doesn't* happen. See, when the CNS is damaged, something called a glial scar develops, and by producing different families of molecules, the glial cells inhibit nerves from regenerating. The nerves are the same as in the PNS, but their environment is different. Basically, nerves can't regrow over a glial scar. Now, we can't say until we analyze today's tests, but there's some indication that yours might have done just that."

"I don't get it," said Tanya.

Neither did Cameron, but he liked it. That molecules were involved was part of the appeal: Their role in his recovery—which, as a consistent D-grade student in high-school biology, he judged too intricate for him to probably ever comprehend—freed him from the effort he'd been expending trying to understand it from a spiritual angle. And it didn't escape his notice that this explanation harked back to his own original theory: that the wonder—the miracle—was in the design. It flattered him to think he'd been correct from the beginning, before everybody else, as he'd later say, "started filling my glass with Jesus juice."

"So today's tests'll show what, exactly?" he asked, leaning forward as though ready to immediately start them.

"If the regeneration we think we saw was actually that, and if, by progressing, that might've allowed you to regain functionality."

"Awesome," Cameron said, but noted, with a prickle of confusion, the doctor shaking her head and scowling. "But how come no one ever told me this was possible? How come they—"

"Because it's not."

"Not what?"

"Not possible. Maybe you missed what I said a second ago—sorry, I know this is a huge headful. The glial scar environment prohibits axonal regrowth. Neuroregeneration doesn't happen in the central nervous system."

"So now you're telling me something impossible happened."

"No." A fluster eroded her tone. "Because if it were impossible, it couldn't have happened."

"I am so fucking confused," said Tanya.

"Doctor," Cameron said, pausing for a moment to calm his own flustered mind. "This is the most wonderful freaking thing that ever happened to me. To anybody. I mean, it's like I got . . . it's like I got born again." The evocation didn't strike him until after he'd said it. "I don't mean like *that*. I mean physically—it's like someone hit the reset button. I mean, hell, look at me." He kicked his legs out, his heels banging the base of the exam table. "But you know what the hard part is? And I feel like shit for even saying this out loud here, walking past them other guys out there who'd kill to be in my shoes."

"Literally in your shoes," added Tanya.

"The *only* hard part?" he continued. "It's not knowing what the fuck just happened to me."

"Cameron, I totally get it," Janice said, though she hadn't anticipated this level of concern—what sounded like desperation crackling in his voice. Their phone conversation had suggested a more blithely elated Cameron, leaving her with the sense that lack of concern might present a clinical challenge for her. "We know a lot about the body and how it works, but we don't know everything. There's a number of medical conditions we simply don't understand yet. We call those idiopathic conditions. And then there are conditions we sort of understand but not really. Rabies, for instance. It's been around forever but we still don't know why it's fatal—whether it kills brain cells directly or shuts down the brain with overstimulation. If I had a rabies patient here, I'd be in the terrible position of telling that patient that he's going to die and I can't explain exactly how or why."

Cameron grunted. "Sounds like you just told me to suck it up."

"No no, not at all. What I'm saying is that I wish I could explain what happened to you, but I can't. Not yet. But we're going to test the hell out of you today, okay? Because I want to know the reason you're walking as much as you do. Maybe even more, because whatever your body did, other bodies should be able to do the same thing. We're all the same model."

"Parts is parts," he said.

Janice nodded. "Something like that."

"So until then, what?" said Cameron. "I'm supposed to say it's a—what was that, an idiotpathic condition?"

Tanya snorted.

"Idiopathic. No, it's—"

"Why *ain't* it a miracle?" Tanya broke in. "That's what the newspaper called it. That's what it looked like to me. I was right there."

Cameron nodded at his sister then turned back to Janice. "That's what a miracle is, right? Something impossible happening?"

Janice took her time asking, "Are you religious?"

"Not especially. Probably a lot more today than I was a week ago."

"Is that something you want to believe? That it was a miracle?"

"I don't know that I want to *believe* anything . . ."

"Because it's not my place to advise you on what to believe or what not to believe," said Janice. "That's for clergy. My job is to deal with what I can see."

"But it *could* be a miracle," he pressed, "if the stuff you said was impossible really happened?"

"I can't stop you from using that word. But it's not my word."

"What's your word?"

"I don't have one." She sighed. "Not yet. But since we're defining miracles here, I'll give you my own definition of one, for what it's worth. I'd say it's an event that happens in advance of an explanation for it."

Cameron digested this for a while, staring down at his knees. "So I'm like a UFO."

Janice let out a rare laugh. "I can get behind that, sure."

"U.W.O.," Tanya said, and in reply to their puzzled glances explained, "Unidentified Walking Object."

"I like that even better," said Janice. "Let's get you over to radiology, okay? They've kind of cleared the decks for you today."

In retrospect, Janice would say, this initial post-recovery consultation was a failure: She'd dismissed the possibility of a miracle without marshaling any evidence to counter it. The scant information she did divulge, moreover, contradicted her position. By disclosing that the phenomenal nature of Cameron's recovery appeared to be mirrored at the cellular level, she'd inadvertently fortified any claims for a miracle. "Because what nature can't explain," she'd say later, "supernature can. And will."

And did. As Cameron recycled her words through his mind—while lying motionless inside the white donut hole of an MRI scanner and later as a technician pricked his back and legs with needle electrodes—he experienced a clarity similar to the clarity that the tequila provided him. Science was confirming his recovery as extraordinary, but was unable to explain it—not even with a guess. The doctor had images, but the images didn't make sense. That was because his body had accomplished what bodies cannot accomplish. What'd happened to him in the Biz-E-Bee parking lot wasn't, as he'd previously thought, a miracle on par with Biloxi High throwing all those laterals to score a million-to-one touchdown. It was on par, instead, with Biloxi turning the Gulfport defenders into stone statues.

Here was the sign he'd requested, the proof for which he'd prayed: his doctor banging his knee with a rubber hammer while whispering Jesus's name.

On the ride home, overcome with euphoria unlike anything he'd ever experienced, he pulled out the business card he'd been given in the waiting room. Tanya glanced over to see him rocking slightly in the passenger seat, pressing the card to his forehead with his eyes closed and lips trembling.

"What the hell you doing?" she said.

"Shut up, I'm praying."

"You're praying?"

"Just shut up for a minute."

"Aw shit," she said.

five

THE FIRST HINT OF WHAT WAS TO BEFALL THE BIZ-E-BEE arrived on foot, on the morning of August 28, carrying a seven-foot-tall red inflatable crucifix on his shoulder. He was wearing a tunic-style white shirt from which the sleeves had been cut and a pair of faded floral-print surf shorts. Flowing indiscriminately from his jaw was a beard that was white with scraggles of yellow blond. His skin evoked a dried apricot or mango: ochre, leathery, gnarled, and here and there dusted with windblown sand. He smiled almost constantly but just shy of happily.

Lê Nhu Quỳnh was alone in the store that morning. A car honk drew his attention outside, to where the man was hauling his big red crucifix across Division Street, indifferent to the stuttering traffic. Quỳnh watched the man beeline his way across the parking lot to the front of the store where he rested his crucifix against a window, wiped the sweat from his brow with a forearm, surveyed the empty lot with a look of keen satisfaction, and then sat down on the curb.

When a customer pulled in, the man shouted some sort of welcome that Quỳnh couldn't quite make out. The man did the same with two additional customers, one of whom, a regular, said to Quỳnh at the register, "Didn't take long for the loonies to show up, huh?"

Quỳnh has never had much patience for loonies, who rank near the top of a list of human annoyances that includes drunks, solicitors, teenagers in groups of more than three, coupon users, check writers, shirtless men, hundred-dollar-bill breakers, fake-ID presenters, customers who smoke at the register, correct-change verifiers, bathroom users, spare-change dumpers, beer drinkers who bust open six-packs to buy single cans, navigators of freshly mopped wet floors, and coffee drinkers who use two or more nested cups rather than a cardboard sleeve. But loonies—or "crazies," as Quỳnh prefers—come equipped with the most complications. It's easy to evict a solicitor or to hustle out a drunk. With crazies, a more delicate touch can be required.

Quỳnh wasn't feeling delicate that morning. Hat was at the dentist with Little Kim, and because the Lês have no dental insurance (and possibly because they grant their daughter free rein to the store's soda inventory), Kim's dental appointments had been proving reliably calamitous to their checking-account balance. Quỳnh had spent the last hour girding himself for the damages, calculating, as is his wont, several worst-case scenarios; Kim's last visit had caused them to miss a lease payment on their car. But while this was the most immediate stressor, others lurked close behind: the state tax authority was threatening collection action on a first-quarter sales tax miscalculation Quỳnh had made; one of the Biz-E-Bee's vendors had revoked ninety-day terms, downgrading them to C.O.D. status; and, due to an outstanding balance, their propane supplier had padlocked the big blue cage of tanks outside. About a month before Cameron's recovery, in fact, Quỳnh had mostly stopped opening the mail. Even the certified letters he slipped unopened into stacks. Exiting the store, then, he was in zero mood for a loony.

Quỳnh is a small man, even by Vietnamese standards, yet the coiled energy he projects adds at least six inches to his stature. He wears his worries and aggravations like a very tall hat. Even behind the counter, where a degree of inertia is expected, he exudes a harried and frenetic air, tending to customers while also surveilling a bank of screens—his laptop, the security-camera feeds, and a small video monitor on which an action movie is often playing—that one regular jokingly calls the "NATO command center." For this customer and others, it can feel like buying a candy bar from an air traffic controller. The Cuban-style guayabera shirts Quỳnh favors should temper this effect, with their suggestion of bongo ease, but they don't, especially when Quỳnh overstuffs the many pockets with notes and cigarettes and vendor invoices and other workaday debris, as though ornamenting himself with stress. He seems mired in a constant state of besiegement.

"What you want?" he snapped to the man outside.

"Good morning to you, brother," came the reply.

Again Quỳnh snapped, "What you want?"

"I have come to meet Christ our Savior."

Quỳnh shook his head. "He not here."

The way the man chuckled called to mind a cartoon Santa: *ho ho haw.* "But this is the place, is it not?" The man pointed up to the sign. "The Biz-E-Bee."

"This is my store. I own it."

"Ah! Then you are a blessed man, brother." The man gestured to the pavement between his feet. "This is holy ground."

"You going to buy something?"

Again the man broadened his smile. "I have not walked all the way from Chunchula, Alabama, for nabs and a Coke, I can tell you that."

Quỳnh didn't know where Chunchula, Alabama, was, except that it was in Alabama, which meant the man was either lying about having walked or he was crazy. Or both: an even likelier possibility. "Customers only," Quỳnh told him. Now it was his turn to motion to a sign, this one on the door. "You see? No loitering."

"Oh, I don't wish to loiter. My intention is to wait."

Quỳnh waved his arms as if to disperse the foul odor of this response. "That's the same thing!"

"I see. Well then." Lifting his eyebrows and slowly turning his head, the man assessed the storefront area. "Maybe I can go 'round side, then, how'd that be?"

"No."

"All right then. How about over yonder?"

"No."

"Brother." The man's smile was diminishing now, as he lifted himself up from the curb, the effort shuddering his knees. "I've walked thirty-seven hours. We're talking about the Son of Man here."

Quỳnh folded his arms, unimpressed.

Shrugging, the man lowered his eyes. "Reckon I'll take to the sidewalk, then."

"Not there either."

"Oh come on, brother. That's a public sidewalk."

"Then go there, fine." Quỳnh turned toward the door, not quite pleased with this arrangement but guided by an old Vietnamese proverb: *Argue with a smart man, and you'll never win. Argue with a stupid man, and you'll never stop.*

"Mind I leave my cross here?" the man called after him.

"No way."

The man sighed. "You're not a Christian, hoss, are you?"

Quỳnh paused in the open doorway, his loony-evicting instinct validated by the faint growl he'd caught in the man's tone. "I'm a businessman," he said.

"All the riches of the world," said the man, extinguishing any menace with his broadest smile yet, "are to be found in Christ the Savior."

The bell above the door sounded Quỳnh's response as he returned into the store. From behind the register he watched the man haul his crucifix to the corner and lean it against a streetlamp post. He watched the man sit down beneath it on the sidewalk, facing the parking lot. And then, quite against his will, Quỳnh watched him wait.

Ignoring him should've been easy, but wasn't. The man's unbroken surveillance carried a radioactive charge that Quỳnh sensed through the glass and from forty yards away, an atomic-level disturbance that left Quỳnh feeling more jumpy and irritated than usual. Even with his back turned, he registered the man's stare. Customers provided a trickle of distraction, but after each transaction Quỳnh caught himself glancing out the window and grimacing from the way the man's eyes seemed to lock instantaneously with his. Something about the intensity of the man's waiting, too, felt infectious, so that after a while Quỳnh felt that he was also waiting—for what, he didn't know, but when he noticed the man rising he found himself gripped by a strange excitement and craning his neck for a view of what'd caused the man to stand. When it became clear the man was merely stretching his legs, Quỳnh cursed himself aloud, and, lest he go crazy himself, vowed to ignore him for good.

If not for that trickle of customers, he might've accomplished this. Every third or fourth one made some remark about the man and his cross. One asked if the man was some sort of advertisement, to which Quỳnh responded by waving his arms in that same odor-dispersing way.

Despite all the questions he'd fielded since news of Cameron's recovery broke, Quỳnh hadn't devoted much hard thought to what'd happened to Cameron outside his store. "Amazing," he sometimes said. "Crazy," he said at other times. Hat considered it a bona fide act of God, but then she considered everything an act of God. ("If she goes to the Piggly Wiggly for chicken and finds chicken on sale," he says, "that was God.") Quỳnh's own loose assessment of what'd happened chimed with Cameron's initial take: that it had been some kind of extraordinary biological event—a natural marvel, to be sure, but no more or less a marvel than the grapefruit-sized sulfide meteorite that came crashing through a friend's roof in the New Orleans neighborhood of Versailles. That it had happened at the Biz-E-Bee, he figured, was mere happenstance, as when convenience store owners in luckier states sold winning lotto tickets—though the analogy doesn't quite align, as Quỳnh points out, because store owners receive a cut of lotto winnings. All Quỳnh had received, so far, was a slew of questions and now a visit from a guy with a blow-up cross.

Hat, Little Kim, and a $443.00 receipt from the dentist entered the store just after noon. Quỳnh was goggling the receipt in openmouthed shock—this was the worst-case scenario plus a hundred dollars—when Hat asked, "What's going on with the guy outside?"

Absently, he said, "What guy?"

"The one with the big red crucifix."

"Ah, some crazy," he said. "Says he walked here all the way from Alabama."

"Alabama? Why?"

"To meet Mr. Jesus." Quỳnh started calling Jesus "Mr. Jesus" years ago, as a way of needling his wife about her faith, but the reference had long ago lost its sting and was now marital parlance.

"Because of the newspaper?"

"I guess. He wanted to loiter out front but I said no way buddy. If he stays much longer I'm calling the police."

"How long has he been there?"

"Eight thirty or nine, maybe. Right after you left."

Hat peered out the window at the man for a while. Then she went to the visi-cooler and fetched a bottle of water. As she made to open the front door Quỳnh said, "What are you doing?"

"I'm bringing him some water. It's ninety-seven degrees out there."

"I told you, he's crazy."

"Crazy or not, he's got to be thirsty."

"Then he can buy himself some water! No way. He's in front of a *store*! Don't encourage him or—"

The bell above the door sounded her rebuttal.

This kind of bickering can sometimes feel like the default dynamic for the Lês. As with most married couples, however, the true nature of their disputes is rarely related to the subject at hand. They argue about the leaves when it's the roots they're angry about.

For Quỳnh and Hat, these roots are their opposite worldviews. Quỳnh tends to see the world as a minefield of doom, with life defined by its constant brushing against death; he is never positioned more than an inch away from catastrophe. Hat's outlook can be difficult to unbraid from her faith, but, theological certainties aside, a strand of optimism runs through her. The secular branch of her perspective can sometimes feel gleaned from motivational posters—"obstacles," she's fond of saying, "are just opportunities in disguise"—yet with this earnest radiance comes a kind of strength, an immunity against the panic and angst that infect her husband. They both credit this polarity to their age difference—Quỳnh is forty-six, while Hat is thirty-three—with Quỳnh citing naïveté as a symptom of Hat's relative youth. Yet residue from their disparate childhoods in Vietnam must surely play a role as well.

Both of them left Vietnam at around the same age: Quỳnh as a seven-year-old, in 1975, and Hat, in 1989, as an eight-year-old. And both are the children of military men who failed to make it out of Vietnam alive. The similarities, however, stop there.

Quỳnh barely knew his father, who was a South Vietnamese Army colonel stationed in Nha Trang, but what he knew of him was magical. Quỳnh remains half-convinced, for example, that his father could communicate with animals—especially the geckos that overran the walls of Quỳnh's grandmother's farm in Vũng Tàu, which would halt, and then thoughtfully respond, when his father spoke gecko to them: *cac ke . . . cac ke.* When Quỳnh would ask what the geckos were saying, his father would say, "They are asking about you. They think you are too small, too much like them, and that you should eat more." Though the family lived most of the year in Saigon, it's the farm in Vũng Tàu that Quỳnh recalls most vividly: the funky smell of the longans ripening in the orchard, the black clouds of bats swarming the orchard at dusk, the betel-leaf and areca-nut aroma of his grandmother's kisses, the slow pounding of the gong lulling him to sleep during Buddhist prayer sessions, the pride and responsibility he felt when dispatched to the chicken coop to fetch the morning eggs. As to the war up north, his father rarely spoke about it, but when he did it was as a mild and temporary irritant—like a vexing business matter unworthy of discussion in the home. It would be over soon in any case, he promised. Southerners like him had been repelling invasions for generations: from the Chinese, Chams, Khmers, Japanese, and French. The communists, his weary pose suggested, would be no different.

The fall of Saigon therefore came as a galactic shock—a breach of reality. Still, his father acted nonplussed. In the days preceding the South's surrender he arranged for the family to escape the country via a patrol boat from Vũng Tàu that bore them to a U.S. liner headed for Guam. He was obligated to attend the funeral of a general, he said, but his plan was to follow in a few days and reunite with them in Guam. Instead he was captured, and almost immediately executed. Quỳnh doesn't believe that his father lied to the family about the dangers he was facing, or that he understated them, nor does he think his father was under any illusions about those dangers. His father's plan was solid, Quỳnh says, but it failed. His intelligence and effort weren't enough; the world ate him anyway.

Listening to Quỳnh recount the story of his life, one senses that Adam, interviewed years after his eviction from Eden, might employ a similarly nostalgia-crippled tone—the Fall of Man recast as the Fall of Saigon. All the tropical fruit scents and gecko magic fall away as Quỳnh's autobiography sputters forward, the vibrant colors fading into a black-and-white tableau. Penniless, and reliant on charity, the Lês—Quỳnh, his mother, and his younger sister—drifted around the United States before locating distant relatives in Biloxi, one of the congealing points in the postwar Vietnamese diaspora. Quỳnh was among the first wave of Vietnamese immigrants, and suffered the hard lot of a pioneer. He struggled through adolescence, hounded by bullies and hamstrung by his difficulties mastering English, and dropped out of high school two months before he was set to graduate. (One year later, because of students like him, the Biloxi school district instituted bilingual education.) For the next eleven years he worked as a crabber for his mother's second husband, fishing for blue crabs and selling them to restaurants and wholesalers, but that fell apart when his stepfather lost the boat to gambling debts. In the meantime he met Hat, who was seventeen at the time. On the night he proposed, she says, he noted their age difference, with fretful gravity, and also warned her that his life expectancy might be abbreviated, though he couldn't say precisely why. "He asked me to marry him," she recalls, "and then spent two hours trying to talk me out of saying yes." (She found this odd but endearing, as though his care for her well-being trumped his desire to marry her.) More than a decade passed before Hat finally became pregnant— enough years for Quỳnh to abandon hope. So when Little Kim entered the world with her underdeveloped lungs, and the doctors in the neonatal intensive care unit assigned her long odds for survival, it made a kind of grim sense to Quỳnh, relaying the click of an awful logic. He awaits calamity with an intensity rivaling that of the man outside awaiting Christ.

If Quỳnh is a man in exile, from a place as well as a time, his wife is an exhilarated escapee. For him, leaving Vietnam was a nightmare; for Hat, it was a glorious dream. This is where their age difference bears some meaningful weight: Hat was born in 1981, a bleak and scorched period in southern Vietnam. She has no memories of luscious longan orchards or magical geckos or even of her father, a former mid-level Army officer who was sentenced to a reeducation camp before she was born and subsequently died there. What she remembers, almost exclusively, is the frantic waiting in a Saigon slum, with her mother exhausting every means possible to get Hat and her two sisters out of the country. This included handing over twelve hundred dollars to a smuggler—a sum painstakingly scraped together over a six-year period—who then vanished with the money. Funds eventually dribbled in from relatives in Biloxi, along with news that the relatives' church would sponsor the family's immigration to the United States if they could somehow get to Thailand or Hong Kong.

They left in the middle of the night, crammed onto a wooden boat with more than a hundred other refugees. Hat's mother fell into a near-catatonic state, terrified of Thai pirates who were said to throw women and girls overboard after raping them. As Hat's older sisters tried consoling their mother, Hat found herself drawn beside an elderly nun sitting against a gunwale and calmly praying the rosary. The nun seemed un-afraid, her spindly fingers constantly traveling her rosary beads, and after a while Hat fell asleep with her head in the old woman's lap, tranquilized by the murmured Hail Marys and the boat's seesaw creaking. This pattern continued for days and nights, Hat's mother and sisters cowering nearby while Hat was nestled into a trance that she likens to that of a cat wait-ing out a thunderstorm beneath a house. One morning, with dawn just a coral sliver on the horizon, a tremendous commotion on board jolted her awake. They were just off the island of Kokra in the Gulf of Thailand, and a flotilla of boats was headed fast their way from land—pirates for sure. The panic that greeted this sight almost capsized their boat. Hat heard her mother wail and watched her collapse to the deck retching. Hat let out a wail, too, but holding her close the old nun hushed her, saying the Vir-gin would protect them. The boats arrived, surrounding theirs. Two pas-sengers leapt shrieking into the water, choosing the threat of sharks over the threat of pirates. But these weren't pirates. They were local fishermen who'd come to offer aid.

Hat lost track of the nun as she and the other refugees disembarked on the island, and never saw her again. But as a model for how to withstand fear and suffering, as a lodestar for courage and equanimity, Hat has never forgotten her. The story of the nun emerges, in fact, as a digression in Hat's account of Kim's weeks in the NICU—as a roundabout way of illustrating the divergent ways she and Quỳnh dealt with that trauma. Quỳnh, she says, resembled her mother on that boat, all cold sweat and tremors: He waited for his daughter to die while desperately hoping she wouldn't. Hat, in contrast, awaited Kim's recovery with no allowance for any other out-come. When she prayed, it was for the speed and ease of Kim's recovery, not for the recovery itself. She never granted God that decision because she felt certain he'd already made it.

This same rigid certitude was what Quỳnh glimpsed in his wife as she walked out the door and across the parking lot to where the man with the inflatable crucifix was stationed. Quỳnh watched her give him the bottle of water and for several minutes stand talking with him. Alone with Kim in the store, he wagged his head and cursed. Black thoughts came slinking into his mind: that perhaps this man was a serial killer and might now be inspired to dismember her, or that he was a local con artist who'd sniffed an opportunity to swindle a Christian do-gooder like Hat, or that Hat might return to the store saying the man was grateful but also wanted some Doritos.

Back inside the store she announced, "He has liver cancer."

"Oh," said Quỳnh.

"He's dying. That's why he's here. He's hoping to be cured."

"Oh," Quỳnh said again.

"He walked here for thirty-seven hours straight."

"That's a long walk." He cracked a roll of quarters into the register. "He should've taken Greyhound."

"He said you were very rude."

"What did he want me to do? This isn't a hospital. We don't *cure* people!"

"I'm just telling you what he said."

"Did you tell him we don't cure people?"

"I didn't tell him anything."

"You just gave him a Dasani water."

"I did," she said. "It's ninety-seven degrees out there and he has liver cancer."

"And hospitals have air-conditioning! And free water!"

"Do you want me to pay you for the water?"

"Why doesn't *he* pay for it?"

This argument mellowed—but didn't end—for several hours, until a van pulled into the parking lot. The van was extra-long and gray and bore the name of a Hattiesburg church on its sides. Out of the van came seven or eight people, two of them young and clean-cut but the others old and plump and slow-footed. From behind the register Quỳnh and Hat watched as the people took cellphone photos of the store and the parking lot and then joined hands in a circle. One of them spoke while the others closed their eyes and bowed their heads.

"Don't you dare bring them any water," Quỳnh told Hat, who made sure her husband noted her sneer before disappearing into the back office.

The church group's members, however, didn't want mere water. What they wanted, instead, were random portions of *everything:* beef jerky, candy bars, potato chips, sunglasses, automotive air fresheners, 5-Hour Energy shot bottles, key chains, Tylenol, cans of Dinty Moore stew. With great but reverent excitement they roamed the three aisles of the Biz-E-Bee, loading their arms with a haphazard array of nonperishables, while Quỳnh regarded them with a bewildered squint. Lined up at the counter, they peppered him with questions about Cameron's recovery, often interrupting his answers—"amazing," he told them; "crazy," he said—with more questions. They asked him for the precise spot where Cameron had stood, and after Quỳnh pointed to it several of them went outside and took turns standing there with their heads bowed again. Then one woman, white-haired and heavyset, asked Quỳnh if there was anything for sale with the name of the store on it.

"With the name on it?"

"Yessir," she said. "Like a koozie or something."

Quỳnh thought about this for a while.

"Maybe a business card?" she asked.

Quỳnh glanced around, but the only thing behind the counter were his stacks of mail. "I have some mail I could sell you," he offered.

The woman brightened. "Can I see?"

He fished out an unopened bill and laid it on the counter.

She pursed her lips. "Anything else?" she asked.

He replaced the bill with a glossy catalog from a convenience store wholesaler. On its cover was a photograph of a cream and sweetener dispensing machine upon which was glued a large label bearing the Biz-E-Bee's name and address.

"Oooh," the woman said, reaching to touch it but then withdrawing her hand. "How much for that?"

Quỳnh lifted it for a dramatic appraisal. "One dollar," he said.

"That's fine," the woman said, plucking a bill from a small change purse.

When the church group finally left the store, it was with nine pieces of Biz-E-Bee mail—including a certified letter, for which Quỳnh charged an extra fifty cents—and with Quỳnh trailing them out the door with a wide and winning smile. He posed for a group photo in front of the store and then waved as the van backed out of the lot and turned onto Division Street.

When Ollie came in to work, half an hour later, he found Quỳnh on the phone, still smiling, and nodding as he tapped keys on his laptop with the phone cradled against his shoulder. Noting Ollie's entrance, Quỳnh placed his hand over the phone's mouthpiece and told Ollie he needed him to do something. That man outside, with the big red cross? "Go bring him a Coke," Quỳnh told him. "And some Doritos too." Then he added seriously, "We have lot of work to do, big guy."

six

ON THE MORNING OF SEPTEMBER 2, TWENTY-EIGHT OF THE
Gulf Coast Veterans Health Care System's physicians and nurse
practitioners filed into the recreation hall in Building 17 for the hospital's monthly Interdisciplinary Quality Improvement Conference, or IQIC.
These IQICs—which gather clinicians together to discuss patient cases in
much the way cases get dissected in teaching hospitals—were a recent initiative, mandated by Washington, and the center's chief of staff and medical director, Dr. Larry Turnbull, made no secret of his antipathy toward
them. Any time a doctor spends talking to other doctors, went his thinking, is time stolen from patients. He opened this morning's conference
without any sort of greeting, which despite his antipathy was uncharac-
teristic of him; Dr. Turnbull's beloved Mississippi State Bulldogs football
team had three days earlier shut out Southern Miss, 49-0, and his audience was expecting at least ten minutes of a gloating recap during which
to catch up on paperwork. "Well," he said instead, "let's just get to our
business here."

Dr. Turnbull, who is seventy-four, is a native of the area—he grew up
and still lives in Pascagoula, a bit east of Biloxi—and has been the center's
chief of staff since 1994, which makes him an anomaly in the VA system,
where the moorings of appointments rarely withstand shifts in political
winds. Credit for his longevity used to be chalked up to his friendship
with Trent Lott, the former Republican senator and onetime Senate ma-
jority leader—they grew up together in Pascagoula—but Turnbull's ten-
ure has outlasted Lott's, so nowadays no one knows. Still, no one disputes
Dr. Turnbull's skills as a cardiac surgeon, which age doesn't seem to have

blunted, nor his ferocious commitment to patient care, though some—Dr.
Janice Lorimar-Cuevas among them—grumble that his concept of patient
care hasn't much evolved since his years as a combat medic in Vietnam.
"It's a country vet mentality," she says. "Sew them up in the afternoon and
put them back on the plow come morning. When you talk to him about
holistic care you get the feeling he's imagining an aromatherapy studio in
Berkeley."

Janice was on the docket (as her husband, Nap, had phrased it) that
morning—her first-ever IQIC presentation. Everyone knew why and since
everyone wanted the inside skinny on Cameron's recovery, the presentations preceding hers—including one about a recent admittee to the ER
who'd briefly but dramatically been suspected of Ebola infection—were
met with impatient disinterest. "Is there any other input we could possibly get here?" asked a frustrated clinical virologist after his Ebola-scare
presentation, to averted-eyed silence. The speed at which the meeting was
progressing, however, appeared to brighten Dr. Turnbull's mood, so much
so that when he called upon Janice for the morning's final case, he accorded her a wide and gleaming grin and said, "Now let's us all hear about
your miracle fella, Dr. Cuevas."

Janice suppressed a wince. She was already rankled by the way the
word *miracle* was being used to caulk the gaps and cracks in Cameron's
story, and she showed her irritation in the tight-lipped smile she returned
Dr. Turnbull. Maybe, she thought, he'd meant it ironically. After setting
up her laptop for her slide component, and switching on an iPhone app
with which to record the presentation, she paused to survey her audience.
No one was doing paperwork. Every eye was upon her. Dr. Turnbull, she
noticed, was flexing his fingers and still grinning, as though anticipating
entertainment.

"So our patient," she began, "is a twenty-six-year-old Caucasian male
admitted to us for outpatient care continuum. He presented as a T9 ASIA
A with zone of partial preservation of pinprick to T12. LEM score of 0.
Cause of the SCI was combat trauma—shrapnel from an IED. Date of injury, March twenty-second, two thousand ten."

As she clicked the remote control in her hand to display some of the earliest imagery in Cameron's file she felt the entire room craning toward her.

"The shrapnel entered the body from the right paraspinal area and crossed the midline through the spinal canal. It split the T9 vertebral body. As you can see from the MRI, the posterior element was shattered and the nerve roots sustained collateral damage from the burst fracture. The dura was also torn. A T9 decompression/fusion was performed at Brooke but patient showed minimal sensorimotor improvement even in the zone of partial preservation.

"But this," she went on, "is where things get really interesting." With another click of the remote she put up a slide from Cameron's current MRI. "On August twenty-third, the patient spontaneously regained lower extremity motor and sensory function."

Aside from a long *whoa* drifting from the back of the audience, the room went silent.

"Can we—can we see that first slide again?" someone shouted out.

Mental exertion, Janice saw, was contorting every face, even Dr. Turnbull's.

"When you say, 'spontaneously regained . . . ,'" someone else asked.

"I mean he stood up from his wheelchair and walked without assistance."

Murmurs overtook the room while Janice fielded a half-dozen more questions about Cameron's injury, surgery, and recovery. Frown lines began appearing as the physicians, struggling to navigate through this information, found themselves hitting blind alleys. A few shook their heads in what looked like cognitive surrender or its close cousin, amazement.

"Four-year spinal shock?" someone ventured, weakly enough to pass it off as a joke.

A hand went up. "I realize we're in unusual territory here," asked a nurse practitioner who worked in the neurology department, "but are we actually in, you know, *uncharted* territory? Recovery from SCIs can be awfully variable. I'm just wondering if there's any precedent here . . ."

"Great question, and it's why I consulted with Dr. Price," Janice replied, referring to the nurse practitioner's department head. "Let me just put something on the screen here—one sec. Okay, this is data from a two thousand seven ICCP study examining rate of spontaneous recovery after an SCI." Onto the screen went a bar graph illustrating the percentages of paralyzed patients who'd recovered function, based on the A to E grades established by the American Spinal Injury Association's Impairment Scale, known as ASIA. "As you can see," Janice explained, "after one year, using the model systems, about eighty-three percent of ASIA A patients remained ASIA A"—Cameron's former grade, meaning a complete absence of motor and sensory function below the injury. "Nine percent converted to ASIA B." (Complete loss of motor function but incomplete sensory loss.) "Seven percent to ASIA C and one percent to ASIA D." (Both motor and sensory loss incomplete.) "But ASIA A to ASIA E," Janice went on, which was the leap Cameron had made: "Zero percent.

"So, yeah," she concluded. "This is way out there."

"What really astounds me," said an orthopedic surgeon in the front row, before pausing to laugh: "Well, a *lot* astounds me here. But one thing—I'm presuming there was significant muscle atrophy in his legs after four years. So, then, the sudden onset of mobility . . . I mean, even if you exclude neurogenic atrophy, four years of secondary disuse atrophy alone is enough to . . ." He rubbed the side of his face. "Let's forget what looks like neuroregeneration for a second. Let's dial it down. Ambulation on its own seems *really*—problematic."

"Yeah, that was my first reaction too," Janice said. "I will note that his muscular recovery has conformed to a more typical pattern since that initial burst. For the most part he requires crutches now, as we're starting to rebuild strength in PT. I suppose one possibility is that an adrenal rush in that moment allowed for an unusual degree of muscle contraction—"

"An extraordinary degree," said the orthopedic surgeon.

"I wasn't there in the parking lot," said Janice, "so I can't say with certainty how long he stood or how many steps he took. This was self-reported."

"But he was able to walk at your consult, five days later? Unassisted?"

"He was," she said. "With difficulty, but yes. He walked."

The audience chewed this for a while.

"Is there any chance we're looking at a somatoform disorder here? A conversion disorder?" someone asked, raising the possibility that Cameron's paralysis had been psychological, a type of mental disorder—that he'd converted psychological trauma into physical symptoms, and that the only thing that'd been preventing him from walking since 2010 was his mind.

Janice shook her head. "The etiology of the SCI was organic," she said. "That's evident in the imagery. This wasn't psychogenic."

"And dermatome tests," someone else added, "would seem to rule that out."

"But is it possible—I'm just riffing here—is it possible the physiological damage wasn't as severe as the initial presentation suggested? If you factor in the overlay of a somatoform? You've got penetrative spinal trauma with a patient exhibiting a corresponding lack of motor function. It's easy to imagine his attending physician at Landstuhl thinking, well, if it quacks like a duck, it's a duck—"

"Again, I think we can see it clearly on the scans," Janice said. "It is a duck. Or was."

"Somatoform, though . . . that could potentially explain the sudden ambulation," said the orthopedic surgeon. "If his leg muscles had stimulation or some movement in his sleep over the years . . ." He shook his head, grimacing. "Maybe. I don't know."

"But aren't we ignoring what appears to be axonal sprouting?" someone else said. "That seems to be the elephant in the room. Somatoform can't account for those MRIs, folks."

"But clerical error can," someone said.

"An SCI *with* an overlaying somatoform disorder *plus* a scan mix-up?" said another. "Isn't that pushing coincidence to its outer limits?"

"I'm more comfortable with coincidences than with miracles," the orthopedic surgeon grunted.

"I'll second that," Janice said, a moment later realizing she'd unwittingly endorsed the somatoform disorder theory, which she found wholly unconvincing.

"What about infectious discitis?" someone else asked. "This was a penetrating wound."

"As you can see from the imaging," Janice replied, clicking the remote, "there's no indication of any epidural abscess. No indications of effusions."

"And we evaluated spinal fluid?"

"We did," Janice said.

"Can we go back to that study for a moment?" someone asked. "What's the rate of conversion from ASIA B to E? I'm curious. Is there one?"

Janice clicked the remote a few times. "About one percent," she answered.

"Huh," came the response. "So if there *was* some degree of sensory function present, and he was misclassified, maybe we're not *entirely* in uncharted waters . . ."

"Based on the study parameters, yes—possibly. Dermatome test results can be variable, even within individual patients, but we should note that at Landstuhl, Brooke, and here—he never scored above zero. Not once."

"Have we trended electrolytes?" someone said. "I might be grasping at straws but . . . but, hell, I guess we all are . . ."

This went on for another fifteen minutes, with Janice finding herself increasingly isolated onstage as certain theories gained backers and alliances started forming in the audience: somatoform versus abscess versus ASIA misclassification versus clerical error versus what an anesthesiologist deemed "shit happens."

"I did a residency in pathology before switching to anesthesiology," he explained. "And in pathology we sometimes had to say—excuse my language—*shit happens*. By which we meant the precise cause of death just couldn't be determined, not with precision. Maybe there's a corollary there . . ."

The orthopedic surgeon, with a teasing grin, swiveled around to say, "Bill, I can't think of anything more terrifying for a surgeon than to hear an anesthesiologist uttering the phrase 'shit happens.' "

Above the resultant laughter came Dr. Turnbull's croaky drawl. "I hate to spoil all this fun here, folks, but I'm afraid I gotta cut this off," he announced. "I'll grant this is fascinating stuff but we could hash it out till the cows come home. I think we should all thank Dr. Cuevas here for the excellent and very unusual presentation." All eyes were pinned on Turnbull now, since custom was for him to have the final word on case presentations—and with anything but cardiac cases, to which he often dispensed granular-level opinions, this final word tended toward coach-like platitudes. He cleared his throat. "The purpose of these lovely conferences, as we all know, is to evaluate care quality to determine whether there's room for improvement. So let's ride that pony. Anyone got a thought as to how we might've achieved better care efficacy here? Or what we can do better for this boy going forward?"

No one said anything.

"If we look at this from an outcome-based perspective," he went on, "and I think we should—I'd have to say this appears to be a successful damn case. This boy came into our care as a paraplegic and during his care here regained full function in his lower extremities. I'd say he hit bingo. Anyone care to argue that definition of success?"

Again, no one said a word. Scattered shrugs were all.

"Now, Bill," he said to the anesthesiologist, with a touch of mock-sternness. "There's another way you could've put that, uh, sentiment from pathology. It's the way my mama used to put it: The Lord does work in mysterious ways."

"God happens," came the anesthesiologist's rejoinder.

This time it was Janice's voice cutting through the laughter. "With all due respect, sir," she said to Dr. Turnbull, perhaps more icily than she intended. "The Lord actually works in predictable ways."

Anxious expressions in the audience alerted her to how insolent this might've been received, and when her gaze returned to Dr. Turnbull she could see this was the case. Below his combed-back white hair his face seethed with the redness of a lobster splashing into boiling water. "I realize the cases on y'all's schedule today might not be as interesting as this one," he announced, his eyes pegged hard upon Janice, "but neither are your patients as healthy as this boy seems to be. So let's go give the rest of 'em our best effort, boys and girls. Let's try to get 'em all to hit bingo."

As the audience members began standing Dr. Turnbull stood up and announced, "One additional note, folks. Can y'all listen for a second? There's obviously a great deal of press interest in Dr. Cuevas's case so let's make sure that everything that you've heard and said in this room stays right here. The usual protocol remains in effect—everything goes through public affairs, *everything*." His face still flushing, he shot a quick glare at Janice, who'd briefly (and, she'd thought, benignly) appeared on a Fox News segment after getting ambushed outside the hospital. "Thank y'all for your attendance."

And with that Dr. Turnbull left—so swiftly that Janice was forced to abandon her laptop onstage in order to pursue him. (She did stash her iPhone, still recording, into her lab coat.) She squeezed her way through hallway discussions of Cameron's case, one of them intriguingly heated, and trailed Dr. Turnbull's white coat out the door. A cooling bay breeze was drawing patients and visitors outside, and dozens were lounging and smoking in the circular courtyard that Dr. Turnbull was bisecting, most of them congregated around a fountain in the middle. The courtyard had just been restored after hosting construction equipment for two years for a $304 million expansion of the GCVHCS campus, still ongoing, that Dr. Turnbull had helped shepherd through congressional thickets. The hot drowsy summer had been hard on the newly planted grass; only a few green tufts were struggling upward.

Dr. Turnbull must've heard Janice's heels clicking fast and insistently behind him because he turned to face her, just before the fountain, without her calling his name.

Flatly, he said, "Dr. Cuevas."

"I didn't mean any disrespect back there," she said. For a marathon runner, she was oddly out of breath. "I'm sorry if my comment came across that way. By predictable, I meant, I guess, explicable—that a positive abberation is still an abberation, and warrants further study. It felt like you gave that short shrift, sir. To me. I'm sorry if I'm being too frank"—Janice hates this tendency of hers to over-apologize; she and Nap still laugh about the time he pointed it out to her and she immediately apologized for it—"but I think this case deserves more."

Dr. Turnbull ran a hand through his hair and scanned the courtyard before he spoke, nodding amiably to a patient rolling by in a wheelchair. "Do you know who called me last week?"

Janice shook her head. "Sir—"

"Secretary McDonald did. And Senator Burr too." He was referring to Robert A. McDonald, who'd just two months before been confirmed as secretary of veterans affairs, and North Carolina senator Richard Burr, the ranking member of the Senate Committee on Veterans' Affairs. He lifted his heels to slightly raise himself, as though to emphasize the importance of these calls.

"And do you want to know what both of 'em said to me? 'Larry, I don't know what y'all are doing down there, but whatever it is, keep doing it.'"

Janice shook her head, opening her mouth to speak—

"Now hold up, let me just tell you what I told 'em both: I got me one helluva fine doctor on my staff, name of Janice Cuevas. C-u-e-v-a-s. I appreciate taking the call, gentlemen, but all the credit goes her way."

"I'm honored, sir," Janice said. "Genuinely. But you *know* that credit isn't mine. All I did was read the same newspaper they did."

Pursing his lips, Turnbull vented a long sigh through his nose. "Maybe you need to be looking at this another way," he told her. "That boy of yours—once he's out of physical therapy, hell, the next time you see him might be for his flu shot next year. Benchmarks don't get higher than that. That's a success, Dr. Cuevas. That's as good as success gets around here."

"But it's not our success."

"Is that what this is about? Whose success this was, or is?"

"I'm not quite following you, sir."

"Look, you've got a lot of patients, Janice," he said. "You're clocking so many goddamn hours that our contract docs are 'bout ready to see your head on a platter. Those patients—all 'em—they're your focus. You really want to take hours away from them to figure out why this one boy managed to switch his transmission out of park?"

"If this was a mystery illness," Janice said coolly, "I imagine you'd have a different take."

"Damn straight I would. But it ain't. It's a mystery recovery and I'll take ten, twenty, a hundred more of 'em today. Look at these men out yonder." She steeled herself as Dr. Turnbull placed a hand on her shoulder to pivot her toward the fountain. "I'd like nothing more than to see every one 'em jump out of those chairs and walk off this campus. Hallelujah and pass the peas. Every one 'em."

"But don't you see?" she said. "If we can pinpoint what happened then maybe we can determine if it's reproducible. We didn't even get to potential drug reactions back in there, or whether axonal regrowth could've been—"

"We're not a research institute, Janice. And writing papers—that ain't your job."

"I'm sorry, sir"—there she went again—"but—"

"Did you forward his case file up to Washington?"

"Just like you said. And I also sent it up to the CfNN in Providence," she said, referring to the VA's Center of Excellence for Neurorestoration and Neurotechnology, a research laboratory.

"Then let's let 'em work their magic."

"Sir, this is *my* patient and I feel an extraordinary obligation to him, and to my other patients like him, to—"

"Now hold right there," Dr. Turnbull said, and Janice did, waiting while he sighed and glanced about the courtyard with a distressed, even pained expression, his face reddening once again. When finally he spoke it was in a lowered voice, a muted baritone hiss: "Let's just get to the nub of this, okay? Has it crossed your mind that you might've missed something along the way?"

"Absolutely," she said, though without much confidence. "I thought—I thought that was the point of me presenting the case this morning. I thought we were making progress until you cut it off."

"And therefore it's possible," he continued, as though she hadn't answered, "that this boy spent four years suffering in a wheelchair when maybe he didn't need to?"

He raised his head and tightened his eyes as though assessing a suture he'd just made. Realizing she was out of breath again, and gasping lightly, Janice said nothing.

"What if it turns out a two-week course of Clindamycin could've had him up and out of his chair four years ago?"

"Sir," she protested, "there's been nothing to suggest infection—"

"Tell me which headlines you prefer," he said. His face was back close to hers now, his voice tuned to a growl. "The ones we got now, or ones that says 'VA miracle turns out to be VA mistake'?"

Now it was Janice's turn to tighten her eyes. "You don't actually think this *is* a success, do you?"

"What I think, Dr. Cuevas, is that the deeper you look into this, the greater the risk that you're gonna find something you wish you hadn't."

She tilted her back. "Then that will be on my shoulders, won't it?"

"Yeah," he muttered. "Don't I wish." He took a step back from her so that his face was no longer in hers and she could no longer smell the coffee on his breath. The smoke from a newly lit cigarette came drifting over from the fountain, and, still short on breath, Janice suppressed a cough. "What I think, Dr. Cuevas, is that the status quo is the *very* best-case scenario for everyone involved, you and your patient included."

seven

CALL IT PROPHECY, COINCIDENCE, OR THE ROUTINE EXUBER-
ance of a mother's love: Cameron Harris's mother, Debbie Ann
Harris née Cruthirds, sometimes referred to her son as her "miracle
baby." This was because his entrance into the world, the raw fact of his
existence, defied obstetric opinion, or at least the opinion of one obstetri-
cian, hers, who following Tanya's birth told Debbie she was unlikely to
bear more children. No one recalls precisely what the medical hindrance
was—"something about her uterus, her tubes," according to her sister
Bylinda—but Debbie's "miracle" tag for the infant Cameron is a memory
set in concrete. "I reckon every mama thinks her baby is a gift from God,"
says Bylinda. "But Deb, she was sure of it. Cameron was like a fortune
cookie from on high. He spun her life around a hundred eighty degrees.
She wasn't big on church and all that until he come along. Fact, she was
pretty wild in her younger days. She and ol' Snead used to throw down
pretty hard."

Debbie Cruthirds met Snead Harris during her freshman year at Biloxi High School. Snead was two years ahead of her, a thick-necked, blue-
eyed linebacker on the Indians varsity squad known for his toughness,
his fuse-free temper, his Kawasaki motorcycle, his fondness for mixing
high-proof Everclear with beer for what he called "Sneady Snacks," and
for being the only student at Biloxi High with a shaved head. (The shaved
head was to disguise a case of very premature baldness that, according
to family members, resulted from a bizarre medical condition: While he
was playing in an uncle's barn as a child, a hayseed fell into Snead's dirty

ear, sprouted, and grew into his ear canal, eventually requiring surgical extraction to relieve the pressure. Family members cite this as the cause for his baldness as well as for his violent bent.)

Debbie's family, the Cruthirds, has been on the Mississippi Gulf Coast for generations, its men mostly shrimpers as her father was. Snead Harris was a transplant from Stone County, in the piney woods above the salt line, an immigrant from the hardscrabble, hard-luck inland. Rufus Little Harris, Snead's great-great-grandfather, was a Confederate deserter from Missouri who took refuge in remote Stone County to avoid being hanged for desertion but died in prison anyway after shooting a preacher six times in the back for sheltering his beaten wife. One of Rufus's four sons, Fant Harris, was shot by a black sharecropper while having intercourse with the man's thirteen-year-old daughter; Fant survived long enough to organize the sharecropper's lynching but died shortly thereafter from infection related to the gunshot wound. This legacy of violence and imprisonment went trickling and occasionally gushing into subsequent generations: Cameron's grandfather Randall "Poke" Harris served four years in the state penitentiary at Parchman for beating a used-car salesman with a tire iron before stealing a 1955 Chevrolet Nomad. One can find it difficult, reviewing the Harrises' ancestral rap sheet, to avoid hearing the echo of William Faulkner passing judgment on his notorious Snopeses: "a family, a clan, a race, maybe even a species, of pure sons of bitches."

But Debbie didn't see it that way: not at the age of fourteen, when she met Snead, nor even at the age of twenty-eight, when he abandoned her for good. "She loved him like crazy," says Bylinda, who was eighteen months her sister's junior. "Oh don't get me wrong now. Them two was constant drama. Up and down all the time, breaking up and getting back together—that was pretty much every weekend. He'd cheat on her then she'd cheat on him and some poor guy'd get his ass whipped and then there they'd be together all hand in hand like nothing'd ever happened, two teddy bears. When she was with Snead, she was either crying tears of joy or tears of grief—hardly nothing in between." Following high school, when Snead took a job as a derrickman on an offshore oil rig and Debbie started working as a nurse's aide, their relationship appeared to smooth out—or at least Snead's long absences eased the abrasiveness. "They'd throw these big-ass parties when Snead would come back from the rigs,"

Bylinda recalls. "About as wild as you can imagine. Next morning there'd just be beer cans and bodies on the floor and, God help me, Snead and Deb passed out buck naked in a corner with these big dumb grins on their faces."

One effect of those nights, aside from the grins, was Debbie's unplanned pregnancy with Tanya. "I'll say this for Snead," Bylinda says. "He went down on his knees proposing the moment he found out he was gonna be a daddy." They were married on February 27, 1985, six months before Tanya's birth, and honeymooned at a Texas hunting ranch where Snead's cousin worked. A year later they bought the house on Reconfort Avenue and settled into what no one describes as marital bliss. "He'd hit her sometimes," says Bylinda's husband, Bill. "I know that because he told me so, one of the times they come visit. I wouldn't say he bragged about it. It was more like he was . . . like he thought he was giving me advice. Like if two guys are bass fishing and one says to the other one, 'You know, man, if you let them topwater lures rest a bit before you get to reeling, you'll probably get more strikes.' That kinda tone. Sorta like, here's something that works for *me*. I don't recall what I said back to him but I can tell you it wasn't what I should've said. I never wanted nothing to do with him."

But Debbie did, despite everything. Tanya, who endured six years with her father before he left, saw things differently. "Daddy coming off the rigs wasn't ever a good thing," she recalls. "Mama'd go crazy cleaning and primping and cooking and talking about how good everything was gonna be. But it wasn't good, not one time. Because you knew he was going to blow up but you never knew when or why or what for. That's how she told it to me. He'd start hollering at the TV news because they put a black weather girl on there: 'Now I gotta listen to a nigger telling me it's raining.' Or freaking out on Mama for letting me eat steak on account of steak's too expensive for kids and him saying how fat I was anyway. I didn't cry a single tear when Mama sat me down and told me he wasn't coming back from Texas. Not a damn one."

Snead Harris had taken an oilfield job in west Texas—a twelve-month contract gig paying him twice what he was earning offshore. Over the course of his first three months in Texas his phone calls home gradually petered until his final call, when he told Debbie he'd met another woman and wasn't coming home. "I remember the show *Full House* was on the

TV when she was telling me," Tanya says. "And something on that show making me laugh right after Mama stood up, and her throwing this look back at me and saying, 'Girl-Bunny, you understood all I just told you, right?' And me saying, 'Yes, ma'am. I sure as heck did.'"

By this time Cameron, the miracle baby, was three years old, a whirligig of toddler energy. Debbie reconnected with her Catholic faith after Cameron's birth, believing that with her son she'd been divinely accorded some sort of second chance—that from her womb had emerged not just a child but a set of personalized commandments. She feared this newfound piety, however, might've alienated her husband and factored into his leaving. "His people was hard-shell Baptists," explains Bylinda. "They thought Catholics drank blood." In the immediate wake of Snead's desertion, Debbie set aside religion to take a back-first plunge into depression, dropping into a yearlong emotional coma. "I took care of both of them, really," recalls Tanya. "Mama couldn't cook so I cooked. Mama couldn't get Cam dressed so I did. That was me yanking off his wet Pull-Ups. Mama'd cry and Cam'd cry and I'd be switching back and forth between them, holding them, telling them it was all gonna be all right."

So this was how Cameron Harris grew up: with two kinds of mothers, a phantom of a father, several years of maternal weeping jags, and an infinite amount of fried oysters. "My Mamaw taught me to fry oysters when I wasn't even tall enough to see over the stove," Tanya says with a laugh. "Dixie Seafood used to be across from where the Biz-E-Bee is so I could always get a jar. That's all Cam would eat. I'm serious. They was like chicken tenders to him."

Despite this deep-fried, cornmeal-crusted diet, Cameron grew up lean and lithesome, with delicate, doll-like features. Debbie Harris, everyone agrees, was a looker—her sister claims she was a ringer for the model Cheryl Tiegs, with beach-blond hair and spacious, searching, delft blue eyes plus a pair of narrow, elongated legs that could so powerfully distract men that, the story goes, they were once the cause of a gnarly waterskiing accident—and Cameron clearly favored her. "The memory of mine that's most vivid," says Mary Annie Fillingame, Cameron's third-grade teacher, "is how *beautiful* a child he was. I don't think I'd seen a prettier boy in all my life. You know, he had that terrible fall the year I had him, when he cut his little cheek. I remember him coming in with all the bandages and me thinking, of course, *oh that poor child,* but also thinking: *My stars, that perfect face. That poor perfect face."*

Tanya, by her own vinegary admission, took after her father. His lumpy linebacker's figure was hers from birth. Instead of the bouncy gold curls of her mother and brother, Tanya was endowed with a head of coarse beige hair she likens to "badger fur," in which gray streaks started appearing during puberty. Her body reacted to heat not just by sweating but by breaking out in vast pink continents of hives, a liability for Gulf Coast summers. Her flat feet made her waddle like a duck. If any of this ever distressed her, however, Tanya doesn't show it. From an early age she equipped herself with the armor of self-deprecating humor, insulting herself before anyone else could. In grade school she invented a character she called "Fat Sally," pulling a pair of pink tights up to her chest and pretending to hunt for cake, and, with acid cheer, she would volunteer to be a human shield during dodgeball games. She didn't lack for friends, but popularity wasn't a goal of hers. While other kids were gathering after school, Tanya was making a beeline home to help raise a baby. Debbie was working nights as a nurse at the Merit Health hospital in Biloxi; she and Tanya traded shifts taking care of Cameron.

For a while Tanya had a boyfriend in high school, a Russian-born adoptee named Oleg who played cornet in the marching band and death-metal guitar in his bedroom. Oleg was a spindly, tiny boy, barely five feet tall—as an orphan in Russia, Tanya says, he'd been severely malnourished—making them an incongruous-looking couple. A card he once gave Tanya bore an illustration of Winnie the Pooh and Piglet holding hands, which he annotated by drawing an arrow pointing from Piglet to the word ME with another arrow connecting Winnie the Pooh with YOU. Whatever Oleg's intent, Tanya interpreted it, heart-stung, as a depiction of their physical pairing, the lopsided way they must've looked walking hand-in-hand through the school hallways. Following their breakup, Oleg wrote her a long and sentimental letter in which he thanked her for, among other things, teaching him "how to be a man." Here was something else Tanya didn't know how to interpret. Maybe he meant she'd shown him the proper way to kiss a girl and what to say to make a girl feel special. But then she'd also taught him how to chug a beer, bait a fishing hook, and change a flat tire, so she wasn't sure.

Cameron, entering middle school at this time, had grown into a happy, engaged, even irrepressible boy. His sights were set on becoming an actor, and he went so far as to take after-school acting classes in Gulfport where he appeared as Fyedka in a production of *Fiddler on the Roof*. Along with his best friend, Bucky Petz, Cameron made movies using Bucky's VHS camcorder. They christened their partnership CB Productions and dedicated every film to the memory of Cameron's dog, Lucky. Tanya starred in one of these movies—as the victim of a sand monster slowly consuming her into the gut of Biloxi beach.

Despite the years separating them, sister and brother were never far apart. Their inchoate selves seemed nurtured and secured by the other's presence, symbiotically linked. Tanya had a television in her bedroom, and many nights would find her and Cameron curled together in its quivering silver glow, Cameron usually drifting off to sleep beside his sister—most nights, according to Tanya. When nightmares struck, or when the passing trains rattled him from sleep, it was in Tanya's bed that Cameron sought refuge.

Highlighting Tanya's role risks diminishing Debbie's. Debbie worked long hours, and the stress of single parenthood left her brittle at times, but tenderness was never in short supply. Tanya and Debbie confided in one another: The first person to whom Tanya reported her first kiss, from Oleg, was her mother, and Tanya was Debbie's sounding board for conflicts at work and, later, for thoughts about her dating life. Together, almost as partners, they fawned over Cameron.

Like all children, Tanya and Cameron didn't lack their mild traumas and troubles. Debbie's temper, prefiguring Cameron's, could spontaneously combust; her children now laugh about the way she'd sometimes hurl a flip-flop at them when angry, about her gunslinger's adeptness at removing the sandal and firing it their way in a single smooth stroke, but it wasn't likely a laughing matter then. Money was always tight in the Harris household. For as long as they can remember the ringing telephone was ignored until the answering machine could confirm that the caller wasn't a debt collector. Cameron, like his sister, struggled mightily with schoolwork, and while Tanya seemed immune to social cruelty, Cameron's awkward exuberance made him an occasional target for bullies. In seventh grade Bucky moved to Florida; the loss of his best friend struck Cameron hard, as all losses seemed to do, and he has never, to this day, fitted anyone else into the best-friend slot. He tended, like his mother, toward emotional extremes. When his dog, Lucky, broke loose, and the eight-year-old Cameron found the dog's crushed body at the side of Division Street, he cried for three days straight, stranded far beyond the reach of any consolation from his mother and sister, marooned on an island of terrible, shrieking grief. He was also, Tanya says, prone to overthinking—to pondering choices, even minor ones, to the point of anxious immobility. "You know how you get a gut feeling about something, and just go with it?" she says. "Cameron never seemed to have that. He still doesn't. He just chews and chews things in his head until there's nothing left to chew."

Cameron's adolescence coincided with what might be called his mother's second adolescence. After years of moping about Snead's abandonment followed by years in which she threw herself into the church, and with Cameron outgrowing his need for her attention plus her transfer to the hospital's day shift, Debbie Harris decided it was time to try dating. "She had to been lonely," says Tanya, who helped her mother craft her first online dating profile. "Dinner'd be cleaned up, the laundry all folded, and Cam and I'd be back in my room watching TV. I reckon she didn't feel there was a whole lot left for her at night. And maybe she'd finally gotten Daddy's poison out of her system."

The effect of this, for Cameron, was that men started coming around the house on Reconfort Avenue—lots of them, though never for very long. Donna Arlut, a co-worker of Debbie's at the hospital, observed this period in their life. "Deb went on dates a lot but I don't recall her ever going past a fourth or fifth," she recalls. "Heck, I set her up on a few of those. Honestly, I don't think she knew *what* to do with a decent guy. You gotta remember, Snead wasn't just her first husband—he was her first boyfriend. Her first and only everything. So she didn't know what love was. She didn't know it didn't have to be torture. I'm guessing a lot of those men found themselves very confused after a few dates with Deb."

Ingratiating themselves with Cameron was a common maneuver for these men. They took him fishing for croakers at the harbor, rode him around on their boats, taught him how to hit golf balls at a driving range, threw catch with him in the front yard. One of them, a highway patrolman, let Cameron fire his service revolver at a hunting camp up near

Jackson. This patrolman, according to Tanya, was also in a way responsible for Cameron's high-school football career. Apparently unimpressed with Cameron's visit to his hunting camp, he expressed concern about Cameron's manliness to Debbie just as Cameron was about to enter Biloxi High School. "He told Mama he thought Cam was a little weak or something," Tanya recalls. "Told her the best thing she could do for him was to get his scrawny self onto a football field." Debbie Harris didn't think enough of the patrolman to continue dating him, but, pricked by his comments, and perhaps suffused with nostalgia for Snead's old glories as a varsity linebacker, she did defer to his counsel. That summer she convinced Cameron to try out for the junior varsity football team.

Cameron was nothing like his snarling, thick-necked, bruise-dispensing father. He was slender and lissome, and he carried himself nimbly and elusively, less like a bull than a deer. "So, an ideal wide receiver," says his former coach, Tom Bud Necaise. "I saw it that first tryout, clear as day. He had good straight-line speed but you put him on a route and he could run it like nobody's business. He just had these superb instincts. To be honest, after just a few weeks in, I was figuring him for a future college ball player. I really was."

As Cameron was embracing football, furiously studying the game in order to catch up with teammates who'd been playing since grade school and spending long grunt-filled hours in the weight room, Debbie was finally embracing one of the men she'd met online. Jim Yarbrough was recently divorced, with three kids of his own, and had served in the Navy during the first Gulf War. Jim had a modestly dangerous side to him—he was a professional poker player—which seemed to satisfy Debbie's appetite for a bad boy. But Jim was good to her, and for the first time since Snead Harris bolted to Texas, Debbie's friends and daughter saw her illuminated by love or something close to it, discerned a newly honeyed melody in her voice. She and Jim attended every one of Cameron's games together, except when Jim had a conflicting poker tournament, and on "Military Night" at Harrison Central High School, during Cameron's sophomore year, Jim Yarbrough was among the veteran parents lauded on-field at the halftime ceremony. This was by Cameron's request. He liked that Jim didn't use him to peacock for Debbie, didn't drag him fishing or golfing or boating or shooting; Jim had his own kids to tend to. What Jim did best (in Cameron's eyes)—quietly, even wordlessly—was to respect Cameron. With a poker player's intuition, he seemed able to read precisely who and what Cameron was, zeroing straight into his essence without objections or judgments, and with an easeful tolerance for adolescent muddles. It helped, too, that Jim had played community college ball: His postgame commentaries, on the drives back home, were always filigreed with fresh insight.

By the end of his second JV football season, Cameron's talents were glittering. The first time his picture appeared in the Biloxi *Sun Herald* wasn't after his recovery at the Biz-E-Bee; it was after a winning game against D'Iberville High School, the camera catching Cameron in soaring flight above three hapless-looking defenders. His mother had the newspaper page framed and with great ceremony hung it in the living room. Cameron was a lock for the next season's varsity squad, and in the spring Coach Necaise dropped by the house to talk about the college recruiting process with him and Debbie and to leave a copy of the *NCAA Guide for the College-Bound Student-Athlete*. He'd already mentioned Cameron to Coach Cutcliffe up at Ole Miss, he said, and he'd gotten an unsolicited feeler from the receivers coach at the University of Alabama-Birmingham. "I was seeing a bright, bright future for Cameron," Coach Necaise says. "That boy had some hellacious legs under him, some real speed and agility, and a set of big soft hands that the ball loved sticking to. The hours he put in the weight room, too, and out on the track—he had the drive. I'd say the only thing he lacked was confidence but we were making headway with that until the tragedy with his mama." At this Necaise sighs, and with a sour, deflated expression shakes his head. "That pulled the rug right from under him."

On June 17, 2004, at around four thirty p.m., Debbie Ann Harris was driving in the right eastbound lane on Interstate 10, just past the exit for the Bernard Bayou Industrial District, when an eighteen-wheeler from Texas, estimated later to be traveling more than eighty miles an hour, plowed into the rear of her Honda Civic without braking, as though oblivious to her. The impact launched Debbie's car into the center median with the eighteen-wheeler hurtling close behind. The truck flipped, its cab sliding sideways into the westbound lanes and its trailer capsizing onto Debbie's accordioned Honda. Debbie was pronounced dead at the scene.

It can seem like a small and ugly point, the truck's origins, but it's one Tanya nevertheless dwells upon when talking about her mother's death: Because the truck and its driver hailed from Texas, Tanya sensed and still senses her father's invisible hand in what happened—as though thirteen years after wounding Debbie with his desertion, and just as she was beginning to realize how nourishing life could be with a kind and decent man, Snead Harris had dispatched that eighteen-wheeler to finish her off for good.

Cameron took the news—which was delivered, in that tightly knit way of small towns, by the same highway patrolman who'd dated Debbie and triggered Cameron's football career—by holing up in his room for twenty-four hours, weeping so hard and ferociously that Tanya, perched outside his door, feared whether it was possible to sob oneself to death. Then he emerged dazed and red-eyed into the living room, smoked half of one of Tanya's cigarettes, and holed up for another twelve hours. When he came out the second time, Tanya says, he came out different. "He come out broken," she says.

Cameron played three games of varsity football that fall, tying a school record for the most receiving yards in a single game in the season opener against St. Martin, before quitting. "We tried everything we could to turn him back around, the coaching staff and his teammates and all his teachers," Necaise recalls. "We told him how much it'd mean to his mama, what it meant for him going to college, everything. But nothing got through. He just kept saying he was done."

Perhaps a longer stretch of stability might've assuaged some of Cameron's grief, might've remedied some of that brokenness; maybe time could've resurfaced him. But fourteen months later, as he and Tanya (who was eighteen when Debbie died, and living at home while working at a Dollar General store) were still struggling with the fallout from their orphaned existence, Hurricane Katrina came uncoiling off the Gulf. The scant solidity they'd been able to piece back together got smashed by the twenty-eight-foot storm surge then went sloshing out to sea.

After the hurricane Cameron went from broken to shattered. The once-irrepressible boy seemed wholly vanquished from his being, replaced by a dejected, glowering, slouch-backed young man who seemed unwilling or unable to reflect upon anything more than the cigarette smoldering between his lips and the hammer in his hand as he cobbled their ruined house back together alongside the church volunteers from Indiana. After the volunteers would leave for the day he'd sit chainsmoking in the twilit backyard for hours, amid stacks of new lumber and piles of molded, pulpy drywall, staring at the debris with a dark and vacant countenance—as though his heritage had caught up with him and he'd submitted to wearing the same blank expression his Stone County ancestors had accorded the rear flanks of mules while plowing furrow after furrow after furrow. Nothing could cheer him. Nothing could even shake him.

Tanya tried. She tried fishing out the artist brother of hers who'd so joyfully and nerdily engineered her consumption by a sand monster, tried fishing out the supercharged athletic dynamo who'd been on track to be the first of Rufus Little Harris's descendants to attend college, tried locating that single sand-grain of exuberance that must surely have been lodged somewhere inside him, resistant to the hydraulic force of his despair. But long gone were the days when she could pull him to her chest to let him soak her T-shirt with his tears, when she could silence his crying by humming Madonna songs to him while rocking him in her big lush arms.

And Tanya was swamped with struggles of her own. In the course of fourteen months she'd lost her mother, her home, much of her hometown, and her job (all that remained of her Dollar General store, after Katrina, was the foundation slab), and she was watching her brother be hollowed out by anguish, was watching that once-bright future of his being erased like chalk off a chalkboard. A cigarette was about all she wanted to reflect upon, too.

Cameron graduated from Biloxi High School in 2007, just barely, and without the varsity letter in football that'd once seemed the most token of his destined honors. Afterward he zigzagged through a series of construction and post-Katrina cleanup jobs, cash gigs for some of the out-of-state contractors that descended upon the coast. Many of his co-workers were itinerants from Mexico and sometimes he'd hang out with them at their trailer parks, drinking cut-rate tequila while they laughed and argued in Spanish. Occasionally Coach Necaise called to check in, as did Debbie's old boyfriend Jim Yarbrough, but unless Tanya was home these calls perished in the answering machine.

Not that Tanya was home all that often. She'd taken a waitressing job at Waffle House, one of the first businesses on the beach to reopen after the hurricane, and with the job had come a new social circle of co-workers, a raggedy bunch. After a while she stumbled into a low-grade romance with a cook named Durnell who went by the nickname D-Lite. What D-Lite liked most was to spend four or five frenetically sleepless nights in New Orleans's French Quarter alternating hits of crystal meth with a local drink called a Hand Grenade, by the second day swatting constantly at a set of imaginary bongos and by the third day running out of bars that would serve him. Tanya couldn't stand the meth—not the high itself, which incinerated all her desolation in a white-hot burst of euphoria, and for the only time in her life made her feel sleek and invincible, but instead the bleak, interminable comedown and the unbearable way she'd grind her teeth while using, leading to throbbing jaw pain that only exacerbated the comedown. Usually she'd bow out after the second or third day, retreating to the backseat of D-Lite's parked car where she'd dose herself with Xanax and half-sleep for long, miserably cramped stretches. Sometimes, she says, D-Lite would venture out to check on her, poking at her limp body with the tip of his boot; but usually not. One time she staggered from the car to a tattoo parlor on Frenchmen Street, just to feel someone paying close attention to her.

It was after one of these trips to New Orleans, early in 2009, that Tanya returned to Reconfort Avenue and noticed a stack of folders, brochures, and official-looking paperwork piled atop the kitchen table. She lit a cigarette and edged herself blearily toward the pile. She eased open one of the folders, lifted out a form, and for a long while stared at it. "Cam?" she called out, to no response. "Cameron?" But she didn't need his confirmation. Trembling in her hand was a DD Form 4/1, a signed contract. In the middle of a goddamn war, her baby brother had gone and enlisted in the Army.

eight

AMONG THE MANY OTHER CURIOUS VISITORS TO THE BIZ-E-Bee in the weeks following Cameron's recovery was a thirty-four-year-old Catholic priest named Adolf Bosah Chukwurah Nkemdiche. In his native Nigeria he was known as Father ABC but Mississippians had pruned that down to Father Ace. Quỳnh was away that morning, making his weekly run to Louisiana to buy lotto tickets, so Father Ace obtained the information he was seeking from Hat. Then he walked down Reconfort Avenue to the Harris house and rang the doorbell.

Father Ace is the pastor at Our Lady Queen of Angels parish, four blocks west of the Biz-E-Bee on Division Street—such a slight distance away that it didn't occur to the priest to drive. Queen of Angels, as it's known, is the smallest parish in the Biloxi diocese, with a congregation of just ninety-three families. (By contrast, its parochial neighbor to the west, Our Lady of Fatima church, boasts 1,700 families.) It's also the poorest parish in the seventeen-county diocese, with annual collections insufficient even to fund maintenance on the eighty-three-year-old church building—so poor and so small, in fact, that after Hurricane Katrina ravaged the church, the diocese secretly considered shuttering it.

Since his appointment as pastor in 2011, however, Father Ace has engineered something of a comeback, adding twenty families to the congregation, renegotiating the parish's debt with the diocese, and ministering to his parishioners with a stamina that's tiring merely to observe. There's an athleticism to his efforts that he comes by naturally, having been an all-star soccer striker in his youth, and then briefly, until suffering an on-field injury that left him with a permanent limp, a member of Nigeria's national

Under-17 team. When he scored, sixty thousand people would belt out the chorus to the Jackson Five song "ABC," and the memory of this spreads an unsaintly smile across the priest's face, ignites a twinkle of dormant ego in his eyes. The sound that buoys him nowadays is the nonstop vibrating of his cellphone, its hornet buzz usually signaling someone in need: of a ride to work, of bail money, of an emergency babysitter, of help fending off an eviction. The age-old metaphor of a shepherd and his flock feels inadequate for how Father Ace operates. He is more like a cowboy: galloping hard to drive his herd forward, hooting at the stragglers, lassoing the wayward, moving 'em on and heading 'em up, his face glossed with a perpetual sheen of sweat. The rumor—which the priest denies, though he's flattered to hear it—is that he sleeps only two hours a night.

Some of his parishioners—especially the older ones—credit Queen of Angels's reinvigoration to Father Ace's doctrinal conservatism. He has revived bygone rites and rituals—the solemn Benediction of the Blessed Sacrament, novenas, meatless Fridays—and, from the pulpit, frequently inveighs against the cafeteria-style attitudes of many American Catholics. Many of his instructors at Enugu Memorial Seminary in eastern Nigeria were elderly Irish missionaries, and their pre–Vatican II orthodoxy he readily absorbed. The mercies he extends to his parishioners, almost hourly, stop short at theology. Sins he forgives; doctrinal dissent yields a whipcrack rebuke.

It's a conservatism he wears quite literally on his sleeve. When Tanya Harris opened the door, she found Father Ace dressed in his standard throwback garb: his body draped in an ankle-length black cassock and his clean-shaven head capped with a stiff, black, three-peaked biretta. She needed no further information to conclude, "Reckon you'd like to talk to my brother."

By this time, twelve days after Cameron's recovery, the doorbell was becoming a familiar sound, ringing with almost cuckoo-clock regularity. First had come the reporters, in a triplet of waves: the local and New Orleans press, first; then the national press, brusque and skeptical; and then, to Tanya and Cameron's bemusement, the international press, some from Asia but most hailing from Latin America. ("Miracles lead every newscast in Chile," a cameraman explained to Tanya. "Miracles and UFO sightings.") After that had come an intermittent but now increasingly steady flow of what Tanya was calling "the randos": little old ladies bearing chess pies or deviled eggs, peering past Tanya for a glimpse of Cameron; a group of seven Mexican men timidly requesting to touch Cameron's legs (Cameron allowed this, but admits it was "flat-out weird"); and people in various shades of distress asking for Cameron to pray with them, which invariably he did. They sat beside him on the couch and held his hand or more frequently his knee, often in front of a video game paused on the flat-screen. He didn't know what to do when they wept.

"Don't bother to stand," Father Ace said when Tanya led him to Cameron, who'd begun to rise from the couch, but then the priest changed his mind: "Actually, I might like to see that." When Cameron did, the priest crossed himself and issued a quick and whispery prayer. Cameron was used to this by now—his physical therapist occasionally did the same thing.

Tanya sat beside Cameron on the couch while the priest introduced himself and the reason for his visit and took a chair. He asked, "Have you spoken to any clergy?"

"We had this Baptist preacher come by," Cameron answered, and Tanya nodded. "You know that big new church up there on Big Ridge, across the Bay? That's the guy. I don't think he liked I was drinking a beer."

This drew the priest's attention to an open can of Bud Light on the coffee table; lunchtime was still an hour out.

"Your mother, she was a parishioner at Queen of Angels," said Father Ace.

"Yeah, we all were. Hell, I was an altar boy. That was Father Huey back then."

"I've heard so many good things about him."

Lighting a cigarette Tanya said, "Mama used to say he did the fastest Mass on the Coast."

Father Ace flashed a citric smile. This had been his welcome to Queen of Angels three years earlier: anonymous notes from parishioners chiding him for the duration of his homilies and contrasting him with the belovedly brisk Father Huey, as though the quality of a Mass, like that of an internet connection, could be measured in speed. Back at his rural parish in Nigeria he could stretch his homilies two hours or longer; for his parishioners there, some of whom traveled sixty miles to Mass from far-flung villages linked by muddy rutted roads, a ten-minute sermon would be an offensive shortchanging, grounds for parochial mutiny. He knew he'd passed the ten-minute mark, here in the States, by the violet glow he'd spy on faces in the pews—from the light cast upward from their phone screens.

"Maybe, please, you will tell me in your words what happened at the Biz-E-Bee store," the priest said.

As he told the story, Cameron found himself first surprised—then simultaneously comforted and unsettled—by the priest's unfazed reaction. Father Ace kept nodding affirmatively, saying *yes* and *of course* and *I understand*—as though Cameron's story, which had thus far astonished everyone who'd heard it, including Cameron's own doctor, was of a kind he'd heard many times before, an ordinary case from the parish files. At its conclusion, when Cameron, as was now his custom, slapped his thighs and exhibited the bending of his knees, the priest leaned forward with his palms pressed together and asked, "Had you prayed?"

"Prayed how?"

"To walk again."

"Yeah. Sure I did. All the time."

"To whom did you pray?"

"Who'd I pray to?" Cameron frowned. "Well . . . shit. To God."

"Of course."

"I didn't mean to cuss. Sorry for that, Father."

"It does not bother me."

Tanya said, "Is that even a cuss word in Africa?"

Father Ace stared at her. "It . . . it is the same," he said.

"I prayed to God," Cameron went on. "To Jesus. Is that what you mean?"

"Yes yes, but I'm curious if you might have prayed to a saint? Or maybe to a loved one in Heaven? Or might others have prayed to someone for you?"

"I don't know that I recall," Cameron said.

"There was this prayer thing on Facebook," Tanya said. "Right after Cam got hurt." She turned to her brother. "You remember that? Megan Bearden's mom put it up."

"Naw, I'm not gonna remember that," Cameron said, waving a hand across his chest. "I wasn't really checking Facebook at Landstuhl. That was pretty sweet of her."

Snatching her phone from the coffee table Tanya announced, "I'm gonna find it," then sank back into the couch cushions flicking at the screen. "Not bearded, *Bearden*," she fussed at it.

"Maybe you can also tell me, if you are willing," Father Ace said to Cameron, "about how you came to be injured."

Without glancing up Tanya said, "Oh, he don't remember much. It's like—amnesia."

"I'll tell you all I know," Cameron said, ignoring her. "We were on patrol, and I was—"

The priest raised a braking hand. "Tell me where this was? I would like to hear everything."

"Oh right, sorry." Cameron paused to scratch his shoulder and blow the air from his cheeks, as though mentally equipping himself for the task. "Zabul Province, Afghanistan. That's on the Paki border but we was up in the north part of it, way up in the mountains. Like seven, eight thousand feet above sea level, I don't know—I almost quit smoking there 'cause I couldn't ever catch my breath."

Triggered by the mention, Cameron lit a cigarette as he continued: "Middle of nowhere, seriously. Middle of *middle* of nowhere. There's one paved road in the whole province, that's Highway One. Up where we were, though—man, I don't think I saw a car the whole time. You couldn't get one up there, there's just these little goat paths up and down the ridges. A few of the local national dudes rode motorcycles, the ones had some money anyway. Otherwise you ride a donkey. Unless you're female, and then I don't know what you do—stay put, I guess."

"That's some horseshit right there," Tanya muttered.

"Our COP was about three clicks from the nearest village. The rumor I heard, from the platoon we replaced, was that some of the locals figured them for Russians when they made first contact. That's how freakin' remote it was. These people were like two wars behind."

"This was when?" A small notebook and pen had appeared in Father Ace's hands.

"When I got injured? That was March of oh-ten. We'd been at Hila since—let's see, I think it was October. That was the COP, the name of the combat outpost—Hila. Before that we were down at FOB Barmal, right on the Paki border. Hila . . . it had its own kind of suck, for sure, but it was a whole lot quieter than Barmal. Anytime you went outside the wire there, someone was gonna be shooting at you. Something was gonna blow up. You went out in full pucker mode every time, you know what I'm saying? Hila . . ." Here Cameron paused, lowering his eyes. "Hila was different."

During the silence that followed Cameron took two deep and over-attentive drags from his cigarette as a pensive expression softened his face, compelling the priest to ask, after a while, "Different how?"

"Hila?" Cameron blinked his eyes rapidly. "Man, it was—well, it was *cold* up there, Jesus was it cold. I'd never felt cold like that in my life. You're bunking in a mud hut, it's ten below . . . you walk outside to pee, feels like your damn face is gonna break."

Sensing something other than thermostat memories was what'd distracted Cameron, Father Ace gently pressed him: "What else was different?"

"Well, the patrols was totally different—we was on foot," Cameron said, but from the way his voice and expression had resolidified the priest gathered that this also wasn't the difference he'd intimated. "The terrain up there, it's way too rough and rocky for nothing else. We couldn't do mounted patrols like we did at Barmal, with the Strykers. So about every three days, each squad'd go on a little hike."

"What were those like?"

"A lot of it was pretty routine. We'd keep changing it up but there was kind of a circuit we'd do. Visit a village, talk with the elders, bargain for some intel. Try to find out where the bad guys was holed up, what they were planning. Do some fingerprinting, retinal scans, hand out some soccer balls to the kids. Hang outside while the lieutenant drank tea with the elders. These villages up there—they were really small, sometimes just like ten or eleven families living on the side of some cliff, these little houses kinda stacked up on top of one another. Some of them were shady, but they weren't nothing like the villages in Barmal. Down there they hated us. Hell, even the kids hated us. I gave some candy to this little girl one time and like all of a sudden these boys chased her down and just started beating the shit outta her. Like, preschoolers, man. Blood coming out of her nose. And these little suckers tried whaling on me when I went to break it up, serious. You'd try to help these people out but they didn't want it. You'd airlift a bridge in there for them and the next day, hell, they'd burn it down."

"What about the day you were injured?"

"That was a weird one, actually." Cameron stopped to light another cigarette with the tip of the one he'd just exhausted. Tanya, the priest noticed, had abandoned the effort with her phone; she was staring spellbound at her brother through the tobacco haze encircling his head. "So, this guy had shown up at the COP the day before. A local national—dude had one eye, just like Mullah Omar. Said he wanted to turn informant and could guide us to some weapons caches hidden up in some caves. We was still a month out from fighting season but the spooks had been picking up radio chatter about us—"

"I'm sorry—spooks?"

"The guys in Prophet Section, yeah, they listen in on enemy radio transmissions. I wasn't privy to any of this but I heard there'd been chatter about hitting our COP come spring. So it made sense they'd be stockpiling mortar tubes and stuff. Lieutenant Cantwell, though, he wasn't buying the local dude at *all*. His Spidey sense was going haywire. We all saw that. But our CO ordered him to take a recon team on patrol to see what the dude was selling."

"And you were on this team," the priest said.

"Yessir I was. It was a night patrol. We—"

Tanya asked, "How come at night?" This detail, like many others she'd just heard, was new to her. She hadn't known even this prologue to her brother's story before—just the random puzzle pieces he'd divulged over the last four years—and would afterward wonder if the presence of a priest was what'd filled in those blanks or if this was a side effect of his recovery—if along with his legs perhaps his memory had been restored.

Cameron's answer, the priest noted, was directed his way: "The lieutenant, he was like dead-certain this was a trap. But with a night patrol, see, you've got the tech advantage. Night vision goggles and all that. Problem was, though, Gollum didn't have night vision." Noting Father Ace's confusion, he explained: "That's what we started calling the local national—Gollum, you know, from the *Lord of the Rings* movies? The little slimy dude. Led them hobbit guys right into that giant spider-monster thing. Our Gollum, man, he couldn't see worth a damn. Felt like we were stopping every hundred feet for him to get his bearings. That was freaking the hell out of the lieutenant because you don't ever want to stay put too long when you're on patrol. Might've been on account of the dude being one-eyed, I don't know. Our ANAs didn't have night vision either but they were hacking it fine."

Father Ace asked, "What is an ANA?"

"Afghan National Army. We always did joint patrols at Hila—usually six of them, nine of us. We didn't have nine that night, though, because one of our guys was sick and another one—man, I don't know what the issue with Tugboat was, but he stayed back inside the wire. You know, it's kind of weird—the lieutenant, he was all pinged out, but the rest of us, I don't know, we was all pretty chill. Like I said, after all the shit we'd been through at Barmal . . . Hila had been *quiet,* you know? I mean, winter's always quieter in Afghanistan, but this . . . we'd taken some harassment fire, we'd found some IED materials in this shady-ass little village . . . but the only casualty we'd had was back in November when a sniper popped Beano in the foot and—I don't know how to say this—that was almost funny. He got his pinky toe shot off. We're down on the dirt looking for it later and he's like, 'Fuck it'—sorry—he's like, 'Fuck it, what do I even need it for?' And we're laughing because nobody's got a good answer to that."

Cameron's chuckle met the disturbed expressions of his listeners and evaporated.

"If I'm being honest," he went on, leaning forward, "I think a lot of us were itching for a fight. We'd lost four guys in our last month at Barmal so we still had a score to settle, you know?"

He picked up the can of Bud Light but, finding it empty, half-crushed it before plumping it back onto the table. "Sis, you mind grabbing me a thermo?"

Lifting herself from the cushions Tanya mumbled, "Baby can walk again, but not to get his own beer." She mumbled this to no one in particular—if Cameron registered the comment, he didn't show it—and in a tone the priest couldn't quite identify: neither sharp nor blunted, as though she'd swished a butter knife in her brother's general vicinity. It left the priest feeling awkward, though, and half-speaking for Cameron he told her, "You're very kind."

From the kitchen doorway Tanya asked Father Ace if he also wanted something to drink.

"Tea, if you have it."

"Like, sweet tea?"

"Hot tea."

"Naw, we don't got that. Coke or Gatorade is all. The red kind. 'Less you want a beer."

"A Coke sounds delicious," Father Ace said, watching Cameron stubbing his cigarette into the ashtray with a degree of force and concentration that seemed disproportionate to the task. Despite the way he'd earlier disregarded his sister, he seemed to be pausing his story until she came back. The priest took this moment to compliment a poster tacked to the wall by the kitchen entrance. Above the word RISE was a photograph of an infantryman atop a rocky peak, silhouetted against a purple-streaked sunrise; below was printed, ". . . FOR THE RIGHTEOUS FALLS SEVEN TIMES AND RISES AGAIN. PROVERBS 24:16 ESV."

Cameron turned to squint at it. "Yeah, someone at the VA gave me that."

When Tanya returned, Cameron and Father Ace took simultaneous swigs from their cans, though Cameron's lasted significantly longer—long enough for the priest to remark, in a tone less opaque than Tanya's had been, "It is rather early."

Cameron nodded and pursed his lips. "It's hot."

"This is true," the priest conceded, though Cameron's justification was a stretch. The cold air from the A/C vent was at that moment scooting billows of cigarette smoke along the faintly yellowed ceiling. "Please, if you will continue."

"Well, there ain't that much more to tell, really," Cameron said. "Gollum, man, he kept getting turned around. We'd head up some trail but then he'd decide it was the wrong trail and we'd head back down. Must've happened four or five times. Then we come to this village and dude's like, 'Yes, we're very close now,' but that village—we all knew that village, we'd been there before, which meant Gollum knew the village for sure, and would've known how to get there—it was all getting way, way too shady. At this point—"

A ringtone came bursting from Tanya's phone—Kelly Clarkson shrieking the chorus to "Why You Wanna Bring Me Down"—causing her to jump as though bee-stung. She glared at its screen as a tinny guitar riff buffeted the room. "Who do we know with a three-one-oh area code?"

"Search me," Cameron said, clearly annoyed by the interruption. "Bet if you answered it they might tell you."

The twinge of another sort of sting, a deeper one, appeared on her face. "Sorry," she said, silencing the phone and laying it facedown on the table.

"You were in the village," Father Ace prompted.

"Yeah, okay. It's about oh-five-hundred at this point. We'd been out six hours. I remember walking through that village with this nasty sense, feeling like if something's coming, this has to be where. Waiting for the trip wire. Waiting for the boom. Waiting—waiting to get some, you know what I'm saying? To get mashing on that trigger. That's what it's like sometimes—you don't want it, but at the same time you want it bad." Cameron's voice shifted into another gear: lower, slower. "It was totally silent up there. No dogs, nothing. Just that burning cedar smell from their fires—smells like you're walking through a cigar box. And all those stars up there. First time I saw stars like that, I about fell out."

Slowly, in pained anticipation, Father Ace tilted forward, flattening his hands together between his knees in the bunched drapes of his cassock. "So this was the place," he said quietly, "where the bomb . . ."

Cameron shook his head no. "Once we got through to the other side of that village, though, the lieutenant—he was freakin' *done,* man. His Spidey sense was short-circuiting. He got up in Gollum's face and just ripped him a new one. Even put his nine-mill to the guy's forehead. I probably shouldn't say that part. But it was tense, you know?"

Cameron paused for a swig of beer and to light yet another cigarette. "The guy peed hisself. Gollum did."

Father Ace tilted farther toward his knees, his eyes drifting downward. Cameron caught a flicker of something in the priest's expression that he registered as fear or possibly disappointment, as though the story he was telling wasn't quite the one the priest had wanted to hear.

"That's usually a good sign," Cameron said. "When they pee themselves. The Talibs, they never do that. I don't really know what all went down. Most of what I heard was the terp whispering like crazy, trying to keep the lid on it. Gollum, after a while he was just kind of whimpering, moaning and shit. The one thing I do know—the lieutenant broke up the squad after that. He orders our staff sergeant to stay back with me and a couple of ANAs to conduct overwatch in case an ambush really was coming. So we're tail-end Charlie. The rest of the squad starts heading back up and then—and then, yeah, we follow a ways behind."

The way Cameron ended this, with a slight lilt on the final phrase, sounded a strange note of finality, as though nothing more was forthcoming. The priest watched Cameron's gaze wandering about the room as smoke came leaking from his nostrils and parted lips.

"What happened next?" Father Ace said at last.

"I don't know," said Cameron, stricken with a sudden vagueness. He was looking straight ahead, addressing the flat-screen. "We hiked awhile. I don't know how long. Then after a while the ANAs, they just sat down."

Tanya said, "What do you mean, they sat down?"

"Just what I said, they sat down. One of them said they was tired." An edge of aggravation had replaced the smoky vagueness. Was Tanya the cause for this? the priest wondered, now wholly perplexed by their dynamic. As his eyes darted between them Father Ace noticed a vein on Cameron's neck that was pulsing with such vehemence as to evoke a guinea worm wriggling beneath the skin. "It happened sometimes, I don't know. Afghan Good Enough, that's what we'd say. They plopped themselves down on some rocks and pulled out some hash to smoke like they was out back the Waffle House taking a fucking break from washing dishes." Cameron released a long breath as he rubbed his forehead; the priest could tell this was growing harder for him. "Sergeant Lockwood, he radios ahead to the lieutenant, lets him know the situation we got. The ANAs ain't budging. Lieutenant tells him they're probably turning around anyway, on account of the time—the idea is get back in the wire before daybreak. So he tells us to take a knee and wait."

Silence.

"And then?" the priest had to ask.

Cameron sighed. "And then boom."

The priest waited. "Boom?"

"That's how it happens. Just . . . boom."

"The sergeant . . ."

"Yessir, he stepped on it. I was a little ways off from him."

No one spoke for a while. When the priest looked up he saw that Tanya's hand was now on her brother's shoulder. With her other hand she was daubing an eye.

"I was out cold for a while," Cameron finally continued. "When I come to, it's like—concussion waves, I guess. My eyes'd sort of focus, then they wouldn't. There was stuff in them. I'd make out what people were saying, then I couldn't. I remember—I remember asking about Damarkus—about Sergeant Lockwood. How he was."

"He was killed," the priest assumed.

"Nossir, he made it. I don't know how."

"Praise be to God."

"Amen, Father. Amen to that."

"And the Afghan Army men?"

Cameron frowned, studying his cigarette. "They wasn't in the blast zone. We'd moved . . . I don't know, Sergeant Lockwood wanted to check out the ridge or something. I don't remember why."

Only later, after the Vatican investigator would go burrowing into this point, would Father Ace deem it noteworthy. Only in retrospect would he conclude—as he did six months later, in the final report he submitted to the archbishop—that on this minor detail the subject seemed "elusive." For now, though, as the priest watched Tanya rest her head against her brother's shoulder and stretch her left arm across his chest, as if to demonstrate the way she would've shielded him then, and would shield him now and evermore, Father Ace was gripped by a warm pity that felt baked into his very bones. He felt the urge to reach out and touch Cameron, to make palpable the emotion he was feeling, but Tanya was shielding him from this, too, so instead the priest prayed, in silence at first until the prayer spilled into a whisper and then into a full-throated supplication for God's continued mercy that he found himself delivering the way he used to pray, un-microphoned, back in his church in Nigeria, amid the squalling infants and the exalting grunts and hollers of his parishioners. But neither Cameron nor Tanya echoed his gasp of an amen. It was as though he wasn't there.

What Cameron said next, however, did strike the priest as noteworthy—strange, even. Tanya retracted her arm so that her brother could reach his Bud Light on the table, and after he'd taken a sip he shook himself, not unlike a wet dog, and rearranged himself so that he was sitting rigid and straight-backed on the edge of the couch cushion. Father Ace was unsure to whom Cameron was speaking, whether to him or to Tanya, or possibly to himself, when he said: "A lot of things happened to me in Afghanistan. Getting paralyzed, that was just one of them."

The priest took a moment to analyze this. Accustomed to confessions, he jumped to a conclusion. Softly, he said, "You had to kill."

Cameron nodded, but airily.

The priest failed to recognize that he'd swung and missed. "So your lieutenant was correct," he said, in an oblique attempt to wrest more from Cameron than this nod. "The man you called Gollum had led you into a trap."

"Naw, that's the weird part," Cameron said, more brightly now. "It was a freakin' *Soviet* land mine. I didn't know that till later—no one did. Everyone figured it for an IED. We knew there were mines in that district, or might be. But most of the time those old mines don't detonate. It's pretty fucked up, when you think about it. (Sorry.) I'm over there fighting the Taliban and it's the Russians that got me. And got me, like, thirty years later. I mean, the Soviet Union—I don't even think that was still around when I was *born*. It's like one of my Brooke doctors said, he told me, 'You're a casualty of a war you weren't even fighting.'" He took a scowling drag from his cigarette. "I don't know what happened to Gollum. I wouldn't have wanted to be him when that mine blew. Not that I wanted to be me when that mine blew."

"But now," the priest said, and discerning his meaning Cameron raised his left knee up and down in demonstration and said, "Yeah, now."

"Have you spoken to God since?"

Tanya said, "He prays all the time now. Prays like crazy."

"Yeah, I do," said Cameron. "A whole lot. Don't know about crazy. People been asking me to pray for them, and I been doing that some. Sometimes it's hard because . . . well, because most times I don't really know

what to say to folks, you know? Or to God neither. I never promise nothing to them. It's like they think I got the secret cell number for God—but
if I do, hell, what is it? I mean, *you* got that number, right?"

A grin slipped onto the priest's face. "It is a very public number."

"I guess." Cameron sounded unconvinced.

The priest took a sip of his Coke, then after a deep breath said, "I have
a very important question to ask you."

"Yessir."

"What do *you* think happened at the Biz-E-Bee store?"

"I've spent a lot of time thinking about that," Cameron answered after
a while. "Pretty much all my time since, really. I asked my doctor at the
VA. She's got no idea. She talked with other doctors. They don't know. I've
looked it up on the internet. But at this point half the Google results I get
are about me."

"And what have you decided?"

"You mind I turn that question back your way, Father?"

"What do you mean?"

"I mean, you've heard pretty much everything there is. And I figure
you know way more about this type of stuff than I do. What do you think
happened to me?"

Father Ace took a moment to arrange himself, smoothing the cassock
folds on his knees. "I would like to speak with your doctors. Would you
grant me that permission?"

"Of course, yeah," Cameron said. "Whatever you need me to sign."

"But from what you've told me," said the priest, in a hesitant, calibrated
tone, "I am inclined to believe that a miracle took place, yes."

"For real?" Cameron looked stunned. This had become his own private
theory, after Janice's failure to explain what might've happened, but the
priest's affirmation felt somehow thunderous just the same. The distinction, he'd later say, was akin to *feeling* you'd acted bravely in a combat
situation and the Army awarding you a medal that authenticated that feeling. It was official proof. It was legit.

"Miracles are not as uncommon as you have been led to believe," Father Ace said. "In my country, they are quite regular. In hospitals there
you will often see a sign: We care, God cures. Here in America I think
they would post the opposite sign: We cure, God cares. Here, when a case

such as yours arises, skeptics will often dispute it, or at best they may say it is impossible to explain—"

Tanya broke in: "That's exactly what his doctor said."

"—even when all the evidence, all of it, points to the most simple and most beautiful explanation: God's infinite mercy and love."

Cameron fell back into the couch cushions and rubbed his kneecaps for a while, as though massaging the priest's conclusions into them, to see how that felt. Then he frowned. "But then, see—why me?" Turning to Tanya beside him, he seemed to ask this question of her as well, in a faintly coded way: "I mean—*me*."

"We cannot pretend to know God's plan," Father Ace replied. "We can only see his works."

"But look here, Father . . ." Dissatisfaction with this anodyne response knotted Cameron's forehead. "You asked me earlier if I've killed, right? The answer's yes. Yes I killed people. For a while I counted how many but then it got hard because in a firefight you can't always figure the kill shot. I've killed people and then I've cheered. I've watched people die and I've— I've laughed at them."

Father Ace winced—less from distress, however, than as a way of ac-knowledging receipt of Cameron's admissions. As a pastor in a military town, by now accustomed to counseling returning soldiers, Father Ace's response came premixed: "The warrior in a just war is not a murderer," he told Cameron. "This was Saint Augustine's contention, and I adhere to it. What is required for virtue is not a bodily action but an inward disposi-tion. 'The sacred seat of virtue is the heart.' That's what Augustine wrote."

"The heart," Cameron echoed, in a nebulous whisper, before reaching for his Bud Light. In Cameron's face, as Father Ace watched him drink the beer and then knock the bottom of his pack of cigarettes to poke out a fresh one, the priest glimpsed that same brooding, distal look he'd seen when Cameron spoke of Combat Outpost Hila. He lowered a glance to his notebook to make sure he'd recorded it there: HEELA, yes.

"It still don't seem right, Father," Cameron said, shaking his head. "I mean, if I'm being straight-up with you, yeah, there were some times I prayed I could walk again—but did I always believe it? That God'd do something? That God—I don't know, that God even . . ."

The priest nodded several gentle times, as he followed this trail of silence to its end, then finished Cameron's sentence for him. "That God even existed."

"No offense, Father." Cameron's exhale sounded like a tire deflating. "But yeah."

"Oh hell I forgot—wait a second now," Tanya blurted, grabbing her phone from the table and pecking at it, but, after watching her for a moment, the screen swallowing her presence, neither man felt obligated to wait.

"Thing is, Father," Cameron went on, relieved and emboldened by the way the priest had acknowledged—indulged, even—Cameron's spotty faith, "you get me in that confession booth and you better be bringing a sandwich and a cot because you're going to be there for a while, you know what I'm saying?"

"You're saying," Father Ace concluded, "that you do not feel worthy."

"For this? Not even *close*. That's what I'm saying."

"Hmm. Tell me. What do we say before receiving communion?"

"Say?" Cameron blanched. Eight years removed from his last church attendance, he was unprepared for this pop quiz.

"Yes, what do we say?" When no answer came, the priest fed him a cue: "We say, Lord, I am not . . ."

"I am not . . ."

". . . worthy . . ."

". . . worthy . . ." Cameron's eyes suddenly glowed as this latest click lit the pilot. ". . . worthy to receive you, but—"

Here the priest joined in, so that they finished in unison: "—only say the word and I shall be healed." Father Ace's smile was like that of a piano teacher who'd just guided his student through an étude. "Now say it again, and listen to the words."

"Lord," Cameron said slowly, "I am not worthy to receive you, but only say the word and I shall be healed."

With an even more complacent smile the priest leaned back in his chair.

"Whoa," said Cameron, and nodded. "Whoa," he said again, before disappearing behind a veil of cigarette smoke.

At this point Tanya emerged from her smartphone. "Here's that prayer thing I was talking about. Remember? Megan Bearden's mom's thing on

Facebook?" She passed the phone to Cameron who after reading pronounced it "really nice" then passed the phone to Father Ace. Balancing the phone on his left knee and his notebook on his right, the priest jotted some notes before passing the phone back to Tanya.

What Dorothy "Dot" Bearden—grandmother, not mother, of a high-school classmate of Tanya's—had posted, on March 26, 2010, was a prayer request for Cameron's recovery. What intrigued the priest, and occasioned his note-taking, was that Dot Bearden had directed her audience to pray to Archbishop Nicholas Fahey, whose name was hyperlinked in the post.

"Who's Nicholas Fahey?" Tanya asked the priest, at the same time clicking the hyperlink then reading while he answered.

"A Blessed," Father Ace explained. "An American archbishop. For many years I understand he was on the television."

Tanya glanced up, brightening. "Really?"

"Monsignor Fahey had an international cassette ministry, too. Oh yes. I used to listen to these cassettes all the time when I was in seminary." Nostalgia fuzzed the priest's tone as he went on: "I listened to them so much that the tape would grow thin and break and I would perform surgery on the cassettes with tape and tweezers. Oh my, yes. They were so very inspiring." He wrote something else in his notebook and said, "This is quite interesting."

"How come?" Cameron asked.

"Well," the priest began, "to be verified as a miracle, an event must be shown to have been the work of an intermediary—the work of a saint or a servant of God. These miracles serve as proof of their heavenly stature. Miracles are a requirement for a servant of God to be canonized as a saint, you see. Three used to be required but now it is two. And unless I am mistaken, Archbishop Fahey is already credited with one. So it is very interesting."

"Hold on now." Cameron's head was swirling. "God doesn't perform the miracles, that's what you're saying?"

"No, of course it is God. But an intermediary must request them, in response to prayers."

This only magnified the swirling. "It's like the Army chain of command," Cameron muttered.

The priest laughed politely. "It is merely the natural order of things."

"But—" Cameron's head was wagging. "What's the point of praying to someone else? I mean, why'd Megan's mom pick this Fahey dude for me? I'm sorry, I don't get it."

"You can think of it like football," Father Ace said, offering a well-rehearsed analogy. "You want the ball to get into the goal, so you pass it to the player in the best position to score."

Tanya seemed to get it. "You remember Mama praying to Saint Anthony all the time?" she asked her brother. To Father Ace she noted, "He's the patron saint of lost car keys."

The priest enjoyed this. "What a mama you had! I am sorry I was never able to meet her."

But Tanya struck a business tone. "So this prayer," she said, pointing to her phone, "this prayer counts?"

"I would say yes, but these are technical matters—"

"What about likes? Do they count as prayers? Because that post got one hundred fifty-one likes."

"Now this," said the priest, jotting something into his notebook, "this is a magnificently current question. I cannot begin to answer it."

Cameron was still softly wagging his head. "So you're thinking, Father . . . you're thinking this Fahey dude, he's the one did this for me?" He turned to Tanya. "He's on Facebook, sis? Is that what I saw? Lemme see your phone a sec."

"You ought should write a note to Megan's mom," Tanya suggested.

"Oh, Archbishop Fahey died many years ago." Father Ace held up his hands with splayed fingers, freezing Tanya's transfer of her phone to her brother. "But let us slow down. You must understand that everything at this stage is part of an open inquiry. My visit today is just the beginning of what could be a long and very complex process."

"So it ain't official? I was thinking . . . I guess I was thinking you was making it official."

The priest regarded Cameron's disappointment with tenderness, chuckling drily. "Oh, hardly. The verification process leads all the way to the Holy See—to the Holy Father himself. And I admit to you that these are matters I've only read about. I am here merely as a—what would you say in the Army, as a scout?"

"A scout, sure." Cameron shrugged. "Maybe a forward observer."

"The forward observer, that is me. Later this afternoon I will be writing to my bishop. And as you've granted me permission I will be contacting your doctor, if you'll give me his name."

"Her name, yeah. I'll write it down." Cameron dourly scratched the back of his neck. "So what now? I mean, if this was a miracle—what am I supposed to do now?"

"I am glad you asked this question," the priest said, aiming his shoulders at Cameron as he leaned forward in his chair. "To begin, I would ask to see you at Mass on Sunday."

"At Mass?"

"To praise God for this spectacular act of grace."

Cameron agreed with a reluctant nod. "Yessir, I can do that. Tanya'll drive me."

"And I will tell you that it is just as important, for me, and for our ministry here in Biloxi, that *others* see you at Mass." Father Ace would later say that he considers miracles God's advertisements. He subscribes to what we might call the Toyotathon school of miracles: that every so often God performs a miracle as a means of filling the pews. Miracles, in his discount-theory formulation, are designed to bolster the faithful and attract the less faithful. They are, in a sense, sacred marketing. But he deemed this too much for Cameron to digest at the moment, if anytime soon. Instead he told him, "God has given you a breathtaking gift. It was not meant to be yours alone."

"Amen," Tanya said.

"And because of that gift," Father Ace went on, "you must exalt God with everything that you do. Every action you take must now be an act of faith and gratitude. Do you understand?" He stared at Cameron until their eyes finally locked. "You must not defile the body God has restored for you." With his own gaze he guided Cameron's to the array of Bud Light cans on the table, until he was sure his point was clear. "It must be put to use in the name of love."

"Roger that," Cameron said weakly.

With that the priest gave his knees a conclusive slap and stood up. "May we pray?" he said, extending his hand. Tanya took his hand and then lifted her brother's into her other hand. She corrected its limpness with a squeeze.

"Amen," said brother and sister, when it was over.

As Tanya was leading him out, Father Ace turned back to Cameron to announce, "I will see you in three days."

"Do what?" Cameron said from the couch.

"At Mass."

"Oh yeah, right," said Cameron. "See you there."

Cameron sat motionless on the couch for a long while, not even noticing Tanya clearing the Bud Light empties, while checking her voicemail with her phone shouldered to her ear, and then silently delivering him a fresh one. He popped the top. Its exuberant foam spilled onto Cameron's hand and then onto his knee, as if the beer, too, was impressed that the pope, of all people (though at that moment Cameron couldn't name the current pope), might soon become familiar with Cameron Timothy Harris of Biloxi, Mississippi. "Holy shit," he said to no one. Then, more from skittish astonishment than amusement, he found himself laughing. "Actual holy shit. *Holy* holy shit."

"Oh my motherfucking God," he heard Tanya screeching from the kitchen.

"What?" he called.

With a strangely blasted stance she was commandeering the doorway between the kitchen and living room. Cameron swiveled himself to look at her. Her eyes, wider than usual, were trained on her phone. Backlit by the kitchen's windowed sunlight, her hair looked like a nest of live electrical wires, something fatal to touch.

"Holy shit, Cam," she said, looking up.

"That's what I just said. I think I'm supposed to maybe stop saying it."

"Remember that three-one-oh area code call?" She refastened her eyes upon her phone. "You're not gonna believe *this* shit."

At this point, Cameron would later say, he was prepared to believe almost *anything*. What he couldn't have believed, however, was that his life, so freshly and dazzlingly reassembled, was about to be torn apart in ways he never could have foreseen.

after, pt. 2

for we are made a spectacle unto the world,
and to angels, and to men

nine

THE LOS ANGELES OFFICE OF THE TELEVISION PRODUCER Scott T. Griffin looks like—is, really—a miniature museum devoted to Southern culture. Entering the office, which is on the second floor of an otherwise colorless office park on Wilshire Boulevard, is like wormholing one's way into an alternate universe where Muddy Waters is king of one realm and Hank Williams Sr. another, where Bessie Smith and Lucinda Williams are their respective queens, where the kingdoms' official notices are issued as Hatch Show Prints, and where almost every visual detail comes filtered through the *art brut* aesthetic of the Georgia folkartist Howard Finster. The cramped multitude of its Southernness can be dizzying, a dose of regional smelling salts. A bronze bust of the blues singer Robert Johnson, hunched over a guitar neck with a cigarette dangling off his lip, shares the top of a corner file cabinet with a dwarf bottle tree, and even the file cabinet, with its distressed pecan veneer, looks Southern, as though scavenged from a defunct Delta cotton brokerage. Oil-on-plywood portraits by the Memphis painter Lamar Sorrento—of Waters, Smith, both Williamses, Elvis Presley, and others—compete for scarce wall space with framed album covers (Son House, George Jones, Bukka White), a decoratively battered National steel guitar, and various other primitivist folk paintings, a noteworthy number of them bearing religious themes and/or brimstone-weighted Bible verses. Even the plant on the windowsill, a struggling potted cotton plant, adheres to this theme.

It was from this office, on the morning of September 4, 2014, that Scott T. Griffin placed a call to Tanya Harris, whose cellphone number his assistant had cadged from Jesse Castanedo, the *Sun Herald* reporter. Griffin doesn't remember precisely where he first read about Cameron and his recovery—"Huffington, BuzzFeed, one of the ag sites"—but he recalls his initial take as fleeting and weightless. "You see these things every now and then," he says. "Somebody comes out of a coma after ten years and suddenly they're playing Chopin on the piano. A lost cat finds its owner two thousand miles away. Someone wakes up in a casket during his own funeral. They're like brain-freeze stories—you think about them too hard and your mind cramps up. So you skim these things and shake your head and move on." Griffin did just that, he says, but the story—and its attendant brain freeze—followed him. "I was in my car early the next morning—that's the only time I ever get ideas, when I'm alone and driving. Johnny Cash was like that with songs, he had to cruise around to find them. For some reason that story popped back in my head and got me thinking about what it must be like to experience something like that—it's got to blow your mind, right? I mean, that's got to be some super-cosmic peyote shit. I wasn't really thinking TV at the moment. I was thinking super-cosmic peyote shit. But as I'm imagining it, cruising down the Ventura Freeway, I start seeing it on a screen, and I realize I'm not *thinking* about it anymore—I'm *watching* it. And then it's like, boom. Like Johnny Cash pulling onto the side of the road to scribble down the lyrics to 'I Walk the Line.'"

Scott T. Griffin, who likes to be called Scott T., is an independent reality-television producer, so the equivalent action he took was to call his assistant, who was still asleep at that early hour, and instruct her to track Cameron down as quickly as she could. "Because about ten seconds after the idea struck, I started groaning," he recalls. "I was sure I was too late to this. You gotta understand: This business, it operates like a warp-speed gold rush. Someone finds a nugget and then two hours later there's sixty or ninety miners on the scene with pickaxes. And this thing, the more I thought about it in those ten seconds—this is what development people call a 'loud' idea. You've got your God shit, you've got your war vet stuff, you've got America. The material pitches itself—hell, it *writes* itself. So ten seconds later I'm groaning, I'm smacking the steering wheel, because I'm sure that Mark Burnett has already signed this guy to a thousand-year exclusive."

But Burnett hadn't, as Griffin learned several hours later when Tanya Harris responded to the effusive voicemail he'd left her. No one had. So Griffin instructed his assistant to book three plane tickets to Biloxi—one for her, one for him, and one for Griffin's regular cameraman, Huntley Benyus, otherwise known as Honeybun. The assistant, a twenty-two-year-old Alaska native named Kaitlyn Douglas, had only been working for Griffin for three months, since graduating from Montana State University in the spring, but in those months she'd developed something of a crush on her boss, which she did not mind advertising. "I'm excited that I get to see your home," she said to him. "I'll pretend you're taking me home to meet the parents."

When Griffin, who was married at the time, batted down this comment, she responded mock-poutingly, "I'll guess I'll just be meeting your office's parents, then."

His "office's parents," as Douglas put it, is clumsy yet effective shorthand for the wellspring of Griffin's creative energy, that being the South. The opportunity for him to visit and with any luck work in his native region was, indeed, a residual factor in Griffin's interest. "The story was the story, okay? Wherever it might've happened," he says. "But that it was in Mississippi—yeah, you can glance just about anywhere in this office to see how that would've been some icing for me." Griffin, who is forty-four, fashionably long-bearded, doughy in a way that suggests overconsumption more than under-exertion, and most often seen wearing an obscurely soulful vintage concert T-shirt, has a habit of lubricating his speech with arbitrary squirts of laughter, as though to keep reminding his listener how absurd everything is—from the television industry to life itself. Any veil of earnestness is subject to constant piercing. This is a tic he may have picked up from his father, a longtime salesman for a Memphis liquor distributor who somehow managed, Griffin says, "to be total bullshit and zero bullshit at the same time," or in other words the perfect salesman. Unlike his parents—both of them natives of Illinois—Griffin was born in the South, but only because his father was transferred there for work in the late 1960s. His Southernness, then, might also be said to be total bullshit and zero bullshit at the same time. He was raised in Germantown, a blandly prosperous suburb of Memphis, but as a teenager began aligning himself with the gnarlier terrain just across the border in Mississippi. "Germantown felt like capital-A Anywhere," he says. "Mississippi, though—that was Somewhere."

One cannot sketch Griffin's career—or hope to understand any time spent in his office—without pausing to examine this distinction of his. His career began when he was an undergraduate at the University of Mississippi, majoring in Southern Studies. "I was deep, *deep* into the blues scene there, that raw hill-country drone stuff," he explains. "But I couldn't play an instrument, I was tone deaf, and to be honest I couldn't dance worth a shit either. So I started toting a camera around." The footage from that camera, casually gathered, found its way into a thirty-six-minute documentary film entitled *Ain't No Goddamn Picnic,* which won the university's William Ferris Student Documentary Award, helping to secure Griffin's placement in the master's program in Documentary Studies at Duke University. (It was also the seed for his television debut, a seven-episode series called *American Juke Joint* that ran on the Discovery Channel in 2005.) "The texture of the South was what really galvanized me as a filmmaker," he says. "The visual texture, yeah, but the cultural texture too. It's so rich, so craggy. You can focus that camera on anything and already you've got half a story. Already you've got tension. You see that in William Eggleston's photos, right? That narrative flatness that isn't really flat at all. It looks like nowhere but it's just fucking *bleeding* somewhere."

During the decade-long interlude between Duke and Discovery, Griffin says, he devoted himself "to being a pretentious asshole." (Cue the spurt of laughter.) "I fancied myself the Jean Rouch of the South, or at least aspired to be the Jean Rouch of the South," he says, referring to the French filmmaker and anthropologist considered the father of documentary eth-nofiction and a pioneer of cinéma-vérité. Griffin's laugh is never more frequent nor derisive than when he's describing the bohemian languor of these formative years, yet it's also not a subject he easily extinguishes. His ambition, back then, was to create Art, and while few people, least of all Griffin himself, would affix that label to his oeuvre—*World's Rowdiest Bars* (producer, 2006–07, Spike TV); *Moonshine Confidential* (co-executive producer, 2008, Discovery); *Lot Lizards* (producer, 2010, Spike TV); *Hoss Trammell: Airplane Repo Man* (executive producer, 2012–14, History Channel)—he nurtures a view of himself as an artist in exile, albeit economic exile. "When you're in your twenties, you know, pretension comes easy," he explains. "Everything's about the art. Everything's about never surrendering. Then you hit your thirties and look around and most of your art posse, they've dropped out. The guy everyone thought was such hot shit, the one destined to be the next Les Blank—that guy's got a kid in diapers and drives around in a van that says Dan the Dog Fence Man. And you pity that dude. Then you hit your forties and somehow things get reversed. Dan the Dog Fence Man, he's got a pool and three honor students and a condo down in Alys Beach. He's the one pitying the guy who's maxing out credit cards to make some twenty-six-minute short that only seven people at a Nebraska film fest will ever see. So with me, where I am—" With a subtle wince he pauses here, as though to brace himself for sincerity. "I feel like I found the medium zone, you know? I'm making reality TV, yeah—let's be honest, sometimes I'm making *crap* TV—but I'm still holding a camera. And in my own way, in my own less-than-crappy moments, I'm telling some kind of truth. Whatever the aesthetic was, whatever film meant to me—I'm still bound to that."

Truth, art, and the South: These undergirded the talking points that Griffin deployed on Cameron and Tanya Harris when he flew to Biloxi to meet with them. What Griffin was seeking from Cameron was the latter's signature on an exclusive option for Griffin to produce something about Cameron's recovery and its aftermath—"and that's as clear as it was in my mind," Griffin says, "just *something*: a one-hour doc, a series, I didn't know." During the two-hour meeting he told Cameron and Tanya that his upbringing in the South meant he wouldn't "Honey Boo Boo them," or play their Southernness for laughs or exotic zing. And that he was different from the other "sleazehounds" who might come around bearing similar option contracts—that his background was as an artist, not an exploiter, not a money guy, not a quick-hit producer, thereby equipping him with a sensitivity that was rare in the television ecosystem. ("I'm a non-sociopathic human being," he told them. "Do you know how many of us there are in the TV biz? Seven of us. *Seven,* okay? We find one more and we can have a volleyball game.") And that unlike other producers who believed in maintaining a rigid distance between talent and producer—refusing even to divulge personal contact information so as to insulate themselves from later blowback—he believed in a more collaborative relationship. "This is *your* story," he told Cameron. "Not mine. *Yours.* I respect the shit out of that, okay?"

And as for truth?

"Thing is, man, we don't know what exactly happened," Cameron said at one point. They were gathered in the Harrises' living room: Cameron and Tanya, Griffin and Douglas. Tanya had served everyone Gatorade in red Solo cups. "My doctor, she's as confused as anyone," Cameron went on. "All the tests she's run, they ain't adding up. We had a priest here the other day"—Griffin noticed the way Cameron deferred to Tanya even when making a mild factual point such as this one—"and he's thinking it's a miracle, you know. Like, full on. God's hand and shit. So it's just like, I don't know . . . this *happened*." He cranked a leg upward. "This just . . . it happened, you know? And no one knows why."

Flexing his fingertips together as he leaned forward, Griffin asked, "But you want to know why, right? Why and how?"

"Hell yeah we do," said Tanya, with Cameron nodding in agreement.

"Then think of us like a private investigation team that's going to work on your behalf," Griffin said. He laughed here, characteristically, but the laugh was muted, half-choked, as though something had caught in his throat. "We'll be the ones reaching out to experts and doctors and theologian types, trying to figure this out. Because those people? Honestly, dude? They won't talk to you. They're not going to return your calls. 'Cameron Harris? Who the hell's that?' You get what I'm saying? But you know who everyone talks to? Everyone? TV. *Everyone talks to TV.*" Still flexing his fingers, Griffin paused to allow this point time to get sponged into their minds. "Whatever the truth is about why you couldn't walk before, and why you can right now—we can get you closer to it than you can get alone. It won't be just you and your doctor and your priest trying to figure this out here in Biloxi. You'll have the full resources and might of a network behind you. That's not a small thing. It's a freakin' huge thing really." Then with an analogy he tried appealing to Cameron's military service: "It's like air support showing up, man. Every rocket you could need. Aimed anywhere you want. You get what I'm saying?"

The analogy hit its target, Griffin decided; the nod Cameron accorded it was firm, strong-jawed. Having pitched dozens and dozens of subjects over the years, some of whom (moonshiners, truck-stop prostitutes) he'd been asking to perform illegal or degrading activities onscreen, and being furthermore wired with his father's salesman DNA, Griffin could sense when he was closing a sale. He knew what the ionic charge of momentum felt like. Hence his calculated retreat: "Just think on it for the night, okay?" he said. "Y'all talk it over. It's a very personal thing. And it's a *powerful* thing—TV, I mean. TV can change your life. And while most of those changes end up positive, I can't promise every one of them will. But I've been in this business long enough—and I've got a *core* in here" (slapping his chest) "that actually gives a shit, you know?—to know how to manage this stuff. To make sure you feel in control. To make sure you get that a TV show doesn't last forever but this human thing that we've got going, you and me, this mutual relationship—that does. So I'm not laying any pressure on you, okay? The only thing I'll ask, and it's small, is that if someone else swoops in with a pitch, you give me another chance to talk before you sign anything."

"I appreciate that, man, I really do," Cameron said. He swung his head to look at Tanya for a moment; she responded with a lazily encouraging shrug. "I like what you said about helping us find out the truth."

"That's going to be the entire purpose of what we do," Griffin said, snorting out a laugh. "That's the show right there. That's the steak on the plate."

To his sister Cameron finally said, "You got any issues, Tan?"

When Griffin left the Harris house he carried with him the signed option contract for which he'd come plus two signed appearance releases. Once in the rental car he whooped and punched the air, all but peeling out as he drove from Reconfort Avenue. "Did you see the scar on that dude's face?" he said to Douglas. His excitement was apparent in the manic way he was driving, texting, and talking simultaneously—gunning the engine, flurrying his iPhone's keypad, almost slurring his sentences together. "Goddamn. He's got this wounded Steve McQueen thing going. I was figuring we'd be dealing with some meathead, you know? Some big-ass chunk of Army Strong. But this guy . . . fuck me, I hope he doesn't get washed out on camera. You remember me telling you about that subway musician show, the one that never went anywhere? The one about the punk chick and the ancient Chinese violinist? That chick had this amazing elfin vibe to her—this fragile, Björk thing about her that fucking *killed* you in person. But you saw her on camera and it was like: Who's the talking mouse? The camera just shrank her. But he'll show up. He'll totally show up. Can you not see the opening shot? Him in his wheelchair? That little shitball store . . . ?"

That night, Griffin and Douglas and Honeybun ate dinner at a casino restaurant beside the beach. Champagne bottles were drained and replaced. Griffin launched into a rant about the objectionable presence of *burrata* cheese on a menu billed as "New Southern." ("I hate when 'New Southern' means adding some Benton's country ham to a Thomas Keller dish.") And then later that night, according to documents filed eleven months later in Los Angeles in Griffin's divorce, he and Douglas slept together for the first time. The mood was celebratory, loose, a little unhinged. They had a TV show on their hands. "More than that," Griffin says. "We all felt sure we had a hit on our hands."

Over the next three days the trio produced what's called a "sizzle reel": a four-minute teaser for Griffin to exhibit in his pitch to networks. Griffin, who admits to liking movie trailers often more than movies, is particularly deft with these, and the reel he crafted for what he was then calling "The Rising" is a masterwork of this sub rosa genre: It begins with combat footage from the war in Afghanistan—unruly mountain ranges as glimpsed from a helicopter's gun port, AK-47–toting Taliban fighters slipping behind boulders, infantrymen scrambling for cover in copter-flattened poppy fields, tracer fire, random explosions, soldiers shouting at one another in the hot chaos of battle, more explosions, and then a montage of wounded men (including harrowing close-up cellphone-camera footage of a wounded soldier's blood-spattered grimace)—as all the while the 78-rpm scratch-sound of the blues artists Bukka White and Memphis Minnie singing "I Am in the Heavenly Way" swells from a background whisper to a foreground roar. It's a Holy Roller gospel number the duo recorded in 1930, yet White's voice has an unholy, gravelly timbre to it as though his drink of choice was turpentine on the rocks, with actual rocks. Then the screen goes suddenly black, the music does a split-second fade, and a static-edged voice, audibly stressed, announces, "I have a nine-line medevac. Are you ready to copy? Over?"

What follows is a wide, Eggleston-esque shot of Cameron slumped in his old wheelchair in the otherwise empty parking lot of the Biz-E-Bee.

It's sunset, the sky behind the store smeared with clouds so furiously and unnaturally orange as to evoke pollution more than splendor. The shot lingers, the only audio the gray noisescape of unseen traffic on Division Street. Then we hear Cameron's voice: "I was paralyzed from the waist down by a bomb in Afghanistan in two thousand ten. There wasn't any way I was ever gonna walk again." At this point the camera is slowly, almost imperceptibly zooming closer, yard by yard. A rapid-fire series of re-created shots follows—Tanya pushing Cameron down Reconfort Avenue, Cameron in his wheelchair playing a video game, Tanya grunting as she hoists her brother into his bed—before returning to the Biz-E-Bee, the zoom having continued through the intervening montage. "When the feeling came, I didn't know what was happening to me," we hear Cameron say, as the camera arrives at a close-up and lingers on his scar. "I just . . ." It sounds like his voice is cracking here, though it wasn't; Griffin added that effect in post-production. "I just stood up and walked. Something told me I could walk. And I did."

In the remaining three minutes, during which Bukka White and Memphis Minnie resume their singing, we see Cameron and Tanya in interview shots mixed with scenes of them interacting. There's also a shot of a priest confirming that Cameron's recovery was in his view a bona fide miracle, but this was not Father Ace—this was an actor friend of Griffin's in Los Angeles, reading lines Griffin wrote for him (Griffin also wrote Cameron's lines).

What's otherwise noteworthy about those three minutes is how Griffin chose to depict Tanya: almost exclusively as comic relief. Regarding her exchange with Ollie in the Biz-E-Bee, we see her saying: "I've hit men with a lot of things but never no box of Cap'n Crunch before." Later she's seen rolling her eyes as she delivers a variation on her joke about fetching beer for her brother: "When he walks to the fridge to get his own damn beer, that'll be the real miracle." Then there's a briefly absurd scene wherein Tanya is seen encouraging her brother to dance: "Come on, baby bro. Let's see if them new legs came with some hot moves." (According to Tanya, this moment was plucked out of context; she was making a joke after Honeybun asked them for some movement as he was setting up a shot.) Cameron emerges from the sizzle reel as something of a tortured Hamlet figure—a man gnawing at the fact of his existence, with even his beer-drinking depicted as some downhome strain of philosophical inquiry—while Tanya fills the role of the gravediggers: as coarse comedy, as a buxom, Fritos-chomping, tension-easing fool. "I wanted to inject some warmth into the reel," is how Griffin defends this. "I was afraid of the pitch coming across as too religious or deadly serious. I needed to show some post-miracle *joy*, you know?"

Back in Los Angeles, it took Griffin and his agent only eight days to sell "The Rising." "It went fast," he concedes, "though not always easily." There was one network executive who asked if Cameron had "exploded" in any way when he stood up, seeming genuinely bewildered by the lack of sacred pyrotechnics. Another exec "adored" the pitch but wanted Griffin to find three other miracle recipients for a competition series that could possibly be set in the Holy Land. Another exec flatly rejected the entire premise: "Here's what's going to happen. A real physician is going to diagnose this guy with a psychosomatic injury and then we've got what? A show that's called, 'Whoops, It Was All in My Head.'" Another seemed fixated on having a celebrity host or narrator: "Who's that black astrophysicist guy? Neil something Tyson. Huge cred and a great Q factor. Or what about someone like Alan Jackson?" An older exec recalled Geraldo Rivera's 1986 primetime debacle, when he opened the gangster Al Capone's secret vault on live network television and discovered it empty. "I don't like doing mysteries in real-time," he grumbled. "You're just walking around with your belt unfastened the whole time. One wrong step and your pants drop." It's possible there were more nuanced reactions that Griffin is failing to divulge, but reality-TV insiders say this sounds about right. As one says, "I'm kind of shocked no one asked if there was any weight-loss component to the miracle experience."

Then came Bree Winterson, the recently installed head of programming at the Lifetime network. Griffin wasn't expecting much traction from Winterson, who has a reputation for savage bluntness. He'd pitched her several years before, when she was in development at The Learning Channel, and she'd so thoroughly decimated his idea that Griffin had never pitched it elsewhere. Scarred by that experience, his pitch to her this time was soft, tentative, at times even apologetic. "I felt like I was trying to feed kale to a tiger," he says.

But this time was different. "The sister," Winterson said after viewing the sizzle reel. Winterson's manner of speaking is so distinct that impersonating her is a common late-night party trick among industry folk: She emits statements like smoke rings, pausing afterward to admire their passage through the air and expecting others to do likewise. "I love her. She's the heart of this. He's up in the clouds and she's down to earth—that tension, it's just so gripping. Obviously that's what we're looking for here at Lifetime—that strong female element."

"Of course," Griffin purred, his theatrical confidence belying how bewildered and blindsided this reaction was leaving him. This wasn't the "steak on the plate," as he'd put it to Cameron, that she was praising; this was instead, to Griffin's thinking, the parsley garnish.

"But he's got this strange appeal too, the miracle man," Winterson went on. "It's hard to put my finger on it, and that's part of the appeal. It's like half maternal affection and half I-wanna-jump-his-bones. That makes him total viewer bait. But *her*—what's her name? Tanya? She's your breakout, Scotty."

Griffin almost always corrects people: Scott *Tee*, not Scotty. With Winterson he let it slide.

"He's been transformed," she went on, "but we're going to want to see her *transforming*."

This wasn't close to Griffin's vision for the show—Tanya, to his thinking, was peripheral to the larger story of investigating a paranormal event—but Winterson's smoke rings weren't something you easily disputed; nor was the budget she controlled something to risk over what could be, if he stepped back for an objective look, merely a subtle shift in perspective. Winterson had been hired to fully revamp Lifetime's offerings, and to accomplish that, Griffin's agent had advised him, the network's president had endowed her with "fuckbuckets of cash."

"I see this as a series," she said, launching copulating cash buckets into Griffin's head. "Here are these people, right? They've had this amazing thing happen to them. They hit the spiritual lottery. And they're normal. They're funny. They're dirty around the edges. They're just like our aud, in other words. That's how I'm seeing this: Recipients of divine grace . . . they're just like us!"

Griffin glanced at his agent and swallowed. The agent's shrugged response was reminiscent of the one Tanya had conferred upon Cameron two weeks prior: *why not?*

"This is a hit, Scotty," Winterson said. "This is so fucking loud. It's sticky. It's got a dark smart edge. I'm game for a deal memo." This was her widest, most sculpted smoke ring yet. "Today."

In those deal memo negotiations, which the network's lawyers ensured took several more days than Winterson desired, one stipulation arose: Winterson wanted Griffin and his crew on the scene *fast*. "We need to see him while he's still limping," she explained. "While these two are still in shock. The before and after is crucial here. Their acclimation is our biggest danger. I think we need this to be as close to live as we can get it."

In financial terms, this was the largest single deal—and, subsequently, the maddest scramble—of Griffin's career. He had a thirty-day window for pre-production. During that month he and Douglas spent sixteen-hour days together, hiring crew and arranging tax credits through the Mississippi Film Commission and sketching out profile interviews and charting storylines (to which Winterson, as an executive producer, almost constantly objected) and hashing out licensing deals and more—much more. "It was like that old Mickey Rooney–Judy Garland routine: Let's put on a show!" Griffin says. "Racing the clock the whole time. Nothing but adrenaline in the veins. It felt like rock 'n' roll."

And then, on the morning of October 27, 2014, Griffin and his six-person crew took over Reconfort Avenue in Biloxi. Mrs. Dooley, from her porch, watched the black trucks roll in. "Somebody getting busted big-time," she recalls thinking to herself. Other neighbors peered from behind curtains. Children from adjacent blocks lined up at the edge of the railroad tracks, glaring at this otherwordly invasion of men and women wearing headsets and conferring over clipboards and hauling or wheeling enormous video and audio equipment into the garage. The men and women wearing the headsets waved at the children but the children didn't wave back. Filming for "Miracle Man," as Winterson christened the show, began that afternoon.

"Look, I know how story works," Griffin says now. "I know there's a certain compression that's required, and that certain roles need to be filled. I get that. And so I get why some people are going to paint me as the villain in this story. Because of what I do, because of what I represent, because of what happened New Year's Eve, the lawsuits, the whole fuckup parade. I'm not going to suggest that every choice I made along the way was the right one." The laugh he inserts here is pungent enough to mistake for a cry. "But a villain, to my thinking, has to have evil intent or else a reckless and selfish disregard for consequences—and I had neither. I did the best I could with the situation I was given. No, there's a villain here, but that wasn't me. You see, this is what makes this such a Southern story. The villain was the past."

ten

THE WEIRD AURA OF CELEBRITY ISN'T ENTIRELY UNFAMILIAR to Dr. Janice Lorimar-Cuevas. Her father, Winston Lorimar, wears something of that halo, and while his celebrity is of the small-town variety, dimmed further by its literary derivation and then further by the where-are-they-now status of his reputation, she's nevertheless witnessed its effect on people: the way its glow galvanizes and attracts them, at times as nonsensically as a porchlight entrances insects. More acutely she's seen it on the infrequent occasions when one of her father's famous friends would visit Greenwood—the actor Morgan Freeman, she recalls, used to drive down once or twice a year from his home in the north Delta to talk books with her father, and Winston often groused about their meals being interrupted by fawning, camera-brandishing white women "who'd never thought to speak to a black man before except to say how tightly they wanted the roses pruned."

Still, Janice found herself astonished by the commotion Cameron roused when, on November 14, he entered the Half Shell Oyster House, in downtown Gulfport, to meet her for lunch. Awaiting him at a table providing her a view of the door, she was able to track the reactions whirling through the restaurant as he made his way toward her: the double takes, the sidelong glances; the leaned-in whispers across tables ("You see who that is?"); swift tilts of the head or chin employed as directional signals; and, on a few diners, brute and undisguised staring, as though a giraffe were ambling through. Even the busboy refilling her water glass froze tableside to watch Cameron walk in, and he remained that way, immobilized by fame's radiation, as Cameron found Janice and sat down across from her. The effect was so striking, in fact, that Janice noted it to Cameron even before greeting him. "Well you just got recognized all to pieces," she said.

"Do what?" he said.

"You don't notice everyone staring at you?"

"Aw yeah, that shit." He waved a hand opaquely. "We was at Hardee's yesterday, in the drive-through, and about half the folks work there all crammed in the window to wave at me, all that stuff. Couple them taking pictures. They got this donation can hanging off the side there, you know—for some charity, I didn't look which one. But Tanya tells me to put a dollar in there and then the whole window starts clapping and flashing me the thumbs-up sign like I . . . hell, I don't know what. Like I just pulled a pit bull off a baby."

"That has to feel," she said, "incredibly bizarre . . ."

"Father Ace says it ain't me they're staring at, it's God." A thoughtful frown emerged on his forehead. "That's how he says I'm supposed to think about it anyway."

"Ah, right," Janice said. "The detective priest. He's come to see me twice."

"He's putting me in to the Vatican for a miracle."

"He's very . . ." The word cued on her tongue was *aggressive*—that's how she'd described Father Ace to her husband. But now she chose, ". . . energetic." While Janice and the priest's first meeting had been cordial, their second had borne an interrogative tension, with Father Ace making no effort to conceal his agenda: The explanation he needed for Cameron's recovery was the absence of any explanation, which was precisely what Janice possessed yet which she felt reluctant to offer. She knew what he intended to pour into that empty vessel. Nap, for his part, found her account of the ordeal faintly amusing. "Not everyone gets deposed by God," he told her.

"Father's downright hyper," Cameron replied. "He drives me pretty hard."

Janice was curious what he meant by this but found herself distracted by Cameron's appearance—something about it seemed different to her, or maybe multiple things were just fractionally different: cleaner, sharper . . . something. "You look good," is how she summarized it to him.

"I been working out a little bit," he said, not quite as aw-shucksily, she thought, as the pre-recovery Cameron might've responded. "Tried running last week but I still don't got the legs for it. They're gone after about a quarter mile."

Continuing to assess him, she said, "You look like you've put some weight on, too. Healthy weight."

"They got this catering deal, you know, for the TV crew? You can pretty much get anything you want whenever. Taquitos, these little biscuits, must be ten different kinds of ham."

Unable to suspend her scrutiny, she moved her focus now to his clothing. Janice couldn't recall having ever seen him in anything but a T-shirt, but today he was wearing a charcoal chambray hoodie—an urbane swerve. She complimented it.

"Yeah, that was weird," he said, with two fingers flecking the fabric in much the way Janice's brothers used to pick at their Easter suits. "They measured me the day they arrived and then two days later come all these FedEx boxes filled with clothes. Something about how they can't have logos and stuff on TV. You should see what they did to the house, too. Painted every room because white walls don't look good onscreen. Tanya even told them about Mama's old porcelain collection and a week later comes this glass case filled with porcelain animals. They're all the wrong animals—Mama just did dolphins and coast stuff, y'know, lighthouses and shit—and now there's like rhinos and kittens in there. But it got Tanya crying anyhow."

"So how is it?" Janice leaned in with a small-talk smile. "Life on camera?"

The waiter interrupted and they paused to order. Meeting a patient for lunch was unprecedented—lunch itself is a rarity for Janice; nibbling a protein bar between patient consults is as close as she usually comes— though seeing a patient outside the office is not. Janice helps coordinate the hospital's home-based primary care program, and her in-home consults, she says, make up her most rewarding time as a physician. A smirk crawls onto her face when she admits how baffling this would sound to her med-school professors at Pitt, who'd tried steering her away from primary care, the Peace Corps of medical fields, toward the elevated realm of specialty medicine. The glory (and money) in medicine, they told her, was in doing things *to* people, not *for* them. But she was never interested in parts; she was interested in patients.

"My father's ideal of a physician, which I might've absorbed a little bit," she says by way of explanation, "was Doc Woodson in Greenwood, long dead. He zipped to his house calls on an old German motorcycle and expected to be served a slice of pie after his examinations. My father tells this story—who knows if it's true?—about Doc Woodson treating a boy with a broken jaw. The story was that a mule kicked him but somehow Doc Woodson figured out the boy's father had hit him. So he heads outside, finds the father, and whacks him in the jaw with a hickory stick. Then he sets the father's broken jaw but tells him next time he won't. My father called that the pinnacle of a medical house call: treat the injury, treat the cause."

The contours of this lunch meeting (Janice objects to calling it a consult), however, seeped outside the normal lines. She'd taken a personal day from the hospital and was afterward heading to the Tulane Medical Library in New Orleans to research glial scar histology. She'd declined to log the meeting with the hospital. No one—especially not Dr. Turnbull—was aware of it. This was on her time.

"Life on camera, yeah," Cameron was saying. "Not sure I reckoned what a *job* it'd be. Like, six in the morning till six at night. And them telling me what I'm doing that day. Like, today you're going shopping with your sister, or you're going to play football with some school kids. They won't let me smoke or drink beer neither. Not on camera, anyhow. Says it ain't in character. But they let Tanya do it. Hell, they open beers for her."

"They've called me, you know," Janice said of the show's producers. "A lot, actually."

"Yeah, I heard," said Cameron, averting his eyes. Scott T. Griffin had been urging him to issue a personal plea to Janice to appear on the show. "You don't want to be on TV?"

"Well, that's up to Public Affairs, and no, they're not keen on it," she said. "But, honestly? I *don't* really have any interest in being on TV. Of course my father was a writer so TV was always sort of the enemy in our house. Just watching an episode of *Friends*, I mean, that was like betraying the Western canon."

"Huh," Cameron responded. He sipped Coca-Cola through a straw.

"I used to make all these movies when I was a kid, me and this friend," he told her, so sheepishly that Janice felt he was confessing something. "Dressing up like spies and filming all this crazy stuff by the bayou back of his house. That was a lot more fun than the filming I'm doing now."

"I'll bet it was," she said, with the flatly encouraging tone of a psychiatrist listening while making notes, which is more or less what she was doing in her head. A theatrical bent in childhood was probably, of course, just that: one bend in a life that, like everyone's, contained many. But it suggested, or maybe suggested, that the spotlight Cameron was entering was not entirely alien to him. Perhaps just idly and childishly, and so long ago as to be meaningless, but he'd once aspired to an existence onscreen. "Huh," she said.

"They wanted to come along today," he told her. "The producers."

"I'm glad they didn't, Cameron. This is sort of . . . off the record. I just wanted—well, I guess I just wanted to see how you're coping with everything. You know, up there, in your head. I—"

She saw an unmistakable pall of disappointment drape his face.

"What?" she asked him.

"That's why you wanted to see me?"

"Yeah, just to catch up—I'm sorry, did I . . ."

"I guess I just had it in my head that you might have some news for me."

"News?"

"About what happened. About why I'm walking."

"Oh no," Janice said, and cringing with guilt she reached a hand across the table. "I'm so sorry if I gave you that impression. I wouldn't have—I would've called you into the office if—ugh. I'm sorry."

"Naw, it ain't a big deal," he mumbled, not quite convincingly. "Reckon I just got it in my head wrong."

"I haven't stopped investigating," she assured him. "In fact we've forwarded your case up to a VA research lab in Rhode Island that works on neurorestoration. And I've been looking into every angle I can think of." Stung by his disappointment, and wanting to further assure him of her commitment, she divulged how she'd recently discovered a seventy-year-old case similar to his.

Light returned to Cameron's face. "Similar how?"

Janice sketched the story for him, the seeds of which she'd found in a citation in an obscure Korean War–era Army Medical Services report—a portion of the story, anyway.

Floyd John Denton, of Bagdad, Arizona, was eighteen years old when he enlisted as a private in the Army Air Forces in 1942, and displayed such remarkable flying prowess that in less than a year he was promoted to master sergeant. In the first five months of 1943, he was credited with shooting down nine enemy planes over North Africa. On May 23 of that year, Denton's P-38 Lightning fighter was strafed in a dogfight over Algeria and caught fire, forcing him to bail. Enemy tracer fire shredded Denton's parachute during his descent, causing him to spin like a maple seed as he went hurtling toward the desert. Landing in a shallow wadi might've saved his life, but it didn't save his spine. When Bedouin tribesmen happened upon Denton, a day later, they found him paralyzed below the waist, and turned him over to Italian troops. He languished in a hospital near Bari, Italy, until September 1944, when the Italian authorities repatriated him, and he returned home to Arizona.

On the morning of May 12, 1950, almost six years to the day of his injury, Floyd John Denton woke up with sensation in his legs—a light prickly pain, "as though chiggers," as the author of the Army Medical Services report stylishly put it, "were snacking on his lower extremities." Denton recovered motor function much more slowly than Cameron did—over the course of two weeks, Denton's granddaughter told Janice; the AMS report failed to specify—but the differences more or less stop there: Like Cameron, the once-paralyzed airman found himself fully restored.

Cameron's face was registering a pendulum of reactions to Janice's account. Part of him felt thrilled, he'd later say, to hear that he wasn't alone, could no longer deem himself an aberration of nature or of supernature; yet another part of him was dismayed by something he still finds hard to articulate. A loss of singularity, perhaps. The feeling, maybe, of scaling a mountain reputed to be unclimbed, only to find a candy wrapper at the summit. A question came trembling off his lips: "Did he—did he stay that way?"

"For the rest of his life, yes," Janice answered.

This was Cameron's only question about Floyd John Denton, and for that Janice felt relieved. F.J., as he was called, "was a hard, rough man," says Cherie Nugent, the granddaughter with whom Janice spoke. Nugent, a massage/reiki therapist in Phoenix, is the eldest daughter of F.J. Denton's son, and a candid family historian. "They say he was bad to drink before he started walking again," she says, "and then worse to drink after." Alcohol-fueled fisticuffs appear to have been his prevailing post-recovery pastime—with bar patrons, mostly, but also with his co-workers at the Bagdad copper mine and, sadly, with his wife and child. Yavapai County Sheriff's Office records show Denton was arrested for battery and assorted other charges eight times between 1952 and 1957. (Later records were lost in a fire.) Even in a hard-drinking, knock-em-stiff mining town like Bagdad, Denton cut a ferocious and dangerous figure; he was fired from the mine in 1959, allegedly for assaulting a foreman, and worked sporadically as a handyman in nearby Prescott thereafter. When he died, in 1965—killed in a one-car automobile accident after midnight on the Yavapai Indian reservation, the cause of which struck most people as self-evident—the *Prescott Evening Courier*'s obituary made no mention of Denton's wartime heroics, except to note that he was a World War Two veteran, nor did it make any mention of his extraordinary postwar recovery.

There's no evidence of any medical investigation having been done on Denton's recovery. He was clearly examined by military doctors for his case to have been cited in the 1951 AMS report; but the citation was anecdotal, appearing in the report's introduction as a way of illustrating the epidemiological mysteries of spinal cord injuries.

"I don't get the feeling people thought of it as a miracle, no," says Nugent. "At least no one in the family ever talked about it that way. It was more like, nothing and nobody could ever whup F.J. Not even a drop from a burning plane with his parachute torn to ribbons—not even that could break him. Like he was too damn tough to stay paralyzed."

Denton's recovery, then, seems to have been viewed less as an act of God than as an act of will—when it was viewed at all. The local newspapers took no notice. Nothing in the archives of Bagdad's two churches suggests Denton's recovery attracted clergy interest. "He wasn't raised in the church and I doubt he ever entered one," says Nugent. "There wasn't a lot of love for him in the family, and probably wasn't much love for him anywhere around Prescott, if I had to guess." To say that Floyd John Denton—despite his aerial valor and despite his spectacular recuperation—rolled through Bagdad and later Prescott like a tumbleweed, leaving no apparent trace, seems valid; but it seems equally valid to liken his passage to that of a rattlesnake, a presence best avoided. "My father was just twelve when his dad died and I don't think I'm exaggerating when I say he's never stopped being terrified of the man." (Carl Denton, Nugent's father, hangs up the telephone when asked about his father; he did speak to Janice, but only to say he didn't wish to discuss the matter and to recommend she speak with Cherie.)

"So what's it mean, then, that this has happened before?" Cameron asked her.

"That's what I'm trying to figure out. And I'm still very unsure how this," meaning Cameron, "is related to that," meaning Denton. "Unfortunately there's no data to quantify any parallels. There's just a story."

Cameron was shaking his head. "And here you said you didn't have no news."

"Is that news?"

"I mean, can miracles happen twice?"

"Well." She brought a forkful of salad to her mouth to give herself time to consider a response. Privately, her answer was yes: The existence of a precedent—if the case of Floyd John Denton could be called that—suggested that a very rare and unknown mechanism could be at work. But Cameron was asking about miracles, not mechanisms; the distinction was more than semantic. "That's a question for your priest, not me."

Seeing his brow knotting, she wondered if divulging F.J. Denton's story had been a mistake. Intimations aside, Denton's neurons and Cameron's might've shared nothing more than narrative resemblance. "Is it all still bothering you?" she asked. "I mean, not *bothering* . . . you know. The whole spiritual thing."

"Not as much, I guess," he said. "I mean, Father Ace, he's certifying it. The hard part now is understanding why it happened to me—why God chose me. And what-all I'm supposed to *do* with it."

"Is that how you *want* to think about it—as a miracle?"

"I don't know," he said. He looked uncomfortable, as though congested with something inexpressible. "I mean, it's either God or it isn't, right? The result's the same."

"That's probably a healthy way of looking at it," she said, though a part of her grimaced as she said it. Nap, her husband, had voiced something similar while venting his frustrations about the off-duty energy Janice was devoting to Cameron's case. His irritation, she thought, wasn't entirely unfair; she was experiencing her own side effects. Her exercise regimen was getting squeezed, for starters—she hadn't clocked a ten-mile-plus run in weeks, and, with her concentration often fritzing, her running times were inching up. During yoga classes she didn't find her head clearing, as it once had, but instead felt it clouding ever deeper. When Nap mentioned events in the news she often found herself staring back vacantly: The only reading she was doing was medical literature. She hadn't been like this— single-minded, frazzled, abstracted—since med school, and maybe not even then. Her friend Cheryl had even asked her, in a roundabout way about which they still laugh, if Janice might be having an affair. "A healthy way of looking at it, I guess," she added to Cameron, and perhaps to herself, "though I can't imagine it's an easy way of looking at it."

"Helluva lot easier than what I used to have to think about," said Cameron. He was dipping a fried oyster in Tabasco-laced ketchup, and his tone was light. "Shit, I was popping my Skittles just so I could think what to eat for breakfast. I don't miss that."

"Miss—" Janice felt a twinge of alarm. "Don't miss what?"

"My Skittles. The meds."

"You've stopped taking them? Which ones?"

"All 'em. Except the pain meds sometimes, when my legs get to aching."

"The Zoloft?"

He nodded.

"The Prazosin?"

"Yeah, that too. I still got some of those Klonopin tabs left but, naw, I've not taken nothing since . . . it's been a couple weeks I think."

Cameron had been taking a daily 150-milligram dose of Zoloft, an antidepressant, since 2011, when he'd foundered into a deep depression following his release from Brooke Army Medical Center. Janice had later prescribed him a high-dose regimen of Prazosin, which blunts the impact of excess adrenaline, to ease Cameron's nightmares and sleep disturbances. She'd also prescribed him Klonopin, a benzodiazepine, for anxiety. It's a common and clinically effective cocktail for treating post-

traumatic stress disorder. A year or so before, Tanya had confided to Janice that the drugs had probably saved her brother's life.

"Cameron, those medications weren't for your legs. They were for your
brain."

"But the problem with my brain was my legs."

"No, no, no." She was registering a gush of adrenaline and anxiety herself now. "Your PTSD—that's independent of your physical trauma. Just
because your physical trauma resolved doesn't mean the psychological
trauma did. What happened to you is still up there."

"But it doesn't *feel* that way. What it feels like is that none of it happened."

"But it *did.*"

"I'm just saying."

"No, listen to me please. Major life events can often lead to depres-
sive episodes—even happy events. Sometimes *especially* happy events.
And let's be honest—life events don't come more major than yours. You're
grappling with some substantial issues right now, from the spiritual stuff
on down. I mean, if fame feels weird now, imagine how it's going to be
when the show premieres. And when it ends. What about then?"

He stared back at her.

"Look, there may come a time for us to adjust your medications to
align with your different situation in life and how you're feeling about it,
absolutely—but right now isn't it. It's more important than ever for you to
be stable up there. I really can't stress that enough, Cameron. When did
you stop? Do you remember?"

His face was expressionless, and that in itself Janice read as defiance.
"Two, three weeks ago," he said. "When my Zoloft ran out. I just figured . . ."

He concluded this sentence with a shrug.

"Have you noticed any changes?" She'd pulled her iPhone from her
purse and was now typing notes into it.

"Changes? Not really. Don't get that dizziness anymore. Or that zoned-
out feeling. Uh, takes me a lot longer to catch a buzz? That's a weird one."

"Nothing negative? The nightmares haven't returned?"

"Nothing."

"No mood swings, no anxiety, intrusive thoughts . . ."

"*Nothing,* doc." The smile on Cameron's face, steady and beatific, evoked that of a preacher, intimating that what seemed fraught and complex might in fact be quite simple. "Maybe that's part of the miracle."

With a deep and unruly sigh Janice placed down her phone. "I really wish you'd talked to me before making that decision."

"I'm talking to you now."

As Janice opened her mouth to respond she sensed a strange tightening of the atmosphere, a warning that came floating through the air, and when she glanced right then left she saw that the diners around them were staring and maybe also, she worried, eavesdropping. Perhaps she and Cameron had been exuding more tension than she'd realized, or perhaps she'd failed to notice, until then, just how closely their lunch was being monitored, how entrancing was Cameron's porchlight of fame. Gulfport and Biloxi aren't small towns, by Mississippi standards, but they act like it; if word were to reach Dr. Turnbull she could conceivably (if gymnastically) defend a social lunch with a patient, but certainly not an off-campus, off-the-books consult about Cameron's drug regimen. Cameron's gaze followed hers, and possibly latching onto her discomfort he announced, "I'm gonna grab a smoke."

"I'll walk out with you," she said.

Out on the sidewalk Cameron tapped his pants pockets and cursed; he'd left his cigarettes in the car. Janice watched as he fished a keyless car remote from one of those pockets. When he thumbed its button the headlights on a very new and very shiny car flashed twice, accompanied by the blooping of its horn, and Janice trailed Cameron to the car where he plucked a fresh pack of cigarettes from the passenger seat. A disabled placard, she noticed, was hanging from the rearview mirror.

"This is yours?" she said.

"I reckon," he said, lighting a cigarette with a shrug. The car was a 2014 Ford Fusion sedan, its deep blue exterior evoking the Gulf beneath a full moon. "Two cars show up one day and they hand me the key to one and tell me it's mine. I didn't ask for how long. They said Ford donated them or something. The producers, they didn't want Tanya's old Kia in the driveway so we gave it to Quỳnh to use."

"Quỳnh?"

"He's the Vietnamese fella owns the Biz-E-Bee."

"Oh right," she said. "I actually stopped by there a week or so ago. It's like a shrine to you."

"Yeah, he's given us a lifetime discount. Ten percent off everything except cigarettes."

At this Cameron grinned, widely and toothily and almost, to Janice's eye, victoriously, the way a poker player revealing a royal flush might grin, and it was then, in the bleached light of the midday sun, that she finally identified that overriding discrepancy in his appearance that'd been throwing her off: his teeth. They were spectacularly white and uniform, like plastic piano keys. He was sporting an anchorman's mouth.

"Your teeth. Are those . . . ?"

"Veneers, ha." Cameron sucked at them, blushing. "Network paid for 'em."

"Well I'll be damned." She wagged her head in an effort to shake off her visible incredulity. "It's just—it's a whole new you, isn't it? Top to bottom."

"Kinda is, huh?"

Looking at him now, with the sun-dappled peacock shades of the Gulf at his back, his glinting new teeth eligible for a Colgate commercial audition, his blond hair—now longer than he used to keep it, and styled with L.A. precision—shimmering lightly in the breeze, she flashed back to the first time she'd seen him, in her office: crumpled, scarred, unwashed, pale, minimally responsive, mildly intoxicated, ever-nudged by his sister, one of those combat casualties for whom survival, in their heads, seems more curse than blessing. He'd come to her, that morning, in a state of rot. It was beyond difficult for her to reconcile these two Camerons—no, it was flat-out impossible.

"Are you—are you happy, Cameron?" she found herself asking. The odd way he looked at her suggested he hadn't quite heard her, so she repeated it: "Are you happy?"

Cameron remembers answering yes to this question. Janice, however, recalls him replying with a question of his own: "How could I not be?"

She's adamant about the accuracy of this memory, she says, because she remembers asking Cameron's question of herself as she drove along the coast toward New Orleans that afternoon: *How could I not be happy,* she remembers thinking, *about this transformation in my patient?* What was it that was unsettling her about him? She ran through their conversation in her head (later, in New Orleans, she'd transcribe it from memory), sifting through everything he'd said for clues to . . . to *what,* exactly? To something atmospheric, ineffable, emotional—the goose-pimply stuff she hated.

She turned on the car radio. She turned off the car radio.

Was it her own pride, she wondered darkly: some noxious facet of her ego resenting Cameron's metamorphosis because it'd not only happened without her but possibly *in spite* of her? But what warped species of physician begrudges a patient's recovery?

Or was it merely a symptom of the terminal weariness she was feeling— maybe Nap was right when he'd said they should take a vacation or start having babies—from trying and trying and trying and trying to find an explanation for Cameron's recovery, in hundreds of books and internet journals, in long-shot consultations with other clinicians, in a forgotten 1951 Army Medical Services report that simultaneously provided her with everything and nothing she needed, in her groggy thoughts as she awoke every morning and in her groggier thoughts as she fell asleep every night? How could science have nothing to say? How could *she*—she who'd examined those legs when they were spindly and insensate, who'd studied and re-studied the data, she who'd felt the motion of those reanimated legs beneath her palms and found herself gasping that same incoherent word as everyone else, *Jesus*?

As Mississippi became Louisiana, the piney woods escorting I-10 giving way to cypress swamps, their still and glassy waters rust-stained with reflections of the autumn leaves, Janice's mind drifted back to Doc Woodson in Greenwood and to what her father had deemed the pinnacle of medicine: *treat the injury, treat the cause.* But what if there was no cause? What if that boy from her father's story, the one with the broken jaw—what if he'd just been sitting outside the Pemberton General Store or in front of Fountain's Big Busy Store downtown, not doing anything, not even chewing gum, when from out of nowhere he felt his jawbone snap? Doc Woodson wouldn't have said *Jesus,* no. Doc Woodson would've said bullshit. Doc Woodson, she realized, would've called that boy a liar.

eleven

STOPPING BY THE BIZ-E-BEE STORE, IN THE LATE MONTHS OF 2014, wasn't quite, as Janice noted, like visiting a shrine. As a Yelp reviewer wrote, in December, it was more like "someone . . . opened a Cracker Barrel at Lourdes."

From the outside the Biz-E-Bee looked much the way it always had, save a couple adjustments: a big red plastic banner, hanging to the side of the entrance, now trumpeted "MIRACULOUS" DISCOUNTS!, and an eight-by-twelve-foot rectangle of neon-orange spray paint mapped roughly the spot where Cameron had risen from his wheelchair. Venturing inside, however, one confronted a dizzying farrago of kitsch, mementos, standard-issue convenience items, and souvenir oddities that, depending on one's leanings, could provoke groans of disgust or yawps of glee. (Case in point: a custom-designed snow globe, priced at $35.99, containing a male figurine seated in a wheelchair; tilt the globe to the left and, amid scattered flurries, the figurine stood up.) A double-sided rack of T-shirts, most of them emblazoned with generic miracle messages (SUCH A BIG MIRACLE, read one, IN SUCH A LITTLE CHILD), stood beside a rack of postcards bearing celestial scenes, the kinds of postcards one might wish to mail friends and family from the afterlife. Topping the aisle racks were jaggy skylines of devotional candles in various sizes and colors and scents. The Biz-E-Bee was surely the only store on earth wherein one could purchase a Pepto-Bismol–pink statuette of Jesus, a six-pack of Miller High Life, an I "BELIEVE" IN MIRACLES keychain, an autographed plastic bottle of holy water, a Tabasco-seasoned Slim Jim, Prinknash incense, an empty-wheelchair Christmas ornament, two packs of Marlboro reds, a faux-pearl rosary, and the latest issue of *Penthouse* magazine.

And Lê Nhu Quỳnh, the co-proprietor of this raggle-taggle emporium, was as happy, in the words of his new friend and boarder Virgil "Gil" Poleman, "as a pig in shit." Poleman was the inflatable-cross-bearing pilgrim who'd shown up five days after Cameron's recovery and after a seventy-mile walk from Chunchula, Alabama. When Hat learned that Poleman had no place to sleep, she'd strung a hammock out back behind their small apartment at the rear of the store. This was not Quỳnh's preferred arrangement. Poleman offered him some utility, as a sort of storefront barker, but extending a sick and potentially deranged man free rein of your bathroom seemed to Quỳnh a stretch too far. He badgered Hat with questions all through that first evening, as she cooked dinner, half-watched television, tried to sleep: What about when it rains? What happens if he dies here? What if he's being hunted by mobsters who'll gun down the whole family for harboring him? What if more people like him show up, what then—are we founding a colony for the diseased and the desperate? Quỳnh stomped and shouted when Hat eventually took to responding, drowsily, with Bible verses.

Little by little, however, Poleman charmed him. First Poleman cured Steven Seagal, Quỳnh's eight-year-old fighting cock. Quỳnh had only fought the bird once, an experience so traumatizing that he had immediately retired the Kelso rooster, which has lived peaceably ever since in a tiny wire pen out back. Quỳnh claims to keep it for security, which makes his wife laugh. "It's his best friend," Hat says, describing evenings when her husband, stymied by Little Kim's *Dora the Explorer* reruns occupying the television, watches action movies on his laptop outside, positioning the screen so that the rooster can share the view and occasionally explaining plot points to it. When Poleman appeared, the bird was in poor shape: its face swollen, sticky discharge leaking from its eyes and nose, its breathing growing more and more rattled. Quỳnh was adding crushed garlic to its water but was otherwise stumped at how to treat the rooster, whose death would leave him the sole male in the household—a psychological calamity, according to Hat. Poleman, who grew up on a farm, diagnosed it instantly. "This bird's got the roup," he told Quỳnh. After just a single dose of the antibiotic Poleman recommended, Steven Seagal showed improvement and Poleman was promoted to regular guest at the Lês' supper table. That Poleman didn't eat much was another facet of his charm.

But he was also, Quỳnh soon found, an invaluable ambassador to the pilgrims that started swarming the Biz-E-Bee in his wake. Quỳnh couldn't "talk all that Mr. Jesus," as he puts it; Ollie couldn't talk at all; Hat was too preoccupied with Little Kim and with managing the increasingly complex operations of the store, now that their inventory had shifted to religious items, many of them custom-ordered; but Gil—Gil was magnificent. He issued warm and munificent welcomes to the pilgrims, listened intently to why they'd come and what they were seeking. He guided them out to where Cameron had risen and led them in prayers, usually with his eyes glued shut and with a Bible held aloft in a cancer-trembled hand. He shepherded them, gently, toward the aisle of souvenirs he'd helped Quỳnh select, encouraging them to consider a keepsake of their visit. (The snow globe, for instance, was Poleman's idea, and a savvy one: The initial order of two hundred sold out in less than two weeks.) Oftentimes he told them his own story about coming to the Biz-E-Bee, which Quỳnh still found knuckleheaded—dying men shouldn't go walking from state to state, he thought, dragging giant red sanctified beach toys—but which riveted the pilgrims, who often wiped tears and embraced Poleman and called him an inspiration.

"I spent two thirds of my life bass-fishing and drinking and smoking and chasing women," he'd tell them. "The other third I spent sleeping. That was until I found Jesus." Over the course of several evenings, out back in the little bit of yard that belongs to the Lês, Poleman gave Quỳnh a more nuanced version of his story. He'd served in the Navy, and got to see Korea and the Philippines, which he was surprised to hear Quỳnh had not. He'd been married three times and had six kids. He'd managed a couple fast-food restaurants then worked many years for the Alabama Power Company. After he got laid off he didn't do much besides drink and fish until finding Jesus. The cancer diagnosis arrived six months after he was born again. All he wanted now, he told Quỳnh, was a little more time to make good.

It's a verdant, fragrant, deeply shaded spot out back. Disheveled thickets of bougainvillea, trumpet vine, wax myrtle, bamboo, coral bean, and oleander intertwining beneath a loquat tree lend it a sense of refuge. As the two men drank sweet tea out there, watching Steven Seagal scratching and pecking the floor of his pen, their conversations sometimes drifted toward the philosophical. Gil was agreeing to Hat's demand that he seek cancer care at the VA—"Jesus," she reminded him, "helps those who help themselves"—but the chemoembolization treatments that he had recommenced in late September (he'd started chemo in Alabama) weren't supplying him much hope. His only shot, he felt sure, was a Biz-E-Bee miracle.

Despite Little Kim's against-the-odds survival, and despite having seen Cameron staggering beside his empty wheelchair, Quỳnh was still allergic to long-shot hopes. One night he pushed back with an analogy about lottery retailers, one of his private fascinations. Despite widespread beliefs to the contrary, he explained to Gil, a store that sells a mega-jackpot lotto ticket, a so-called "lucky store," is almost certain to never sell another. They're one and done, Quỳnh told him: That's how luck works. (For the record, Quỳnh's inversion of what economists call "the gambler's fallacy" is anecdotally but not statistically accurate.) Tucked into that analogy was the dour suggestion that Cameron's jackpot negated Gil's chances.

Gil chewed this idea over for a while as a CSX train rumble-clattered past. Then he said, "The drinking and the carousing didn't teach me a whole lot but the fishing did. Lotta folks, they think there's some luck to fishing. But when you find the right hole, and you're pulling lunkers outta that hole every day—that ain't luck, brother. What you've got there is the ideal environment for those fish, the water temp and the current level and the structure, all that stuff. And I think that's what we've got right here. A spiritual honey hole."

He was far from alone in that assessment. The first big buses—sleek coaches that seat fifty or more people—began sweeping into the parking lot in late September. For the most part these were chartered by church groups from around the region: Louisiana, east Texas, Alabama, Arkansas. As word of Cameron's recovery spread, however, the buses started showing up from more far-flung locations. Coaches pulled into the lot from Nevada, from New York, from West Virginia, Minnesota, Kansas, and elsewhere, and from them streamed Catholics, Presbyterians, Congregationalists, Methodists, Baptists, Pentecostals, Adventists, Mormons—old, young, sick, healthy, black, white, Asian, Latino—the passengers sometimes blinking with wonderment as they'd debark, as though entering a fabled realm. Some of them were religious tourists who told Gil of their prior visits to the Christ in the Smokies Museum in Gatlinburg, Tennessee, or to the Holy Land Experience in Orlando. Others were craving fellowship, they said, in the palpable presence of Christ. And still more, like Gil, came in search of healing.

Rachel Taylor was one of these. Taylor, a freshman at Baylor University, is a vibrantly freckled nineteen-year-old who wouldn't look out of place modeling clothes in a J. Crew catalog, the kind of girl emanating a glow because even the light itself wishes to be near her. Two years ago, while training for an international competition in equestrian vaulting, Taylor's foot snagged during a dismount from her horse, and the resulting fall paralyzed her below the waist. The idea of making a pilgrimage to the Biz-E-Bee came from her father, a Houston energy trader, who after reading about Cameron's recovery flew thirty-two friends and family members on a private jet to Biloxi where a chartered bus then conveyed them to the store. "Lord and Savior Jesus Christ, your servant Rachel is a girl deserving of another chance, of the fullest and most abundant life you see fit to give her," her father prayed outside the store, with all thirty-two of them holding hands in a circle around Rachel, her wheelchair stationed inside the neon-orange rectangle. Seven of her sorority sisters were wearing their pledge jerseys in solidarity, their cheeks stained with mascara as Rachel's mother's face was likewise streaked. If there was any hope or expectation for a spontaneous, Cameron-style recovery, no one showed signs of it; after her father's fulsome amen, the participants one by one embraced Rachel and, in the words of one, "just told her how much we loved her and how we were praying for her." Despite all the tears being dabbed, the group reassembled on the bus in a buoyant, even festive mood, headed for dinner at one of the casino restaurants before their flight home.

On the other end of the spectrum were pilgrims like Jimmy Batson. Batson, a forty-two-year-old FedEx driver, didn't come far, just twenty miles down the beach from Pass Christian, and didn't come seeking a release from paralysis or cancer as more dramatic others did. Batson suffers from a genetic skin disorder known as ichthyosis vulgaris, which causes patches of his arms and shoulders and sometimes his face to flake off in gray scales. One Thursday in October, after work, he drove to the Biz-E-Bee and stood inside the rectangle for about five minutes rubbing his forearms as though to make sure the nature of his affliction was clear. "I've tried every damn cream and lotion known to man," he told Gil and Quỳnh inside the store. "Figured on this maybe giving me a boost." Along with a Coke and a bag of Zapp's potato chips for the drive home, he purchased for his mother a devotional candle and for his sister-in-law a reusable plastic beverage tumbler on which was printed HANDLE WITH PRAYER.

For every one-off customer like Batson, however, Quỳnh was feeling the disappearance of another of his regulars. The Biz-E-Bee was serving the world, it seemed, no longer just the neighborhood. It still sold convenience items, but not very conveniently. No one wanted to tote their day's-end twelve-pack of Coors through a throng of hymn-singing worshippers. No one wanted to wait in a line five-deep to buy a can of chew. No one wanted to squeeze his work truck into a parking lot jammed with out-of-state cars and idling buses. No one wanted Gil's grandiloquent welcome when all that was needed was a tin of Altoids and a pack of Trojans. Was it disrespectful to walk through that neon-orange rectangle, which, situated by the doorway, required some awkward maneuvering to avoid? No one felt sure. A third of a mile down Division Street was a BP minimart where the prices had frankly always been a little better and where you never had to walk past someone kneeling on the asphalt speaking in tongues.

Cameron Harris was the most significant of these vanishing regulars, despite the ten percent lifetime discount Quỳnh awarded him. Quỳnh wished that wasn't the case, because of course the pilgrims were always hoping to see Cameron, asking what time he usually came by, and often lingering outside the store after their visits in case he might appear, and furthermore it seemed weirdly important to many of them that Cameron still shop there. "He is not here, but is risen," Gil started saying, in a mischievous cribbing from the Gospel of Luke, until someone took offense.

But Quỳnh understood Cameron's absence—or tried to, anyway. Midway through October, while Cameron was in the store autographing water bottles, passengers offloading from a midsize church bus—Pentecostals from a small town near Memphis, according to Gil, most of them middle-aged women—mobbed Cameron so ferociously that both Gil and Ollie had to pry bodies off him like football referees untangling a fumble. From that point forward Cameron did his autographing after hours, snatching a Bud Light tall-boy from the cooler and asking if it was cool to smoke inside, something Quỳnh let him do. Wherever he was nowadays buying those cigarettes, however, it wasn't the Biz-E-Bee.

Cameron's appearances at the store grew slightly more frequent once filming began on *Miracle Man* at the end of October. But these were scheduled and rigidly choreographed visits prior to which the store all but shut down as the camera crew and production assistant set up inside, peeling advertisement signage off the cooler doors and moving things around while Quỳnh watched in helpless bewilderment. The production crew was made up of sharp young people, terse and barky and quick to throw elbows. Ollie and Gil were always banished from the shoots, just one of the many things about the production that Quỳnh didn't understand. One time the producer asked him to sit Little Kim on his lap while they filmed some B-roll footage of him tallying up purchases. He had never put Little Kim on his lap behind the counter, not with that bank of computers so attractive to her tiny lethal fingers, but his resistance was quickly and thoroughly swatted down. When someone shouted, "Talent en route!," Quỳnh learned, it meant Cameron or Tanya or both were on their way. The production assistant would hand Tanya beer and tampons and random items such as an auto air-freshener to buy, all of which got charged to a production company Visa. Sometimes, while the cameras were rolling, Cameron and Tanya would bicker at the counter, and Quỳnh was never sure if they were pretending or truly arguing though the disputes did seem to vaporize once the filming stopped. Mostly, Quỳnh just grinned. That seemed to be what everyone wanted him to do.

It wasn't that Quỳnh didn't miss his regulars. He did, at least occasionally. One of the production assistants, the one named Kaitlyn, always guarded the doorway before and during shooting, interviewing potential shoppers about appearing on camera and requiring those selected to sign release forms. At times Quỳnh found himself wincing as he'd watch long-time customers arguing with her, saying they just needed a can of Alpo or to reload a prepaid cell-service card, before storming away.

One of Quỳnh's regulars who was refused entry during filming was a Biloxi police sergeant named Wade Ladner. Ladner has a strong relationship with Biloxi's Vietnamese community, and for years this'd made him a reliable and entertaining fount of coffee-time gossip for Quỳnh—he always had the Monday-morning skinny on who'd gotten busted over the weekend and for what. Quỳnh would recognize the names of many of those arrested from his crabbing days, and his distance from their foibles always filled him with pleasurable solace. When Ladner swung by the store one morning, for his standard order of coffee and a pack of the Lucky Strike non-filters that Quỳnh stocked almost exclusively for him, he ran up against Kaitlyn at the door. As a uniformed officer he couldn't sign the release, but he wanted in anyway. Ladner rapped his wedding ring on a window a dozen or more times, which brought filming to a halt inside and brought Quỳnh outside with coffee, Luckies, and a cringing apology. Behind Quỳnh, however, came Scott T. Griffin, who was livid about the interruption.

Ladner lit one of the cigarettes while Griffin berated him, exhaling what looked to be a missile-guided stream of smoke into Griffin's face. He was clearly unimpressed with the importance of the work that Griffin was accusing him of obstructing.

"Maybe sometime I could tell you about the time I arrested that boy in there," Ladner said, peering over Griffin's shoulder and through the door to where Cameron was standing idle. "Come to think of it, pretty sure we locked his sister up just last year. But you look like a smart guy. Probably knew all that already."

Whether Griffin knew all this or not, Quỳnh didn't. But Quỳnh sensed he wasn't going to learn the details from Ladner. The look in the policeman's eyes, as he flicked the barely burned cigarette to the sidewalk, said to Quỳnh that he wouldn't be returning for a long while, if ever.

Still, Quỳnh was a businessman, and he couldn't argue with his balance sheet. Come December, by which time more than a quarter of the Biz-E-Bee's inventory was in souvenirs and devotional items, Quỳnh was calculating that every big coach that pulled into the lot was grossing him, on average, $1,243—the equivalent of two hundred packs of Lucky Strikes, at a substantially higher profit percentage. Griffin's production company was writing him checks, but the big payoff, Griffin told him, would come once the show aired, when he should expect the store to be "slammed twenty-four-seven." In November Cameron dropped off his sister's car along with its title, and now Quỳnh was thinking of exchanging the family's other, older car for a used motorcycle—the first major luxury he'd ever considered. Because Hat was negotiating settlements with their creditors, and chipping away at their debts, Quỳnh wasn't fearing the mail for the first time in years. The mailman's name was Kip—Quỳnh finally learned that.

Yet there were less quantifiable consolations too. His neighborhood customers squabbled with him, they stole from him, they wrote him bad checks, begged him for credit then cussed him for refusing, forgot what they'd come in for and then resented him not knowing, decided against the pint of ice cream in their hands and so abandoned it on a shelf, made fun of his accent when they thought he wasn't listening, paid for a single bag of ice and then took three. They didn't take selfies with him, as the pilgrims did. They didn't purchase things from the Biz-E-Bee for the sole purpose of purchasing things from the Biz-E-Bee. They didn't wander his store with enraptured awe that reminded Quỳnh of the way he'd regarded his grandmother's farm in Vũng Tàu—as a sanctuary from the confounding, hardscrabble life beyond its small borders, as a hideaway from the world's brute chaos, as a place of magic. That he did not share their faith was beside the point. He shared their esteem and yearning for places of enchantment—where geckos talked, as his father used to tell him, where none of the normal rules applied, where the world felt open to redesign.

Here's what's strange, however: His wife, Hat, who *did* share the pilgrims' faith, and whose indefatigable optimism had always been the counterweight to Quỳnh's fatalism, was feeling the opposite. It was as though whatever force lifted Cameron to his feet had also reprogrammed the Lês. Now it was Hat lying awake at three a.m., worries sabotaging her sleep, while beside her Quỳnh lay dreaming—the reverse of what three a.m. had always looked like for the couple. She had no doubts about what she'd witnessed with her own eyes—Cameron suddenly upright and limping into the sunlight, and nothing but God to account for it—but felt guilty when she saw people praying in that rectangle, as though she and Quỳnh were offering these people something that wasn't theirs to offer. If God had commanded Cameron to rise—and that's what Hat believed—then she felt it was for a divinely precise reason. It wasn't because this corner of Division Street and Reconfort Avenue had freed itself from the strictures of spiritual physics, that underneath the parking lot bubbled miraculous waters. Since September there'd been reports of repeat healings—a woman from D'Iberville was claiming the remission of her cancer following a prayer visit to the store; someone from New Orleans, Hat heard, was crediting the Biz-E-Bee for curing asthma—but Hat found herself instantly rejecting these stories, as much as Quỳnh savored them and as much as they bolstered the Biz-E-Bee's legend. She knew it bucked against Jesus's teachings, to believe only what she herself had seen, and sometimes, at three a.m., this is what rasped her mind.

Cameron, too, was an abrasion. Why him? She knew it was futile to guess at God's reasons, but she found herself trying anyway—and always failing. True, she'd barely known him. He was just another customer, so what she understood about him came via the tea leaves of his purchases: beer and cigarettes, mostly. That he'd been wounded in combat didn't strike her, as it seemed to strike others, as in and of itself grounds for healing. (She'd overheard one man telling Gil that Cameron's healing confirmed God's approval of fighting Islamists, because, he said, "not a single sand nigger" was up and walking like Cameron was.) In fact she found the nature of Cameron's injury slightly problematic. Her childhood in Vietnam had shown her, firsthand, the disfiguring effects of U.S. military intervention, and she admits a faint animus toward military men. The father she'd never known, whose service had marooned his wife and three daughters in that Saigon slum, had been a military man, something Hat's mother—and to a lesser degree Hat herself—never stopped resenting.

She was happy selling the religious items the Biz-E-Bee now stocked, and dismisses the question of whether doing so was capitalizing on Cameron's strange fortune. "Would it be better," she says, "to sell more Funyuns? More beer?" No, the question that bothered her was whether the real product for sale was hope—and false hope, at that. What did she owe to the sick and the lame who traveled there, some from thousands of miles away? What did she owe Gil, who disguised or denied his condition so well and so bravely, but who was clearly, day by day, losing the fight against his cancer—his appetite dwindling, his skin yellowing, his hands and sometimes his eyes twitching and trembling from what Hat knew was pain? She'd never felt so sanguine and lighthearted in the store office as when paying down their debts, one after the other, as though she and Quỳnh were finally stationed at the helm of their own destiny—but what other debts, she found herself wondering, might they be invisibly accruing?

During one of those three a.m. interludes, surrendering the prospects of sleep, she fixed herself a cup of tea but finding no milk in their refrigerator she slipped into the store for some. While writing an I.O.U. at the counter, Quỳnh's longtime requirement, she noticed something strange on one of Quỳnh's security-camera feeds: A man was lying in the parking lot. Normally this would've alarmed her, and sent her fleeing back into the apartment to wake Quỳnh, but the man was lying inside the rectangle, and even in the grainy black-and-white feed she discerned something familiar about him. She turned on the exterior lights and as she opened the front door the man lifted his head from the asphalt.

It was Ollie. He nodded yes when she asked if he was okay. She didn't ask what he was doing out there, and he couldn't have told her anyway. But she knew. And the knowing shot a hairline crack through her heart.

She was almost anticipating, then, the icy breeze she felt flowing through her on the morning of December 18, when, alone in the store while Quỳnh was at the bank, she heard the bells above the door chime and looked up to see a man entering the store.

His black hair was veined with gray and combed assiduously back, and the lines of his face were straight and severe, as though sculpted from some impossibly adamantine material. He wore a midnight-colored suit that even Hat, unattuned to the fineries of menswear, recognized as expertly tailored, and in his hand was a briefcase made from a leather more supple and mellow than any leather she'd seen. Approaching the counter he carried himself bluntly but with aristocratic poise, the air and light seeming to part for him out of an ancient deference. Hat noticed a silver pin, on his suit lapel, consisting of two crossed keys that were banded beneath a bejeweled triple crown.

He told her he needed to talk about Cameron Harris, and his tone made clear he was on official business.

twelve

ON DECEMBER 19, CAMERON HARRIS RECEIVED A PHONE call from Nicola Ash, the senior director of publicity at Lifetime television overseeing the publicity campaign for *Miracle Man*. The series, as Cameron knew from Scott T. Griffin, was scheduled to premiere on March 15, in a Sunday prime-time slot, and this abbreviated time frame was flustering Ash. Bree Winterson had from the start envisioned *Miracle Man* as "real-time" television—not quite live, but also not filmed months in advance in the style of most docudramas—as a way of imbuing it with an added layer of authenticity: The audience wouldn't have any clue about where the show was headed—and how or even if Cameron's mystery would be resolved—because the producers wouldn't either. This, went her thinking, would make it social-media catnip. Winterson's notion was met with widespread derision and hand-wringing inside the network— Griffin's team, for its part, felt unduly hamstrung by what they saw as a gimmick—until the podcast *Serial* debuted in October, and by November was proving an outsize hit. A spinoff of the public radio show *This American Life, Serial* chronicled the reinvestigation of a fifteen-year-old murder case in what the show's producers also deemed "real time"—and its enormous success was validating Winterson's vision.

Still, with that vision came headaches, hassles, unworkable deadlines. Among them was the challenge Ash was given: How do you execute a strategic publicity campaign for what is essentially a work in progress? She had a few standard strategies locked in place, however, which was why she called Cameron that afternoon. Lifetime would be flying him and Tanya out to Los Angeles in late January, she told him, for a round of meet-and-greet receptions with affiliates, key advertisers, and members of the Television Critics Association. She was also booking him to speak at several large churches. In the meantime, she said, she'd nailed down coverage in a couple of "long-lead pubs," or monthly magazines, that required his participation. Among these was a "totally cute" Q&A with *Cosmopolitan* that needed doing as quickly as possible, as the editors were dropping it into an issue they were closing before Christmas. She had *Cosmo*'s questions; all Cameron needed to do was to email her back his answers.

"Oh, and one more thing," she added. She couldn't find the long-form questionnaire he was supposed to have filled out months earlier. Ash was surprised to hear Cameron say he hadn't gotten around to it—that was the province of the network's legal department, not known for its patience, but then she figured the lawyers might also be having trouble adapting to "real time."

Tanya, Cameron admits, wrote the answers to *Cosmopolitan*'s questions for him that night. (The interview, which ran in the March 2015 issue, was headlined, THE MIRAC-LAY-US (PLEASE!) STAR OF LIFE-TIME'S "MIRACLE MAN" OPENS UP ON GOD, COUNTRY, AND WHERE ON A WOMAN HE LIKES TO LAY HIS HANDS.) Among them:

Q: *What sorts of women are you attracted to?*
A: I'm a pretty simple guy, so I guess I'd say a simple woman. I
don't go for too much complicated stuff. Someone I could take care
of, treat right. I don't go for too much makeup or fancy skirts. I
guess the main thing in life is to find someone who loves you,
really truly crazy loves you.

Afterward Tanya dug out the twenty-one-page questionnaires the network had FedExed them back in October and sat down on the couch to fill them out, her brother's first. Cameron was sitting beside her with earphones on, playing *Halo: Spartan Assault* on the Xbox. Splayed open on the coffee table was a Domino's pizza box, one side holding a few congealing slices and the other side serving as a receptacle for empty Bud Light cans. A gummy orange puddle of Catalina dressing was pooled near the slices, per the quirk of Biloxians to eat their pizza with Catalina or French salad dressing. Blinking in the corner were the lights on an artificial tree from Home Depot, contributing just a footnote of festivity. Though Cameron had inspired a boomlet of miracle-themed Christmas ornaments, his and Tanya's tree was dressed with just one—a gold glass ball on which was etched IN CHRIST ALL THINGS ARE POSSIBLE, a gift from Father Ace.

The house was unusually quiet—almost eerily so. The production crew was at their beachfront rental cottages across the bay in Ocean Springs; most of them were flying out the following day, a Saturday, for a one-week Christmas break. After a month and a half of filming, the quietude felt balmy and restorative, as though the *at-ease* command had been bestowed upon Reconfort Avenue.

Cameron seemed, to Tanya, acutely in need of a break. She'd been noticing his moods pebbling over the course of the last several weeks. She wondered if the high of his recovery might be wearing off, now that swinging his legs from bed in the morning was no longer supplying that same giddy shock—if perhaps he was experiencing the post-miracle equivalent of a comedown.

Not that he didn't have recent cause for irritation. Two weeks back, his cellphone started ringing nonstop, with callers dialing him from Indonesia, South Africa, Australia, from places like Moldova, which Cameron didn't even know was a country, people from all corners of the world calling him at all hours of the day and night—most asking for prayers and blessings though a few others accusing him, pungently, of fraud. How his number had gone public was a mystery until Tanya discovered a fake Twitter account under Cameron's name offering up his phone number in the account bio. Scott T. Griffin found it all wildly entertaining and devoted two days to filming Cameron fielding these calls and playing some of the voicemails aloud, leading Tanya to suspect Scott T. was behind the fake Twitter account. (Griffin denies this; the person behind the short-lived account, however, has never been identified.) There was also the fresh worry, once Cameron received official notice from the VA that his disability status had been revoked, that the Army might call him back into service—but Tanya told him this fear was paranoid. Griffin weighed in with the same opinion. "That'd be terrible optics," he assured Cameron.

Even non-irritations, though, seemed to be rankling him. Four days earlier a bow-tied political operative named Shawn McNamara had come by the house for a meeting he'd requested. Tanya laughed out loud when

McNamara revealed the reason for the meeting: to gauge Cameron's interest in running in the Republican primary for the Mississippi state senate. Griffin kept the cameras rolling throughout, as McNamara presented his campaign-ready version of Cameron's story—"decorated soldier, American hero, wounded in action, healed by the hand of the Almighty, and ready to serve again"—and crystal-balled a subsequent rise into a congressional seat, if Cameron was interested. "Endorsements don't come better than God's," he told Cameron. During the meeting Tanya's laughter remained constant ("Cam don't even know how to vote," she says, admitting the same about herself) and afterward, once McNamara left, this laughter spread to Scott T. and the crew. "I think Mr. Bowtie just wanted to get himself on TV," Griffin can be heard saying on the unedited footage. But Cameron never laughed; he played along with McNamara, per Scott T.'s direction, but did so flatly, and afterward seemed neither amused nor flattered but rather offended. "Because my legs work again, now I'm qualified to be a senator?" he said later, on camera. "That's some bullshit right there."

Tanya had been noticing more and more of this irked stance from her brother these past few weeks. He'd been absentminded, mopey, his default expression often colorless and drained. She was unaware he'd stopped taking his medications six weeks earlier, and, as she'd say later, "would've thrown a fit" had she known. But she didn't: All she knew was that her brother was, in her words, "acting like a bitch," which struck her as indefensible—what did he have to complain about now? Nothing she could see. She'd devoted so much and many of her twenty-nine years to steering him through the straits of anguish—after Daddy left, after Mama died, after Katrina blew through, after his return from Afghanistan—that to see him now, docked finally in a harbor of blessings and yet *still* brooding, *still* sulking into a beer can in the backyard—it was pissing her off. What the hell *else* did he want?

Tanya only made it to the second query of the questionnaire's Personal Information section before nudging her brother, who lifting an earphone from his ear glowered at the disruption.

"It says here," she said, "'Have you ever been known by or used any nicknames or other names?'"

"Jesus, Tan." That vein in his neck was twitching slightly. "You know all my shit."

"I'll just put Cam then, fine."

He replaced the earphone to resume the game as she muttered, "Don't bite my head off." The television screen popped with turquoise explosions and yellow laser fire. Then it froze as Cameron paused and once again raised his earphone.

"Cambo," he said.

"Cambo? Who calls you that?"

"Sergeant did. Over in Afghanistan."

"What's it mean?"

"Cambo, like Rambo."

"That's funny. You want I put that down?"

"Naw," he said. "Don't."

The turquoise explosions reappeared on the screen as Cameron went back to playing the game. Then they froze again. Cameron lifted the earphone once more to say, "Serious, Tan, don't put that down."

"I'm not."

"Serious."

"I'm *not*."

Tanya kept on with the questionnaire, drinking a beer as she went:

Do you have any physical conditions, special needs, accommodations or fears that we should know about?

She wrote: Not anymore!

Nothing about Tanya filling out her brother's forms—or for that matter standing in for him for his *Cosmopolitan* Q&A—was out of character for them. After their mother died, and Cameron's already-middling grades took a deep and sudden plunge, Tanya had taken to doing Cameron's homework for him. "Sometimes it was just easier," she explains, "to do his math worksheet or whatever than to try to get his head screwed back on." Charity morphed into habit—Cameron never filled out a single of the hundreds of forms required by the VA, every one of them bearing Tanya's approximation of his signature—but Tanya has never seemed to mind.

The questionnaire before her now, however, was probing way too deeply for her to manage solo, forcing her to nudge her brother yet again. This time he removed the headphones and sighed. "Shoot them at me."

The questionnaire was industry standard for reality-show applicants, having been developed in the wake of several mini-scandals that jolted networks in the genre's early days—the groom on *Who Wants to Marry a Multi-Millionaire?* with a restraining order smudging his past, the *American Idol* finalist with a weakness for driving drunk, the wholesome-seeming contestant on the dating show *The Bachelor* with an undisclosed sideline making foot-fetish videos. "I don't want to get to the second-to-last episode of the season," the producer Mark Burnett once told the *New York Times,* "and find out that one of my contestants is on the internet with a goat or something terrible like that."

"Here's a good one," Tanya said. "Says here, 'Have you ever made or appeared in a sexually explicit video recording or photo?'"

"Shut up. It really says that?"

"Serious as a heart attack."

"Put down no."

"*Put down* no?" She gave him a teasing poke in the side. "So is it no, or is that just what I'm putting down?"

"It's too bad you ain't funny."

With puckish glee she read off another: "'Have you ever been photographed in lingerie?'"

"Come on. You're just jacking with me now. Gimme that thing—"

Batting away her brother's hand and pressing the questionnaire to her chest, Tanya leveled a mock-stern expression at him. "Will the defendant please answer the question?"

"This really why you made me pause my game?"

"Naw." Tanya frowned, deflating herself with a sigh. "There's all kinda stuff in here I don't know how to answer. Like this . . ." She went flipping through the pages. "'Have you ever been the subject of any judicial or nonjudicial disciplinary action while in the military?'"

"Negative," he said.

"All right, what about here—what do we put here: 'How many times a week do you drink alcohol?'"

"Hell, what's that about? I don't know. Seven?"

"Maybe we say four?"

"Don't reckon it really matters." Cameron gave a yearning glance to his paused game, swigging a Bud Light, then shrugged. "They've cut me off anyway."

The prohibition on Cameron drinking beer (and smoking cigarettes) on camera, which the cameraman known as Honeybun was drolly calling the network's "Sharia clause," had come down from Bree Winterson—and while the directive may seem minor, it exemplifies the course she was navigating for *Miracle Man*. In early November, after viewing some of the roughly edited daily footage known as "string outs," she'd emailed her objections to Griffin: "Seeing that beer in his hand all the time just doesn't feel right to me, and if it's making me itch then it's going to make the aud break out in hives. We're not tailoring this for evangelicals but obv they're in the target demo. Their little heads are going to pop off if they're watching Cameron chugging beer all day. Ditto on the smoking, let's lose it." What about Tanya?, Griffin wrote back. Winterson's answer: "Let 'er rip."

Winterson's email correspondence with Griffin reveals the extent to which she was modifying and in some sense upending Griffin's original vision for the show. "Let's cut the medical expert component by about half, maybe more," she wrote him in early December, following another round of string outs. "Reeks of PBS." When Griffin resisted, she doubled down: "The more I think [about] it the more I want to lose the medical angle outright. The science grinds it down. There's no suspense because no one [is] saying anything remotely fuckable about what happened." Winterson referenced a scene in which Tanya split a highly compromising seam on her leggings just as Cameron was taking the stage for a presentation at a Baptist megachurch, and Tanya's delicious remark to the camera that she "could use a miracle in my crotch right about now." How do you shift, Winterson asked, "from 'I need a crotch miracle' to some doctor droning about nerve endings? It [the medical component] stomps the brakes." The way Griffin was interpreting Winterson's edicts was for him to reshape *Miracle Man* into "a sort of religious conversion narrative," he says, "with Tanya cast as the heathen. Will she come to the light? Will she become a Jedi like her brother? That was the gist I was getting." Tanya, he admits, was never informed of this direction, nor were she and Cameron ever privy to any edited footage. "She didn't know anything about it," he says.

Yet this underestimates Tanya, who by December was sensing that her life and her brother's—and their relationship—might be heading for a skewed depiction onscreen. In the interview segments, for instance, Tanya would be asked to say what she found most inspiring about her brother, to which she'd respond with a joke, usually too ribald to air, and then, when pressed, a milder joke, until Griffin or his field producer would say, "Maybe you can talk about how his persistence and determination have inspired you," to which Tanya would respond that his persistence and determination sure did inspire her, at which point they'd say that was wonderful but it'd be great if she could express her emotions more openly, so that viewers could really feel the intensity of that inspiration, could see through the clouds the heights to which she looked up to Cameron.

"And this one," Tanya was saying now, her legs tucked beneath her on the couch. "'Have you ever experienced psychological distress that's interfered with your daily functioning?'"

Cameron lit a cigarette and grimaced. "Ain't like I'm not talking about my PTSD on camera . . ."

"I'll put yes, then."

Then she read another: "'Do you have any history or difficulty controlling anger and/or violent conflicts, including loss of temper, family fights, fights with boyfriends/girlfriends?'"

Smoke oozed from the corners of Cameron's mouth. He squinted at his sister. "Why they wanna know all this for?"

"Hell if I know, Cam. I'm just reading you what it says."

"Well, just put no."

She pressed her pen to the paper, then stopped. "But then it asks this: 'Have you ever been accused or charged with assault?'"

Cameron turned away from her to screw his eyes onto the screen with its frozen *Halo* tableau. "You mean the Landry thing? That was youth court. So put down no."

"It says *ever* been charged."

"I didn't get *charged* with nothing."

"Then how come we had to get that lawyer?"

"What the hell?" He swung his head back toward her and with an icy glare and a riled edge to his voice asked, "You think those guys on *Ice Road Truckers* didn't crack a few heads back in the day?"

"I didn't write it, Cam. I'm just reading you the stupid form."

She watched her brother tighten himself into the couch, venting smoke through his nose.

He didn't like the memory and neither did she. That Tanya had been present for Cameron's arrest was coincidence—a younger co-worker of hers at the Dollar General had invited her along to a party at the piers on Biloxi Beach, across from what was then the Biloxi Yacht Club, where she wasn't shocked to see a throng of Biloxi High School students—she'd partied there herself, back in high school—but was surprised to encounter her little brother, staggering drunk.

This was August 21, 2004, two and a half months after Debbie Harris's fatal accident. Cameron was there with some of his football teammates, blowing off steam before the following Friday's season opener against St. Martin, and Tanya was trusting they'd see him home safely. She and her co-worker's crowd were keeping their distance from the rowdier high-school kids, who'd started a campfire on the beach. When they heard the unmistakable uproar of a fight breaking out, they moved to extend that distance—until Tanya heard her brother's name, first being shouted and then being shrieked.

Someone had already dialed 911 by the time Tanya was able to shove her way through the crowd to its seething, open center. To her left she saw Cameron, shirtless and distorted in the campfire's glow, with two of his teammates holding him by his arms and another blocking him from the front; and to her right she saw a guy sprawled on the sand with a panicked clutch of girls tending to him, his squashed face almost completely slickened with gore. The crowd was seized with an unnatural hush; high schoolers were craning their necks for a view, whispering *ohmygod* and *holyshit* but not much else.

Cameron didn't appear to recognize Tanya when she finally made her way to him. His blood-spattered chest was still heaving and his drunk gaze seemed locked upon something very far in the distance, past even the lights of the shrimp boats on the black horizon. He maintained that faraway stare, without acknowledging his sister, as sirens whooped and floodlights scalded the beach and two Biloxi police officers arrived to jerk Cameron away in handcuffs. "I don't know what happened," one of Cameron's teammates told her afterward. "They was talking, Landry was laughing, and then Cam just got to whaling on him. Went all rabid-dog on him. Took like four of us to pull him off."

Tanya never did get the full backstory from her brother—she fitted her own assumptions and theories into the missing puzzle piece spaces, some more congruently than others. If his face hadn't been so battered she would've recognized the guy Cameron had laid out on the sand: Tommy Landry, a senior baseball standout whose older brother had been in Tanya's graduating class. Landry went to the ER with a broken nose, a cheekbone fracture, a concussion, and a cut beside his eye requiring significant stitching. There was nothing to indicate that Landry returned even a single punch; from what Tanya heard, Cameron never gave him the chance.

For help Tanya called Jim Yarbrough, who connected them with a lawyer whose fees Tanya paid out of her mother's life insurance payout. Cameron wouldn't talk about the fight with her except to say that Landry started it—exactly how he wouldn't say—and got what he had coming. But he did confide in Yarbrough, who told Tanya that Landry had been bullying Cameron for a while and that, drunk, and emotionally eroded by Debbie's death, her brother had just snapped. This was also the explanation their lawyer presented to the youth court judge, who, noting Cameron's lack of prior arrests, his recent trauma, and his value to the Biloxi High School football team, sentenced him to a probationary period known as informal adjustment. An eight p.m. curfew for the next six months was as punitive as it got, though the judge voluntarily exempted Friday night football games from the curfew. This exemption was meaningless, however, by the time of the ruling—by then Cameron had already quit the team.

"Says here," Tanya was saying, "that they need dates, jurisdictions, and parties involved."

"I'm telling you—youth court don't matter none," he told her. "Just drop it."

Tommy Landry, Tanya knew, wasn't the only one to have suffered her brother's temper. After high school he'd gotten into some kind of ugly scrap with one of his construction co-workers, one of the Mexican guys he sometimes hung out with after work. Again, the details she got were sketchy, but Cameron had come home late and tequila-rattled with the knuckles of his right hand broken, got fired from his job the next morning, and two days later found his truck tires slashed and a Spanish word spray-painted onto the driver's-side door. One of the meager consolations Tanya later formulated about Cameron's enlistment in the Army was that maybe he'd be able to purge this violent streak from his system, could get that rage vented—that whatever ammunition with which Snead Harris's genes had endowed him could be emptied into some terrorist and be gone forever.

Despite this knowledge, she checked no where it asked if Cameron had ever been fired from a job. She also checked no about gun ownership, though she knew Cameron had picked up a pistol at a pawnshop after his truck tires got slashed. She didn't feel like getting up to inventory all of Cameron's medications, so, in an instance of accidental accuracy, she just wrote "none" where the form requested a full listing. Sometimes Tanya mumbled the questions aloud to herself as she read—a habit she developed as a dyslexic child—and with every third question or so she heard Cameron sigh or grunt until finally, in a surprisingly plaintive voice, he asked, "What the hell they gotta know all this for?"

"Beats me," she said.

"You gotta have security clearance to go on the freaking TV?"

"Just about," she said.

Cameron stamped out a cigarette and sat staring at the coffee table with dazed intensity. After a while Tanya felt compelled to ask, with equal parts concern and annoyance, "What?"

"I don't know," he said. Tanya heard a remnant of his boyhood whine cocooned in his voice, the mewling he used to do when flustered with homework or when their mother ordered him to bed. "It's just that— everyone's been up in my shit for months. Asking this, asking that . . ."

"What'd you think was gonna happen, dumbass? You had a miracle happen." She shook the questionnaire at him. "And now you're fixing to go on TV about it."

"Yeah, well, I thought the TV guys was gonna help figure out what happened to me."

She sat there blinking. "A miracle happened to you."

"Yeah, but . . ." He shook his head and winced. "They said they were gonna be like private investigators—you remember Scott T. saying that? They were gonna find out some answers."

"Some answers? You been saying God's the answer."

"I'm saying—what I'm saying is the only thing anyone's got for me is questions. A million damn questions. Like *I'm* the one with the goddamn answers. I mean, last week, shit, when I did that thing for the paralyzed vet group? One of those guys—this big old Marine, said he took a bullet to the spine in Desert Storm—he's asking me what I think I did to make this possible. Asking me if I think the secret is just to never give up. And I'm standing there trying to come up with an answer knowing the real answer's this, this right here." He flicked his game console with a finger and tumped an empty can of Bud Light off the table. "I played some fucking games and drank some beer and popped some pills, man. That's what I did. I didn't do shit. I didn't think about doing shit. There's your secret recipe."

Tanya folded her arms and waited while her brother lit a cigarette before asking him, "You done?"

"Done what?"

"Done bitching."

"You think I'm—bitching?"

"For someone who's up and walking after four years, yeah, I'd say you're bitching."

"So I'm supposed to do what, Tan—just, like, dance all the time? Crank up some Christian rock and do the hokey fucking pokey?"

She tilted her head, unimpressed by this angst. "Telling folks about yourself and about what-all happened and going to Mass on Sundays and wearing free clothes and getting asked to run for congress and all the other shit you been complaining about . . ." This light inventory caused her head to shake. "Most folks'd say that's a pretty low price for what happened to you."

"You ain't getting it," he said, his face ruddying with exasperation. "It ain't the going to Mass. It ain't really the talking to folks. It's all these people looking—looking *up* to me, it's all these people thinking my prayers are going to fix whatever they got wrong—"

"Maybe they will."

"Like all the prayers I never said helped me? You seen all the letters—you heard all those voicemails—you seen the way folks treat me, that dude telling me I should run for congress now—shit, why not be president? All these people think I got some kinda magical powers and I don't, I don't got nothing like it . . . I mean, I don't think I do. Do I? I don't know. Shit, that it's right there."

"What's it right there?"

The eyes he presented her were big and glossy. "It's like I don't know who I am anymore."

"Well," Tanya said, lighting a cigarette of her own, unmoved by her brother's plight. "Who the hell were you before?"

Cameron didn't answer. He just nodded a few times, dimly, before returning the earphones to his head and resuming his game. Everything she'd done for him all these years, Tanya was thinking, plus everything God had done for him, and here he was: whining like a spoiled kid who'd received just nine of the ten things on his Christmas list. It was classic Cam: overthinking everything. Can't have nothing nice, not even a miracle. Tanya sped her way through the remainder of the questionnaire, giving no thought whatsoever to its final question: "Is there anything else in your past and background that would cause embarrassment or other harm to you, the network, or the show?"

after, pt. 3

wherefore let him that thinketh he standeth
take heed lest he fall

thirteen

T HE SPEED AT WHICH *MIRACLE MAN* WENT HURTLING INTO
production was uncommonly swift but not unprecedented. In contrast, the speed at which a Vatican-linked investigator arrived in Biloxi
to examine the particulars of Cameron's recovery has few contemporary
parallels, according to church observers. While the digital age has expe-
dited the Vatican's inquiries into supernatural phenomena, the process
still tends to be measured less in months than in years or even decades—
two-thousand-year-old institutions, after all, lack a certain spring in their
bureaucratic step.

This quick-fire dispatch, however, owed almost nothing to the specifics
of Cameron's case. Underlying it—and underwriting it—was a Michigan
trucking magnate's decades-long quest for a substantiated miracle, part of
a larger goal to which he's so far pledged more than half a million dollars.
More than anything else, though, the rapid-response nature of the investigation can be credited to a fluke of geography and to the enchantments
of an Italian sports car hugging Southern backroads. The investigator, Euclide Gianni Abbascia, a former Roman prosecutor who lives part of the
year in Washington, D.C., happened to be spending much of the autumn
in Knoxville, Tennessee, assisting with the official inquiry into a medical
miracle being attributed to a nineteenth-century priest and current sainthood candidate named Isaac Hecker. Abbascia adores road trips, partly
because he's an amateur photographer but more significantly because he's
the owner of a 1972 Maserati Ghibli Spyder, and was therefore happy to
oblige a request from Rome to swing south to Mississippi for a preliminary vetting of Cameron's case.

The Vatican's protocol for investigating and authenticating miracles can strike atheists and other skeptics as absurd. (The social critic Carolyn Brinkwater once likened it to "performing a background check on your imaginary friend.") Every major faith recognizes miracles, to varying degrees, but the Catholic church is the only entity that purports to verify them. Miracles are not seen as proof of God's existence, because the church considers that a given, but rather as proof of a deceased person's presence and stature in heaven—as signals of saintly or pre-saintly intervention in the frail, chipped gearing of human existence. This is why Father Ace asked Cameron about the recipients of his prayers, and why Tanya's remembrance of a friend's grandmother praying via Facebook to the late radio evangelist and current saint candidate Nicholas Fahey was essential to him. Without a saint's verified role, an event may be miraculous—but not, canonically speaking, a miracle.

The authentication process—opaque and byzantine, but also forensically rigorous—has changed only around the edges since 1588, when Pope Sixtus V centralized and formalized a practice that for centuries had been the function of local bishops and rectors. Because these bishops were often political appointees, this vox populi method of authenticating miracles—and thereby helping to confer sainthood on those deemed responsible—was prone to looseness at best and corruption at worst, and as such was among the many grievances lodged by reformers during the Protestant Schism. Sixtus V established a new body, nowadays called the Congregation for the Causes of Saints, for regulating, among other matters, what is and isn't a miracle. Essential to this body's deliberations was the *advocatus diaboli,* or devil's advocate, a canon lawyer whose role was to argue against the canonization of sainthood candidates, often by debunking the miracles attributed to them. The job, in effect, was to be the in-house rationalist, to conduct one's duties with a perpetually raised eyebrow.

This is not exactly the role Euclide Abbascia sees for himself—and it's worth noting that Pope John Paul II effectively abolished the role of the advocatus diaboli in 1983—but he is nonetheless an heir to its prosecutorial skepticism.

Most alleged miracles, he says, fail an initial sniff test. He cites the Cambridge mathematician John Edensor Littlewood's theorem that human events with million-to-one odds are more commonplace than they might otherwise seem, when you factor in a sample size of seven billion people—that is to say, given truly large numbers, the improbable inexorably fades into the probable. Things that *can* happen, but almost never do, do not constitute miracles. Abbascia points to the survival of one of the victims of the 2012 mass shooting in an Aurora, Colorado, movie theater, that of a twenty-two-year-old woman who was shot in the face: A shotgun pellet entered her nose but traveled through an unusual seam of fluid in her brain cavity, never farther or much closer than a millimeter from the brain's vital areas. An extreme outlier, in statistical-probability terms: yes. An example of prevenient grace, perhaps. But not a miracle. Bending the laws of probability is not the same as bending those of nature.

Parsing these distinctions, and hundreds of others, has been Abbascia's occupation for almost a decade. His older brother, Matteo, is a member of the European Parliament whose name is frequently bandied as a potential candidate for Rome's mayoralty, and Euclide once seemed poised for a similar political destiny. The Abbascia family has been part of Rome's elite since the Renaissance; when Euclide was baptized, at the Basilica of Saint Vitale, then–prime minister Emilio Colombo was among those in attendance. He followed his brother to the University of Milan before peeling off to earn a degree in civil law from Pontifical Lateran University, which operates under the Pope's direct authority. "I don't think Euclide," his brother jokes, "ever quite got over the thrill of being an altar boy."

As a young prosecutor in Rome, in the 1990s, Euclide gained mixed renown for his role in convicting a serial killer named Donato Padovano. Mixed, because Padovano—nicknamed "Il Vigilante" by some papers and "Il Mostro Buono" ("the Good Monster") by others—located his eight victims on internet chat rooms for pedophiles, luring them to their deaths with false promises of a rendezvous with a six-year-old girl and/or boy. These were grisly deaths, preceded by torture and for six victims by castration, but, once the pattern became clear, they roused little pity or terror in Rome. An editorial in the daily newspaper *Il Tempo* even suggested police turn a blind eye to the killings, likening the still-at-large killer to a gardener pulling weeds. When Padovano was finally arrested, in 1999, a small crowd gathered outside Rebibbia prison in support, many leaving flowers and wreaths, which the police were quick to cart away.

For Euclide Abbascia, the multiyear trial proved a crisis point—the nadir, or final gasp, of an enervating career in the law. It wasn't that he felt the moral ambivalence of *Il Tempo*'s editorialist and much of Rome's citizenry, even after it emerged that one of Padovano's victims had repeatedly and brutally molested his nieces years earlier. (At sentencing, two of these nieces pleaded for leniency for their uncle's murderer.) No, Padovano was indeed a *mostro,* and not a good one: He later confessed to the murders of two prostitutes predating his pedophile spree, before he found a way to morally rationalize the pleasure he derived from slow and vicious killing. As the trial trudged forward, in the plodding way of the Italian judiciary, Euclide Abbascia felt himself increasingly unmoored, cast adrift on a sludgy, toxic sea. He deplored the victims as much as their murderer but most of all deplored the hours they all spent crowding his head; his job, he felt, was merely to punctuate a sentence he wished he'd never read.

"From my earliest childhood," he says, "it was always my goal to live in a state of astonishment. But this was the wrong kind of astonishment. This was astonishment at humanity's capacity for evil, for depravity, for greed, for apathy. It was too much for me. I wanted to be amazed by something greater."

So he quit. After spending two years nurturing his photography skills, Euclide Abbascia took an unpaid internship at the Vatican's Congregation for the Causes of Saints, working in the office of the Promoter of the Faith (formerly the Devil's Advocate). There he used his legal chops to pick apart sainthood causes, scouring the biographies of sainthood candidates the way political campaigns conduct opposition research—poking the lives for weak spots, for exaggerations, for buried scandals, for anything that might disqualify a candidate from the church's most sacred honor. That his labors were mostly futile supplied him with immense joy. Crowding his head now, and suffusing him with clean amazement, were people of extraordinary virtue and sacrifice, acts of profound empathy, and, above all, the astonishments of the miracles under his review.

Toward the end of his three-year internship, in 2005, he started working part-time for Dr. Antonio Liuni, a private canon lawyer in Rome who specializes in propelling and litigating sainthood causes before the Congregation. Dr. Liuni, who is seventy-eight, had by then grown too old for the global travel that investigations demand; while still a vaunted lay-figure in Vatican circles, esteemed for his granular mastery of canon law and theology, arthritis plus hearing loss had eroded his ability for investigative grunt work. After concluding his Vatican internship, Euclide Abbascia stepped in full-time, making the final step on his journey from mostros to miracles.

There is a financial aspect to this work, of course, which is what leads us to Euclide Abbascia's apartment near Logan Circle in Washington and then, by degrees, to Biloxi, Mississippi, and Cameron Harris. Though one can look upon the dome of St. Peter's Basilica from the window of Dr. Liuni's office on Via della Stazione di San Pietro, Dr. Liuni has no official connection to the Roman Curia; he is in private practice. The Vatican is not even his client. Instead, the sainthood candidates themselves are. He argues their cases before the Congregation, submitting evidence tying them to good deeds and miracles not unlike a prosecutor ties a defendant to misdeeds. Yet Dr. Liuni's clients are all dead—some of them for centuries. Naturally this makes it difficult to bill them for services rendered.

So paying Dr. Liuni's fees—as well as Euclide Abbascia's expenses, plus the fees and/or expenses of medical experts, consultants, transcribers, translators (the Vatican accepts documentation only in Latin), fundraisers, printers, and more—falls to donors. The cost for a canonization drive, at present, is on par with that of a minor political campaign: about one million dollars, according to most estimates. But the parallels don't stop there. Supporters of a sainthood cause appeal to wealthy donors just as political candidates do. (These large donors tend to come from the diocese where the saint-candidate was born or lived; a local saint, like a professional sports team, is apparently a boon to civic pride.) Smaller donations are solicited via websites, some more slick than others, invariably featuring a DONATE NOW button: five dollars here, twenty dollars there. Some canonization campaigns have lately taken to using the website gofundme.com, rewarding various donation tiers with books and biographical DVDs about the candidate.

These websites also frequently solicit reports of miracles. (To qualify for canonization, as Father Ace explained to Cameron and Tanya, a proposed saint—unless martyred—must have instrumented at least two authenticated miracles.) The website for the cause of Father Augustus Tolton

(1854–97), for example, includes this appeal: "To report any spiritual or physical favors granted through prayer in Father Tolton's name, please write to . . ."

Dr. Liuni is one of those on the receiving end of such reports; and when the evidence seems credible, and the funding is solidly in place, he dispatches Euclide Abbascia. Though Abbascia is reluctant to admit it, that funding component is the reason he spends so much time in the United States—so much time, in fact, that it made sense for him to lease his Logan Circle apartment in 2010. The United States has produced only eleven saints in its history, and just two of them native-born, yet it currently fields an abundance of proposed saints, in various phases of progress, with actively financed causes—fifty-four of them. Why? One might argue that with the country's vast Catholic population (seventy million, at last count), the presence of more than eleven saints bears a certain mathematical logic—a nod to John Edensor Littlewood's theory of large numbers. One could also argue, however (and Father Ace, whose native Nigeria has yet to see a saint canonized, does indeed make this argument), that the United States's wealth—not its Catholic population, not its miracle-spangled history, not its spiritual timbre—is the real fuel for these campaigns. "When a miracle happens in rural Nigeria, who hears about it?" he asks. "Who pays to have it documented? Who gets on an airplane and brings the case to Rome? These things, they cost money." (It's important to note that hiring an advocate like Dr. Liuni, as with hiring any lawyer, is no guarantee of success. Some of Dr. Liuni's causes—including well-financed American causes—have been languishing for more than forty years.)

Supporters of Archbishop Nicholas Fahey's cause for sainthood—one supporter in particular—wire-transferred the funds that brought Euclide Abbascia to Mississippi. Fahey was beatified by Pope Benedict XVI in 2006, beatification being the penultimate step on canonization's long stairwell, after the Vatican awarded him credit for the spontaneous restoration of vision in an Indiana boy who'd gone blind from macular degeneration. That left Fahey one miracle shy of sainthood.

Fahey's cause has been in Dr. Liuni's hands for more than twenty years, which is not unusual, but, unlike most other causes, it has a principal backer: a sixty-nine-year-old Detroit trucking magnate named Norton

Skag. According to the foreword he wrote for a booklet promoting Fahey's cause, Skag was a reckless and self-absorbed twenty-seven-year-old when, in 1974, Reverend Fahey came crashing into his life. At the time Skag was married and working for his father, who started Freight Connections Trucking with a single used panel truck. But Skag had an ungovernable wild streak that often brought him, as in this case, to the brink of self-destruction. Following what Skag has obliquely called "a night of sin," in Michigan's Upper Peninsula, he found himself driving through the dark in a remotely wooded area where he was able to tune just a single station on his car's radio: an AM station broadcasting one of Reverend Fahey's sermons. For more than an hour Skag found himself captivated by Fahey's voice and message. Then Skag's car brushed a guardrail and flipped and kept flipping. Skag, who was unbelted, seemed to float around the car's interior, he wrote, "like an astronaut in zero gravity," before losing consciousness. What woke him was the sound of state troopers assessing the wreckage with what sounded like black laughter—the car was so gruesomely mangled as to be comical, a riddle of twisted steel. Yet the radio was still playing—Reverend Fahey's voice a bit softer, and fringed with static—and Norton Skag, while bruised and bloodied, climbed from the car himself. "The Reverend Fahey's voice, and me, were the only two things that survived that crash," Skag wrote, "and that served to join us forever after." What walked away from the wreckage, he continued, was "a new man."

That new man built his father's company, now called FreightConnex, into the fifth-largest trucking company in the United States, with annual revenue of more than ten billion dollars. All credit for this success—and more importantly for the Augustinian turnaround Skag made in his personal and spiritual life—Skag attributes to the guidance and guardianship of Reverend Fahey. For anyone who's ever found himself or herself on the interstate behind a FreightConnex truck wondering about the quotation painted onto the rear of every trailer, "Faith is to living as headlights are to driving"—that's a line of Fahey's. Skag struck up a correspondence with Fahey, and after Fahey's death, in 1980, Skag petitioned the church to open an official cause for sainthood, seeded the money for the Archbishop Nicholas Fahey Foundation, and eventually retained the services of Dr. Liuni.

Dealing with Norton Skag isn't like dealing with the guilds of nuns and monsignors to which Dr. Liuni has been long accustomed; it's more like manning the crow's nest for Captain Ahab. Skag is hard-nosed, implacable, indifferent to the ancient delicacies of Vatican protocol, and most of all impatient. He badly wants to see Fahey canonized before he dies, to fully liquidate the debt he feels he owes.

Hence Skag's middle-of-the-night phone call to Rome after he'd come across a news report about Cameron's recovery and its possible connection to Fahey. Dr. Liuni drowsily advised him to let the process advance at the diocesan level. As he's been telling Skag for two decades, these things take time—*beati* from the ninth century are still short a second miracle. But Skag was characteristically insistent, especially after Dr. Liuni let slip that Euclide was in Tennessee. He offered to put on immediate standby a FreightConnex truck for conveying the investigator to Mississippi. Imagining Euclide, whose passion for his '72 Maserati Spyder is opera-worthy, being sentenced to the passenger seat of a long-haul truck brought a pained smile to Dr. Liuni's face. "This won't be necessary," he told Skag.

Euclide Abbascia's first visit in Mississippi, after Father Ace, was to Dot Bearden. Bearden was the one who, less than a week after Cameron's injury, issued a request for prayers for him on Facebook. Aside from doctors, the requester of the alleged miracle is the most significant figure in Euclide Abbascia's investigations—more important, when they diverge, than the actual recipients of the miracle, called *miracolati*. The miracle, after all, is a form of communication between the saint or saint-in-waiting and the requester. Sometimes the requester and the *miracolati* are one and the same, but just as often they aren't. The physical favor may be directed at someone else, in this case Cameron; but the spiritual favor, the answered prayer, is bequeathed to the requester.

Bearden was out on her front porch when Euclide pulled in. She leapt out of her rocker to gawk at the exotic car in her driveway, her head popping over the railing like a prairie dog's, and devoted the first twenty minutes of the interview to telling Euclide about the classic Ford Mustangs her late husband used to restore. Bearden, who is eighty-two, exemplifies what people mean when describing an elderly person as *spry:* She exudes a honeybee's industriousness, able to tend to the three great-grandchildren often in her care while constantly baking layer cakes and casseroles for the funeral luncheon ministry at St. Michael's Catholic Church while also attending Mass four times a week and, once a week, getting her hair coiffed to maintain her Aqua Net-ed white swoop. She is that rare elderly person on whom exercise clothes look truly functional.

Yes, she told Euclide, of course she remembered the prayer. She pulled it up for him on the Microsoft tablet her daughter had given her the Christmas before:

> **Dorothy Alice Bearden** Dear friends, I just heard that Biloxi H.S.
> graduate Cameron Harris has been very seriously injured while
> serving our nation over in Afghanistan. He needs our prayers!!!!!
> Please join me in praying to the Archbishop Nicholas Fahey for his
> full recovery and return home! Relying upon his merits and power
> before the Sacred Heart of Jesus we pray. Yours in Christ, Dot.
> March 26, 2010 at 8:32 pm • 151

That she'd issued this prayer on social media was a novelty to Euclide, but one he welcomed. Normally he relies on requesters' recollections of praying—when, how, and to whom—and must ultimately gauge that what they say they did, while kneeling silently in a pew, or alone in their bedrooms, is what in fact they did. But here was the ne plus ultra of forensic evidence: a documented, time-stamped prayer, as perfectly preserved on the internet as a DNA sample sealed in a jar.

Below Bearden's post were thirteen replies, three of them expressing shock and dismay but ten indicating that a prayer chain did go into effect that spring. In subsequent questioning, Bearden told Euclide her Friday morning prayer group at St. Michael had maintained their prayers for Cameron's recovery until someone heard he was back in Biloxi, and, sadly, unable to walk ever again.

Gently, Euclide pressed her:

Q: *But you didn't pray after that? After you knew he'd been paralyzed?*
A: Oh, we knew he'd got paralyzed early on. Megan [her granddaughter] heard it from his sister. Once we all heard he was home and was safe, well, I reckon he fell off our prayer list. But I kept praying for him.

Q: *You did?*
A: Yessir I did.

Q: *By yourself?*
A: That's right.

Q: *Did you ever pray a novena?*
A: Sometimes. But mostly it was just like talking.

Q: *You and Reverend Fahey?*
A: That's right. Just talking, me and him. I'd tell him who was
hurting, who could use his grace.

Q: *And you'd mention Cameron Harris?*
A: Lots of times, yessir I would. That boy had a hard row, losing his
mama the way he did, then him getting blowed up in Afghanistan.
You pray for those in need.

Q: *But you also prayed for others in need?*
A: Everyone in need. Everyone I thought needed grace.

Q: *Was Cameron Harris special?*
A: I reckon he needed more grace than just about anybody else.

Later, per protocol, Euclide quizzed Bearden on why she'd directed her
prayers to Fahey and not to another *beati* or saint, such as Mother Teresa:

A: Well, I don't *know* Mother Teresa. When you read about a saint
in a book or something, you don't really know them. How they
talk, what their voice sounds like. What it feels like to sit in a room
with them. Seeing Reverend Fahey on the TV all them years—I
knew him. I knew how to talk to him. I knew what he'd say to me. I
knew what he'd do for me.

Now, for Euclide, came the delicate part: determining why the late
Nicholas Fahey—swamped by prayers from millions, from priests implor-

ing him to aid the sick among their flocks to the parents of dying children kneeling despondent at their children's bedsides—why Nicholas Fahey might've plucked from this supplicatory profusion a single appeal among many from Dorothy Alice Bearden of Biloxi, Mississippi. For two and a half hours he drew from her the story of her life, her sixty-one-year marriage, her children and grandchildren, the peaks and valleys of her eighty-two years on earth. After a while he zeroed in on her faith, her moral triumphs and failings, the questions and regrets that still wrested her from sleep. Euclide Abbascia is often mistaken for a priest; it's a misapprehension he usually dispels but other times lets slide to his advantage. Priests are confessors, and confessions, as any detective knows, supply the protein to an investigation. Yet nothing Bearden revealed gave him pause to doubt either her or, for that matter, Reverend Fahey's potential receptiveness.

Still, the interrogation was intense. At the end of it, Dot Bearden, whom no one has ever seen tire, who is known around St. Michael as the Energizer Bunny, whose great-grandchildren drop from weariness before she does—Dot Bearden collapsed. The sheer magnitude of what was under review—her splayed-open life and beliefs, the grand forces she appeared to have set into action—paled her face and sagged her eyes and when she tried to speak no sound emerged from her dry lips. Euclide removed her shoes for her, as she was eventually able to request, and fetched her a quilt so that she could nap on the couch. She asked him to pray with her, and he did.

As Euclide made to leave, she stopped him with a question: "Was it really me?" Her voice warbled; in the span of four hours it seemed the eighty-two years she'd so valiantly outraced had somehow caught up with her. "Was it really me that done this?"

"Of course not." Euclide smiled. "It was God."

Euclide Abbascia's next visit, the following morning, was to Dr. Janice Lorimar-Cuevas. Hers was a tough interview to wrangle. (As usual, with physicians, he identified himself over the phone as Dr. Abbascia, employing the honorific that Italians bestow upon any college graduate. As Dr. Liuni had taught him, identifying oneself as a lawyer—even a canon lawyer—is the quickest way to spook an American physician into silence.) Janice sighed. She was frankly tired of discussing Cameron's case, she told him, and when he explained his connection to the church she noted that she'd met with Father Ace not once but twice and couldn't think of anything to add.

Euclide is used to this and much worse with doctors, some of whom refuse to speak with him at all. "Many of them are defensive," he explains. "They view their inability to explain a medical situation as a professional failing, as something they don't wish to have scrutinized. Others don't want to lend credence—even by discussing the case—to any non-secular interpretation." Janice felt traces of both reactions, she says, yet, despite her protestations, Cameron's case was still entangling her mind as kudzu entangles an oak; when Euclide called, in fact, Cameron's medical file happened to be staring up at her from her laptop screen. She said he could have an hour.

Janice was surprised, then, at how quickly she found herself warming to Euclide. He was exponentially more fluent in medicine than Father Ace—or really anyone without a medical degree with whom she'd discussed Cameron's case, plus some people *with* medical degrees—but also, she admits, "impossibly charming."

"It was like having Marcello Mastroianni sitting in your office," she says, with an embarrassed flutter of a laugh. (Not for nothing did the Italian press deem the young Euclide a *batticuore,* or heartthrob. Spending time with Euclide Abbascia in public, one cannot fail to notice the effect he has on women—nor, for that matter, the effect they have upon him. As Dr. Liuni is known to say: Were it not for Euclide's fondness for fast cars and beautiful women, he'd make a sensational priest—or husband.)

Bewitching charms aside, however, Euclide impressed Janice with his line of questioning. Unlike Father Ace, who seemed to be campaigning for Cameron's recovery to be inexplicable, for Janice to throw up her arms in terminal bewilderment, Euclide seemed determined to ferret out a medical explanation. Several of his questions prompted her to scribble notes for her own follow-up. After a while, mildly dazzled, she told him he obviously had experience with cases like Cameron's.

"A little, yes," he replied. "But with recovery from paralysis there's almost always a natural explanation. In fact, if you're asking about my own experience, I should retract the word *almost* and just say always. You have to go back a long way, to 1977, for the most recent case of paralysis recovery that the Congregation approved as a miracle."

This was the first time he'd deployed the word *miracle,* and Janice felt herself rankling. His incisive questioning had eclipsed the fact that he was there on behalf of the church, equipped with a very different agenda than hers. "So you're—what?" she asked him. "A doctor of supernatural medicine?"

"I would call myself an investigator of thaumaturgic events."

She frowned. "Thaumaturgic?"

"This is the scientific term for 'miraculous.'"

She snorted lightly. "There's a lot of irony baked into that definition."

"Perhaps." Euclide shrugged, smiling. "But then, as Søren Kierkegaard said, just because something inconceivable happens, in the scope of our perceptions, doesn't mean it didn't happen."

"Well, you should know that I am no believer in miracles," she told him. "I wasn't before and I'm not one now."

Euclide, used to hearing statements like this from physicians, gave her his canned response: "Your beliefs, Doctor, like mine, are irrelevant to this investigation. Only your findings."

"Okay, but you'll use my findings to draw a conclusion," she said. "Isn't that the dividing line here? Isn't that where our purposes diverge? I've been hunting for a medical explanation, and you're here hunting a miracle."

"My objective," he countered, as warm as she was cool, "is precisely the same as yours has been. To determine the precise cause of this recovery."

"Ah, but you have another cause in your pocket."

"I'm sorry?"

"If my findings are inconclusive, that's it—they're inconclusive. But to you, that means they *are* conclusive—of a miracle."

"Not so," he said. "If you have no medical conclusions, and I have no conclusions to offer, then there's a void and we agree on it. We are in harmony. And this harmony is what I report. The *Consulta Medica* examines our findings—very rigorously. After that, it's up to the Congregation to determine if there might be a spiritual conclusion."

"But that's what I'm talking about," she said. "In the absence of an explanation, the explanation is God. I'm sorry but I find that—I hope I'm not offending you, but I find that reductive. To say the least."

"Offending me?" Euclide flashed her a big, almost mischievous grin. "Discussions like this, they're my candy. But you're voicing a common

misperception about miracles. You see, the absences of medical intervention or a natural explanation do not in themselves signify divine intervention. It isn't the *absence* of anything that proves a miracle. Just the
opposite: It's the *presence* of the divine."

"Which isn't provable," she said flatly.

"But that's what joins us here together today, isn't it?" Again came
Euclide's smile, slightly flirtatious and wholly self-assured. "We are both
confronted with things we cannot prove. We are both of us out past the
borders of observation and data, and into the realm of belief."

Janice leaned back in her chair and considered this, though not for
long. Euclide's swart charms and breezy intelligence were brushing a
glossy sheen onto the conversation, but underneath that lacquer, she
thought, was the same circular reasoning—*God exists because the Bible
says he does, and the Bible is God's word, et cetera*—she'd been hearing
from religious types all her life, especially as a girl in the Mississippi Delta,
where her lack of a church affiliation (she didn't dare admit atheism until
college) marked her for freakdom, made her a bull's-eye for conversion.

Perhaps, she'd later think, it was this low-grade irritation—triggering
an impulse to rebut the absurdly paranormal mindset of Euclide (and by
extension all those grade-school missionaries who'd invited her to "fellowship" with them) with a different variety of outrageous thinking—that
led her to divulge, to this total stranger, an idea that had been fermenting
inside her for weeks, ever since her lunch with Cameron, and that she'd
shared with no one save her husband, Nap. She tapped her desk with a
pencil and ran her tongue along the inside of her teeth, an anxious habit.
Then she said, "I've answered your questions. Can I ask you one?"

"By all means," Euclide answered.

"Have you ever been involved in a case in which someone faked a miracle?"

"Faked?"

"Faked. As in a hoax."

Euclide leveled a darkly curious gaze at her, and when he spoke he
picked his words with slow caution, as in the way one navigates a room
suddenly blackened by a power outage. "I've investigated dozens of alleged
miracles that turned out to have been the result of natural forces . . ."

"That's not what I'm talking about," she said. "I'm talking about—I guess the word would be fraudulent. So-called miracles that turned out to have been deceptions."

"I see," he said. He was staring at her now, and she thought she could see the color of his eyes drop a shade, from bright blue to indigo, as if a cloud were passing through his head. "I've only heard or read of such cases, which do exist. By the time a case reaches my attention, though, it's already undergone a preliminary investigation at the diocese . . ." His voice went trailing off, squelched by this new element Janice had slipped into the room. "Do you have reason to believe," he finally asked, "that we might be looking at such a case?"

Janice blew the air from her cheeks, finding her own voice squelched by that same atmospheric shift. Then, with sluggish care of her own, she said, "Let's just say I'm more comfortable with a human explanation for this recovery than with no explanation, and definitely more than with any mystical explanation."

Euclide tilted forward in his chair, close enough to Janice for her to catch a slim breeze of cologne floating her way. "So you've thought about this," he said to her.

She almost laughed. "I've thought about everything."

"Can you tell me how it would it be possible?"

"Well, it's all theoretical."

"Theoretically, then."

She tapped her pencil again, and then, after a what-the-hell exhalation, she laid it out: "Some patients, as I guess you know, can make full recoveries from spinal cord injuries, even when they seem to be paralyzed at the time of trauma."

"You're talking about spinal shock," he said.

"I am. Functionality is recovered as the cord swelling goes down, usually within six months . . . or, in this case, possibly, after a successful decompression-fusion."

Euclide nodded for her to continue.

"But what if the patient," Janice said, "had a reason to want to be paralyzed?"

A bloated pause. "Because . . ."

"Because *not* being paralyzed meant he might have to return to combat."

Euclide's eyebrows performed a quick dance of intrigue before burrowing into a frown. "But how can one fake paralysis?"

"It's not easy, but not impossible either," she said. "I've found several cases in the VA files. Online, too." Among those, she explained, was a 2012 case in which an Army specialist, supposedly paralyzed from the belly button down after suffering a traumatic brain injury in Iraq, received a mortgage-free, wheelchair-adapted house in Texas from a national non-profit called Shelter for Our Troops. A neighbor boy, flying his new drone, caught video of the man standing at his backyard grill flipping burgers. "In this case, though, I think the patient"—Janice couldn't bear the accusatory voltage of referring to Cameron by name—"would've required guidance at Brooke Army Medical Center. An accomplice on the hospital staff."

Euclide asked her the same question she'd asked herself: Who would do this and why? The answer Janice gave him was based upon a theory her husband had devised while away at a legal convention in Mobile, which he'd sketched for her in a rambling late-night email:

> "Someone at Brooke—a physician like you, a nurse, I don't
> know—who'd seen too many boys come home in jagged pieces,
> who didn't see the point of these drawn-out wars in Iraq and
> Afghanistan, who'd come to hate the idea of gluing these guys
> back together just to ship them back to the front lines, who then
> came upon a patient so traumatized by what he'd seen/done/
> experienced and so terrified of going back that he was willing to
> do anything, even to voluntarily immobilize himself, to avoid going
> back—someone who couldn't bear to see the fear and dread in
> [the patient's] eyes, couldn't decline a plea for help. That's who."

"That's my best and really only explanation for the imaging," she said. To solidify the diagnosis, she explained, this theoretical accomplice would've needed to swap a more severe MRI into Cameron's file. And perhaps to fudge the results of Cameron's tests—or to coach him on squeaking through them on his own. He or she would've then seen Cameron discharged and sent home to Biloxi, with a medical retirement and full disability—and straight into the arms of a sister whose devotion to him was demonstrably limitless, and whose domineering manner during Janice's medical consults might have been, in narrow-eyed retrospect, a way of shielding her brother from suspicion, of shifting attention from him to her.

Euclide digested all this for a while, with his lips pursed and his pen poised in his raised hand as though to scribble notes in the air. "But then," he said, "we come to the event of August twenty-third."

"The recovery, right," Janice said, before a sudden spastic gulp. A gurgle of something acidic caught in her throat: something that felt like self-loathing. This wasn't what Cameron Harris had authorized when he'd given her permission to discuss his case with church officials. But she was in too deep now, connecting the dots too smoothly and rapidly, to stop herself. "So, it's been four years," she said. "The patient's terror has subsided. The war is winding down and there's no chance he'll ever be sent back into action. And he's tired of the subterfuge, the sores, maybe the loneliness. He wants to be free to be himself again, to walk again, to live the life he compromised in order to avoid returning to his unit."

"Perhaps he fell in love," Euclide offered.

"Who knows? We could list ten thousand reasons why he'd want his mobility back. Maybe his sister got tired of it, too—having to drive him around everywhere, do all the shopping, I don't know . . ."

"Yes, okay, but what about his legs? We just went over this a little while ago. They were very clearly atrophied."

"That," she said, a flourish of certainty in her voice, "is the single biggest piece of evidence here."

Euclide scrunched his face and shook his head. "I would think the muscular degradation actually *negates* this theory—"

"No, look," she cut in. "His legs *were* atrophied. But not so much that he wasn't able to stand on August twenty-third. The fact that he stood up and somehow walked—that's been one of the biggest riddles of this whole thing. If you spend four years in a wheelchair, whether from actual paralysis or pretend paralysis, your leg muscles are going to atrophy, they're going to waste away. Deterioration begins after just two weeks of immobility. On top of that you've got deterioration of the trunk muscles, which would make balancing almost impossible. Loss of length and trunk muscle, lack of coordination, loss of sensation and proprioception—the sense of where one's joints are in space—all of this is what makes his ambulation so . . ."

"So unbelievable."

"Right," she said. "But let's say you're up and walking just a little bit every day—maybe to the bathroom and back, maybe to the kitchen when the window blinds are down, whatever. In that case you might retain just enough muscular functionality and coordination to be able to pull off the appearance of a spontaneous recovery. To get up out of your wheelchair in a convenience-store parking lot and take a few steps, in front of witnesses who've spent years seeing you paralyzed. To do the whole hallelujah pony show."

"To enact a miracle," Euclide said quietly.

"That's right," said Janice, falling back into her chair. "A goddamn miracle."

fourteen

BARELY A HEARTBEAT AFTER EUCLIDE LEFT HER OFFICE, DR. Janice Lorimar-Cuevas felt such a physical onslaught of remorse and horror that jackknifing herself sideways she retched into her wastebasket. What evidence did she have to accuse or almost-accuse Cameron the way she just had? None. She hadn't even called Brooke Army Medical Center to speak to the staffers who'd treated Cameron, to see if she might catch a funky whiff. And was it even possible to hack the VA's VistA system? She didn't know. Yes, she'd diagnosed Cameron with PTSD, lending minor credence to her premise for a motive, but she'd diagnosed hundreds of combat veterans with PTSD and couldn't remember Cameron saying a single extraordinary thing about combat—certainly nothing to indicate he might go to such spectacular lengths to avoid it.

It'd been one thing for her and Nap to hash out their black-hearted theories in the evenings, as Nap stirred Sazeracs and Janice exercised whatever story-making muscles she'd inherited from her father; but for her to have leaked it to the entrancing investigator from Rome, to have unleashed her suspicions and sent them scurrying out into the world— Janice was revolted with herself. She recalled something Nap had said one night while they were cooking up the theory: "If it's true, you know, you'll look like a fool for having fallen for his con. If it's not true, though, you'll feel like a fool for thinking it—also a big asshole."

What'd opened the spigot for it with Euclide, she decided, was him uttering that empty little sack of a word: *miracle.* The whole exchange after that had turned into a kind of proxified argument between her and Euclide and between reason and faith, and in order to win that argument—to trump his magical thinking with a perhaps equally outlandish theory, but at least one grounded in reality—she'd pushed Cameron Harris into the pyre. She'd sacrificed him to make a point—had given him up as a burnt offering, just like they did in the damn Bible.

Or had she? Because—because *what if it was true*? Knowing Cameron the way she did—even the veneer-toothed, flashbulb-attracting version of him she'd encountered at lunch a month earlier—it felt beyond difficult to believe. But what was easier to believe: that a dead televangelist convinced his heavenly landlord to reach down from the clouds and breaking all natural laws hoist a paralyzed man to his feet? She wouldn't have divulged her suspicions to Euclide if some part of her didn't believe them—right? It wasn't as though she'd *enjoyed* constructing this ugly theory, with all its kamikaze implications for her career, aside, perhaps, from a few aha Nancy Drew exultations that probably had more to do with the presence of Nap and his killer Sazeracs and to the fact that the two career-junkies were actually *doing* something together—she wasn't like her father, she didn't revel in fabulism, she didn't make up stories for the hell of it, she didn't make up stories at all.

So what *did* she believe? Not think—*believe*. She laid her palms on her desk as though trying to ward off seasickness. Euclide was right about one thing: She *had* exhausted the limits of seeing—she'd passed, just like he'd said, into an entirely different realm now. And suddenly this question—*what do I believe?*—felt like the most fundamental and essential question she'd ever asked herself. For all of her thirty-three years, Janice realized, she'd been defining herself by what she didn't believe: not in Santa Claus or in God ("same difference," she might've said), not in reckless love or in mind-altering substances (the occasional Nap Cuevas cocktail excepted), not in market-driven health care or in running barefoot to prevent injury or in Bikram yoga being more effective than regular yoga, not in idleness or indiscipline or the luxurious lethargy of introspection, not in meta-phors or symbolic language, not in the little green gremlins her father'd claimed had sucked the life out of her mother through cocktail straws, not in stories of any kind. But years of inventorying what she didn't believe had been a way of eluding the question now holding her fast to her desk, making her late for a patient consult, making her own legs feel suddenly and ironically useless, with a vomit-spattered wastebasket beside her feet: What did she believe? Not just about Cameron Harris—though, yes, of course about Cameron Harris: Was he a fraud or a saint? And did that make her a fool or an asshole?—but about all the facets of existence that can't be glimpsed or measured no matter how hard you stare or try. She was feeling a strange and unfamiliar pain somewhere in her body that she couldn't quite locate—a place she knew that Euclide Abbascia, and all those like him, would smugly identify as her soul.

Euclide, for his part, didn't quite believe Janice's theory about Cameron. "A leap of faith," he says, "is required to believe in God. But to believe a conspiracy theory, one has to leap considerably farther." His sense was that Janice was groping, half-blindly, for a tactile resolution to this mystery. Her frustration had been apparent to him even as she'd charted the broad strokes of the case. Still, he couldn't dismiss it. Years as a prosecutor had inured him to the vast turpitude of human behaviors, equipping him with a capacity to believe almost anything about the berserk ways people act under duress, and while it seemed a stretch to think that out of cowardice a man would willingly paralyze himself for four years, well, he'd witnessed worse stretching from people, in much worse directions. Like all conspiracy theories, he thought, Janice's carried a little bit of sense masquerading as a lot.

But that little bit of sense was enough to color his subsequent interviews—with Lê Thị Hạt, especially, whom he found behind the counter at the Biz-E-Bee the next morning.

In most of Euclide's cases, the nature and character of the *miracolati* are peripheral or even immaterial to the investigation. (The exception to this is when the requester of the miracle and its recipient are the same person—when a cancer sufferer, for instance, appeals to a saint for his or her own healing.) No attention is paid to the dicey question of whether or not a recipient might've deserved or even wanted the granted miracle, a deliberate oversight informally known as "the Dismas Rule," in reference to the thief who was crucified beside Jesus, whom Jesus is said to have dispatched directly to heaven despite his moral slackness. In one of Euclide's early cases, in fact, the *miracolati*—a young Irish woman who somehow made a full recovery after twenty-one minutes underwater put her in a brain-damaged coma—refused to cooperate with his inquiry, possibly (rumor had it) because her near-drowning had been a suicide attempt; the Congregation approved the miracle anyway.

Hat couldn't have gathered this from Euclide's line of questioning, however. After eliciting her account of what she'd witnessed outside the store on that August afternoon, he began probing her about Cameron:

Q: *Does Cameron Harris strike you as a trustworthy person?*
A: What do you mean?

Q: *Well, let's see. Would you extend him credit?*
A: Oh, we never do that. No way. Not for anyone.

Q: *What do you know about him?*
A: What does a shopkeeper know? He likes beer. He used to smoke generics but now I think he smokes Marlboros.

Q: *That's all you know?*
A: I know the things that I've read in the newspapers.

Q: *But what did you know about him before you read the newspapers? Besides the beer and all that.*
A: I knew he got hurt in the war. I didn't know where or how. His sister took care of him, I knew that. She did all the talking. He never said much.

Q: *Anything else?*
A: My husband said he heard he got arrested once.

Q: *Arrested for what?*
A: He didn't hear that part.

That Hat seemed unnerved by Euclide's questions—as the interview went on, her posture and hands seemed increasingly positioned to protect her abdomen, something the young Euclide had learned to associate with agitation and deception—only served to create a kind of feedback loop:

the more anxious Hat seemed, when discussing Cameron, the deeper Euclide tried to dig, thereby compounding her anxiety.

Hat, for her part, says she *was* nervous, for two reasons. One because this lawyerly man in her store reminded Hat of all the state and federal tax officials who'd ambushed her and Quỳnh over the years, sweeping into the Biz-E-Bee with catastrophic audits and collections; no one carrying a briefcase into the Biz-E-Bee ever pulled anything happy from it. More significantly, however, Euclide's questions suggested to her that he had doubts—big official doubts—about Cameron's recovery, that perhaps something false or rotten was festering beneath the miracle sheen. Pockmarking her mind, as she fielded Euclide's questions, were thoughts of poor Gil and the last-ditch hopes he'd pinned on the Biz-E-Bee. Of all the people who were daily coming from near and far to plant themselves in that eight-by-twelve-foot rectangle painted in the parking lot, praying closed-eyed and open-armed for that blessed lightning to strike twice. Peering past Euclide, as he was asking her if she'd ever heard rumors about Cameron walking before his recovery (no), if she'd ever seen his feet jerk or move (no), if she'd ever happened to notice the condition of his shoe soles (his shoe soles?), Hat saw behind him the canyons of miracle merchandise that'd reversed her and Quỳnh's and Little Kim's fortunes, that were making the coming Christmas unlike any they'd ever had before, that'd been for the Lês what rain is to a drought-cursed farmer. But then she also remembered the dark prickle she'd felt watching Cameron Harris crack open that Bud Light almost immediately after walking, and wondered to herself if perhaps she'd glimpsed something then without really seeing it—that maybe what this investigator's questions appeared to be implying was something she'd known from the beginning. Every interruption by a customer felt like a reprieve. She was sweating. She was suddenly, and terribly, afraid.

Euclide left the Biz-E-Bee with his head more clouded than when he'd entered. A more cynical inquisitor, surveying all the miracle kitsch for sale, might've conjectured the possibility of the Lês being complicit in a miracle hoax—their witnessing, after all, was netting them a profit. But Euclide had seen all this before, most vividly in Medjugorje in Bosnia where the Virgin Mary is said to have appeared to six children in 1981. In the wake of any miracle come pilgrims, and behind them, inevitably, the souvenir-mongers. The announcement of a miracle is also the announcement of an imminent crap bazaar.

Not to mention, Janice's conspiracy net was already wide enough.

Still, Euclide's interview with Lê Thị Hat failed to neutralize the doubts Janice had seeded. And those doubts, the more Euclide considered them, began sprouting and branching. A high-profile hoax would do more than just threaten Reverend Fahey's sainthood cause. (If and when another event was credited to Fahey's intercession, the Congregation, singed by scandal, was likely to move slowly if at all, thus denying Norton Skag his life's last remaining goal.) No, a hoax like this could threaten the Catholic church as well—exposing the church to ridicule and vitriol during an already-fragile moment in its history. His job was to serve the cause of Archbishop Nicholas Fahey. His blood allegiance, however, was to the Holy See.

That he needed to interview Cameron Harris was a given, of course. Perhaps surprisingly, Euclide hadn't planned to speak with Cameron during this initial swing through Mississippi—the Dismas Rule notwithstanding, at this stage he'd considered Father Ace's interview notes to be sufficient. Euclide's instincts, however—both prosecutorial and canonical—were telling him to continue to postpone that interview. He knew he'd rattled Hat with his questions, and he was regretting it; he didn't want to poison what could be—probably was—a run-of-the-mill miracle investigation, thereby bungling Reverend Fahey's chances for sainthood based upon a skeptical physician's high-strung suspicions. Norton Skag would have to be patient, would need to stifle that inner Ahab of his. If Euclide was going to seek the hand of the divine, he needed to dust for human fingerprints first.

Years before, in Rome, Euclide worked with a police inspector who was fond of quoting William Butler Yeats: "The light of lights looks always on the motive, not the deed, the shadow of shadows on the deed alone." Cameron's motive, the light of lights, struck Euclide as the obvious linchpin to Janice's theory. She'd admitted to him, in her office, that the motive she'd assigned Cameron was entirely her own invention—that she'd devised it, sans evidence, in order to service the theory's other moving parts. To connect the dots, she'd created a dot. Euclide wasn't sold on it. There were far easier ways to get out of combat duty—more immediately shameful, perhaps, but what was shame when stacked against four years of self-confinement in a wheelchair? And couldn't he have instead just manufactured a limp?

He didn't share Janice's suspicions with Father Ace, though the priest was eager for Euclide's assessment, but he did have Father Ace photocopy the notes from his interviews with Cameron for him. These he took to a restaurant, Mary Mahoney's Old French House in Biloxi, where his young waitress, noting the Maserati out front and his leading-man looks, asked if he was in town "for the Miracle show." After a slow black chuckle he told her no, but her question served to confirm, lucidly, the importance of this case: Cameron Harris's recovery wasn't just a mystery, it was a spectacle. Whatever Euclide did needed to be airtight.

He was barely three sips into his Negroni, reviewing Father Ace's notes, before a line of Cameron's seized him as if by the throat: "A lot of things happened to me in Afghanistan. Getting paralyzed, that was just one of them." He peered up from the papers and from his rust-colored cocktail, staring into the middle distance. Was this line of Cameron's a kind of cracked door, behind which Janice's motive might be hiding? What else would Cameron equate with a paralyzing injury? Euclide sipped his drink without tasting it, ignoring a chunky pair of sunburnt men in fishing shirts who were ogling his Maserati through the window and angling for his attention as its owner. If Janice's hunch had any chance of being correct, he realized, the motive was to be found somewhere in Afghanistan, on some shell casing–littered ridgeline. Afghanistan would've been the motive's birthplace—would've been where, before anything could be done to conceal it, it was visible.

Only one member of Cameron's platoon was mentioned in the notes: Staff Sergeant Damarkus Lockwood, who'd been injured by the same blast that'd wounded Cameron—apparently more severely. Euclide was tapping his iPhone screen as the waitress, for reasons he pretended not to understand, delivered him a second Negroni that, with an un-shy smile, she said was on her.

Lockwood's unusual first name made him a cinch to locate. A phone call was all Euclide had in mind—until he noted the address. Lockwood lived outside the small town of Helen, Georgia, in the state's mountainous northeast corner near the border with North Carolina. Checking the map on his phone, he saw that the town was barely a fractional detour on his way back to Knoxville, and, scissoring his fingertips to zoom the map closer, that the area's backroads resembled a lovely bowl of spaghetti—the sort of squiggly mountain roads that Maserati engineers in the 1970s had designed his Spyder to make love to.

Euclide thanked the waitress for the gratis though untouched Negroni, slightly savoring the look of disappointment on her face. He slid into his car and started it, listening closely and rapturously to its engine growl as another man might tune his ear to Bach, and then, with the twilit, oyster-colored beach to his right, and the perishing sun smearing the sky violet behind him, he pointed the car's trembling hood toward Georgia.

Both hands gripping the leather steering wheel, Euclide Abbascia was anticipating twists ahead—just nothing like the twist he was headed for.

fifteen

THE DECEMBER 31 CALL SHEET FOR PRODUCTION OF *MIRACLE Man* was forecasting a light and agreeable workday. Because the schedule had them shooting past midnight, in order to film Cameron and Tanya welcoming the new year in a Biloxi bar, the crew members—most of whom had flown back from the West Coast the night before—savored a rare opportunity to sleep in, with no one needing to report to Reconfort Avenue before noon. Actual filming wasn't slated to begin until three p.m., when Cameron and Tanya would be reenacting their Christmas supper—or rather staging a Christmas supper, since on Christmas Day they'd grazed at a church lunch following Mass at Our Lady Queen of Angels before settling back home to watch *Revenge of the Nerds III* and *Fast and Furious 6*. The plan called for interviews after that—MEANING OF CHRISTMAS, noted the call sheet; HOPES FOR THE NEW YEAR—followed by a long dinner break doubling as a cast-and-crew holiday party. Then, at nine p.m., they'd be moving to a location shoot at a dive bar called Guidry's Lava Lounge that on the call sheet had been slyly renamed "The Champagne Room."

By one p.m., however, the morning's bright popcorn clouds were giving way to ominous gray streaks, a smudgescape rolling in overhead that could've been seen as a harbinger of things to come if such skies weren't so endemic to winter afternoons along the Gulf Coast. Huntley Benyus, the director of photography, or DP, known as Honeybun, was standing out on the driveway with Aidan Casey, the camera assistant. One of the camera batteries wasn't charging properly, and with cigarettes jouncing on their lips the two men were passing the battery back and forth, list-lessly stumped.

Then, with a glance over Honeybun's shoulder, Casey's mouth flopped open. "Whoa," he said. "Check it out."

Coming down the center of Reconfort Avenue was Mrs. Dooley, slowly but steadfastly, clicking her walker ahead of her. Though neither man had ever seen Mrs. Dooley off her porch—they'd filmed interviews about Cam-eron's recovery with her there—this wasn't, on its own, what'd snatched Casey's attention and was now fastening the men's gaze to her. Something about her shuffling carriage looked fraught to them—the explicit purpose of it, its wizened down-tempo urgency, the way her jutting chin seemed to be drawing the rest of her down the crackled asphalt. "Yoda's on the march," Casey whispered. The two men watched her for a while. "What's she *doing*?"

"Grab me the three-oh-five," Honeybun ordered, sensing the potential for story intrigue but at the moment more beguiled with the scene's aes-thetic, the strange and elegiac figure the old woman was cutting against that roiling, glooming, Book of Revelations sky. Within a minute he had the camera shouldered and was filming Mrs. Dooley's slow-motion ap-proach. Arriving at the front of the Harris house Mrs. Dooley didn't pause; she just crooked her walker to the left, making a sharp, smooth Pac-Man turn, and scaling the curb she started up the front walkway.

"Howdy," Honeybun can be heard calling to her on the footage. With-out acknowledging the greeting or turning her head or even her eyes Mrs. Dooley asked, "Cameron Harris inside?"

"Sure is," came Honeybun's answer. Then to Casey he hissed, "Run and mike her."

"She released?"

"She's released, get a mike on her."

Casey approached her warily, perhaps intuiting her reaction to him trying to pin a tiny microphone to her housedress: She swatted at him as though he were a gargantuan horsefly. When he tried again, bargaining with her as a nurse might bargain with a patient refusing a medical test, she rammed him with her walker to continue on her way. Casey threw a comically flummoxed shrug at Honeybun before Honeybun waved him out of the scene. Two thirds of the way up the walkway Mrs. Dooley came to a stop and, as if addressing the front door, asked again, "Cameron inside?"

"Yes he is," answered Honeybun.

"Y'all go fetch him for me."

Honeybun motioned for Casey to do this without entering the camera frame, sending him scampering into the house through the side door. Half a minute later the front door opened and out came Tanya, still in her oversize nightshirt, with Cameron trailing behind.

"Mrs. Dooley?" said Tanya, in her voice a mixture of confusion and diffuse concern and the residue of interrupted sleep. The way Casey had roused her and Cameron from the couches had been abrupt and mildly alarming, an evacuation order.

Mrs. Dooley said, "I want to talk to Cameron."

"He's right here," Tanya said, as Cameron slipped past his sister to where Mrs. Dooley stood parked behind her walker. On his way he flashed a peeved look at the camera, unsure why this unscheduled visit was being filmed, and then glanced up the street toward Mrs. Dooley's house on the corner, gauging the distance she'd traveled in her house slippers and what on earth that could mean. Then he looked down at her, noting a tremor on her lip and a redness spidering her eyes. "Something wrong?" he asked.

She took a deep, pained breath. "I want to know," she said, "did you pray for my grandson?"

Cameron Harris has been acquainted with Eula Dooley his entire life, and he could tell, from the seething tightness in her voice, that she was upset. He knew what the musk of her anger smelled like, from her having thrashed his bottom sixteen years earlier, and he was smelling it now. But . . . her grandson, him praying? "Do what?" he asked.

"I says, did you pray for my grandson? Like I asked you."

"Like you asked me?" His face was slack with bewilderment.

"Right after you risen," she told him. "I asked you to pray for him for me. To tell Jesus he needed watching over."

Cameron nodded, his memory apparently jogged. "Then . . . yeah," he said. "Of course I woulda."

Mrs. Dooley loosened her grip on her walker and rocked back on her heels, as though satisfied, but not soothed, by this answer. Her gaze drifted down to Cameron's no longer spindly legs and after a while she let out a thick grunt. "Just look at you now," she said, far from admiringly. Her tone felt more suited to someone addressing a drunk crumpled at the bottom of a stairwell. "Yes, sir. Look at you now. Jesus worked a wonder on you, didn't he?"

"Yes ma'am he did." Cameron's face was registering even deeper confusion. "He sure did."

"Yeah," she said, drawing it out, her red eyes narrowing as she assessed Cameron's legs once again. "Jesus worked a sure-enough wonder."

By this time Scott T. Griffin had arrived outside from the kitchen, where he'd been editing on his laptop wearing earphones and had therefore missed Casey's call to action. His mood was foul from not knowing what was happening and because whatever was happening was being filmed without audio support. (The production's sound mixer, Austin Kroth, wasn't scheduled until two.) In the footage he can be heard whisper-shouting at Casey why nobody was miked.

By this time, also, Tanya had joined her brother on the front walk. Cameron felt her hand on his back as she said to Mrs. Dooley, about the grandson, "That's Antwain you was talking about, right? He still up in Chicago?"

Mrs. Dooley nodded with her chin, looking to the ground and then up again. Her bottom lip shook. "Antwain got shot last night."

"Shot?" Tanya's shoulders sank. "How?"

"Coming out of a store, just like our store there." She waggled a finger toward the Biz-E-Bee. "Police was looking for someone held up another store. Said he pulled a knife. Boy didn't have no knife."

At this point Griffin slipped into the frame carrying three sets of lavalier microphones, the same kind of miniature clip-on mike that Casey earlier had tried clamping onto Mrs. Dooley's dress. Untangling cords, he said, "Ya'll just hold for a second while we get these on . . ."

"The police shot him?" Tanya was asking Mrs. Dooley.

"Just hold up," Griffin barked.

"My daughter," Mrs. Dooley said, ignoring Griffin who was threading a wire underneath the back of Cameron's T-shirt, "she called me from the hospital this morning, thinking he was gonna make it. I says yes he'll make it. I says we got some heavy prayers on our side, Jesus himself'd be in that room with 'Twain, with my own eyes I have gazed upon his wonders. I did. That's what I told her."

"I really need a pause here, folks," said Griffin as he wedged himself between the Harrises and Mrs. Dooley and began stringing a mike toward her.

Cameron's hand shot out to grab Griffin's forearm. "Leave her be," Cameron said. Firmly and articulately, he lowered Griffin's arm then released it. A stunned look passed across Griffin's face that was quickly replaced by a pinkish glower. On the footage Tanya can be seen startling then shrinking back, as though catching a darkly familiar frequency in her brother's voice. Cameron said, "This here ain't got nothing to do with what happened to me."

"That's actually my call," Griffin snapped back, making another attempt to pin the mike to Mrs. Dooley. She lifted her hand to swat him, as she'd swatted Casey, just as Cameron grasped Griffin's wrist and this time held it.

"This ain't your story," Cameron growled, screwing his eyes into Griffin's, squeezing his wrist, that big neck vein of Cameron's throbbing. "Remember?"

Tanya, her mouth forming a circle of shock, placed a hand on Cameron's shoulder. This was to placate him, but must've also seemed, to Griffin, a signal of her support, leaving Griffin no one to whom he could appeal. Wriggling his wrist, the pink flush of his face gone crimson hot, Griffin opened his mouth to respond but apparently thought better of it. Once Cameron let go of his wrist Griffin wound up his arm as though to whip the mike and its cords to the ground—but apparently thought better of that, too. He kept his eyes trained on the lawn as he went stomping out of the camera frame, the mike cables trailing him like empty leashes. "Can we just put a fucking boom on them?" he ordered Casey.

None of the three acknowledged what'd just happened with Griffin, Tanya resuming the moment Griffin's back was turned their way. "Is Antwain okay?" she asked, fearing the answer.

Mrs. Dooley shook her head.

Cameron said, "He didn't make it?"

Mrs. Dooley's head was still shaking.

Tanya slid a hand over her mouth and Cameron turned his head away from the camera and toward Division Street, where a car was pulling into the Biz-E-Bee—maybe for a cold six-pack, maybe for some life-saving grace. He was just starting to understand Mrs. Dooley's anger, that cold-ass way she'd regarded his legs, and it both stung and confounded him. Him walking had nothing to do with Antwain dying: nothing. And him praying . . . prayers didn't stop bullets, he thought, they weren't a Kevlar vest, they weren't insurance, they were wishes, coins you flipped into a fountain, they got heard or they didn't get heard, and nobody knew what they did no matter how much they all claimed to know. In the meantime, as Cameron stood there in a contemplative funk, Tanya kept lobbing all manner of questions at Mrs. Dooley, Tanya-style, trying to map what'd happened.

The official story, per the Chicago Police Department, is that Antwain Custis, thirty-four, was confronted by officers seeking a suspect in a recent armed robbery. When Custis turned belligerent and attempted to flee, one of the officers fired on him with a nonlethal beanbag round, striking Custis in the leg. At this point Custis allegedly reached into his coat pocket, which suggested to the officers that he was reaching for a weapon; one of them opened fire, shooting Custis in the abdomen. Eleven hours later Custis died from the wounds. Inside that pocket, police said, were narcotics and a knife. A later inquiry, however, revealed the narcotics to be a single joint (which family members believe Antwain was probably trying to get rid of when he reached into his pocket) and the knife to be the same box cutter he used in his job as a receiving manager in a South Side liquor-distribution warehouse.

"I got three great-grandbabies lost their daddy today," Mrs. Dooley was saying. "That boy, he was good. I raised him right here and he was good. He had his struggles but . . . well, y'all remember." Whether she stopped herself due to the camera's intrusive presence (Honeybun was still film-ing, roaming a half-circle beside them), or because she simply didn't wish to dwell on Antwain's struggles at the moment, is unclear. Fact is, how-ever, Cameron *didn't* remember. Not even Antwain's name, which he was grateful to Tanya for supplying. Antwain had been eight years older than Cameron, and thus, by the time Cameron was old enough to explore the avenue, a teenager and then an adult—an unknowable figure for a kid riding a Big Wheel, never mind the racial divide. All he really remembered about the grandson was that he always wore a droopy Lakers jersey and sometimes sat out in his car listening to Lil' Bow Wow and OutKast and David Banner with the bass cranked so high that every window on the street thrummed and fuzzed and Cameron's mother's little porcelain figurines would tap-dance on their shelves.

After a while Mrs. Dooley leveled another stare upon Cameron, this time as if waiting for him to say something—as though he hadn't answered a question she'd asked, or that as a representative of twisted fate he had an obligation to weigh in. The first of the afternoon's raindrops splatted his forehead. "I hate the prayers didn't save him," was all Cameron could think to say.

Her stare got harder and narrower, reminding him of the way she'd surveilled him as a child, pointing that crooked finger at him as though to say she knew what he was thinking, she knew what he was plotting, that she'd always be onto him. "How come praying can do this," she finally said, *this* being Cameron up on his feet, "but it can't save a child from bleeding?"

"I don't know," Cameron said, falling silent for several beats as the raindrops multiplied. "You know I don't know. I'm sorry."

Mrs. Dooley was nodding expressionlessly up at him, raindrops seeping down the canyons of her wrinkled face. She looked to be running some kind of calculations through her head, valuations and probabilities and the gut algebra of moral justice. Then her gaze widened to take in the broader tableau: Honeybun's face scrunched behind the big black camera lens, Griffin and Casey rubbernecking from the driveway, all the audio-visual equipment heaped in the open garage, enough cable to lasso the moon.

"This rain's fixing to come down," Tanya said. "Why don't I carry you back in the car and I'll sit with you awhile?"

Mrs. Dooley's focus returned to Cameron. "Cameron going to walk me back," she announced.

Cameron looked to Tanya, who nodded, then eased himself closer to Mrs. Dooley. She swiveled her walker around, in a many-pointed turn, and without acknowledging the crew or even Tanya began shuffling back down the walkway. "I'll still come on over in a few," Tanya called after her. "I just got to throw some clothes on."

For the first few minutes Cameron trailed a few feet behind, silent except for the order he gave Honeybun and Casey to stop following them. Mrs. Dooley clicked herself forward down the street so slowly that Cameron found it difficult to keep pace with her—his legs, once motionless, begged indifferently for a longer, faster stride.

About halfway down the street Mrs. Dooley asked, somewhat accusingly, "What them people do in there all day?"

"They're making a show. You know that, Mrs. Dooley."

She grunted half-heartedly. "Ain't no one told me what the show about."

"It's about what happened to me," he said. "About everything I been doing since."

She glanced over at him, for the first time on their walk, asking, "What's that you been doing since?"

Cameron's response took a while—a half-dozen slow steps, at least. "Making a show," he finally admitted.

"Huh," she said.

They shuffled along for a time.

She asked, "People going to watch that show?"

"That's the idea, I guess."

"And what they going to see?"

When Cameron failed to answer, after another half-dozen steps, Mrs. Dooley answered her own question. "I'll tell you what they going to see." Her tone made unclear whom she was addressing: Cameron, herself, the asphalt, Jesus. "They going to see *nothing*."

Cameron winced, and Mrs. Dooley, glancing rightward again, seemed satisfied at the sight. "You don't think I see you back there," she said about the backyard, her taut voice rising but studded with heavy breaths, "acting like you still got cause to do nothing, *be* nothing?" She shook her head and snorted, grief and disgust crammed into one nasal honk. "Still pouting like someone done sucked the red off your lollipop. Jesus give you a fortune and you acting like you don't know how to spend it."

Maybe I don't, Cameron wanted to say, but didn't. Instead he peered down at his dragging feet, uncertain why he deserved this but persuaded that, whatever the reason—he did.

They were at her house now, the raindrops multiplying.

"Jesus didn't do what he did so's you could join the circus," she said.

This stopped Cameron, and as Mrs. Dooley turned to ascend her front steps Cameron stood there sagging, his wettening T-shirt beginning to cling, rainwater glazing his face. "What—what am I supposed to do?" he asked of her back, and waited.

"That between you and Jesus," was all she said, fumbling with her screen door, and she was almost inside before Cameron, dazed and slumping, thought to say how sorry he was about Antwain. Her head dipped, but she spoke no reply.

Scott T. Griffin didn't try to speak to him when Cameron returned inside, which was good, because Cameron was in no mood to talk. He holed up in his bedroom, smoking so fulsomely and unceasingly that Honeybun, passing the bedroom door on the way to the bathroom, noted curls of smoke oozing from the top of the door.

Did you pray for my grandson. Like I asked you. Right after you risen. Cameron didn't believe it mattered, certainly not to the fate of Antwain Custis, but while he remembered Mrs. Dooley asking him to pray for her and her grandson, he couldn't remember ever doing so. Thing was, he hadn't prayed at all that first night, *right after you risen*—he hadn't done anything that night besides dumbly reel from what'd just happened to him, stupefied by the aftermath of an unfathomable magic trick. The reactivation of his faith lagged days behind the reactivation of his legs—and by then, well, by then his head had gotten crowded, by then it felt like half the world was begging for his blessing—by then he'd just forgotten.

He'd failed her, he thought. He'd failed her, and then, just now, he'd lied to her. But she'd seen right through the lie, hadn't she?—had peered directly into the void that he wasn't supposed to have anymore, then called him out on it. It didn't make a lick of sense, of course, that him praying could've changed even a stray molecule of what'd happened to Antwain up in Chicago—that a prayer of Cameron's could've cauterized the bleeding or redirected the bullets or given Antwain the wits not to reach into his pocket with cops training their guns on him. That made no sense at all. Yet as he sat there on the side of his bed, sucking cigarette after cigarette, his own legs seemed to be speaking to him in a language of twitches and trembles that he couldn't help but translate as: *Sense, circus freak? What the hell is sense?*

Scott T. Griffin, for his part, sat holed up as well—in the kitchen, fuming, pecking aggressively at his laptop. The clash with Cameron had snapped something inside him, his last mental shoelace. For four months he'd been working sixteen hours a day on a show that was increasingly bearing little to no resemblance to the earnest and scientifically rigorous show he'd intended to make. The deadline that Bree Winterson had set for him, silly to begin with, was now making no narrative sense whatsoever, was just a zombified marketing gimmick chasing Griffin in his sleep. His marriage had come unglued over the holiday shooting break, his affair with Kaitlyn Douglas exposed by an ill-timed text message, and for all intents and purposes he was currently homeless. Moreover, his relationship with Douglas, which'd bloomed under the excruciating heat of the production's deadlines, was now wilting from that same heat. (As one crew member would later say, "When you're shooting with a skeleton crew, like we were, your P.A.'s main duties can't be flashing the showrunner and giving him backrubs.")

And now, *now,* the goddamn cherry on top: Cameron Harris, his one-of-a-kind subject, his soon-to-be star, was bucking him for just trying to mike the old lady down the street. The first bona fide moment of drama in weeks, finally a scene that wasn't just people oohing and ahhing over the sight of a guy walking through Walmart, that wasn't just a setup for some wisecrack from Tanya or a physical therapy montage that came off like a hundred-to-one dilution of the *Rocky* movies' training scenes—finally this, resentment and sorrow under a supporting-actor sky, with Cameron, he thought, finally positioned to step into his role as an unlikely pastoral figure—at the moment Griffin was viewing the footage Honeybun had uploaded for him—and he had crap for audio, he had wind-whoosh and murmury garbled voices that might just as well have come from the bottom of a well or from a no-budget Brooklyn mumblecore flick.

"Fuck it," he said aloud, dumping the footage file into a folder he titled, after the Gil Scott-Heron song, "Whitey on the Moon." When Honeybun poked into the kitchen around two thirty, to check on the afternoon's status, he found Scott T. dourly mixing a tumbler of vodka and kombucha, something he was unaccustomed to seeing during shooting hours from his longtime boss. (Though Honeybun's first thought, he says, was about the drink itself: "*Ewwwww.*") Griffin told him they were "eighty-sixing the Christmas shit" scheduled on the call sheet. Today's vibe was all wrong for a chestnut scene, he said, and, for that matter, everyone knows that Christmas scenes are only effective when they air during Christmas. (It's probably no surprise that the Christmas theme was Winterson's idea.) He was of a mind to scuttle the holiday dinner, too, except that he'd already placed the order for two hundred oysters on the half shell and his bottomed-out morale didn't need to infect the crew's. "So are we just going to drink until nine?" Honeybun asked. Griffin tinkled the ice in his glass and shrugged. "Yippee," Honeybun said flatly.

And that's more or less what they did. By the time Cameron emerged from his room, crew members say, Scott T. was sporting a conspicuous vodka buzz. He strode straight up to Cameron, threw his arms around him in an apologetic man-hug, and like opposing athletes after a game they seemed to shake off their differences, especially after the Bud Lights started relaxing Cameron. They bickered mildly over the proper way to eat an oyster—Cameron claimed hot sauce and Saltines were essential; Scott T. issued an elaborate pitch for sucking them nude from the shell, to "guzzle their essence"—but otherwise seemed fine. Led by Honeybun, the crew members razzed Griffin for his gnarly kombucha cocktail, with even Kaitlyn—her relationship with Scott T. having graduated from open secret to open affair—joining in. She forced him—Cameron and Tanya too—to throw back whiskey shots the way she said they did back home in Alaska. A joint got passed, selfies got snapped and posted. The product-placement Vitamix blender, which the Harrises had never plugged in, was given its inaugural whirl mixing tequila with some frozen margarita mix someone fetched from the Biz-E-Bee. Scott T. blasted Drive-By Truckers and Todd Snider songs, and then, for Cameron, some retro-cool Southern gospel that Scott T. figured he'd dig. Kaitlyn tried teaching Aidan Casey some of her high-school cheerleading routines, resulting in an overturned couch. It was New Year's Eve, after all, and no one, besides Scott T., was older than thirty.

The day's call sheet, no one failed to notice, had all but been scrapped. "It was like we'd all come back from the production break," says Honeybun, "and then decided, what the hell, everybody play hooky."

Except, that is, for one thing: They were still heading out to Guidry's Lava Lounge, even if, at this point, they recognized themselves to be something less than an adept television crew. "We don't gotta get all that much," Scott T. said of the footage they needed to shoot—not that herding the group toward a bar required much lobbying. A location shoot like this one comes with an array of challenges: releases need signing, lighting can be tough, drinks get spilled on electronics, scoring a decent camera angle in a cramped dive bar can be next to impossible, audio is a nightmare, cameras get jostled, talent gets soused. Yet both Honeybun and Austin Kroth, the sound mixer, had worked with Griffin on *World's Rowdiest Bars* (Spike TV, 2006–07). Producing that show, they all felt, had equipped them with a tool kit more than sufficient, even with margaritas hobbling them, to shoot a handful of scenes in—"What's this place called? The Champagne Room?" Casey asked on the way, texting his girlfriend back in L.A. Honeybun, who'd scouted Guidry's with Kaitlyn, and was responsible for renaming it on the call sheet, let out a fat burst of laughter. From the front seat he cooed, "You'll see . . ."

No one can explain the lava in the name of Guidry's Lava Lounge, not even Guidry's daughter Breanna, the current owner. The bar, up far enough in North Biloxi to have weathered Katrina, has been around since the early 1970s, leading some to theorize that the name might've had some connection with lava lamps. Others figure it was a sign painter's misspelling, though they're at a loss to cite what the intended word could've been. Curiosity about the name, however, is exclusive to newcomers and out-of-town visitors, neither of which Guidry's much attracts. It occupies an unwelcoming cinder-block rectangle set on a wide dirt lot on Old Highway 67, the only indication of life inside being a neon Budweiser sign obscured behind a barred-up and dirt-clouded porthole of a window. In the daylight, the building's maroon paint—everything's maroon, even the window bars, as though the building hadn't so much been painted as dipped—evokes the color of a fresh kidney left to rot in the sun.

But daylight isn't what Guidry's is about, despite the obligatory lunch specials and the handful of tattooed old men barnacled to the bar on most afternoons. On Friday and Saturday nights, when there's live music—country-rock cover bands with names like Free Beer Tonight and the Rebel Rousers—Guidry's can get magnificently rowdy, crowds spilling out into the dusty dark parking lot for bouts of fighting or loving or both. Painted over the entirety of the ceiling is a giant Confederate flag, but it's almost impossible to make it out since someone got the idea in the nineties to shellac magazine covers over it—mostly the cleavage-and-chrome covers of *Easy Riders,* a biker mag, but also, weirdly, a few *Good Housekeeping* and *People* covers, including one featuring Ivana Trump, decades of cigarette smoke having stained her smiling face a decidedly non-Caucasian shade. You can theoretically get a cocktail in Guidry's, but, as the *Miracle Man* crew discovered, you really shouldn't try. When Aidan Casey ordered an Old-Fashioned, that au courant order of L.A. hipsters, Breanna Guidry slapped a Budweiser onto the bar. "That old-fashioned enough for you, hon?" she said.

Guidry's is a Tanya haunt, not one of Cameron's. Cameron had only been there a few times before tonight, when Tanya would drag him in during his leaves from Fort Benning, and the way he contorted his mouth whenever Guidry's came up relayed his opinion of the place. Tanya, however, has been a semi-regular since just after Katrina, when the Point Cadet bar frequented by her and her equally underage friends got swept out to sea. It was Guidry's she was leaving, in 2013, when the highway patrol busted her for DUI. The year-long license suspension that followed curtailed her visits, as the constraints of *Miracle Man* production did later, once her license got restored. She'd been looking forward to her return tonight, though, sending group texts to friends as Kaitlyn drove her and Cameron to the bar, inviting them to "get yr hot asses on the TV!!!!!" Certain folks at Guidry's haven't always treated Tanya kindly—a contributing factor to her DUI, she says, was overhearing some friends of a cute biker guy she was talking with that night laughing how they didn't know what he'd do with her because he didn't have a "wide load" sign for his bike. So Tanya was relishing tonight's homecoming—making her reappearance with a film crew in tow, outfitted in a black Adrianna Papell sleeveless lace dress the production company had bought her, with Kaitlyn having done her hair and makeup, and with margarita glee already zipping through her veins. She gave her brother's knee a giddy squeeze on the drive. He didn't respond, she recalls; he was looking out the car window, vacantly, with his cheek resting in his palm.

None of the patrons was surprised to see the cast and crew and camera sweeping into Guidry's, as the deal Griffin's company had struck with Breanna called for a doorman to be stationed outside the entrance, requiring patrons to sign an appearance release before entering. True, they might have expected a more sober-acting crew than the one that spilled through the doorway, but then again, this was Guidry's Lava Lounge, where the lead singer of the Rebel Rousers was known to occasionally pass out onstage. (Audience members sometimes commandeered the microphone afterward for a band-backed version of karaoke, belting out Garth Brooks songs while trying not to step on the unconscious front man.)

Earlier in the day Kaitlyn had delivered to the bar hundreds of silver cardboard cone hats and Mardi Gras beads and other New Year's Eve party favors (though not traditional noisemakers; Austin the sound mixer threatened her with death if she got those). The crew was glad—and in some sense relieved, spooked as some of them were about the rough clientele—to see patrons wearing them, with possibly the exception of the friend of Tanya's who'd engineered a kind of pointy brassiere using two of the hats and some fishing line from her boyfriend's truck. "She *really* wants to get on TV," Tanya told Honeybun. In this, she wasn't alone: Word had gotten out and Guidry's sparkled with an unusually glammed-up clientele—young women, mostly, jockeying with one another to stay in front of Honeybun's gliding camera, sipping their drinks through straws so as not to sully their lipstick. This provoked flurries of texts from male patrons to their elsewhere bros, and by eleven Guidry's was packed way beyond fire capacity, with Kaitlyn forced to go searching for a copy machine because the doorman was running out of release forms.

And queen of this teeming kingdom, for a brief and glorious time, was Tanya Harris. The same half-dozen of her friends who'd descended upon Reconfort Avenue to celebrate Cameron's recovery were there, plus a half-dozen others, massaging her with compliments about her dress and her hair and about the thirty pounds she'd lost since filming began (or that she'd been encouraged-slash-directed to lose, thanks to Bree Winterson's desire to see "transformation"). "Seriously, girl," one of them said, with vodka-cranberry-infused tears of joy on her cheeks, "you look *amazing*.

Ah-may-zing." Tanya didn't necessarily believe this—"no matter what you do," she'd told Kaitlyn earlier about her hair, "it's always gonna be badger fur up there"—but, smiling, blushing, she couldn't help *feeling* a little amazing.

For two months she'd been on camera, yes, but most of that had been private domestic scenes, her galumphing around in her sweats with Cameron, doing whatever Griffin told her to do. This felt different. This felt, she'd later say (with a speck of unintended irony), like "a coming-out party"—like what cotillion girls must feel, making their debuts. Everyone laughed a little louder and longer at her jokes, and no one, not a soul, made jokes about her. (If only the dickhead bikers were there, she found herself thinking, to get a look at her load now.) Cute guys didn't look askance when she looked their way; one guy, a tattoo artist who'd inked the butterflies on her left calf but for years had mostly ignored her at Guidry's, was suddenly hound-dogging Tanya all night, repeatedly letting slip that he was going through a divorce. ("Wonder why . . . ," said one of Tanya's friends.)

Yet it wasn't all surface cheer. That afternoon she'd spent more than two hours with Mrs. Dooley on her porch, helping her cope with Antwain's death as the rain patted the porch roof, maintaining a hand on Mrs. Dooley's bony shoulder as the old woman narrated photo albums, even fishing a couple teary laughs from her at the end about Antwain's young exploits. (Unlike Cameron, Tanya had lots of Antwain memories.) Something about that, the sense of fulfillment that comes from expended empathy, or the plain satisfaction that comes from leaving people better than you found them, had kindled inside Tanya a warm firefly glow. Taking care of people was what Tanya did—first her mother, then Cam—and she hadn't realized, until today, how much she was missing that, with Cameron now more or less independent. And this realization—that she possessed not just a skill but a purpose, maybe even a calling—was only adding to the buoyancy she was feeling at Guidry's.

Partly as an homage to Antwain, she cued up David Banner's "Cadillac on 22s" on the jukebox, a mellow hip-hop song dating back to before her mama died and before Katrina hit and before Cameron went off to Afghanistan, and with her eyes closed Tanya began swaying then dancing to its chill, stuttering beat, adding a fizz of nostalgia to the cocktail of emotions she was savoring. When she opened her eyes half the bar was dancing with her, her friends in a semicircle around her, Scott T. and Kaitlyn grinding sloppily in a corner, Honeybun raising the roof with one hand while filming with the other, the cute if leering tattoo artist trying to snake his way toward her, someone she'd never seen before handing her a fresh drink out of nowhere, the wannabe reality-TV starlets bobbing in a miniskirted tangle behind her, everyone hollering out the last line of the chorus with her, "Pray to the Lord for these Mississippi streets, hey *hey* hey."

Emboldened, perhaps, by having shared the dance floor with Tanya, the wannabe-starlets thronged her afterward, pleading with her to pose for selfies and group shots with them, filming her with their cellphones, and at least one of them asking for her advice on how to break into TV. Tanya's response was characteristically wry: "Maybe ask God if there ain't something he can do for your brother?"

Amid all this, she realized later, she'd lost track of that brother. Everyone did, except the bartenders. Cameron started drinking hard the moment he entered Guidry's, and not just his standard regimen of thermal angel blood, or Bud Light. Scott T. kept buying him whiskey shots, to reseal and then seal again the détente they'd hugged out that afternoon, which led to other people buying Cameron whiskey shots, and which led, after a while, to Cameron buying himself whiskey shots. Honeybun admits, and the raw footage makes clear, that he didn't devote many megabytes to filming Cameron. Griffin, for one thing, was having too loosey-goosey a time, using bourbon to flush out all the bile of his recent weeks and the earlier part of his day, to remember to direct, and the way Tanya was hamming it up kept Honeybun's camera lens glued to her. Aidan Casey sat with Cameron at the bar for a while, until some older guy engaged Cameron in a religious discussion that quickly went deep—way too deep for Casey, at least while his head was topped with a pointy cardboard hat. Austin Kroth, who hadn't been there to witness the friction between Cameron and Griffin, recalls wondering if Cameron might've still been pissed about the incident, whiskey fueling and maybe exaggerating some residual resentment. "He just started getting this coiled-up thing about him after a while," he says. "We were all pretty squiggly in there, having way too big a time dancing around and shit. I don't know that anyone was in the mood to hear a Scott T.'s–a-prick rant from Cameron, if that's what it was. That's what I figured it had to be."

It wasn't until ten minutes to midnight that Honeybun, with a panicked yelp, realized he needed his missing star for the countdown. After two minutes of frantic searching he found Cameron outside, smoking by himself in a misty blue drizzle.

"You're allowed to smoke inside, you know," he said to Cameron, noting even as he said it that Cameron didn't need his hometown's ordinances explained to him. Cameron shrugged dazedly.

"We've got, like, five minutes till midnight," Honeybun told him. "You ready to put on the happy face? Pop some bubbles?"

Cameron nodded as he took a long drag from the cigarette, showing zero capacity, in Honeybun's eyes, for putting on the happy face.

Honeybun took a step toward him. "Hey," he said, finding a more sober register. "You okay?"

"Yeah, I'm cool." Cameron shuddered his head as if to dispel something inside it. "There's just someone in there, someone I kinda got a problem with."

Honeybun instantly latched onto the same mistaken assumption Kroth did: that Cameron was still distressed about his earlier dustup with Scott T. "Oh, just get *over* it," he said. He did a little shuffle in the dust, trying to dance a smile onto Cameron's face. "That was *so* last year. Ha! Come on, we gotta get video of you popping some champagne . . ."

From all accounts, and from what the footage shows, Cameron seems to have rallied. Honeybun scooted him up beside Tanya on the dance floor where Kaitlyn armed him with a bottle of Dom Pérignon. Tanya led the bar's countdown, and Cameron, with graceful skill and perfect timing that would've mystified his sister had she paused to consider it, popped the champagne bottle just as midnight struck, the launched cork bouncing off the *Easy Riders* ceiling and the champagne foaming up and out of the bottle and down Cameron's forearm. Tanya took the first swig, the champagne's fresh suds causing half the swig to come spraying from her mouth, and Cameron got the second. From every corner of the bar there was cheering, hooting, kisses, yowls. Brother and sister enjoyed a long embrace as the bottle got passed around, but in that clasped moment—their only semi-private interaction of the night—Cameron mentioned nothing to her, she says, about anything or anyone bothering him. She saw no warning signs whatsoever. "He was drunk, yeah," she says. "But so was I. So was everyone."

For the next hour or so Cameron flickers in and out of the timeline, mostly out. Cameron himself can't really account for his doings or whereabouts in the bar, though Breanna Guidry says one of her bartenders refused to serve him a shot—an uncommon event at the Lava Lounge. Casey recalls seeing him besieged by a gaggle of the same young women who'd been flocking Tanya, and him awarding Cameron a fist-bump for what looked, to Casey, like a "groupie buffet." Tanya spent that hour on the dance floor, her dress sticking to her from champagne and sweat, she and her friends teaching the crew the Cupid Shuffle line dance, an expression of roaring bliss fixed solidly on her face.

For the first part of that hour Honeybun locked his camera out in the SUV in order to dance, his Honeybun acrobatics briefly stealing the spotlight from Tanya. Then he got an idea. Returning with the camera, he started canvassing the patrons with a question, as much for his own amusement as for usable footage. "What miracle," he went around asking, "are you looking forward to in the new year?" Many of the answers were funny or glib, as you'd expect them to be at Guidry's at one a.m. (a fifty-something woman, cocking a thumb toward her husband, said, "Viagra"), and a notable portion of them required the intercession of parole boards more than God's hand, but Honeybun found himself surprised at how affecting some of the other answers were. A man in a biker vest talked about freeing the father he idolized from the grips of Alzheimer's; a young woman wearing a 2015 tiara talked about unlocking her sixteen-year-old brother from such a profound case of autism that he's unable to speak, citing her brother's condition as the reason she found Tanya and Cameron's story so inspiring, why she'd come to see them tonight.

Honeybun's drifting passage down the bar ended at a man sitting alone at one end. None of the crew members recall noticing much about this man earlier in the night. Casey thinks he saw the man leaving angrily with a blonde woman at some point—they brushed into him on their way out, nearly spilling Casey's drink. He must've returned without her, Casey thinks, because when he saw the man next he was slouched solo at the bar, looking as though he might be nursing the wounds from whatever had happened with the woman. Though the man is twenty-eight he looks considerably older on the footage, as though hard living, or maybe just inebriation, has fast-forwarded his physical features by ten years. His eyes are nestled in puffs of flesh, shadowed by the brim of a camouflage baseball cap pulled low over his forehead. He has a flat and slightly zigzagged nose. The white polo shirt stretched over his torso is a size or more too small, revealing a roll of white belly. A pair of athletic sunglasses hangs from his shirt collar, though the sun had been obscured then retired since noon.

As Honeybun approaches you can see a base smile cross the man's face. It's obvious he's overheard the question coming his way, and the way he shifts in his seat suggests his answer has been prepared for a while, ready for him to uncage it. He doesn't even wait, in fact, for Honeybun to ask him anything. The man—whose name, everyone would later learn, is Tommy Landry—just pitches toward the camera, licks his lips, and says as loudly as he can:

"I'll tell you what a real miracle would be. If Cameron Harris ever hooked up with a chick. He's a fucking *faggot*."

"Okay, wow, you're a real asshole," was all Honeybun could get out, dipping his camera down and away from the man, before Cameron appeared suddenly and as if out of nowhere, so swiftly and so forcefully it was like one of the faces on the *People* magazine covers had spat him out of the ceiling.

The punch he threw knocked Landry, all two hundred and fifty-some pounds of him, right off the barstool. This first blow isn't visible on the footage—at that moment the camera was aimed at the sticky floor—but, out of documentary instinct, Honeybun re-steadied the camera on his shoulder and skittered backward a couple yards to record what happened next.

On his way down to the floor Landry smacked the wall, and he tried using it now to scramble up onto his feet, ripping down a poster of Miller Lite girls as he climbed upward. No one really did anything at this point— you can hear a wave of excitement and laughter rolling through the bar since the expectation was that this fight, like most bar fights, would end right there, with a single punch and then lots of entertaining braying. As well, because of the tight crowds and the way Guidry's is laid out, only the closest onlookers were aware of the combatants' identities—Cameron's in particular.

Once on his feet, with his cap having been punched clean off his head, Landry swiveled toward Cameron. His face was contorted with a crazed and cornered look that might've been owing to pain, or to basic rage, or possibly to fear: No one but Cameron and Landry would understand, for a while, that this was a continuation of that same face-breaking fight they'd had ten years before on the Biloxi beach, paused—but not forgotten—for a decade.

Jumping over his crashed barstool, Landry made a rage-sloppy, all-out lunge toward Cameron. Cameron fielded the lunge with remarkable agility, considering his blood-alcohol content, but then again Cameron had been trained by the U.S. Army and was serving combat duty in Afghanistan while Landry was serving as rush chairman of the University of Alabama's Pi Kappa Alpha chapter. Cameron feinted left, throwing off Landry's balance midway through his charge, and then grabbing Landry's right arm with his own right arm he palmed the back of Landry's head with his left hand and with a single snap of motion, graceful if only in a savage way, guided Landry's face into the two-inch-thick oak bar.

Landry let out a gurgling yelp as, for the second time in his life, Cameron Harris shattered his nose. The crowd made a collective leap back as Landry's face bounced off the bar and with a beefy thud his back slammed the floor. The amperage of violence had by now electrified Guidry's; some people fled the fight circle, mostly women, while other people, mostly men, jostled in for a view. Cameron was on top of Landry almost the second he smacked the floor, his punches terrifyingly rhythmic: one to the ear, pause; one to the jaw, pause; one to the eye.

"Oh . . . my . . . *god,*" you can hear Honeybun saying, in something close to a howl. A bystander tried pulling Cameron off but Cameron wheeled his left arm up and back, striking the bystander in the cheek and sending him sprawling sideways, enfolded back into the crowd. "Get this cocksucker off me!" Landry croaked, during one of the pauses, before Cameron punched him square in the mouth. "Faggot," Landry wheezed, during the next pause, his teeth stained red, a mustache of blood above his lips. Cameron struck him in the mouth again.

By this time the footage's audio amounts to shrieks and frenzied crosstalk. "Help him!" you can make out a woman pleading. Another female voice calls for Tanya, *Tanya*. A half-dozen men jump in front of the camera lens in quick succession, the last of them staying put with his back blocking the camera. "Get his arms," someone shouts. "Calm the fuck down," someone else is shouting at Cameron. "Get his fucking *ARM!*" To Cameron: "It's over, dude, it's over!" Not quite buried in the audio is Landry's voice, feeble, broken teeth clogging his throat, still saying *faggot*.

The next thing visible is four men, two on each of Cameron's arms, yanking Cameron up and off Landry, their expressions so strained it appears they're unsuctioning him. Landry's hands cover his face just as Cameron's heel strikes it, a parting kick that may or may not have been intentional. Cameron struggles for a few seconds, flailing like a captured animal, until a fifth man manages to take hold of his ankle and, with a drill sergeant's timbre, screams at Cameron to calm down. Then Cameron goes limp, with his one free limb, one of those miraculous legs, dangling inertly from his body as the five men cart him out of the bar, the stunned crowd parting and Tanya running close behind, then Griffin, then the crew interspersed with Tanya's friends, then fifteen or twenty people hoisting their cellphones to snap photos or record video, and then finally Honeybun, moaning something unintelligible as he records Cameron being dumped into the backseat of the production SUV and Tanya in her black cocktail dress, sobbing, crawling in after him.

The first social media posts went up even before the crew pulled out of the parking lot. Stacking up throughout the wee hours of the morning, some with shaky noisome video and others with dark and blurry pictures, they were all variations on this one, a Facebook post from a witness:

Keith Niolet For real. I just saw Miracle Man beat the shit out of some dude at Guidrys.
January 1 at 1:34am • Like

Among the many people who saw these posts that morning was Jesse Castanedo, the reporter for the Biloxi *Sun Herald,* who's covered enough hurricanes in his career to instantly recognize one on the horizon, to spot a Category 5 shit-storm blowing straight his way.

sixteen

FROM THE INSIDE OF HIS '72 MASERATI GHIBLI SPYDER, IDLING out front of a mobile home at the end of the steep and sinuous dirt road he'd traveled to get here, Euclide Abbascia was watching four massive dogs, of a size and demeanor he'd only ever encountered before in Luca Giordano's seventeenth-century painting of the hellhound Cerberus guarding the gates of Hades, leaping and leaping and then leaping yet again at the car's windows, Euclide brought close to tears by the *scritch-scratch-scritch* of their claws carving up his doors. Compounding his distress was uncertainty that he was even at the right place. When the Google Maps voice announced, "You have arrived at your destination," he'd been looking at two mailboxes perched by where an old logging road (by the looks of it) met the county route. Happening upon a fork as he followed the road into the woods, he'd opted for the road more traveled, the Maserati's low underside aching from all the washouts and ruts despite Euclide's efforts to baby it up the climb.

Reasoning with the dogs from inside the car did nothing to calm them, quite possibly because Euclide's entreaties came out in Italian. He honked the horn.

The youngish woman who emerged from the mobile home aligned with Euclide's mental image of the woman he'd spoken to on the phone the previous day, who'd identified herself as Damarkus Lockwood's sister Shyrece. Distracted by the dogs, he'd also failed to notice the wooden ramp on which she was now descending. So this must be the place, he decided, rolling his window down two inches.

The woman clapped her hands and waved and hollered at the dogs, which stopped jumping but didn't quite retreat, running circles around the car now as though formulating Plan B. She seemed in no hurry, not walking so much as flowing down the rocky driveway in her aquamarine sock feet, dressed in bright pink pants with an unzipped sweatshirt over a jewel-studded black T-shirt. As she approached the car she came into focus as a lithesome woman, no older than thirty, slim but somehow voluptuous at the same time . . . and a quite pretty woman too, as Euclide couldn't help noticing. Her face, scrunched into an expression of annoyance but also what looked like amusement, was corona'd by a short, ringleted afro. Tattoos of stars ran up both sides of her neck, as though to suggest a sparkler flaring beneath her T-shirt, a firecracker of a heart.

Once alongside the car she ran her gaze across its silver contours, ignoring the driver stranded within. Euclide rolled his window down a few more inches. "Huh," she finally said, still neglecting to look at him. "I know you bad lost."

"Can I get out?"

"I don't know," she said. "Can you?"

"The dogs, I mean."

She made a brief, tepid show of yelling at them to get back. "They ain't gonna hurt you."

Once out of the car Euclide wiped his sweaty palms on his trousers and made sure not to glance at the car door. This he could do later, when he was somewhere safe to weep. "Euclide Abbascia," he said, extending his hand.

She didn't take the hand, instead tilting her hips to the side and raising one arm akimbo. "Didn't we talk on the phone yesterday?"

"We did," he said. "Yes we did."

"And I told you not to come 'round."

"You did, yes," he said, lowering his rejected hand, "but the nature of my work can be so complicated and strange-sounding, you see, that I feared I did not express it very well over the phone."

"Naw," she said, with a deadpan shrug. "You did fine."

"Ah, well." Euclide broke out a grin. "Thank you."

"You welcome," she said, drily, clearly immune to his smile.

Euclide laughed, at the same time taking stock of the area. The mobile home—newish-looking, to Euclide's eye—sat in a clearing of woods so tight that he wondered how anyone had gotten it up here, the hemlocks encircling it so ancient and high that the house seemed situated inside a silo. Indicating long-ago settlement was a scatter of slanted gray outbuildings behind and to the side of the house, the forest in the process of claiming some of them, a sapling poking through one rotted roof like a conquering flag. Several children's bicycles of various sizes stood leaned against the house and a netless basketball hoop was hanging something less than regulation height on an electrical pole. Strands of Christmas lights hung blinking in the daylight. One of the dogs lifted his leg to pee on Euclide's front tire. "I imagine you don't get many visitors up here," he said to her.

"Same as anybody else, I reckon," said Shyrece, nudging her shoulder in his direction as if to point out Exhibit A.

"Yes, I suppose so," he mumbled, before shifting himself out of small-talk gear. "Look, I have no wish to be a pest, but if I could speak to your brother for just a few minutes, it would—"

"Like I told you," she cut in, "I don't think my brother wanna talk about the things you wanna talk about."

Euclide issued an affected sigh. "Would it be possible for him to tell me that himself?" He threw on a dumpy, browbeaten expression. "Just to confirm? This way, you see, my boss won't make me write letters to him, and mail them certified, and on and on like that, wasting everyone's time . . ."

Shyrece lifted an eyebrow. "Sounded yesterday like your boss is Jesus."

"Ah!" A quick laugh came bubbling forth; he liked this woman. "In a sense, okay, I guess this is true." Wagging his head with a mock-sour expression, he said, "He's a very tough boss . . ."

Shyrece assessed the situation for a while, her lips pursed and her hand still locked to her hip. Then she turned back toward the house and started casually back uphill, saying quietly, with a darting glance at the Maserati, "Jesus sure must pay you all right though." Despite any real signal from her, and with the four dogs drooling disturbingly close to his heels, Euclide followed.

Euclide's lips fell apart as he entered the mobile home. The living room was all but covered with Native American artifacts and memorabilia—a war bonnet, tomahawks, a beaded breastplate, arrows, whorls of arrow-heads under glass, paintings of battle scenes, much more—mounted so neatly upon the fresh white walls that Euclide felt inside a gallery, that if he looked harder he'd see tiny price cards below each item. He was dizzied by a kind of cultural disorientation he'd experienced before in the States though never so vividly. Occupying a couch amidst all this pow-wow ornation, with the wide eyes and bulging neck of a bullfrog, was an old man wearing puffy orthopedic shoes and a T-shirt on which was emblazoned an airbrushed portrait of the rapper Ludacris. To Euclide's left, in the kitchen, a one-year-old girl in cornrows was banging a sippy cup on the tray of a high chair.

The old man looked up from the television. "Who's this?"

"He wanna talk to D," Shyrece said, scattering some Cheerios onto the tray, which the baby scooped up in little fistfuls to throw to the floor.

"What for?" the old man demanded, his eyes roaming over Euclide.

"Don't matter," Shyrece said. "D ain't gonna wanna talk." To Euclide she said, "D's back there working. Go on sit down, I'll get him for you."

The old man monitored Euclide, taking a seat cater-corner from him, and then let out a hospitable-sounding grunt. "That there's a right comfortable chair, isn't it?"

Euclide agreed it was. He asked, "Is Damarkus your son?"

"My son?" A scoff. "Naw, that's my grandson. His mother, she was my daughter."

"Where is she?"

"My daughter? Aw, she passed giving birth to Shyrece. Me and my wife, we brung them two kids up. 'Course, then she went and passed." The way he explained all this suggested less sadness about these deaths than disappointment with the women in his life for their inability to stay alive.

Euclide gestured toward the walls. "Are you the one who's fond of Indians?"

"Fond? Shit, man, that's what we are. We Cherokee."

Euclide didn't know what to make of this claim, stifling his gut reaction to chortle at what he thought was a joke or maybe involved a sports allegiance with which he was unfamiliar. Looking at the old man, it seemed as preposterous as Father Ace alleging he was Chinese. Then again, Americans sometimes mistook Euclide for Spanish, Portuguese,

Lebanese, Greek, or more often Mexican—really any of the world's tribes of butterscotch brunettes. The grandfather tilted Euclide's direction to ask, with a confidential hush, "Why you wanting to talk to D?"

"I'm just inquiring," Euclide answered, "about a man he served with, in the Army."

"This boy do something wrong?"

"No, not at all." A pause. "Not that I'm aware of, I mean."

"Then why you asking about him?"

"Something unusual happened to him, medically, and I'm trying to sort out some of the particulars of his injury."

"What kind of unusual?"

"Well, he was paralyzed. And then, for no apparent reason, he wasn't."

"Huh." The grandfather moved his lips around as if literally chewing this information. "Can't hardly believe what doctors doing these days. You look at D—hell, only half him came home. Now he get around better'n I do. Me, I was with the Fourth Infantry over there in 'Nam. Back then, now, they wouldna even *tried* saving D. No point in it, man. They woulda just shot him up with some morphine and tagged him for Mortuary Affairs. Tell you what, they working miracles these days. That right there, that's the truth."

Despite this fresh hint about Damarkus's mobility, and despite Euclide's familiarity with the state of trauma rehabilitation, Euclide was nevertheless taken aback by Staff Sergeant Damarkus Lockwood's swaggering entry into the living room. From the injuries that'd been reported to him, Euclide was expecting someone who looked . . . well, injured. But Damarkus Lockwood most certainly didn't. Yes, the long-sleeve jersey he was wearing dangled slack where the lower half of his left arm used to be, and, yes, he was walking on twin prosthetics left unconcealed by the basketball shorts he was wearing. And beneath those shorts, Euclide knew, was the residue of equally dire wounds. But no: Damarkus Lockwood did not look injured, he looked repaired instead, he looked bionically strapping, carrying his six feet, four inches of height into the room with a jock's supple confidence. Shyrece lagged behind with the tetchy face of someone who's just lost an argument.

Damarkus apologized for making Euclide wait. He'd been on a conference call for work, he explained, and you know how hard it is to beg off one of those. He parted the front curtains for a peek outside. "Shy says you come up in some dope ride." He nodded admiringly at the glass. "You really come all this way from Italy? Lotta layovers getting to this here corner of White County, Georgia."

Damarkus Lockwood, at thirty-two, is as handsome as his sister, Shyrece, is beautiful; Euclide, that aging *batticuore,* didn't fail to recognize this. He has a lustrous mahogany complexion and high narrow cheekbones, the latter lending some credence to his grandfather's claim of Cherokee blood. He keeps his hair and beard fastidiously close-cropped, his hairline pitched perfectly level except for the slice cut out at his right temple, a dandyish geometric flourish. He wears his sergeant's authority lightly, but it's unambiguous when it appears—not as barking but as a quiet and calibrated pressure that squeezes you into submission. His grin, on the other hand, can be so broad and ebullient as to seem deceptively innocent, as though the kind of delight it projects cannot be manufactured so swiftly and smoothly, with every last micron of guile filtered out.

He took a seat across from Euclide as Shyrece passed by to fuss at the baby, the bulk of her attention, Euclide noted, sticking fast to her brother. Damarkus breezed through an explanation of his job coding security software for Verizon— part-time work, he said, mostly from home. The remainder of his working hours he devotes to a local nonprofit using athletics to reach at-risk youths. The kids get a kick out of his prosthetic legs, he told Euclide, just as Shyrece's other child, a nine-year-old son who was at school at the moment, gets a kick out of them.

"He says D got Transformer legs," the grandfather said, with a croaky snicker. "One time Shyrece caught him outside using one them legs for a toy gun. Boy about needed a prosthetic butt after that whupping."

To his grandfather Damarkus said, "Chief, you gotta clear out so we can talk."

"The hell you say." The old man twined his fingers across his belly. "I wanna hear about this boy he's talking about."

"Come on, Chief," said Shyrece, "D just needing some privacy." He ignored her until she flicked off *Judge Judy* with the remote, at which point he submitted, with a teenager's pouty shrug, letting her escort him out to the porch. When Shyrece slipped back inside, Euclide observed, she did so stealthily, as if trying to elude notice by her brother or by him, a fly seeking a wall.

Euclide was laying out the reason for his visit in capsule form, omitting any details about Nicholas Fahey or Congregation processes and protocols. His mission, he said, was simply to determine whether there might be a temporal explanation for Cameron Harris's recovery—something other than the miracle people were touting. The way Damarkus was tightening in his seat Euclide interpreted as polite concentration. When Euclide finished Damarkus asked, "So what'd you come all this way to talk to me for?"

"You served with Private Harris."

"Lot of us did."

"You were injured with him."

Euclide discerned the same subtle wince buckling Damarkus's face that Shyrece must have. From behind Euclide's chair he heard her say, "You don't gotta do this, D. He's just church. You don't gotta do nothing you don't want."

Damarkus's hand went up like a stop sign. "Chill out, Shy. It's all good." Then he turned back to Euclide, the set of his jaw looking hard. "Yeah," he said. "Me and him went down in the same blast."

Euclide pretended to jot this down in the notepad open on his knee. What he wrote instead, however, was the Italian word for sister: *La sorella?* Shyrece was trying to shield her brother from something—but what? Post-traumatic stress disorder came into his mind. He knew Janice had diagnosed Cameron Harris with it, that Cameron was on a lifetime regimen of antidepressants. If Damarkus was similarly afflicted, maybe that explained Shyrece's resistance. To her, perhaps, Euclide was here as a dredger of toxic memories that'd taken years to subside, a walking talking trigger appearing uninvited on their remote, siloed doorstep.

"From the way you were nodding earlier," Euclide said gently, "I take it you've heard about Private Harris's recovery."

"Yeah, that's some crazy shit, ain't it?" The tone was flat, as if he was reading off a teleprompter. Perhaps to correct this, he added enthusiastically, "I mean, I guess it's some *really* crazy shit if you coming all the way from the Vatican to talk to me."

"How did you hear?"

Damarkus hesitated, his eyes exploring the room as if the answer might be mounted alongside the arrowheads. "One of my old lieutenants, I think that's who it was . . . he sent me a link or something."

"Have you heard from Private Harris? Since then?"

"Nossir I have not," Damarkus said.

"D . . . ," Shyrece moaned, her brother hoisting the stop sign again.

Euclide paused to underline the one word in his notepad: There went *la sorella* again. "Can you tell me what kind of soldier he was?"

"Cambo?" Damarkus shrugged a few times as though to unwind some shoulder tendons, like a batter approaching the plate. "He was a meat eater, man. The best kind. You could count on him for anything. You wouldn't know it, talking to him—he's this quiet guy, you know, acts kinda loose, he's pretty chill most of the time—but when shit got kinetic, man, he'd light up. That's why I always liked him being a SAW gunner. A lot of these guys, you know, they get out in the shit, they just open up a blossom, emptying rounds every direction. Cambo, he was smart, he was deliberate, used his eyes. He had everybody's back."

With this brief description Euclide was already feeling some of the air escaping Janice's theory, its tires beginning to go flat. "Is there an example you could offer?" he asked, seeing if more air might leak out. Shyrece was moving about the room, he noted, not quite pacing but close.

"An example. All right, I hear you." Damarkus sat thinking for a while, Euclide's blinking eyes prodding him, before finding one: "First time he sees action will tell you a lot about a soldier. No matter how hard you train him, no matter how many times you drill him, no matter how many goddamn video games he's played, the thing you're gonna see, that first fight, that's instinct. And he don't even know himself what that instinct is, not until that first bullet misses his head. His mama gave it to him, his daddy gave it to him, his people a hundred years back gave it to him. You can adjust that but you can't flip it. You get born one way or you get born the other."

Darmarkus, reverting to sergeant mode, was looking for a sign from Euclide that he'd heard and understood this prologue. Euclide nodded.

"Cameron's first fight was in Paktika Province. We was on mounted patrol and got ambushed," he said, adding tartly, "which is pretty much how every story from there begins. Coming up this steep mountain pass we came up on a civilian truck blocking the road, a big one, what we call a jingle truck, no way around it, no way to push it uphill, no real way to back out, when all of a sudden the Talibs start raining on us. That trap was ill, man—we couldn't even call in air support because they'd figured out it was a dead spot for radio reception. They had two fronts pinning us down—firing RPGs from across and above, capping us with small arms fire. That might've been the worst tactical position I was ever in. The field manual doesn't prep you for that one, not the terrain we were in. Nothing does."

Shyrece delivered him a glass of water then lingered beside him. Damarkus took a sip and continued: "The lieutenant wanted to blast that truck with the two-oh-three, try to blow it out of our way. But, like we all told him, no matter how much fire you get going on that thing you're still gonna have a few tons of hot steel that you ain't pushing up that incline. Only other option was to try to hot-wire it. Thing was, they'd probably booby-trapped it. Their whole attack, their positioning, all that—it was all so tight that you got to assume the truck was wired to blow. So whoever you're sending up there probably ain't coming back. But then again, now, you got forty-three guys who might not make it if you don't try. That's combat math. It sucks.

"This specialist we called Suge, he was our hot-wire man. So he was going up. The platoon sergeant at the time, he ordered Cameron to go up with him to provide cover. Now to me this seemed like a pretty stupid choice, because Cameron's untested, you know, this is his first damn firefight, but I guess Terry—that was the platoon sarge—he didn't want to send one of *his* guys up there. Because his guys, you know, he understood the assets they brought to the platoon, he knew all about their wives and kids . . . but he didn't know anything about Cameron yet. That's combat math too.

"We're all watching from the rear, doing our best to give them two some cover fire. Cameron and Suge get up to the truck and Suge lies down inside, gets to work. And then Cambo, he starts into doing this thing— almost like he's trying to draw fire, running around like a rabbit or something. The lieutenant's watching thinking he's panicking, thinking we're fucked, but I'm seeing different. I didn't know nothing about Cameron then, but I knew he wasn't panicking."

"How did you know?"

"The way he was laying down fire. You hear enough of it and after a while it's like hearing someone play a guitar or something—someone strumming an M249 the right way, man, you can almost hear music. There's a rhythm, there's almost a tune in there. What it is, see, it's the sound of control. You hate hearing it from the other side, but from your side, man, those are your beats, you know what I'm saying? And every second till that truck started up, him and Suge figuring they're dead, Cameron doing his rabbit runs with a Dragunov trained on his ass, a sniper trying to mist him, every one of the enemy knowing what was happening and where to gear their fire . . . that was the sound."

"So the truck," Euclide clarified, "it wasn't booby trapped?"

"The truck wasn't wired, right, that was the good thing. But the damn second Suge sat up to drive, he took a bullet in the neck."

Euclide shook his head, in a show of reverent horror, but Damarkus seemed to be relishing this part of the story, his voice pitching higher and faster. "So Cambo, though, listen, he crawls into the truck and shifts it into reverse. Lying down on the seat. Suge, he's still conscious, but Cameron has to grab Suge's legs to push his feet onto the clutch and the gas, you know, like he's milking a cow. And then we're all watching that truck come lurching backwards, watching it crash right into the front of our lead vehicle, bam."

"Why backwards?"

"Yeah, that's exactly what the lieutenant's screaming. But Cameron figured there wasn't no way he was gonna get that truck forward. There's bullets coming through that door, they're swiss-cheesing it, and any second now a grenade's gonna come busting into that cab, lights out. Best he can figure, he might get that truck moved twenty feet uphill, then the next guy coming up to shove his dead body out the way to drive is just gonna get it moved another twenty. So he cranks the steering wheel all the way left and throws the truck into neutral. Pulls Suge out of the cab through the passenger door, kinda drags him back till the medics get up there. I'm watching Cameron waving his arms for us to roll back right about the same time the lieutenant is losing it completely, he's wanting to shoot Cameron instead of the enemy. But when that lead vehicle backs up a few feet I see what Cambo done and I'm like, okay, roger that shit. We order everyone to pull back a ways, from rear to front. And when that lead vehicle backs up, fast as it could go, the jingle truck stays smooshed to its front, rolling back, until its rear wheels tilt over the side and then that whole motherfucking truck just tips right off the side of the cliff."

Euclide was writing, trying to get as much of this story as he could into his notepad. Whatever image of Cameron he'd allowed to fester in his mind was blurring now, its pixels scrambled by this new information. What he was hearing didn't match the profile of someone who could be literally paralyzed by fear. He went casting about his mind for another potential motive to fit Janice's theory.

"So our route was clear after that," Damarkus went on. "We moved up to better terrain, called in an airstrike, got a pair of Warthogs that blew the face off that ridge, and we counterattacked. And we pretty much wiped them out. We lost three guys in that fight—not Suge though, they stitched him up. Three guys instead of forty-three. Thing is, like I was saying earlier, you can break that story down and find about a dozen instinctual decisions Cameron made that'll tell you what kind of soldier he was. He shoulda got some chest candy for that one, you ask me. That shoulda been a medal."

"And how did he respond to that—his first combat experience?"

"Well, first thing he had to respond to was getting his ass chewed out by the lieutenant. There were guys said I was a textbook motherfucker, but him . . . you either build the Legos like the instructions say or you don't take them out the damn box." Damarkus rolled his eyes before gathering his face into a thoughtful frown. "After that, though, with Cameron . . . same way he responded to anything else. Smoke a cigarette, kinda stick off to the side. He had Suge's blood all over him. He threw up a little while later. But that's normal."

"Was he especially close to anyone in the platoon?"

An inscrutable half-grin crept onto Lockwood's face, Euclide thinking he might be weighing whether to answer this question with a joke. A glance to his sister yielded Damarkus the faintest of nods, even more inscrutable. "I'd have to say that was me, sir," he told Euclide.

"You? Why was that?"

Damarkus's eyes widened as he blew the air from his cheeks. "Oh, man, I dunno. Put aside the difference in rank, you know, me and him just got along, we could hang good. We'd both played high-school ball. We was both from down South, even though, obviously, he's white, and I ain't—"

Prompted by all those Indian artifacts, Euclide couldn't resist breaking in. "This is totally irrelevant," he admitted, "and I hope you'll pardon the curiosity of a foreigner. But your grandfather—he told me he was Cherokee?"

"Straight up," Damarkus confirmed. "We got Cherokee in the blood; we got—what we got, Shy?—Melungeon ancestors from up Tennessee way; my dad's grandad, he was white; and you can see we got some Africa going on. It's funny, when I was a kid, messing 'round with Play-Doh, you know, I found that when I mixed all the colors together I got the exact same shade as my skin. And that was like this lightbulb moment—like, all right, you mix some of everything together, and what you get is me."

The beam of Damarkus's grin was like another lamp turning on in the room, and Euclide felt happy for the swerve. Shyrece, however, seemed coiled more than ever. The baby was drawing her into the kitchen, bleating for more Cheerios to replace the ones strewn across the floor.

"But also," Damarkus went on, "well, you must've driven through Helen getting here, right? Then you probably noticed there ain't a ton of black faces 'round here. We're in the Blue Ridge mountains, man. I mean, we're in *White* County, Georgia, you feel me?" He laughed at this, clearly not for the first time: a lifelong absurdity. "So what I'm saying to you is, I grew up around guys like Cameron, wasn't like he was something weird or foreign to me. I mean, I didn't gotta *like* that country shit he listens to but it ain't like I didn't grow up hearing it . . ."

Euclide leaned in, wanting to capitalize on this higher-watt rapport. "Did he confide in you?"

"What do you mean?"

"Well, did he tell you anything about his home life, or his personal life . . ."

"Yeah, of course he did. Especially when we was at Outpost Hila, with a lot of time to kill. I knew he had a wild-ass sister like the one I got." From the kitchen Shyrece grunted to acknowledge receipt of her brother's zing. "I knew his daddy wasn't around same way mine wasn't. He'd lost his mama, same as me. He never got to play college ball, I didn't neither. We just had some shit in common."

"He confided a great deal in you, it sounds like."

"Look, man, you're gonna learn a whole lot about people when you're stuck up in a little combat outpost for an Afghan winter. With some them guys, you're gonna learn shit you ain't never wanted to know."

"Then how would you describe Cameron Harris, personally?"

Damarkus drew his face into another thoughtful frown, but a soft one, with something far-off in his eyes. "Cameron was tough, you know. Kinda raw 'round the edges. You get him in a group, man, you ain't gonna hear much out of him. But he was . . . he had a righteous heart, you know what I'm saying?"

"A righteous heart," Euclide echoed.

"Yeah, he was strong, you know. Army strong, and all that shit, but . . ." He tapped his chest. "Heart strong, too."

"Would you say he was brave?" Euclide asked, thinking to aim a kill shot at Janice's theory about a motive.

"Over there, you know, sometimes being brave is the same as being stupid," Damarkus said, a small laugh bubbling out of him. "And he was stupid sometimes. That's why I named him Cambo."

"Can you explain that?"

"Naming him Cambo? You seen them old Rambo movies, right?"

"I'm aware of them," Euclide said.

"This was in Paktika Province again, little while later." Euclide wasn't expecting a story, just an explanation, but settled in contentedly. Damarkus's fluent and energetic way with war stories was making him discount his earlier suspicions about PTSD, but there was Shyrece still, now with the baby in her arms, helicoptering close to her brother.

"We got hooked up with an engineer company that was building a holding pen for some detainees," Damarkus said. "They'd found this little courtyard with a guard tower and was stringing up some razor wire, the standard shit. And then it blew up. We came under fire from about thirty or forty Talibs—small arms, mortars, RPGs, the whole menu. We had an MRAP but the moment the fuckers blew in they took it out with a mortar round. Broke the gunner's arm, blinded the driver, just neutralized it with a single sixty. So now we're kinda fucked, right? It's like we're trapped inside a blender. We got enemy up in that guard tower now, we don't got shit for cover, and they're fixing to overrun us—and that's bad, you gotta understand, because if they'd taken that courtyard there wasn't hardly nothing between them and a command center down the highway.

"So Cameron, he's helping evacuate the wounded out of the MRAP. I'm right there with him when a bullet hits one of the wounded in the knee. And I remember him saying, 'Goddammit,' just like that, just *put out,* you know, like he's playing poker and got his tenth crap hand in a row. And without orders, because nobody woulda ever ordered him up there, he climbs up into the gunner's hatch and starts blasting that fifty cal. He's totally exposed up there. I mean, you shoulda seen his helmet afterwards."

Damarkus's eyes were flickering with a distant glint, reminding Euclide of someone recounting an extravagant meal. "I ordered him out of there," he said. "Cambo says he never heard me but I think he ignored me. He's just swiveling and shooting that fifty: bam, bam, *bambambam*. By this time there's Talibs coming over the wall. I realize he's running black on ammo so I get on in there and start loading for him, shouting the whole time for him to get his stupid ass down. I mean, he didn't have a chance up there. I load him a second box, he's still firing. Load him a third. And by the time that third box is running black, man, that courtyard's gone quiet. I don't know how many enemy he took out—had to be more than a dozen."

Euclide looked up from the notes he was taking. No, Cameron Harris wasn't a coward. Janice had it wrong. Here was a young man who'd twice risked sacrificing himself to save others. For the first time since she'd uncorked that venomous theory, Euclide was sensing the warm radiance of a potential miracle, its divine rebuttal. And while he knew miracles didn't work this way, Euclide was beginning to glimpse a framework of justice built into this one, as though walking had been Cameron's reward for the lives he'd saved.

"That's the second time we could've lost the whole squad if Cameron hadn't pulled his Rambo shit," Damarkus was saying. "I remember afterwards he's standing there smoking—he's so cheap, he always smoked this nasty Afghan brand called Pine, smelled like he was smoking kitty litter—and I come up to him like, 'You're a stupid motherfucker, you know that?' And he's like, 'Sorry, Sarge, I just lost my temper.' So sincere, you know, like a kid who just fouled out of a basketball game. Me, I just got to laughing my ass off. I mean, that was close to Medal of Honor shit right there, and he's saying *sorry*. That's the minute I . . ."

He pulled up short. Some kind of switch got pulled, erasing Damarkus's lamplight grin and replacing it with a melting expression of sudden agony or grief. Shyrece moved in, patting the baby on her shoulder, her own expression mirroring her brother's.

Euclide didn't know how to read this. Criminal and canon law in Italy had endowed him with little experience fielding war stories, but maybe this is how it went, he thought: You focus on a single point of light, like a stargazer, until the enormity of the darkness surrounding it smothers the glow. His gaze bounced between Shyrece and her brother. "The minute you what?" he prodded.

Damarkus raised his head, something new and solid in his eyes. "The minute—the minute I knew what kind of soldier he was."

Euclide cocked his head, studying him. "You sound like you admired Cameron very much," he offered.

Damarkus said nothing, that new solidity Euclide noticed calcifying into stone-facedness. An aspect of his eyes, in that moment, was reflecting his lower legs: functional, but bloodlessly metallic.

Shyrece dropped a hand down onto her brother's shoulder. "Pretty sure Cameron," she said to Euclide, as softly as he'd yet to hear her speak, "admired D just as much."

La sorella: Once again Euclide felt the urge to underline that word in his notes.

"Can you talk about when you were injured?" he asked, thinking maybe he was merely positioned too early in this story, that fast-forwarding might bring clarity.

Damarkus's account of the story aligned with the one Cameron had furnished Father Ace, with one exception that Euclide failed to catch: In the version Damarkus told, it was Cameron, not him, who'd wanted to check something out on the ridge, when they'd left the Afghan National Army soldiers and strayed to the spot where Damarkus's boot heel tamped the soil above a land mine that'd been lying dormant since the Soviet–Afghan war of the 1980s. *Boom.*

"It seems astonishing," Euclide said afterward, "that you survived."

Damarkus sketched how he'd done that: the forty-seven surgeries, the way the surgeons rebuilt his urethra using tissue from his cheek, the nine months he'd spent at Walter Reed Army Medical Center followed by the year he lived in a dorm on the hospital's campus for physical and occupational therapy, the hundred-thousand-dollar robotic arm they'd fitted onto him that he almost never uses, not since the third time he punched a hole in the bathroom wall reaching for his toothbrush.

For the first time, Euclide saw a smile creep onto Shyrece's face. Listening to her brother describe what had to be the most painful and difficult period in his life, the grueling aftermath of that land mine, appeared to relax her. She tickled the baby, rocking on her heels. It was pride, Euclide saw. It was warm, warranted pride.

"You didn't stay in touch with Cameron Harris afterward?" Euclide asked, close to wrapping it up, Shyrece's newfound ease dissolving some of the weird mystery of the way she'd been acting until then.

A low vibration suddenly thrummed the room, which Euclide immediately traced to Shyrece. Another mention of Cameron Harris, and her ease popped like a soap bubble. Why? She was staring at her brother's face, with close and tender scrutiny, but she was also, Euclide felt, transmitting signals to him on a sibling frequency that Euclide could sense but not decode.

"Naw, we really didn't . . . ," Damarkus said. "We had some serious healing to do, both of us, and after a while I guess it was like, keep looking that way," twirling a finger toward the future. Something about this explanation must've struck him as insufficient, because Damarkus added, "Some guys stay in touch with everybody in their squad or platoon, you know. The band of brothers thing. Other guys, though," twirling again toward that middle-distance future, "sometimes you just move on, you know?"

With this last statement Shyrece leaned down and kissed the top of her brother's head. With this: not with his account of his injuries and hellish recovery, but with this.

Exactly why this gesture provoked something in Euclide, and what exactly it provoked, he cannot say. The kiss struck Euclide as a reluctant sanction—as if she didn't agree with something her brother was doing or saying but supported him anyway, the kiss of a father releasing his daughter to a bridegroom he abhors. If it hadn't been for her, he'd later say, and the sheer volume of sub rosa communication his antennae kept discerning, he wouldn't have posed the question that he did, would've driven out of those woods armed with an uncomplicated portrait of Cameron Harris. He feared repeating a common mistake of his as a prosecutor, bogging himself down trying to untie a peripheral knot that, tied or untied, would have little to no impact at trial, what Americans called missing the forest for the trees. But still. *La sorella* . . . Janice's suspicions about Cameron stayed viable every time Shyrece flinched at his mention.

"Sergeant Lockwood," he began, steeling himself with formality, "I hope you'll understand why I must ask this question."

The look on Damarkus's face caused Euclide to stall a moment; it suggested he knew precisely what was coming.

"Given your knowledge of Cameron Harris, would you find it at all credible that some or all of his paralysis might not have been legitimate?"

The twist of Damarkus's face made clear this was not at all the question he was anticipating. "Legitimate?"

"That some or all of it could have been faked."

He sprayed the word as much as spoke it: "*Faked?*"

"Maybe some time later, after an earlier recovery of function . . ."

"The fuck for?"

"I don't know," Euclide said, unnerved by the way Damarkus's nostrils were flaring and the sheen of rising fury Euclide could see in his eyes. "Possibly to avoid returning to combat? Possibly—"

Damarkus spat a puff of disgusted air. "You ain't serious with that."

"It's just something that needs to be excl—"

"Naw, you can't come in my house talking shit like that."

"I'm sorry, it's just—"

"You don't know shit, you know that?" Shyrece was behind him now, spearing Euclide with her eyes and with one hand kneading her brother's shoulder, the baby in her other arm beginning to mewl from the tensely raised voices. "You listen to me talk and then you come out with that. You lay *that* shit down. You don't know fuck about nothing."

Euclide lifted both hands to show surrender. He tried to speak, but Damarkus cut him off again—

"You don't know the shit we went through. You don't know what shit is." His eyes were brimming. "You got no fucking idea. Cameron Harris was the bravest, toughest soldier I ever served with. Never saw him half step in my life." His voice was catching, and he gulped for air. His quiet sergeant's authority was gone now, replaced by something wilder, more elemental, more dangerous; the baby let out a cry that could've come from somewhere inside Damarkus. "Did you not fucking *listen* to what I was just telling you? You got something *wrong* with you?"

Shyrece's voice entered: "You see, D? This is why I told you don't do this."

"I don't care you got questions you supposed to ask," Damarkus said, ignoring her, Euclide tensed for Damarkus to come leaping out of his chair. "They're bullshit questions. You don't get to come into my house talking shit like that. You can just get the fuck out of here. You not hearing me? Get the fuck out."

"I told you, D," Shyrece said.

Damarkus threw up his hand in another stop sign, but the effort broke him. He buried his face into the stump of his left arm and let out a low and grinding sob. Euclide sat drawing his lips into his mouth, jolted by a blast he hadn't seen coming, and would've left the house right then, concussed with confusion and guilt, were it not, again, for Shyrece. She peered down at her weeping brother, her features softening so profoundly that it appeared her face was going out of focus, unraveling from pity or love, until, with a decisive nod, she hardened them back, aiming her eyes at Euclide.

"There's something you should be knowing about my brother and Cameron," she said to him.

"Shy, don't—" Damarkus's words muffling into his shirtsleeve.

"What for?" she snapped downward. "I'm listening to you tell a story that ain't the real one."

Euclide perked, though he was feeling something like the way Damarkus had described feeling inside that courtyard: trapped inside a blender. Shards of emotions were buzzing around him, too fast to identify.

"You ashamed, D? That why you sent Chief out?" The baby was wailing now, howling at the ceiling. "He don't care and you know it. You ain't got no cause for shame, D. Only thing shameful is acting like the truth ain't true."

"Shy . . . ," Damarkus moaned, lifting his face just long enough for Euclide to see the flood smearing his cheeks, then burying it again.

Her gaze froze Euclide. "My brother loved Cameron Harris."

Euclide groped to make sense of this, his arms rising as though to capture her words from the air and turn them over in his hands. "Well, sure," he said, elongating his own words less from caution than bafflement. "Combat duty creates . . . it must create incredible bonds, the shared trauma, and—"

"Naw, you ain't feeling me. My brother, he was *in* love with Cameron." She looked down at Damarkus's racking shoulders. "Shit. Look at you, D. You still is."

seventeen

Thirty-six hours after the panicked, shambolic retreat from Guidry's Lava Lounge, on the afternoon of January 2, 2015, Scott T. Griffin was roaming his rented cottage in Ocean Springs, across Biloxi Bay, with his phone pressed to his ear. The rest of the crew—Kaitlyn, Honeybun, Casey, Kroth—were draped on sectional couches, a funereal pall dulling their faces, Kaitlyn nibbling her fingernails one after the other. Honeybun tried lightening the mood with a batch of Bloody Marys, but no one seemed lightened or, for that matter, thirsty; Honeybun had to keep reminding everyone about the sweating crimson glasses in front of them, like a mom pushing cough syrup. On the coffee table was that morning's edition of the *Sun Herald*, read and reread, announcing a criminal inquiry into the fight by the Biloxi Police Department and the temporary suspension of filming.

"Look, Cameron didn't get paralyzed washing windows," they could hear Griffin saying. "He was a *warrior*. He got taken out in *combat*, okay? He was trained for violence, conditioned for violence, and then—no, Bree, please, just think about this for a minute—he had to sit for four years with all that violence running crazy through his veins."

Griffin's manic energy—he was flailing his pink arms, pounding walls and tables to punctuate what he was saying, grunting and gesticulating as though wicking the spirit of the James Brown T-shirt he was wearing—stood in total contrast to the zombies strewn on the couches. An hour before, Lifetime's Nicola Ash had issued a terse statement saying that "in light of the recent incident in Biloxi, Mississippi, the March 15 premiere of the series *Miracle Man* has been indefinitely postponed," sucking even more oxygen from the room. Griffin, however, wasn't see-ing that as the airless omen everyone else was. ("Saying indefinitely is like saying forever with an emoji," went Casey's mumbled reaction.) In fact, Griffin was strangely relieved. Postponement meant a reprieve from the deadlines that'd been shrieking after him every day, particularly in the last few weeks. It meant he had more editing time to hone narratives, to tweezer significance from the hundreds of hours of humdrum existence he'd filmed. Moreover, Griffin wasn't willing to concede that Cameron's assault doomed the show—complicated it, yes, but only in ways that the documentarian in him was relishing. As Griffin saw it, the show until that point had been based on a situation; what he had now, he thought, was a *story*.

"Did he respond poorly to a provocation?" he was saying to Bree Winterson, Lifetime's head of programming, patched into a conference call along with Griffin's agent and a phalanx of attorneys. "Okay, yes. Of course. But was that response really out of the blue? No. That's what war-riors *do*. Is it a short-term loss? Absolutely. But, long term, for the show, listen—I think this just added this massive dose of texture and complex-ity. I really do. The fact that he responded *physically*, after all those years when he couldn't? Cameron's not a saint, but, come on, we knew that. He's not some Christian Superman. He's a bit of a meathead, okay, who took out some asshole in a bar fight. But I'm saying we should *embrace* that complexity. Let's pivot the show *toward* it, not away from it . . ."

When he ended that call, the twentieth or thirtieth he'd made or fielded since waking with a multilayered hangover on New Year's Day, he'd convinced, by his own reckoning, "somewhere between zero and zero-and-a-quarter people." But Griffin wasn't dissuaded. He wouldn't let himself be. *Miracle Man* had become like a vital organ to him, one of the only things pumping blood through his veins. Not just because his twelve-year marriage had turned into a dumpster fire indirectly ignited by the show, and not just because documenting Cameron Harris's story was the deepest project he'd ever undertaken, the thing he was counting on to prove he could do more than local color, that big themes weren't out of his reach, that he wasn't just an L.A. hustler peddling moonshin-ers and jukers and truck-stop hookers from the deep-fried margins. If he lost the show—and the way Winterson kept saying, "Scotty, this just isn't the show we ordered," certified that as a looming possibility—he'd lose *everything:* the money, his crew, his investors, his reputation, any and all basis for convincing future network execs he could deliver a show. To be a producer, he's often said, your job is to produce. It's an infinitive verb. To not produce is to not exist. And that's what Scott T. Griffin, already homeless, already dazed and frayed, and currently listening to Casey and Kroth comparing the westward flights they were scouting on their phones, felt that he was up against: the end of his existence as he knew it. All because of a single one-thirty-a.m. punch in a gnarly little shit-kicker bar. Okay, more than one punch. But still . . .

Honeybun rose from the couch to offer Griffin a look at his phone. "*Hollywood Reporter*'s got a story up," he announced.

"Yeah, I figured, the writer called me this morning." Griffin shooed the phone away. "This line producer from *Fox and Friends* called me a little while ago, looking for footage to use for B-roll on whatever they're doing. I politely told them they could blow me."

"What does that sound like? 'Might you please consider blowing me'?"

"Something like that," Griffin said absently, "more of a British accent."

"There's a meme rolling on Twitter—that Culture Club song, 'It's a Miracle,' playing over cell footage of Cameron on top of the guy. You see it?"

"Saw it. First of many, I'm sure." A sigh. "That tide's gonna keep rising."

"At least it's Friday. Shit'll die down over the weekend." Honeybun's features shifted into a lumpy frown. "So is Cameron answering yet?"

"Crickets," Griffin said.

"Not even texts?"

Griffin shook his head, looking pained. "Tanya's saying to give him time." He passed his own phone to Honeybun so he could read Tanya's last text message to him: *He's pretty tore ^ bout evrtng. Not sure wot hapnd. I'll let u kno when shit calms dwn.*

"She's not sure what happened," handing it back, "or he's not sure?"

"You're reading it same as I am."

Honeybun crossed his arms. "You still don't think I'm right?"

"What I think, and what everybody knows," Griffin said, with a wide roll of his eyes, "is that you've got the loosest gaydar settings in North America."

"I said it that *first night*. At dinner, the very first night."

"You were joking."

"You took it as a joke. You take everything as a joke."

"Because it *was* a joke. I laugh at ridiculous shit, okay? Just like Roy Porter. You remember him—from the Hoss Trammell show? How queer was he?"

"Um, as a three-dollar bill? Look like Tarzan, suck like Jane?"

"Jesus, Bun." Griffin lifted his gaze to the ceiling. "You just hate anyone not being on your menu."

"Oh, please. I just know a vegan option when I see it."

"Look," said Griffin, that pained look back on his face, "can we do this some other time, when it'd be more fun? I kinda got too much going on to be entertaining your sexual fantasies right now. I'm trying to hold this fucking thing together, and by that I'm talking about me," patting his chest, "as much as the show."

"Of course, sorry." Honeybun backed away with his hands up. "I didn't mean to knock your blinders out of place."

Griffin's face knotted as he watched Honeybun walk away. "Anyway," he called after him, "gay guys don't fight like that."

Honeybun wheeled around. "Oh right, I forgot. We just tickle and bite. Case *closed*, Javier."

Griffin's phone rang just as Casey was approaching him. Answering the call, he said to his agent, "Hold on, Roger, just one sec," saying to Casey, "What is it?"

Casey told him he'd found a flight out in the morning. He was booking it.

"I really wish you'd give me some more time here," Griffin said.

"If I'm gonna be sitting on a couch not getting paid," shrugging, "I'd rather be doing it back home with my lady."

With his eyes closed tight Griffin ran a hand across his forehead as though wiping something thick and viscous from it. "If the network gets on board," he said slowly, "and Cameron comes back online, these next few days are gonna be our money shots. We're finally gonna be cooking on a hot stove."

"Dude, I'll be a phone call away," said Casey, as emptily as Griffin had ever heard a person speak.

SEVERAL HOURS LATER on that same cold and drizzle-gray Friday, across the bay in Biloxi, Dr. Janice Lorimar-Cuevas was walking through the hospital's canteen when she passed a face she recognized.

Janice hardly ever frequented the canteen, but she hadn't eaten a thing since her morning smoothie—a habit she understood she needed to change. She'd awakened vomiting the previous morning, and knowing this had nothing to do with the glass and a half of champagne she'd drunk at the Biloxi Yacht Club's New Year's Eve party she immediately dispatched Nap to Walgreen's. They'd watched the pregnancy test results emerge together, the green plus sign seeping into view beneath the little plastic window, Nap brought to speechless tears and Janice sitting stunned on the edge of the bed, running the ramifications through her mind as a microprocessor assimilates data. She was pregnant. And now, a day after this discovery, she was feeling obliged to whet her already-sharp habits, in this case to nourish that zygotic presence growing inside her, even if that meant stomaching canteen food.

Janice reversed a few steps. The woman she'd recognized was sitting by herself with a cardboard cup of mostly uneaten soup in front of her, its skimmed surface testifying to her disinterest. She had her palms pressed flat to the table, as though she'd decided to get up but abandoned the effort midstream. Every inch of her face and bust –the way her raw eyes were sagging, the downturned set of her mouth, the wayward strands of hair stuck to her forehead, the inward droop of her delicate shoulders— was broadcasting distress.

"You—you own the Biz-E-Bee, right?" Janice said to her.

Lê Thị Hat looked up nodding. She took Janice in with a slow, clunky focus. "Oh, you. You're his doctor. I saw you on TV one time."

"Cameron, you mean."

Hat nodded again. "He won't answer his phone." Her voice sounded tired and bitter and not entirely directed Janice's way.

Janice hesitated. "You saw the paper this morning . . ."

"Stupid," said Hat, as though to spit the word into her soup.

This was Janice's turn to nod, though what was stupidest about it, in her mind, was Cameron having quit his antidepressants and anti-anxiety meds two months earlier. Much of what had happened to Cameron in the preceding four and a half months had shocked her—but not this. Having treated hundreds of PTSD sufferers over the years, veterans struggling with their return from Iraq or Afghanistan, she knew the syndrome's hallmarks: hypervigilance, hypersensitivity, a loss of authority over anger. At one thirty a.m. in a barroom, top-dressed with alcohol, unbuffered by any medications, it wasn't hard to imagine those hallmarks getting packed into a fist. With her patients who declined medication, she'd found, often the question wasn't if but when, their fuse long or short but almost always sparking. "It sure did sound that way," she said to Hat.

"Why would he do that?" Hat withdrew her hands from the table and gathered them into little fists of her own. "Someone who gets a miracle, they don't act that way."

Janice tilted her head. "What do you mean?"

"God doesn't give a gift like that to someone who'll use it for wrong." Her fists were tight now, raised to her chest as though to spar. "Not when there's someone else who'd use it for good. When there's someone else who doesn't act like that . . ."

Hat clearly had someone specific in mind. "Are you here," Janice probed, "to visit someone?"

Hat drew air into her nose and bobbed her head in staccato nods, but when she made to speak nothing came out. Lubricating her voice with anger allowed it to emerge, though incoherently, and in spurts: "They're letting him die. The doctors are, the ones over in that building. They're just letting him die."

"Letting who die?"

Virgil Poleman was the answer, Gil. Hat and Quỳnh had admitted him on December 29. Through November and early December the chemotherapy hadn't been working the way the VA oncologist liked to see, slowing the cancer rather than shrinking or stalling it, but then, come Christmas, Gil showed a strange and rosy turnaround—a four-day burst of vitality. No one mentioned it too deeply, so as not to curse it with scrutiny, but it was hard not to view it—through the lens of hope, and furthermore through the lens filter of Christmas—as the miracle for which he and Hat had been praying. Gil's energy spiked, he slept soundly through the night, he was lucid and engaging, and when a suntanned blonde in her fifties came into the store he flirted with her so relentlessly that she looked burnt, not tanned, as she backed her way giggling out the door, reddened by the exuberance of this stick figure's attraction.

Hat tried broaching the miracle prospects with Quỳnh ("Do you think, I mean, could it be . . . ?") but he swiftly shut her down. "My brain can't take thinking about it," he gently snapped. "It's too much, too much." But she knew he was thinking about it, same as she was; he was just too superstitious to admit it. For those four days, as she watched Gil laugh and eat and pray and appear to revert, if only flickeringly, to the Gil who'd come parachuting into their lives back in August—for those four days, all her doubts about Cameron that Euclide Abbascia's questions had fertilized were subsumed by her hopes for Gil, by what she recognized as pure faith. If his turnaround was real, if Gil's cancer was retreating, if by some beautiful sacred power Gil was being cured, then it meant that same power was what'd lifted Cameron to his feet, too. And what *that* meant (she tried and failed not to think) was that the Biz-E-Bee, like Lourdes, was the recipient of God's grace, not merely the site of healings but their cause. Seeing Little Kim nestled in Gil's toothpick arms on the couch, Hat was struck dizzy by the notion of a link between him and Cameron and Little Kim's against-all-odds recovery as an infant in the NICU, her breath stolen straight out of her lungs.

And then it toggled off, just as suddenly as it'd begun. Gil didn't rise at his new-normal hour on December 29, and five hours later still hadn't. When Hat went in to check on him, she found him on his side, his body pearled with furious beads of sweat, his breathing slow and gurgly, bile yellowing his eyes. He didn't recognize Hat, mistaking her for his mother. He just couldn't milk the cows, he told her, felt too sick to do it. Hat got a thermometer into him: 103.8 degrees. With that she drove Gil to the Gulf Coast Veterans hospital, which was where she'd been intermittently camping out—sometimes swapping shifts with Quỳnh, Little Kim sometimes alongside her—ever since.

But no one was doing anything for Gil, so far as Hat could tell. The doctors and nurses, all the interchangeable white coats, seemed to be doing less than she'd been doing—her, just a shopkeeper who'd accidentally adopted a scuffed-up old man from Alabama who'd shown up at her store carrying an inflatable crucifix. With leaky eyes she said it again to Janice: "I don't know why they're letting him die."

"Let me walk over with you," Janice offered, the sight of the congealing soup having quashed her appetite anyway. "Maybe I can find something out for you."

Entering Gil's room, in the acute inpatient ward three floors above her own office, Janice could see, without need to scan his chart, that Gil was dying. The skin of his arms was mottled and bluish, indicating decreased blood perfusion. His sleeping breathing was alternating rapid breaths with none at all, a pattern known medically as Cheyne-Stokes breathing and a reliable sign of a heart shutting down. Still, she conferred with the nurse on duty. Gil had an infection his body wasn't fighting, the nurse told her. T-cell and neutrophil counts were bottoming out. They were administering antibiotics and a blood-growth stimulant, but at this point, with system failure setting in, palliative care was really the only course remaining. Janice and the nurse glanced down the hallway to where Hat stood watching them with her hands bunched at her middle. "She has medical POA if you want to talk to her," the nurse said. "He might surprise us, but I think it's a matter of hours."

Janice gently pulled Hat into the room, the heart monitor dripping a too-slow cadence of beeps. "No one's letting him die, Mrs. Lê," she told her. "There just isn't anything left to do to stop it."

"That's not true," Hat whispered, scrunching her face as if to prevent her from inhaling Janice's words. "They just need to give him a little more time. They can do that."

This didn't strike Janice as an abstract appeal for time, that indefinite extension for which family members commonly pleaded; Janice was sensing a featheredge of specificity again. "More time for what?"

"For the *miracle*," Hat blurted, and seeing Janice's face harden, if only slightly, she sped her voice into a wet rush: "He almost had it. Last week, we *saw* it. If they'll just look at the cancer, they'll see it too. It was happening. I swear it was. You've seen this happen, you know. This is just, what he's got—it's a cold, that's what they told me, he can't die from a cold. If they'd just look at the cancer . . ."

She stumbled forward in what Janice first thought was a faint, Janice throwing out her arms to catch her. Then to her surprise Janice found herself holding this small woman who was weeping into her shoulder. "It's okay," Janice whispered. "It's okay."

Hat threw her head back, her eyes slick and smeary. "I don't even *know* him," she said, swatting in the direction of the bed. "He came to the store after what happened to Cameron. My husband was right, it was crazy to let him stay." She wiped her nose and cheeks with the side of her hand, looking astounded by the wetness there. "Why am I crying? I never cry. Why am I crying?"

"Because you're losing someone," Janice said. It was all she could think to say, though something told her, rightly, that there was more to it than that. Or not rightly, in a sense: because Hat, in that instant, realized that she was losing someone—only it wasn't Gil. It was God.

This realization came more as a physical sensation than a thought, something bursting inside her and leaving in its place a dark and vacant hollow. It wasn't rational, even by the standards of faith, and in some sense it was profoundly and grotesquely irrational. Witnessing a miracle—and despite her doubts that was still what she believed she'd seen—should've buttressed her faith, she thought, should've stiffened it beyond measure, and yet in some paradoxical way it'd provoked instead a crisis in faith, conferring upon her less an affirmation than a test: the photo-negative of biblical trials in which calamity wobbles faith but wondrous signs cement it. God granting Cameron his legs while bequeathing nothing to Gil: It wasn't that Hat deemed Gil more deserving than Cameron, despite what she'd said earlier to Janice. That'd just been her voicing her frustration at the terrible asymmetry—Cameron smacking a guy in a bar as Gil lay gasping. No, it was the randomness of it, the unaccountable unfairness of it all, and with this in mind she flashed back to when she was an eight-year-old girl on that creaking wooden boat out in the Gulf of Thailand, her head burrowed into the lap of the elderly nun counting off her Hail Marys with the same slow meter of Gil's heart monitor. It had never crossed her mind that there were other girls, clutching other nuns in the exact same way, who hadn't survived that same voyage, who'd been raped and thrown overboard by pirates, and that perhaps the nun's placid certitude, so long inspiring, was in fact a kind of indifference: Everything is okay, until it isn't. A baleful shudder ran through her, eliciting more pats on her back from Janice.

Like an audience to this realization, in her mind's eye, came the faces of all the people who'd cavalcaded the Biz-E-Bee these past four months, seeking healing inside that eight-by-twelve-foot orange rectangle painted on the asphalt. What had she and Quỳnh been providing them—selling them, really? No one had spent more time inside that rectangle than Gil, long faith-cooled hours in the sun, and look at him now. Whatever'd happened to Cameron, divinely wrought or otherwise, had nothing to do with the store, she decided, had nothing whatsoever to do with that postage stamp of crumbly asphalt. She'd get Ollie to scrub the paint from the parking lot tomorrow, she thought. She didn't care what Quỳnh would say. It wasn't right to encourage people to stand there. It wasn't.

She looked up blinking at Janice as though emerging from a dream. Janice asked if she was okay, and Hat shivered her head yes, embarrassed to have wept on this stranger, apologizing for the damp splotches on her white coat as she pulled herself away seeking tissues.

"Let's just sit a spell," Janice said, leading Hat to a chair beside Gil's bed.

Furtively, she checked the time. Nap had gone and spilled their pregnancy news to his parents, despite Janice's admonition not to do so at this early stage, and they'd be arriving for dinner shortly. But Janice wasn't late yet. Plus her father-in-law, much like her own father, never begrudged an elongated cocktail hour.

Janice asked about Gil's family: Yes, Hat told her, she'd gotten in touch with them. An ex-wife and a daughter were coming from Birmingham that night, albeit reluctantly. Gil hadn't been the best husband and father, back in his drinking days—Gil himself admitted that, and the ex-wife's and daughter's tones had seemed to confirm it. Janice wasn't naïve, she knew how humanity operated, but something about that estrangement struck her as unimaginable—the baby inside her was almost nothing, manifest only as a morning's vomit and a plus sign on a plastic test stick, and yet, just two days in, she felt overcome by maternal resolve, by a sterling willingness to sacrifice anything and everything for that faint glimmer of an embryo. The centrality and importance of her own life had already begun to fade, its energy transferring to the presence in her womb.

Hearing someone else articulate this, she would've blithely chalked it up to hormones; yet this felt anything but chemical.

Eventually, as Gil beside them wheezed then stopped, each cycle alarming Hat anew, their conversation narrowed to the person connecting them. "Earlier, when we were in the canteen," Janice reminded her. "You said Cameron wasn't answering. Have you been in touch with him since what happened yesterday morning?"

"Oh, Gil wanted to see him," she said offhandedly.

"Gil did? Why's that?"

"He wanted to tell him about some movie." Hat wasn't familiar with the film, but, from the loose and secondhand description Hat gave her, Janice was: Gil was talking about *Saving Private Ryan*, a World War Two drama from the late 1990s. "I didn't really understand," Hat told her. "There was something someone says in that movie that Gil wanted to say to Cameron." Janice leaned forward in her chair, dropping her head between her shoulders, knowing exactly the line Gil wanted to quote to Cameron. The army captain played by Tom Hanks said it, as he lay blood-soaked and dying, to Matt Damon's character, for whom he'd given his own life and those of four of his men to rescue. Janice saw the scene playing in her head. He'd grabbed him by the collar, pulled him weakly to him: *Earn this,* is what he'd said. *Earn it.*

THE TWILIT GULF lay like a vast and luminous purple bruise to her right as Janice drove home along the beach on U.S. 90, until she passed her exit for the Back Bay Bridge and was no longer headed home. The landscapes of her life, it occurred to her, had always been flat—first as a child in the Mississippi Delta, with level fields of cotton stretching in every direction, and then as a woman and physician and now a freshly minted mother-to-be on the Coast, with that blue plane of salt water her southward vista. Nothing had ever impeded her horizons or, for that matter, drawn her toward them; they'd never been anything other than crisp lines. This realization struck her as both meaningful and meaningless at the same time, if anything proof that she wasn't thinking clearly.

She turned left on Caillavet Street and dialed Nap. "Wait," he said, "you're doing *what*?" She needed to see Cameron, she told him, stringing

on a second apology. His voice went blank, he didn't understand at all;
in his mind, the two of them had already indicted Cameron as a fraud,
the morning's *Sun Herald* article having validated not their suspicions
but rather their inklings about an unsavory aspect to Cameron's story, its
more-than-meets-the-eye quality. And what about dinner with his parents? The five of them needed to celebrate. Janice did some quick math
to realize he was counting her as two, setting a sweet but very premature
place setting for the tiny packet of Cuevas cells occupying her belly. She
turned onto Division Street. "Cameron might not want to talk to me,"
she told Nap, who, bewilderment and disappointment aside, was still too
buoyed by the pregnancy news to catch what she knew was in her voice:
the tautness of a steel bridge cable. Nap could be dippy at times, a quality
she mostly adored; he was going to make a terrific father. "He might not
even be home," she said. "And in that case I won't hardly be late at all. Just
tell your parents I had an emergency call, leave it open. I'll text you."

She hadn't identified the emotion tugging her toward Reconfort Avenue as anger until she was parked in front of the Harris house and turned
off her car, realizing the vibrations she still felt weren't from the engine
but from her own body. She gripped the steering wheel for calm, as if to
absorb some of its mechanical logic. For one thing, she reminded herself, the hospital's information technology administrator had the week
before detonated a large hole in her theory: The VA's VistA system, he
told her, was essentially hack-proof. It logged every access and recorded
every change to a patient's file, and while maybe some teenage savant in
Ukraine could figure out how to subvert that logging, it was way beyond
the capacity, he said, with a light sneer, of "any federal employee." Cameron's file, then, was Cameron's file; what it showed was what was there.

Yet her theory remained standing, emotion and intuition and maybe
a smidgen of denial propping it up in the places where its foundation
blocks were missing, with a surge of indignation currently jacking it up
even higher in Janice's mind. If her suspicions were right, and Cameron's
recovery was indeed a hoax, his list of victims now extended beyond her
and the United States government; Gil Poleman was on that list, and also
Hat, whose tears had probably yet to dry on Janice's lab coat back at the
hospital. Whether he'd intended to or not didn't matter: Cameron had
supplied them with false hopes about their own existences, he'd stolen

reality from them. He'd let Gil Poleman go to his death feeling excluded from painfully proximal glory, feeling forsaken upon his own inflatable cross. This wasn't abstract anymore, a crime against bureaucracy; this was sowing hurt.

The lights were on in the house, Cameron and Tanya's twin pair of showroom-glinting new cars out front. Janice steamed up the walkway and rang the bell.

Tanya answered. The squint she gave Janice was bedraggled and confused, as if she didn't recognize her at all—and maybe she didn't, Janice allowed, outside of her lab-coated medical context. Janice identified herself. The pallid shade of Tanya's skin and the nauseated look on her face gave her the appearance of someone who'd been binging on bleach-and-soda highballs. She was partly blocking the doorway. "Can I see your brother?" Janice asked, adding, when Tanya failed to respond, "It's about his medications," not quite a fib.

Tanya's eyes popped a bit, as though Janice had just slipped her a crucial clue to something, and she eased backward to let her in.

Janice's anger went draining out of her the moment she saw Cameron. He was propped shirtless on the couch, sitting upright but curled into something close to the fetal position against the armrest, his wrapped right hand over his head as though to hold his skull together or shield it from invisible blows. When he lowered the hand and revealed his face to Janice, she felt a long shudder run through her. Here was the same broken-looking boy she'd first encountered on an exam table three years ago, his eyes hazed now as then with incomprehension and dread, that giant tattoo of the angel-winged infantryman beside the prayer to the archangel Michael still somehow out of place on his lissome torso, a mistaken branding.

"Let me see that hand," was the first thing she said to him. The hand was wrapped too tightly; she could see puffed flesh where the wrapping ended at his wrist. Unspooling it she found the outside of his hand swollen and the same shade of purple as the Gulf had appeared on her drive over. "Move your fingers for me," she commanded, Cameron gingerly forming a claw. "Have you been icing it?" she asked, Cameron nodding.

"Tanya, will you get us some more ice?" she said. "And do you know if you have any cortisone cream or some other anti-inflammatory cream?"

Tanya asked, "Did I wrap it too tight?"

"No, honey, just a little too snugly. You don't want to cut off the circulation."

Tanya returned with a bag of frozen butter beans, which Janice applied to Cameron's hand. "We don't got any creams," Tanya said. "Reckon they sell it at the Biz-E-Bee? I can run over."

Janice locked eyes with Cameron. "I'm thinking you're probably going to need to make a pharmacy run." To Cameron she said, "You ready to think about restarting your meds?"

Tanya emitted a low hiccup of shock. "Restarting?"

Cameron sat blinking at Janice, lifting an unlit cigarette to his lips.

"You can tell her," she said to him.

He lit the cigarette, twin funnels of gray smoke exiting his nose. "I went off my meds."

"When?"

"Couple months ago."

"The hell for?"

Cameron threw up his hand as if to shoo a horsefly. "Because I didn't think I needed them no more," he said. "Because, I mean, look at me." It was an abysmally wrong time to solicit an assessment, which Cameron seemed to grasp even as the words left his mouth. He'd just disproven his own point. The shoo-fly defensiveness disappeared from his tone as he said, quietly, "It just seemed like if my legs was working then my brain was working too. I dunno. I just didn't think I needed them no more."

"Well you're a stone dumbass," came Tanya's judgment. "And you didn't think to *tell* me that? The way you been acting, now this thing with Landry . . ." Her voice trailed off as pieces went clicking together in her head.

"I think he knows it was a mistake," Janice said, looking to Cameron for confirmation. He dipped his head yes, squinting as he exhaled a stream of smoke. "Look," she said to him, "I don't know what happened with this fight and whether you staying on the medications would've helped it not happen. What I do know is that they help keep you together up there, that they help prevent stress and anxiety from letting you come unglued. Is that what happened?"

"Yeah." He combined a nod with a shrug. "I just lost my shit."

Janice excused herself to get a prescription pad from her car. When she returned the air in the room felt sheared, as though sharp words had just been hurled. She started scribbling out prescriptions, Cameron helping to remind her of his old jilted regimen. She added some Valium, too, to help him over this hump. "You tired of talking about it yet?" she said about the fight.

"A little," he said, his expression suggesting a lot. He stabbed out his cigarette then picked at the bag of butter beans chilling his hand. "I had to turn myself in to the police this morning. Got fingerprinted and all that. Tanya was so messed up about it, had to get Father Ace to come post bond."

Tanya muttered, cryptically, "I ain't messed up about *that.*"

"Is he put out with you?" Janice asked, passing the sheaf of prescriptions to Tanya.

"Not really, no. He told me this story about having to knock the sand out of some dude in his village back in Africa, this big guy who'd drink cooking fuel and go crazy picking on folks. Them priests over there, I guess they gotta act like cops sometimes."

"Is that what you did, knock the sand out of someone trying to pick a fight with you?"

"Something like that," Cameron said distantly.

"It was just some jackass from high school," Tanya interjected, "saying Cameron didn't earn his medals or something . . ."

Cameron flinched, and Janice watched his face and body go tense; she could actually see it in his bared abdominal muscles, the way they contracted into a rutted grid. He shook his head, and without looking at his sister said to her, "We ain't gonna do that, Tan. I told you that."

Janice felt the energy in the room gathering or curdling into something thick, an unseeable partition jelling between Tanya and Cameron. He fished a cigarette from his pack. Tanya was standing by the front door with an ashen, seasick look on her face. "But . . . ," she said, without finishing.

"What I'm supposed to do?" he asked her. "Just hole up? Until what, huh? Hide? From who? From me?"

"I just don't want people hurting you, baby," Tanya said, stepping forward then back.

"Am I really gonna get hurt worse," he said, "than I've already hurt?"

Janice's head was swiveling blankly between them.

"It's different," Tanya begged. "It ain't the same, Cam."

Cameron closed his eyes, summoning or evicting something from what looked to be deep within. He lit the cigarette, letting the smoke curl from between his lips. "This ain't your story either, Tan," he said, Janice unable to follow. "It's mine. It's mine now."

Tanya looked steamrolled, the color of her face alternating from red to green, like dying Christmas bulbs, and her body swaying or rather heaving side to side. Janice instinctively searched the room for a pot or a planter she could grab if Tanya began to vomit. Having arrived here directly from a deathbed, Janice's gut was telling her she was witnessing another kind of death, though she couldn't say precisely who or what was dying. Some kind of cord, maybe, that'd connected brother and sister for nearly a quarter century, severing right before her eyes.

"I been protecting you since the day you's born," Tanya told Cameron, brandishing the stack of prescriptions in her hand as convenient proof, shaking them at him. Her eyes were spearing him. "Everything I ever done been to protect you. To take care of you. Who you think changed your diapers when Mama couldn't lift her ass off the floor? Who you think put food on the table after Mama died? Who's the one stayed up till two in the morning writing your term papers? Who's the one stayed in San Antonio when you come back nothing but bandages, the one carried you in and outta bed when you couldn't do it yourself, cleaned the pressure wounds on your ass, cried when you was crying, who's the one gave up every fucking thing but *you* for four years? Four fucking *years*, Cam. You wanna look at something? You wanna look at something? *Look at me*." She punched herself in the chest three times, each punch expelling a sob. "*Look at me*," she repeated weakly.

Tanya dropped her gaze and let out a high-pitched moan, as though horrified by the emotions she'd spilled onto the floor. Cameron's mouth remained fixed in a tight straight line—yet another flat horizon—while his derelict cigarette was burning itself out in the ashtray. Janice's thoughts swirled as an incoming text message pinged her cellphone—Nap, almost certainly.

The sound jolted her, a psychic alarm clock reminding her why she was here.

"Is there something I should know?" she asked Cameron, registering the absurdity of the question as she asked it. The last three minutes, to her, might as well have been conducted in Latin.

Cameron stared flatly at Janice, barely breathing.

"About your recovery?" she pressed.

A rubbery scowl flashed onto Cameron's face, his bottom lip flopping down. "My recovery?"

Firmly, trying to look wise to him, she nodded.

"My recovery?" he echoed once more, trying to hammer the phrase into something coherent. His confusion looked thorough. "Nothing I ain't told you about that."

"You're telling me," Janice said, the pitching and rising and faltering of her voice reflecting the unruly muddle of her thinking, "that the way it happened, it was just like you said?"

"Yes ma'am," he said, and when he leaned toward her the whole room seemed to shift with him, exerting all its weight upon Janice. "Where you coming from?"

"Where I'm coming from," she said, her words feeling disconnected, like she was reading from a script that her brain's higher powers had already discarded, "is a medical opinion that says the only explanation for your recovery is that you couldn't have been paralyzed the morning of August twenty-third, before you stood out of your chair."

"What?" Tanya squealed, taking a menacing step forward. Janice was suddenly seized by a very real and physical fear, apprehending, in that instant, that her indignation over Hat's grief had completely warped her judgment. She should never have come here to confront Cameron (she'd neglected to even consider Tanya)—not alone, and not when Cameron was already tottering in the aftermath of violence, after he'd just proved his potential for coming unhinged. She should've left this to the Vatican investigator, or, as Nap suggested, taken her suspicions to the U.S. attorney's office. She was pregnant, she remembered, not as a fact but as a vulnerability spiking her fear. She was pregnant.

And she was also—if what everything Cameron's wet eyes were telling her was true—wrong. "You're—you're my *doctor,*" he said feebly, his voice reeled back twenty years to that of a small boy facing broken trust for the very first time, not knowing how to withstand it. Janice looked away; she couldn't bear the way he was searching her face.

"I am your doctor, Cameron, I am," she said, struggling to engineer some way out of this place she'd cornered herself in, feeling Tanya moving heavily behind her, then deciding without really deciding just to lay it all out there, to confess, as Cameron had asked, where she was coming from. "And that's why I've spent these last four months ramming my head into every brick wall I've been able to find, trying to help you and—and me, yes, me too—understand why you're walking, and the only thing that's made any sense to me at all, the only thing I found I could actually explain, was something happening up there"—pointing up to his head, then dragging her finger down to his legs—"and not there."

A long silence gripped the room as a weird reversal set in. Janice seemed the wounded one—voice fraying, eyes imploring—while Cameron regarded her with the tender sturdiness of a country doctor. "I can't tell if you're saying I'm a liar or I'm crazy." His face twitched with something approaching a smile. "But I know I ain't one. And I don't think I'm the other."

"It was real," Janice said, as barely a question.

Cameron bobbed his head, staring her square in the eyes. "I don't know what it was. But it was real."

"Then—then what was all that?" she pleaded. "You and Tanya—what was that?"

"That . . ." He glanced at Tanya. "That ain't about here or here," he said to Janice, touching his head then his legs. He tapped his chest. "That's about here."

"I gotta get out," Tanya suddenly groaned. "I'm going . . ." Her gaze swung around the room until she noticed the prescriptions in her hand: "I'm—I'm going to the drugstore."

The solidity Janice had seen in Cameron was only growing denser and harder. Something had happened to him since she'd arrived, whether because of her or in spite of her Janice didn't know. She watched him pin his sister with a stare.

"No, Tan," he said. "Stay. You ain't heard but a little of it. You only heard the part about Landry. There's something more."

Tanya stood fastened to the doorway. "I can't," came out of her—not even a whisper, just a breath. Her hand found the doorknob, cranked it sideways.

"You can," her brother said softly. "Please."

She left.

To the drugstore, first, then to anywhere else but home.

CAMERON SANK HIS head into his hands. And then, after fetching himself a Bud Light, he told his doctor a story—a long story, his, beginning in Biloxi, Mississippi, in the 1990s and ending with a white flash then soundless blackness on a ridge in Zabul Province, Afghanistan, its latter part the flip side of the same story that, two weeks earlier, Damarkus Lockwood had told Euclide Abbascia inside that mobile home in the backwoods of White County, Georgia.

before, pt. 4

if a man would give all the substance of his house for love

it would utterly be condemned

eighteen

FAMILY MILITARY TRADITION PLAYED NO ROLE IN CAMERON Harris's enlistment in the Army in April 2009. Snead Harris never served, and while the Navy drafted Randall "Poke" Harris, Cameron's grandfather, in 1952, going AWOL three times yielded him what was then called an "undesirable discharge." Beyond this, the ancestral trail goes cold until we come to Rufus Little Harris, who seeded the Harris family in Stone County, Mississippi, after deserting the 15th Confederate Cavalry Regiment during a skirmish in Louisiana—a dubious antecedent. Patriotic zeal factored only lightly: Cameron was thirteen years old on September 11, 2001, old enough to feel horror and a jumbled kind of fury, but young enough that, by the time he turned twenty, the events of that day felt distant and dry and bore only the most oblique of connections to the war in Iraq, the fight Cameron was expecting to join. To his sister and his friends, and sometimes to himself, Cameron parroted his recruiter's reasons for enlisting—job skills training, seeing what the world looks like outside of Mississippi, getting his body back in shape after three years without football. His true reason for enlisting, however, didn't crystallize in his mind until the first time he stood alone in front of a full-length mirror dressed in his combat uniform. He found himself smiling at his reflection, suffused with a profound but secret peace. He was indistinguishable from everyone else, identical down to his fingernail length to every other soldier in his basic training unit. Not one thing set him apart. He was finally, and ecstatically, *normal*.

Cameron can't pinpoint when normality became something elusive to him. The earliest difference from other children that he can recall involves his father, or his lack thereof. Many of his classmates had divorced parents, some seeing their fathers only on weekends, and a couple fathers were dead, but Cameron was the only one, so far as he could tell, whose father's absence was willful—the only child whose father explicitly didn't want him. Yet his mother and especially his big sister served to counterbalance that in his mind. When other kids bitched about their older siblings Cameron rarely had anything to add, less a difference in his mind than an advantage. Still, he disliked standing out. His report cards might've been different, he thinks, had that been otherwise: C-grade work was what he shot for, because C equaled average and therefore drew no attention. Scoring A's could get you lauded, horrifically, in front of the whole class; D's and F's got you miserable conferences with school counselors; but C's, almost magically, got you nothing.

Befriending Bucky Petz in the third grade triggered a seismic shift. Bucky—asthmatic and Jewish and chubby and black-haired, Cameron's opposite in almost every regard—introduced Cameron to the board game HeroQuest and to obscure movies and most notably to theater. Cameron's interest in the latter came as a smack of a surprise to his sister and mother. He recalls his mother, as she was nervously writing out the check for his after-school drama classes, warning him that he "couldn't act my normal way up there, couldn't be shy." But drawing attention onstage, he found, was different than in life. You weren't *you* up onstage, you were a character, and nothing you said or did revealed or betrayed anything inside of you—or at least that's how it felt to him. Your character could be peculiar, foolish, a brute or a sissy, fiercely loved or bleakly unloved, yet beneath the mask you were wearing—be it actual or invisible—you remained you: as ordinary as you wished to be, operating your stage-self as if by remote control. Bucky Petz was Cameron's conduit to this sorcery, and their attendant friendship was in many ways idyllic. When not filming movies about sand monsters and Civil War spies, they fished for croaker and teased girls and planted items on the railroad tracks for the trains to flatten. They watched *Dukes of Hazzard* reruns on TV, Cameron conscious only in retrospect that Bucky would lean closer when Daisy Duke appeared onscreen while he'd lean closer for Bo and Luke. Aside from what Cameron felt for his mother and Tanya and the memory of his dog, Lucky, his friendship with Bucky was the closest thing to love he'd known.

That Bucky's move to Florida coincided so precisely with Cameron entering puberty seems like a cruel twist of fate in a short life over-riddled with such twists, its arc shaped like a spring. Almost overnight, it seemed, Cameron found himself not just alone but equipped with a deep new voice—and deeper new feelings—that he didn't recognize. Many if not most people look back upon middle school with cringing, but Cameron's climb was particularly steep. "Are there any girls at school you like?" he recalls his mother asking, striving to be casual and cool, when he was in eighth grade. He told her no, that he didn't really like girls in that way. Cameron intuitively understood the reason she greeted his answer with such festive relief—despite his tufted armpits and baritone voice, his lack of attraction to girls meant he was still her little boy, her miracle baby, that he'd yet to be stricken with the goatish desires of men. He allowed her to think this, of course, all the while knowing how much more complicated his answer was. The reason girls didn't attract him was because boys did.

Cameron grumbled and pouted about his mother thrusting him into football the following summer—until discovering it provided him an ideal distraction. Soon he was throwing all his energy into it, exhausting his body so thoroughly as to deprive it of the scant vigor required for sexual urges. More importantly, he says, football furnished him an identity. You couldn't be a faggot *and* a football standout; that'd never happened, not in Mississippi or anywhere else. And game by game, catch by catch, Cameron Harris was quickly becoming not just a standout but a junior varsity star.

Something about playing football, he says, was akin to acting onstage: Out on the field, suited up in his helmet and pads and red-and-white uniform, he felt detached from the person inside—as though transformed into the uniform itself, an avatar speaking in a language of passes caught and yardage gained, his every line scripted in a whiteboard pattern of x's and o's. His on-field successes allowed him to project a resemblant character off the field, but still, he says, he was obsessively cautious. Some teachers, coaches, and especially fellow students thought him slow-witted because of his sluggardly delivery and his ceaselessly furrowed brow. But his wits were fine—he just dripped them through a thick, heavy filter. "I've heard Tanya say I don't got any gut instincts, that the way I decide everything is like a cow chewing cud," he says. "But that ain't really it. I always had a gut, everyone does, but mine couldn't be trusted. Whatever my gut was telling me had to be checked. Most of the time it had to be resisted. Everything below the neck was always conflicting with what's above."

Cameron knew he was attracted to boys and not girls but also felt certain he wasn't gay. This might strike some as an absurdly semantic distinction, but for a fifteen-year-old football player in south Mississippi it felt neither semantic nor absurd—it felt like the difference between life and death. He knew he wasn't gay because he didn't act anything like the gay men he listened to his teammates imitate or saw on television—not the urbane and compulsively dowdy Will on the sitcom *Will & Grace,* certainly not Will's swishy friend Jack. He hated dancing and was bad at it anyway. He liked sappy country ballads, yeah—George Jones could make him cry almost on command—but club-pop and most show tunes left him cold. He was *tough*—and that toughness felt essential to him, not as a cover but as an intrinsic and defining aspect of who and what he was. "It was almost like certain black dudes I knew growing up," he says, "who'd look at these other black dudes, you know, the ones with their shorts dragging low, riding around in their hoopties, all that gangsta shit, and be like: Man, I'm black, but I sure ain't *that*. But that's kinda how it is when you're fifteen, sixteen—you don't know what you are so you start drawing these crazy lines everywhere, you know, saying I'm *this* but I ain't *that*. So, for me, liking guys instead of girls, that was one thing. That was this below-the-neck thing I could maybe tune out if I tried hard enough. But being gay? Man. I mean, just listen to how that sounds: being gay. Being. That was going all-in. That was . . ." Cameron shivers his head. "That just wasn't anything like an option."

To Cameron's knowledge there were no openly gay students at Biloxi High School while he was there (other students say there was a quietly out lesbian), but, as with any high school past or present, there were plenty of students suspected of being gay. Some of these fell into the obvious-suspects lineup, their supposed orientations deduced via the age-old tea leaves of stereotype: the more debonair boys in drama club, the square-shouldered members of the girls' sports teams. Others fell into a murkier zone: boys whose masculinity measure failed to meet some other boy's or boys' standard. One of these was a new student, one of the so-called military brats who pass in and out of Biloxi's schools because of Keesler

Air Force Base. He was a member of the tennis team, Cameron recalls, and an occasional but peripheral presence at the beach parties the school's athletes held at the Biloxi piers, seen usually in the company of girls.

Three members of the varsity football squad, a senior and two juniors, took Cameron aside at one such party during the spring of Cameron's freshman year. They liked his skills, they said. Coach Necaise was talking him up for varsity. Mumbling thanks, Cameron felt his chest swelling into something like a pigeon's plenteous breast, his feathers fluffing.

But he wasn't playing varsity yet, they told him—not without passing his initiation first. With a gulp, Cameron asked what that was. "You got to smear a queer, for real," one said, the others nodding gravely. Cameron stood blinking at them, not understanding what they meant—"smear the queer" was a playground game from elementary and middle school; he remembers a PE teacher saying the game's name wasn't nice, jokingly telling the kids to rename it "Tackle the Alternative Lifestyle"—but also feeling terrified by this huddled mention of queerness.

"You see that fag right over there?" They were pointing to the tennis player. "Just walk up to him, tell him he's a faggot, and take him out."

"Punch him?" Cameron asked, the three of them falling out laughing. Yeah, they told him. Drop that mother.

He wonders, in aching retrospect, whether their suspicions were really about him—whether this ostensible initiation might've been a version of that classic movie scene in which a suspected spy is ordered to kill an enemy prisoner in order to prove his fealty. The situation felt, to Cameron, just as fraught as that scene. To say no to them meant more than scuttling or risking his chances to make the varsity squad; it meant outing himself, on some level—sympathy for a fag equal to being one, in Cameron's read of their eyes. "The solution seems so simple," he says now. "You just say, dudes, I'm not *hitting* that guy. I don't even know him." But that escape didn't even occur to him then, blotted out by fear. So much—the identity he'd constructed, his football future, his quivering sense of manhood—felt precariously balanced upon obeying this order. He looked over at the tennis player, awash in a sea of girls, and went shuffling toward him through the sand.

He couldn't bring himself to do it out in the open, the way they'd instructed him. "Hey man," he muttered to the boy, "wanna talk to you about something," leading him down to the surf's edge, a dark distance away from the party. He told himself this was to spare the boy humiliation, but it was also, he admits, to protect himself from shame and scorn. He was too afraid to glance back but felt sure the three players were following, positioned a little way up the beach; he sensed their eyes zapping his back like cattle prods.

It occurred to him to quickly explain his dilemma to the boy and ask him to take a stage fall, but then why would the boy grant him that bizarre favor—and what would stop him from telling people about it? And how could Cameron divulge to the boy that a committee of upperclassmen had branded him a fag? That seemed a more lasting cruelty, an injection of slow-acting poison. They were standing alone at the lapping edge of the water, a frothy black tide coming in, a sliver of moon casting just the faintest blue glow on the boy's quizzical and expectant face. The boy was hiding his braces behind plummy lips, a timid curiosity peeping out of his dark eyes—and he was beautiful, Cameron saw, more beautiful even than that thin white hook of a moon. Footage from an alternative universe flashed onto the screen of his mind, Cameron seeing himself leaning in for a kiss, draping a hand on the tennis player's shoulder, the shorter boy hoisting himself up on his toes in the foamy tide to meet Cameron's lips with his own . . .

But this was not the universe Cameron inhabited. He didn't know if it ever would or could be, nor did he know if he truly wanted it to be. He bunched his hand into a fist and drove it into the boy's stomach—not nearly as hard as he could have, but hard enough for the boy's breath to fly from his mouth and for his body to jackknife and for him to collapse to his knees in the shallow surf. Cameron tried not to look at the boy, glancing up the beach to make sure the varsity players had just witnessed it, frustratingly unable to make them out in the gloom of the distant crowd, but Cameron did catch one searing glimpse: the boy clutching his belly and staring up at him with a shapelessly stricken look, less pained than disillusioned. "Just stay down for a while," Cameron whispered sharply, adding, as he turned to walk away, "I'm really sorry."

Whether the varsity players actually saw him do it was never clear. They acted pleased and surprised that Cameron went through with it, shepherding him to the more central, upperclassman zone of the party and forcing an acclamatory shot of Everclear on him. Cameron never saw if the boy returned to the party, and for the next two years, until the boy's family decamped to another base town somewhere, Cameron couldn't bring himself to meet the boy's eyes when passing him in the hallway or while in the two classes he ended up sharing with him. Mostly from shame, but also from fear: Packed into Cameron's fist, and transmitted in that brute snap of contact, had been Cameron's deepest secret. It didn't matter if the boy couldn't decode it. He possessed it now, and that possession gave him immense, even immeasurable power over Cameron. With a single dark-eyed stare he could've broken Cameron in two.

Cameron tried one other thing, that following autumn, to fend off his heart's and body's cravings: He let a senior cheerleader take his virginity. Little besides terror flowed through him the entire time. He felt sure that something he did or didn't do would give him away, that at some point the cheerleader would suddenly freeze the action and with a look of scowling appraisal say to him, "Wait, are you gay?" To maintain his pelvic focus he concentrated on the parts of her that were least female, bestowing inordinately rapt attention upon her shoulders and clavicle bones. When it was over he felt not just emptied but empty, as though, like Sisyphus in the myth he'd been studying in school, he'd just pushed a boulder uphill only to watch it roll back down. His unease was palpable enough that the cheerleader, reputed to be wise in matters sexual, pressed a fingertip of concern against his cheek and asked if he was okay. "Yeah," he said, "I'm great," but realizing how untrue this was, and how clearly the cheerleader could see that, he devised a quick explanation (casting a flashlight beam of irony toward future events): "It's just, you know, us not being married and all . . . maybe I'm just a little wigged out about the whole religious thing." He can still hear her laugh today: so feline, so sugared, so tender, so generous, so unbearably scalding.

THE TEXT MESSAGES started coming in May of Cameron's sophomore year, the first one popping onto Cameron's phone a day after the football team's spring intra-squad game. It was just a nondescript feeler, Cameron says—*what's up,* or something of that nature.

He tapped a response: *Who's this?*

Cameron's phone was a Cingular clamshell handset his mother had bought him for his birthday two months before. A green glow pulsed slowly from the top screen when messages came in.

Christy, came the answer.

Christy who? How'd you get my number?

I saw you play yesterday. You're awesome.

Thanks.

Can I put something out there?

I guess?

A few minutes passed before the phone glowed green again: *I have a seriously massive crush on you.*

Cameron wasn't terribly interested, not at first, for reasons extending beyond his sexual confusion. This had the makings of a come-on from a certain variety of girl—derided by his teammates as jersey chasers or jock suckers—that didn't just cozy up to standout athletes but tried to collect them, as flesh-and-blood playing cards, some of them more spookily fluent with a player's stats than he himself was. Even for his straight teammates, these girls held limited appeal. As Cameron understood it, you hooked up with one of them after exhausting all other options and come Monday acted sheepish about it, as though explaining that every other movie was sold out to justify why you were spotted exiting a Jennifer Aniston rom-com. Still, Cameron didn't mind the compliments and gushing flattery, the random little flashbulbs of attention—enough to play along, anyway. As the texts continued, though, he began doubting his presumption of a jersey chaser. Christy was way too coy for that—wouldn't divulge her last name or where she lived or attended school, and said she couldn't talk to him on the phone, could only text, but wouldn't say why. Once she let slip an offhand reference to a boyfriend, adding a low-voltage current of something illicit to the exchange.

The texts came at all hours, usually in unpredictable bursts. Most of them, Cameron says, amounted to mundane chitchat. *I'm bored,* Christy would often begin. *What are you doing?* Gradually, though, a picture began emerging: Christy's parents were divorced, and she hated shuttling between her mom's house and her dad's; she loved the show *Grey's Anatomy* but was put out with the book *Wuthering Heights,* which she was reading for school; she had an older brother in college at the University of Alabama, which was where she thought Cameron should play football (*as if,* he texted back); and the love of her life was a little dog named Maybelle whose greetings to Cameron she sometimes playfully transcribed as yips and barks. Cameron told her he loved dogs but after losing Lucky his mom was afraid to get him another.

Music was a frequent topic. It turned out Christy dug a lot of the same classic country he did, the stuff Tanya sniffed at as "nursing-home country." Christy got him to confess that his all-time favorite artist, the one he'd go back to see perform live if he had access to a time machine, was Patsy Cline—something he'd deemed too effeminate to ever reveal to anyone else. Christy *adored* Patsy Cline. She also adored Broadway musicals, she wrote. He told her he didn't as much, but admitted he knew the lyrics to every song from *Fiddler on the Roof,* admitting further, when she pressed, his appearance in a youth production five years before. After breaking off the exchange for dinner, she came back later to ask if he liked "Matchmaker," one of the musical's frillier songs, sung by three sisters pining for their shtetl's matchmaker to find them husbands to love.

Not really my favorite, he wrote back.

I wish I could hear you sing it, Christy wrote. *I bet you sing it so beautifully.*

Late that night, alone in the house, Cameron found himself humming the song and then, after a while, absently stitching the lyrics onto the melody, and then, propelled by something fluid and ecstatic inside him that he was unable to keep bottled, singing and then flat-out belting the song with a felicity and effervescence he didn't know he possessed, a south Mississippi football player in his boxer briefs leaping onto the furniture and dancing through the rooms of the house clutching one of his mother's lighthouse quilts around his head like the babushkas the three girls in his production wore and begging, like them, for a match, for a catch, for the loneliness to somehow end.

As May turned to June, the throbbing green glow of his phone was triggering spurts of anticipatory delight; when the messenger was anyone besides Christy, such as his mom or one of his teammates, he'd frown glumly at the phone, curdling with disappointment. Christy's presence in his life as a phantom, as a kind of genie wholly contained inside that phone, made him loose and incautious with her—it wasn't anonymity, for sure, but felt almost as liberating. Occasionally he chided himself for letting his guard fall too low, pricked by abrupt fears—Christy could be the quarterback's girlfriend, Marissa, whose eye was rumored to be ever-wandering, which would explain her unwillingness to talk—or anyone else, for that matter, anyone whose text messages, if discovered and read by the wrong eyes, could doom him on several levels. Yet it was like he'd threaded some impossible needle, to crib a football saying: He had a sort-of girlfriend who wasn't technically a girl—she *was* a girl, yes, but the only thing tangible of hers was her words, and words were just words, neither male nor female, and appearing the way they did on his phone they were pitchless and sexless, unyoked even from the differing vocal folds of men and women, and therefore his to hear how he wanted to hear them. He didn't want to meet Christy, he didn't want to hear her voice. He wanted her to stay just the way she was: nebulous, ethereal, a romantic abstract, a perfect vessel of disembodied intimacy.

And then, Cameron remembers, came a stormy June night. He was out on the screened-in back porch that used to hang off the back end of the house prior to Hurricane Katrina, doing homework at a folding table and listening to the approaching mutters of thunder. Inside the house his mother was cleaning up after dinner, the faucet running, dishes clinking against silver, a slow soft-rock bass line slithering from the living room stereo. His mom's boyfriend, Jim Yarbrough, was over that night, shuffling cards with a cigarette clamped half-dashingly, half-goofily between his front teeth. He was wanting to teach Debbie some two-person Italian card game he knew but she was cheerily objecting, saying he was just going to win anyway so why teach her the rules? A close crack of lightning startled Cameron, and before he'd even recovered, a shock of rain drenched the house, not as drops or even sheets but as a kind of tremendous block of water that shivered the porch's roof struts and instantly swamped the gutters. Just then his phone buzzed, throwing up its emerald glow.

Are you there? It was Christy. *I have to tell you something.*

OK, he texted back.

I don't go to Biloxi H.S., she wrote.

He held the phone in his hand as the glow faded, sensing a disturbance about to come. But then she'd never actually claimed to go to Biloxi High—in fact he'd kind of pegged her for a Long Beach girl—so what did this matter? A quake of thunder shook the house, a shimmery pewter blur of rain and gutter runoff cloaking his view beyond the screens.

And my name's not Christy.

Not a big deal also, he thought. He'd half-suspected as much.

It's Chris.

He didn't so much stare at the phone as let the phone stare at him. The crackling air felt ionized by the thunderstorm but the storm had a stench to it, as if the neighborhood were being sloshed with recycled water sucked from a stagnant pool.

I'm a guy.

He covered the phone with his hand, throwing a sharp glance inside to where his mom sat with four fanned cards in one hand and a cigarette in her other, laughing at something Jim was telling her. A fresh glow of green seeped between Cameron's fingers.

Are you there?

I'm here, he wrote. Deleted it, tap tap tap, wrote it again.

Are you mad?

Was he mad? No, he was sweating. He was sweating so suddenly and profusely, and felt so much electrical force whirling through him, that in that moment the storm seemed centered inside him, instead of in the dank cloud-deck outside, with every length of gutter on Reconfort Avenue brimming because of him.

No it's cool, he wrote back, at the moment thinking more of Chris's predicament than of his own. Cameron's fingers were being piloted by compassion, at this point, and by admiration as well: What Chris was doing, he realized, was gutsier than anything he could even imagine himself doing. Bulging the cockpit door, however, were other, more selfish feelings, gathering quick and riotous might.

It's cool? Really? I can still have a crush on you?

Cameron's hand blanketed the screen again, a grin splashing onto his face. The closest thing he'd ever had to a girlfriend had turned out to be—

holy shit, a boyfriend. He laughed aloud, then brought the phone to his lips to hush himself. Nothing about what he wrote back felt reckless—just the opposite, in fact. He felt anesthetized by the safety and relief of voicing something true.

Only if I can have a crush on you back, he wrote, sealing it.

And then, like that, Chris disappeared.

Cameron waited.

Are you there? Cameron texted. He waited awhile longer. *Can we finally talk?*

The storm was passing now, drifting inland, towing a wet tumble of vapors in its wake, stray gusts of wind drawing the screens in and out like bellows.

Chris?

Cameron cursed himself, flinging his phone across his homework. He'd gone and scared him, he figured. Christy/Chris had always been the flirty one, Cameron having always been playing down in a lower key, and that burst of reciprocal affection—it must've just freaked him out, Cameron decided. He tried to envision what Chris was doing now—maybe recoiling from his phone like someone who's just fired a weapon he'd thought was unloaded, terrified by the unexpected bang, panickedly assessing the damage. They'd both just outed themselves, and if Chris was anything like Cameron, he probably hadn't ever done that before. Lost upon Cameron was the fact that the outing had not been mutual. Chris knew precisely who Cameron Harris was, but, to Cameron, Chris was just Chris—still just a phantom, the only other new detail added to his identity chromosomal. Cameron texted Chris one last time that night—*I'll be here, whenever*—and set his phone beside the pillow, hoping he'd be roused from sleep, hoping to wake to the sight of his bedroom walls bathed in pulses of dim green light.

Chris didn't text back until three nights later. It was late, past midnight. *Send me a picture,* Chris wrote.

You know what I look like, Cameron answered.

Please?

Chris, come on. What's going on?

That *Please?* was the last text message Cameron ever received from Chris. Cameron wrote back to him—*Are you there? What happened? I'm sorry if I did anything*—without ever hearing back. After one a.m. Cameron finally tried calling him to talk; the call went to a generic voicemail greeting, and Cameron didn't leave a message. He dozed into a daydreamy half-sleep with his phone cradled in his palm. At four a.m. he texted him once more: *If I call again will you answer?* He slept through his six-thirty alarm, missing his daily morning routine of jogging to the high school to run up and down the bleachers. When he finally wakened, his mom mussed his blond hair while pouring him a bowl of Wheaties and laughed that he looked like he'd seen a ghost.

Three days later, she was dead. During the forty-eight hours he spent holed up in his bedroom, when Tanya feared he might die from sobbing, he wrote to Chris one last time: *My mother was the one in that wreck on I-10. She died. I don't know what to do.* But Chris's silence was final. The phone stayed dim.

Cameron gave up after that. Nothing Chris could say or do or be was going to revive his crushed heart anyway. What he had to do now, before anything else, was learn how to survive without his mother. That meant learning how to cook, when Tanya was off at work. It meant learning how to operate the washer and dryer. It meant remembering to turn down the air-conditioning before he went to sleep every night and to water the lantana and the jessamine out front if they got dry. It meant learning how to walk past his mom's collection of porcelain dolphins and crabs and crawfish and seahorses without exploding into spasms of enraged wet grief and shaking the cabinet so violently that everything else she'd loved would be as shattered as he was. He was no longer anyone's boy, which meant he had to learn how to be a man, whatever in God's name that was.

UNTIL HIS MOTHER'S death, Cameron had mostly shied away from alcohol. For one thing, it messed with his athletic training and performance. After the first time he tried scaling the bleachers at dawn with a hangover, his body exuding sweat that smelled like kerosene and his muscles groggy and unresponsive, he vowed it would be his last. But he also feared the lack of control alcohol fomented: His inhibitions weren't merely inhibitions, they were a means of survival, and even after nights with his teammates when he'd nursed just one or two beers, to give the appearance of macho drinking, the following morning would find him replaying the entire evening in his head, anxiously reviewing it for any slips he might've made.

His mother's death changed that. He craved the numbness alcohol delivered, the way it temporarily caulked all the cracks in his heart. Getting drunk crooked his mother's death offstage and narrowed his focus to the immediate here and now. (For a dark but brief period, a little more than a year later, smoking crystal meth would supply Tanya with a similar solace.) At one beach party, in July, he got drunk enough to rally two girls into attempting a half-mile, nude, midnight swim out to Deer Island. The three of them didn't make it far, and, unable to find the clothes he'd shed, Cameron spent the rest of the party wearing only a borrowed towel, his teammates repeatedly yanking it down, Cameron flagrantly unconcerned.

Then came August 21, an unruly Saturday night. Nearly the entire football roster was there, funneling beers, throwing back shots of coconut rum, chanting the fight song, tackling one another in the surf, pumping themselves up for the season opener against St. Martin. But this was way more than a football–cheer squad party. Half the school appeared to be there—stoners, preps, band geeks, emos, hippies and hipsters, gangstas and wangstas, everyone—plus a contingent of college-age folks (Tanya among them, though Cameron wasn't aware of this) throwing a semi-adjacent party a little way down the sand. The night was hot, the crowd muggy, but someone started a bonfire anyway. Cameron had never funneled a beer before, and when the beer erupted onto his shirt he threw the shirt off and pounded his hairless sudsy chest and called for a do-over. He was pumped more than most for the coming football season—he was looking forward to it driving and occupying not just his schedule and his body but his mind as well, to football slapping a lid onto his rolling boil of grief and confusion.

Tommy Landry called him over. Cameron didn't know Landry all that well—he knew he was a senior outfielder on the baseball team, reputedly a clutch hitter, but he was also aware of Landry as someone to avoid. Landry was known to have a mean streak dating way back. It wasn't a physical mean streak—Landry was indeed big, his arms widened by years of batting practice, but he carried himself unimposingly, with a rodent's nimble, nibbly destructiveness. His cruelties were either vocal—his wit wasn't sharp but, like a chainsaw, could gash you just the same—or they were stealthy and prankish. In eighth grade, after a girl suffered the misfortune of experiencing her first menstrual period during class, he allegedly sneaked into the classroom after school and dribbled red acrylic paint across her seat. More than once, rumor had it, he'd accessed the girls' locker room to sneak beef bouillon cubes into the shower heads so the girls showered in hot soup. If you were a girl who passed out at a party and woke to find a penis drawn on your face with a Sharpie, you could feel certain who'd done it. Girls weren't his only victims, however: Hazing had gotten so savage on the baseball team that, earlier that year, two players had quit the team and the school board had had to intervene. Landry's father owned a seafood processing plant over by Keegan Bayou, and was a big athletic booster; gossip pointed to this as the reason Landry had emerged unscathed.

Cameron was just scantly aware of all this, and, at the moment, his own wits were dimming from the effect of the beers he'd funneled. His memory remains blurred. He recalls Landry shooting the shit about the coming football season, wanting to compare his predictions with those of Cameron, who was finding the conversation strained and a little weird, Landry grinning the whole time like maybe he was stoned.

Then Landry curled his finger inward. Cameron frowned. Landry curled the finger again, inviting Cameron to lean in closer. Cameron did. He felt Landry's breath steaming his ear, his nose catching a yeasty, burpy whiff of beer. In a whisper, his bottom lip brushing Cameron's earlobe, Landry slowly sang, "Matchmaker, matchmaker, make me a . . ."

Cameron jerking his head back ignited in Landry's throat a blast of roaring laughter. It was laughter unlike any Cameron had ever heard: a hyena's maniacal skreaks blended with a coughing fit, something vicious and sickly about it all at once. Cameron watched Landry laugh with his hands beginning to clench at his sides. There'd never been a Christy or a Chris. Just Landry entertaining himself, rich enough to possess a spare phone, getting his jollies off when the television lacked a decent baseball game, seeing how far he could take it.

Half an hour later Tommy Landry was in the emergency ward, his pulped face resembling a possum split open on the highway, while Cameron was sitting on a bench in a solitary holding cell at the Harrison County lockup, scraping dried blood from his fingers, a part of him wishing there was more to scrape.

NOTHING ENDED AFTER that, except Cameron's high-school football career—three games into the season, and two games after he tied a school record for the most receiving yards in a single game. The reason he gave for quitting was his mother's death, and while there was truth to that, it wasn't the entire truth. The sudden distance his teammates put between themselves and him, their averted glances, the mumbly chill that seemed to follow him into the locker room: Cameron felt sure that Landry had outed him, probably before but maybe after the beach beating, and he was further dismayed that no one on the team had enough doubts to confront him about it, or enough loyalty to stand up for him or at least let him know.

There's no evidence, however, to suggest Landry ever did take his cat-fishing exploits public. Six of Cameron's former teammates say they never heard any rumors about Cameron being gay. One of the team's running backs, Montrell Davis, speculates that Landry would've had a difficult time defending his investigative methods. "Okay, so Cameron might be gay," he imagines himself responding to Landry, "but you posing as a girl and then a guy for all that time—that makes you some kind of *psycho*, man." Moreover, Davis goes on, Landry would've likely had to field questions "about how it feels to get your ass whupped by a gay guy. I don't know that I want to say this, because that was a nasty beating that night, but Cameron opening his can of whup-ass was probably the best thing he could've done to stay on the down low."

Something important to note: Tommy Landry refuses to confirm the substance and/or details of Cameron's account. But, despite repeated invitations to do so relayed through his attorney, he also doesn't deny them.

"Thing was, man," Davis goes on, "Cameron was our brother, you know, he was our teammate, and to be real frank about it, he was a lot of the reason we were putting up scores. So, gay or not, man, it wouldn't have mattered. I mean that. We would've rallied around him, we would've circled the motherfucking wagons. If some guys had a problem with it, well, that would've been their problem." Whether this reflects the truth of the atmosphere more than a decade ago, or is just the voice of mature enlightenment, is impossible to know. (Another former teammate is far more circumspect: "I'm not saying I would've had a problem with that, but . . . but, yeah, I might've had a problem with that. I think the school would've had to figure out something with the showers and all that, would've had to build something separate for him.") Coach Necaise, who retired in 2011, admits the team's adjustment would've been rocky—"that would've been a new one on me, after thirty-one years of coaching"—but that, as Cameron's coach, he would've stood by him "a hundred and ten percent."

Cameron finds this more troubling than heartening to hear. What it suggests to him is that, with a dash more courage and faith in his teammates, he could've kept playing football and perhaps gone on to a very different life—perhaps college instead of the Army, and onto wherever college leads. But what troubles him also is that he just doesn't buy it—not the generous hindsight from Davis and Necaise, not even the part about Landry staying silent. Landry had the drop on him, and ten years later showed no reluctance to shouting it on camera in a crowded barroom. Why would he have kept it to himself back then—unless, per Davis's theory, Cameron essentially punched his mouth closed? "If he sensed some kind of chill, like he's saying," Davis says of Cameron, "it's because his mama'd just got killed and then he'd gone and beat the shit out of our centerfielder and nobody knew why. I don't think anyone knew *what* to say to him. We just put our heads down and focused on playing ball."

The only person in whom Cameron confided was Jim Yarbrough, his mother's boyfriend. Jim was guiding him through the youth-court briars and wasn't accepting Cameron's vague explanation about being drunk and overreacting to a comment he couldn't even remember. Cameron had always liked Jim—the best thing you could hope for in life, he remembers thinking, was for someone to look at you the way his mom looked at Jim— but their shared grief had endowed them with a thicker and more enduring bond, mutual scar tissue. It'd been Jim holding Cameron's arm at Debbie's graveside service, who'd steadied him as he tottered and swayed. And Cameron trusted Jim. Maybe it was Jim's professional-grade poker face, but he struck Cameron as someone skilled in keeping secrets. So he let it all come flowing—Christy morphing into Chris, everything—and watched as Jim nodded along, unfazed, his eyebrows rising at Landry's actions but never Cameron's. It was far from the first thing he brought up, but at some point Jim asked, "So, you like guys?"

"I don't know what I like," Cameron said.

Jim twirled a pencil between his fingers. "It'll probably make life easier for you if you figure that out, don't you think?"

"What if I do?" Cameron pleaded. "Like guys, I mean?"

"Then I reckon you decide to go with that and call it a day," he said, tapping the eraser end of the pencil on the table twice as though brokering a very straightforward deal between Cameron and his sexuality. "A leopard's got spots," he went on. "Now, he can pretend he don't, and hide up in a tree or out in some high grass somewhere, but he ain't gonna live very well or very long that way. And he's still gonna have those spots."

Cameron tried absorbing this advice, which sounded wise to him at the time, but, wise or not, what Jim gave him was ultimately just a metaphor. Cameron wasn't a leopard. He was a sixteen-year-old kid who was desperately hoping that his variety of spots, like a fawn's, might fade with time—that his attraction to males was something he might outgrow or possibly will into oblivion.

Hurricane Katrina came whirling in the next summer, and when it was over Cameron's exterior and interior landscapes seemed to him bleakly aligned: smashed, scoured, waterlogged, every familiar signpost washed straight out to sea. Driving down the beach, when U.S. 90 reopened, he sometimes found it impossible to orient himself; it was all just drifted sand and naked slabs and, as the dozers moved in, identical debris mounds. A few homes set back from the beach remained standing but hollowed-out, like locust skins. All the talk elsewhere was of New Orleans, but that was because New Orleans had villains for its story—governmental malfeasance, racist urban engineering—while Mississippi had only wind and water, elements unimpeachable, the shapeless consequence of what insurance adjusters marked down as an act of God. Hearing people talk about a "new normal" on the Mississippi Gulf Coast, though, Cameron found a sneer curling his lip: He'd never known there was an old normal.

What the new normal meant, for Cameron, was a hard and dirty existence. He hammered. He sawed. He nailed. He screwed. He drilled. He as-

cended ladders under the murderous sun with bundles of roofing shingles
doubled up on his right shoulder, pack-muling close to his own weight in
sticky asphalt mats. He wrested sheets of plywood into place and affixed
them with a compressor-powered nail gun, the gun thwacking then hiss-
ing, droplets of Cameron's sweat soaking into the parched layers of pine.
He ripped into mildewed wall studs with a reciprocating saw, relishing
the lurching violence of the blade, the way its machine-gun jactitation got
disseminated through his body. A scraggly flaxen beard took shape on
his face, a pioneer's beard, sparse and unkempt, and his skin turned the
brown of a paper shopping bag. He was eighteen then nineteen, and no
longer spurred by a yearning for love; into the vacated zone once filled by
that yearning came a great flume of lust. At the top of the ladder he would
pitch himself forward to slap the shingle bundles onto the tarpaper and
then pause to take in the tableau before him, stingingly erotic, his shirtless
Mexican co-workers like glistened dancers moving on a hot black stage.
Sometimes they would notice him staring and mock him in Spanish and
he would tell them to shut up, that he was just tired. But below the roofline
his body was anything but tired, it was alive with something that refused
to be stifled, that held his dreams hostage at night, and that sometimes felt
driven by little more than dark mischief, dragging bait before him that
he felt incapable of resisting despite the glint of a hook. His new normal
wasn't normal, just as the old normal hadn't been.

He remembers the first time the military came into his head as an option. He was working in Gulfport, framing out a commercial addition on
a building overseen by a giant billboard. It was an Army recruiting sign,
five soldiers inviting onlookers to become one of them. The billboard's
cast was as diverse as an old Benetton ad—two white guys, an Asian, a
black guy, a Hispanic-looking woman—yet in their matching dress uni-
forms Cameron noted a sameness that reminded him, soothingly and
appealingly, of football, and caused him to wonder if an Army uniform
could make him feel the way his football uniform had: apart from himself,
folded into something larger, unidentifiable as anything other than a man
assigned with a particular task, be it pulling passes from the air in a cheer-
thundered stadium or defending whatever his country wanted defended.

Peering up at that billboard, one hand raised in an inadvertent salute
meant to shield his eyes from the sun, Cameron wasn't thinking about

combat, about killing or being killed, as he wasn't thinking about mortar shells and roadside bombs or the conical, copper-jacketed bullets that an AK-47 can spew ten per second, as he wasn't thinking about blood and fear and sorrow and pain and the raw white winters of the Hindu Kush, and as he most definitely wasn't thinking, not even maybe, about falling in love.

nineteen

WHEN STAFF SERGEANT DAMARKUS LOCKWOOD TOUCHED down at the landing zone at Forward Operating Base Barmal, on August 6, 2009, the sleeve of his dress blues already bore six gold combat stripes. At twenty-six years old, Lockwood had served a previous tour in Afghanistan as well as two in Iraq, having been part of the invading force into Iraq in 2003. Before that, on the morning of September 11, 2001, he'd been a freshman at what was then called Mars Hill College, near Asheville, North Carolina, and a third-string back on the school's Division II football team; but soon thereafter, by his own electing, he was neither a student nor an athlete but an enlistee in the United States Army. His rarely glimpsed father had fought in the first Gulf War, and the grandfather who raised him, whom he's always called Chief, served two combat tours in Vietnam before becoming a zealous amateur historian of the U.S. military's frontier wars with the Cherokee. If there was anything consistent in his DNA, Lockwood gathered, it was fighting prowess, something his steady, seven-year rise through the ranks seemed to affirm. He was career-track by this point, a lifer in the pipeline, and though he was still years shy of his first gray hair, Lockwood possessed that alertly grizzled bearing that comes from being shot at numerous times: He looked like a man vulnerable to few if any kind of surprises.

A lieutenant stood waiting for him at the landing pad, and immediately after Lockwood finished scurrying with his ruck down the Chinook's ramp the helicopter rose and banked, its rotor wash spewing a blinding billow of dust that hung suspended in the thin breezeless air for what seemed an impossibly long time, refusing to drift or, like the war itself, to settle. The lieutenant materialized out of the brown cloud to welcome Lockwood, leading him through the FOB's rear gate and talking fast all the while: the squad leader he was replacing, Hooper, everyone called him Hooptie, heck of a soldier, bought it in an IED attack on a Stryker convoy, wish they'd redesign those flat bottoms, makes them deathtraps, but Hooptie, jeez, he had twin baby girls back home, they were all he ever talked about, everyone's just sick about it, in fact nobody's gotten around to packing up his personal effects, partly because we've been taking indirect just about every day, the whole valley's been hot for weeks on account of the election coming, all these fresh fighters coming across the border under a new commander, this Chechen, they call him Cha, that means the bear . . .

Lockwood stopped.

"Oh, sorry," the lieutenant said, circling back. "Everyone says I talk faster than God made ears to hear." He followed Lockwood's gaze to where a shirtless soldier was tending a pit of burning trash, strange-colored flames licking upward, a great palpitating blob of oily black smoke kneading itself above the pyre. "We got a new incinerator but the thing only works half the time," the lieutenant explained, "and no matter what we say the ANAs still dump everything into the pit anyway."

But Lockwood wasn't looking at the fire, not really. There should have been nothing about a soldier burning refuse and raw sewage to catch his attention—but something did. It was close to one hundred degrees that afternoon, a marshy heat that wasn't sparing the high altitudes, but the soldier was leaning on a shovel directly beside the sprawling pit, a khaki bandanna masking the bottom half of his face bandit-style, his long and corded torso slick with sooted sweat, and he appeared less to be monitoring the fire than waiting for something to appear from it, a junior wizard seeking to conjure something from its fetid embers. "That's one of your guys, actually," the lieutenant said, trying to hustle Lockwood along. "PFC One, name's Harris. Kid's a piece of jerky."

Lockwood frowned. "Jerky?"

"Yeah, you know," the lieutenant said, miming a strugglesome bite. "He's a tough one. You're lucky."

IF STAFF SERGEANT LOCKWOOD and the other men of the Second Battalion, Forty-fourth Infantry Regiment's Bravo Company felt lucky that month, it was in the way a fish feels water: not as a blessing or an advantage but as a necessary element that, once removed, meant a swift and gasping death. Their mission, christened "Safe Passage," was part of a larger operation to secure polling stations and the routes thereto in advance of the August 20 presidential elections. What this entailed, for Bravo Company, was stanching the flow of Taliban and Taliban-affiliated insurgents that were stealing across the border from Pakistan to disrupt the voting and further destabilize the province. In practice that meant clearing and patrolling the narrow unpaved road that parallels the Weca Sega River, which they called Route Falcon, and trying to root out any insurgents hiding in the gaunt, medieval-looking villages along the river: Nkhal, Shadikhan Kala, Godikhel, Masheray, Shukikhel, and various smaller others that no one had ever thought to name. Basically, it meant going out every day and kicking hornet nests.

In the two weeks between Lockwood's arrival and the national elections, Bravo Company reported thirty-four troops-in-contact incidents, more than two a day. A few of these were brief firefights; many others were shaggier, more sustained skirmishes, with the company coming under fire from mortars, rocket-propelled grenades, and Soviet-designed KPV heavy machine guns; some involved IED blasts, reminiscent of the attack at a Route Falcon chokepoint that had killed Lockwood's predecessor; one was the August 12 episode during which Private First Class Cameron Harris had back-rolled a jingle truck off a cliff into the Weca Sega and, to Lockwood's thinking, almost single-handedly extracted Second Platoon from a direly indefensible position; and one involved a ten-hour siege and counteroffensive in the village of Tor Kalay, right after which Cameron again proved his grit—or maybe just his volatility.

Tor Kalay was known to be a Taliban stronghold, but for the soldiers of the Two-Forty-Four, having landed in Afghanistan only a month earlier, their August 17 visit was their first. The seventy-five-man Romanian force that the Two-Forty-Four replaced, at ten times its size, had left them radio transcripts and written briefings, but all in Romanian; and on joint reconnaissance missions, during the handover, they admitted to hardly ever leaving Route Falcon—a policy they recommended highly to their American replacements.

Led by a contingent of Afghan National Army and Afghan National Police, Second Platoon entered the village, which sits a kilometer below and west of Route Falcon in a lush riverside maze of pomegranate and quince orchards, in four Stryker vehicles. Out of one came First Lieutenant Shaw Cantwell, the fast talker, whose father and grandfather (Lockwood hadn't been surprised to learn) were farm auctioneers back in Kentucky. Cantwell's overworked interpreter, a young Afghan named Shpoon, directed a teenaged boy to fetch the village elder. From inside one of the Strykers, watching through its open rear hatch, Lockwood noticed the boy was wearing sneakers, not sandals—a reliable Taliban indicator. He poked his head out to survey the village. Not a single child was dawdling outside, another bad omen. "Be ready," he warned his squad.

The elder came out stroking and smoothing his henna-dyed, carrot-colored beard as though preparing himself for a portrait. Tor Kalay was an important polling site, Cantwell explained to him (via Shpoon), and the Americans were visiting today in support of the ANA's efforts to ensure that the Taliban wouldn't disrupt the coming vote.

"The Taliban, bwah." The elder flashed a three-toothed grin and disdainfully threw out a hand. His wrinkle-scored face appeared carved from wood, like a storefront Indian's. "We chased them out with shovels."

"Shovels?" the lieutenant tried clarifying.

Just then a rifle shot rang out, from over where the ANAs were stationed atop a nearby hill.

"Ask him what the hell that was," the lieutenant told Shpoon.

"He say," Shpoon translated, fearfully, watching the elder suppress a low and melancholy chuckle, "that he hopes you have good shovels."

The ensuing battle lasted, almost without pause, until nightfall. The first group of enemy fighters was positioned in an oxbow wadi, on the north edge of the village, and aimed their initial fire—a salvo of gunfire and RPGs and mortars—on the ANAs and ANP, quickly killing one and injuring two. By the time Second Platoon got a sergeant and a medic to them, the Afghans had already burned through their ammo and were hightailing it to their pickup trucks.

It was a classic Whac-A-Mole fight. For every enemy position the platoon wiped out, another one appeared. The Taliban had done a remarkable job keeping their plans secret; nothing in the chatter had suggested an assault on this scale, not with this much reinforcement and tactical rigor. After a while the Talibs were able to advance on three fronts, drawing so near to the Strykers that soldiers were hurling hand grenades from the hatches. Though Lieutenant Cantwell had a mortar Stryker with him, he couldn't get clearance to use it: The firing coordinates skirted too close to civilian structures, from inside of which the platoon's members sometimes heard people cheering. And Charlie Company—similarly pinned across the Weca Sega near Sawdal Malkshay Kot, about thirty-five clicks downriver— had air support all tied up. The Strykers went lurching from point to point, bursting forward then reversing, hounded by close-range machine-gun fire and by RPGs that went streaking over, alongside, and occasionally off them. (Lockwood and Cameron's vehicle would return to the FOB with an RPG's tail fin embedded in it.)

The advantage tilted their way after a sky-parade of air support finally showed up, two Kiowa Warrior helicopters strafing the orchards as well as a bunker that Cantwell suspected was a command center, then an A-10 Warthog trailing behind to pancake the bunker with a five-hundred-pound bomb. "How about those shovels, huh? What do we think about *those* shovels?" the lieutenant shouted, everyone within earshot besides Shpoon thinking he'd lost his mind. With the arrival of Third Platoon, the company's Quick Response Force, the counteroffensive began—the soldiers fanning out into the hills and orchards on foot.

It was Cameron's squad, led by Lockwood, that captured a mud farmhouse north of the village that turned out to be a Taliban medic station, having followed a blood trail the way bow hunters track deer. Inside the hut they found six wounded fighters in varying states of consciousness lying on woolen blankets in a dank, windowless, blood-splashed room, their attending medic on his knees in the center with his hands raised, his long white tunic stained like a supermarket butcher's. His kit was meager: IV tubing and fluids, gauze, burn dressing, morphine, a tin bowl filled with cloudy pink water. The gravest of the wounded, Lockwood saw, must've survived the bunker bombing. His right arm and leg were missing but he wasn't bleeding out, probably because the same fiery blast that blew the limbs off had also cauterized the wounds. Most of his clothing had burned off but charred tatters were fused to what was left of his skin, which was the crispy, wobbly black of a marshmallow suspended too long above a campfire. Lockwood ordered that the medic and all the wounded be zip-tied ("not that one," he had to clarify to a baffled private, an open tie in his hands, standing over the dismembered fighter) and radioed for medical assistance for enemy personnel. Outside, he found a wooden farm wagon piled with three warm corpses and a stray severed forearm, and, nearby, sheltered between the hut and a high stone wall, Cameron doubled over vomiting. Lockwood's first impulse, his sergeant's default, was to chide him: *Keep your insides inside, Private, and let's be ready to move out.* Instead, without a word, he crouched beside him and passed him a water bottle, listening to Cameron swish and spit while he squinted at a Blackhawk helicopter hovering over the distant village dropping body bags filled with ammo and water and medical supplies, a bird shitting mercy.

Including the Taliban medic but not the wounded, nineteen enemy fighters or suspected collaborators were captured that day—an unusually large haul, most of them netted during house-to-house raids that the Afghan National Army conducted after dark with a fire team from the Marine Corps Forces Special Operations Command. Problem was, no one wanted them the next day. So while the ANA bickered with the ANP about what to do with them—the provincial jail in Gardez was full, complicating matters—a squad from an engineer company started constructing a temporary holding pen south of the ANP's command center on Route Falcon. Lockwood's nine-man squad was attached for security, a relief to them: Shaken and exhausted from the previous day's fight at Tor Kalay, the men welcomed a day of recuperative overwatch. Their Strykers were even more battered; the squad left the base in an MRAP, a heavier and more lumbering armored vehicle with an exposed gun turret, while mechanics rehabbed the Strykers.

The site of the holding pen was a long-abandoned walled courtyard, with a small building and crumbling guard tower attached, sitting about a hundred yards back from Route Falcon and backing up against an abrupt slope of blue pines and boulders. When the Taliban attacked—in something akin to a cavalry charge, rolling down from the steep slope like a human avalanche—the driver and the gunner leapt into the MRAP to back it into a better position for firing. Then an RPG struck it, shrapnel blinding the driver and breaking the gunner's forearm. Cameron was helping Lockwood clear the two men from the MRAP when a bullet struck the gunner in the kneecap and dropped him to the dirt—a ricochet, possibly, or a missed shot at Cameron or Lockwood, or, to Cameron's thinking, a gratuitous cruelty, a late hit in football speak, a violation needing payback.

That's when Cameron muttered "Goddammit"—"just put out, you know," as Lockwood told Euclide Abbascia, "like he's playing poker and got his tenth crap hand in a row"—and climbed into the MRAP. Lockwood, escorting the hopping gunner to where a medic was waiting behind the wall outside the courtyard, figured Cameron was double-checking to be sure the vehicle was clear. He was expecting Cameron to show up behind him in a matter of seconds.

And then he heard the MRAP's .50-caliber heavy-barrel machine gun firing in fat, hot, suicidal bursts.

"Shit," he groaned, in fair summary. The squad had guns firing from both the sides of the open gateway and another at the outside of the courtyard's southwest corner, but the Taliban attackers had more guns, maybe three times more, and also, as they began popping onto the attached building's roof and as one went shinnying his way up to the guard tower, increasingly better positions. Lockwood screamed at Cameron to get out and get back; but Cameron says he never heard him, not until the sergeant was below him in the MRAP.

Just how many enemy fighters Cameron killed that morning—firing more than three hundred rounds while exposed in that gun turret, with his furious squad leader rushing into the vehicle to load for him and curse at him and load some more—is unclear. He let the fighters crest the walls and then mowed them down once their feet touched the ground—a sign of at least semi-lucid thinking, since shooting them at the top of the wall would've discouraged the fighters behind them, who, blind to their comrades' fates inside the courtyard, kept climbing over. Cameron raked the mountainside behind them as well, trapping the fighters between the rear wall and the slope and making it possible for the squad's grenadier to launch several catastrophic booms back there. As in any combat situation, teamwork was vital and credit for the outcome diffused: Sergeant Diego Cordon shot the fighter who'd managed to climb the guard tower from where, just a few second later, he would've had an easy bead on Cameron, and the engineer company was able to keep the Talibs from flanking the north side of the courtyard. And luck, that infantryman's oldest friend, also played a cameo: A recon team later solved the mystery of why the first RPG was also the last by finding its launcher's mangled body on the mountainside, a stopped or cracked tube having caused the grenade to detonate into his shoulder. Yet the merit of Cameron's half-crazed valor, even to the members of his squad who'd later distance themselves from Cameron, is undisputed. "We were this close to being overrun," says one, leaving a hair's width of air between his pinched fingertips. "Without that firepower, without him sticking himself up there like he did, I don't think I'd be sitting here talking today. I don't know that most of us would."

Still, Lockwood was incensed. "You, Harris, right there, *you,*" he came charging at Cameron a short while afterward, after First Platoon arrived and a Warthog bombed the slope into a funnelform of gravel. Cameron was trying to smoke, his hands shaking so badly from either nerves or recoil that he was struggling to meet the cigarette with his mouth. His helmet, Lockwood saw, was gouged from where a bullet had glanced it. "You're a stupid motherfucker, you know that?" He was drill-sergeanting him, spit-spraying him, close enough to Cameron to bite his nose off. "Did your mama raise you stupid or did you just figure it out all by yourself?"

The outcome didn't matter, not to Lockwood: Cameron had disobeyed his order to get down and out of the MRAP. Had Lockwood, as squad leader, chosen to break contact with the enemy, and retreat to a hypothetically safer position, Cameron's "Rambo bullshit"—Lockwood's semifond phrase—would've forced upon the sergeant the impossible choice between abandoning his soldier or surrendering his own combat authority. (Cameron, for his part, would later say it wasn't insubordination so much as miscommunication: He thought Lockwood was ordering him to "get down" into a more protected, crabbed posture, more of an insistent coaching tip than a command.) Yet Lockwood's anger was of a giddy, diluted kind—"where you want to high-five someone with one hand," as he puts it, "and smack him upside the head with the other." And Cameron's meek, almost mewling defense—"Sorry, Sarge, I just lost my temper"—somehow drained it entirely. Lockwood found himself clenching his teeth to kill the smile his face wanted to form, one clear fact glowing and buzzing in his mind as the adrenaline leeched from his veins: every member of the squad, himself included, was alive. And if all of it wasn't due to this beautiful motherfucker in front of him, most of it sure was.

Lockwood left Cameron and walked about twenty paces before wheeling slowly back around. The rest of the squad, sitting in a line against the outside wall, was in a victorious lather, rehashing the play-by-play, bumping fists, suckling their canteens and groaning happily how much better cold beer would taste at the moment, yet despite the frequent cheers they were whooping his direction and their entreaties to join them, Cameron was keeping to himself, chainsmoking inside the courtyard—closer in spirit, if not in yardage, to the corpses heaped against the bullet-pitted walls.

Lockwood stood there frowning. He was feeling a keen spear of fascination, lodged deeper than ever, about this quiet, blue-eyed, scar-faced, lank-framed, tender-voiced, violent-hearted soldier of his, both the one he'd found vomiting outside the Taliban medic hut eighteen hours earlier and the one who'd just pulled that kamikaze stunt in the MRAP's gun turret, who still didn't know or didn't care that a chunk of his helmet was missing, the one whose hands Lockwood could still see trembling as a cigarette went wobbling toward his lips. He was reminded of something his mother'd once told him, when as a boy Damarkus was pestering her with questions about his missing father and after a long sigh through her nose she'd made to shut him down: "The best kind of people in this world, D, but also the worst kind—they're riddles. You know what a riddle is? It's something that don't want to be solved. They do things that don't make sense, and no matter how hard you try you can't never figure them out. But you can't help yourself trying. You'll stop eating before you stop trying."

Operation Safe Passage ended with the August 20 elections. The Afghan government's official turnout, for Paktika Province, came in at 626 percent of the eligible voting population—a patently absurd figure, a numerical punchline. From Bravo Company's perspective, the turnout looked closer to nil. Not a single female was seen entering a polling station. By late afternoon, at the Tor Kalay schoolhouse, only five people had been seen going in to vote. When the local ANA commander sought Lieutenant Cantwell's permission to close the polling early, Cantwell spluttered a fierce objection. Yet with an inscrutably straight face the commander explained to him: Tor Kalay's election officials had run out of ballots. The box was full. Cantwell shook his head as a long groan fell out of him, trailing into a sigh. This was what they'd fought for, he tried not thinking: five voters and a white box crammed with bullshit.

Their own mission correspondingly finished, the Taliban fighters slid back into Pakistan to regroup or else ghosted back into the local populace. Several days of relative quiet followed. On one of these, during a dismounted recon patrol, Lockwood's squad stopped to rest in a spinney of pines on a cliff brow overlooking a tributary of the Weca Sega. This was remote country, far from any village, where even the trees seemed calmer and less troubled, their trunks unscarred and their branches unbroken, and where Cameron, for the first time since landing in Afghanistan, noted birds other than vultures. Their songs startled and disoriented him, and for a moment even homesickened him, as if he were hearing the impossible chimes of an ice cream truck. Across the deep gorge, in the distance, were the saw teeth of the border mountains, a craggy range servicemen called the Big Uglies; but they didn't look so ugly now, tinged violet by the canted afternoon sunlight and requiring little imagination to be seen as the spine of a dragon bedded down astride the horizon—half malevolent but half mystical too. Plunging their gaze downward the squad's members could see a silver stream needling its way through the gorge bottom and curving around an outwash of stones directly below. This was where one of the men, squinting through his rifle scope, saw something more. "Y'all ain't gonna believe this," he announced, "but I'm looking at one . . . two . . . three sets of titties right now. I am straight-up not shitting you. Afghan titties at six o'clock."

The speed at which the rest of the squad shouldered and sighted their weapons could not have been quicker had an impending ambush been declared. Three women were bathing in the stream—two of them young, roughly the age of most of the peeping squad members, and the other, perhaps their mother, in her middle years. For a while the soldiers were not just silent but breathless. The only glimpses of live woman-skin they'd seen since landing in Paktika Province were occasional faces in windows, quick bronze flashes of cheeks and foreheads that retreated at the soldiers' first glance; otherwise, as one soldier liked to joke, the burqa-shrouded women were indistinguishable from Pac-Man ghosts. One of the younger women was standing in knee-deep water wringing out her long black hair; the other one splashed her, and a playful, bouncy chase ensued. "Oh . . . my . . . god," one of the soldiers moaned.

"I'm gonna say naked chicks are a sure sign this ain't Talib territory," another one theorized, pretending to be considering the mission.

"Lookit the *bush* on that one," said another, pretending nothing. "It's huuuuge. Looks like she's giving birth to a Yeti baby."

"Unnnhh. If I bust a load right now it's gonna land in Pakistan."

"Someone give that man grid coordinates."

So intently were the men peering into their scopes and binoculars that no one in the squad noticed that two of its members weren't likewise engaged. Staff Sergeant Lockwood glanced over at Cameron, who, eyes bouncing, smiled nervously back.

IN LATE SEPTEMBER, the soldiers of Bravo Company learned they were moving. The reasons they heard for this were myriad and opaque. One was that the brigade's eight-wheeled Stryker vehicles, which'd proven so invaluable in Iraq, were flopping in the gnarlier terrain of Afghanistan—no surprise to the enlisted men, who'd taken to calling them "Kevlar coffins." The Strykers were too wide to navigate many of Afghanistan's scrawny mountain roads, prompting some units to risk removing the vehicles' slat side armor, and their flat bottoms weren't bearing up against blasts from the Taliban's more powerful brand of IEDs. Another reason the soldiers heard whispered was that losses were too high; the Two-Forty-Four alone had seen eight men killed (including Cameron's original squad leader, Staff Sergeant Leroy Hooper) and thirty-one wounded (including, again, three men from Cameron's tattered squad). The Army would later concede that the brigade, swept into that summer's surge of troops, had been dropped into intense combat without sufficient training and preparation. But ISAF's Regional Command South didn't traffic in reactive measures, not publicly anyway: They were breaking up the brigade and dispersing its units, they said, for strategic gains.

What those strategic gains might be wasn't immediately visible from Combat Outpost Hila, one hundred and twenty miles west of FOB Barmal in Zabul Province. At eight thousand feet above sea level, the outpost occupied the top of a mounded buttress—a dwarf cousin to the fourteen-thousand-foot peaks to its north and west—in a thin and lifeless-looking alpine valley known as Darah Khujz. The outpost's appearance befitted its remote location: a cramped, two-acre assemblage of mustard-colored Quonset huts and plywood bunkers and homemade latrines and a heart-shaped mortar pit, all girdled by five-foot hedgerows of dirt-filled Hesco bags.

The outpost was laid out in the shape of a cleaver. In the handle section was a scatter of mud-and-stone huts housing the outpost's Afghan National Army contingent. These dated back to the Soviet occupation of Afghanistan, when Hila came into its original existence as an outpost for Soviet forces battling the mujahideen. The mud huts weren't the only Soviet remnant, however: There was a junkyard, too, a snarled pile of bent steel and rusted artillery and fragged wreckage. At its center was a corroded and sun-bleached but mostly intact Soviet BTR-60, or *Bronya,* an eight-wheeled, tank-like armored personnel carrier that'd long ago been stripped of its tires and sat now like some grim colossus from antiquity, Ozymandias in the 'Stan. The symbolism was obvious but everyone took pains to ignore it, even as they added American junk to the Soviet heap.

One additional Soviet remnant Bravo Company learned about during its orientation: land mines. The area of operations had never fully been cleared. The Soviets usually marked the mines they laid with painted rocks, white paint on one side and red on the other. The mine, they were told, was somewhere on the red side.

Nearly every facet of life was drastically different at Hila. On the low end of those differences: no running water, no hot food, no electricity save for what a diesel generator supplied the command post, no internet, no phones, and no way to or from the outpost except via helicopter or on foot. On the high side, however: Nobody was pelting them with mortars or RPGs. You could linger outside without a neck-prickle forcing you to constantly hawk-eye the mountainsides for movement. You could smoke a cigarette without the low-grade apprehension that it might be your last.

During their first week Bravo Company fielded a few welcoming potshots from the surrounding slopes. No one got hit, though a bullet did whiz in and out of a latrine that a sergeant was occupying, granting him the rare literal claim to having had the shit scared out of him. The company's commanding officer, a pink-cheeked Minnesotan named Gary Lindholm, opted to answer these potshots with sanguine force, calmly targeting the shooters with mortars. A gray puff would appear on the mountainside, followed by silence and then, from inside the wire, rowdy cheering. This felt like great and virtuous sport to the soldiers, their minds still jangling from their losses in Paktika, until they learned that the Taliban paid young goat-herder boys five dollars a day to take those shots.

Three times a week each squad walked what Cameron calls "meet-and-greet" patrols and what the brass was now calling KLE patrols, for Key Leader Engagement: the officers huddling over tea with village elders while the enlisted men outside would scan village men's fingerprints and retinas with handheld devices, or distribute sacks of rice and corn, all the while trying, post-Paktika, to feel or at least act unfazed in the presence of Afghan civilians. Medical teams sometimes choppered in to set up one-day surgical or dental clinics in the villages, a squad assigned to hump along. Any grittier stuff was mostly reserved for night patrols, to confer upon the locals the impression of a benign U.S. presence, but around the Darah Khujz valley that autumn, unlike elsewhere in Afghanistan, there wasn't much grit to be had. During the five months he was posted at Hila, Cameron fired his weapon on just two occasions; Lockwood never fired his at all.

The result of this sudden shift, for the troops, was a kind of mental whiplash. In their three months at FOB Barmal they'd pinballed from one firefight to the next, freebasing adrenaline, their muscles coiled and fists clenched even during sleep. But now, instead of infantrymen, they were feeling like old-timey cops strolling a beat, sarcastic whistling sometimes breaking out in the patrol lines. Hearts and minds were no longer something to line up in crosshairs; they were to be cajoled, flattered, bribed, won.

Before long a new and unexpected sensation flooded them: boredom.

Guitars got tuned for the first time since being shipped from the States. Books got cracked. Giant camel spiders got dropped into boxes to fight, soldiers howling for the spider they'd bet on to prevail. A makeshift gym got built, with recycled foam ammunition sleeves for padding and sandbags and filled ammo cans for weights. A specialist in Lockwood's squad, a tattoo artist back home in New Jersey, started painting murals everywhere—first the regimental insignia, to ease the captain in, but then weirder, darker scenes, like a pterodactyl carrying off a terrified-looking goat wearing basketball sneakers. (This inspired a graffiti artist to spray-paint the latrines like seventies-era subway cars, which was when the captain clamped down on what he called "home decorating.") First Platoon organized a Halloween party where a trio of soldiers won best costume by going nude save for socks over their genitals to mimic the Red Hot Chili Peppers, the ANAs scratching their beards and whispering as they observed from a safe distance. For the party someone procured and slaughtered a cow and stayed up all night to barbecue it, the soldiers gnawing the bones then hurling them to the bare-ribbed dogs prowling outside the wire.

And in the midst of all this, if you looked closely enough, you'd see two soldiers growing increasingly inseparable: eating their meals together in the mess tent, spotting one another in the gym, playing an Italian card game the younger of the pair learned in high school, laughing and talking nonstop together outside even as the bronze autumn sunlight shriveled into the steely cold dim of winter, standing side by side beneath the over-freckled night sky as the older of the two charted the same constellations his grandfather had taught him in the north Georgia mountains, and then later, alone in their cots, as they listened wide-awake to their barrack mates' froggish snores and to the far-off thrum of helicopters, imagining the other imagining him.

DAMARKUS HAD LONG shed the confusion of his teen years, which weren't entirely unlike Cameron's minus the trauma of Tommy Landry— each man's sexual awakenings had been incubated in the antigen culture of small-town Southern football. But whether the Army instilled this in him or whether this innate quality naturally fitted him for the Army,

Damarkus tends to cleanly and coldly assess a situation, then devises a plan accordingly. He doesn't mentally rework situations the way Cameron does, backpedaling through his mind, inventorying all the escape portals he failed to use, sweating the *what-ifs*. For Damarkus, all that matters is *what is*. And what is, he realized sometime late in his teens, was that he was gay.

It shouldn't detract from his otherwise patriotic motive to note that Damarkus saw joining the Army as a way out. Life as a young gay man in rural White County, Georgia—as well as at the loosely religious Mars Hill College—loomed as a cramped and rarely pleasurable existence. One mistake he made, he readily admits, was taking the military's Don't Ask, Don't Tell policy at face value. "It's right there in the name," he says. "They wasn't going to ask and I damn sure wasn't going to tell. That seemed like a square deal. Thing is, though, when you're eighteen years old, whether you're gay or straight, you're thinking about sex—I guess the better word is sexuality—as something that's below the waist. You're just thinking about hooking up. If you're a country boy, like I was, you're thinking about going to the *city*, man, you're looking at the world out there like it's some giant spinning disco ball. You ain't thinking about maybe wanting to move in with somebody someday, how tricky that's going to be. You ain't thinking about how you might maybe want to get married someday—I mean, back in 2001, the only way you was having a gay wedding was if you lived in the damn Netherlands, but even so, man, you're eighteen, you're thinking why the hell would I ever even *want* to? That age, man, you got too much *rooster* in you. But here's the other thing you ain't thinking, if you're me, because you don't understand yet that Don't Ask, Don't Tell ain't nothing *like* a square deal: The Army didn't have to ask you if you're gay. All they had to do was suspect it. And you not telling didn't matter. You were out— you were gone that same fucking day."

Damarkus's closest brush, before Hila, came in 2006, between his second deployment to Iraq and his first to Afghanistan, when he was stationed at Joint Base Lewis-McChord in Washington. He had an off-base duplex apartment in Tacoma's Stadium District where his boyfriend at the time, a waiter at a Tacoma bistro, more often than not spent the night. Late one evening he got a text: A group of fellow NCOs had been out drinking in the city, were now on their way to a strip club, and were picking him up along the way. He froze. No one had ever seen his apartment, which his boyfriend, not much to Damarkus's liking, had taken it upon himself to "spruce." He ordered his boyfriend under the bed while he careened from room to room gathering up framed photos of the two of them and hiding, in his words, "anything faggy—it was taking 'straightening up' to a whole new level." By the time the NCOs arrived, though, Damarkus had come up with a ruse: He played sick, cracking the door to tell the drunk men, in a pained croak, that he was pretty sure it was pneumonia. The NCOs grumbled but relented. As they retreated down the steps one said, "Dig those pretty curtains of yours, Lockwood."

That Damarkus had to extend his ruse for the next two days—calling in sick doesn't work in the Army—was the least of it. Slowly from under the bed came his boyfriend, his face warped with disgust. "This is totally sickening," he said, brushing dust clods from his hair and torso. "I am nobody's mistress." Damarkus stepped forward to placate him but a torrent of resentments came spilling forth, blocking his path: The two of them couldn't hold hands or show any other public affection, were forced to equip themselves with a creepy cover story (second cousins) to go out anywhere together, the boyfriend had to be listed under a female pseudonym in Damarkus's phone, gay bars were no-go zones, merely shopping together was too risky, and if and when Damarkus got deployed again— contact was going to dry up almost completely, and if he got killed, the only way his boyfriend was going to hear of it was through a Google news alert. Damarkus weakly argued that last bit—he'd make sure his sister would know to tell him—but he had no counter to the rest; the way it was was simply the way it had to be. On his way out the door for the last time, the boyfriend said, half-sadly and half-acidly, "Don't forget about Monday," their secret texting code for *I love you*. All Damarkus could muster was a wince.

Deployments, he found, supplied a peculiar kind of reprieve. In Iraq, and in Afghanistan the first time, it was easier to compartmentalize. The existential questions that chilled his nighttime hours in Tacoma—was he doomed to loneliness or to lying or just to alternating bouts of both?—got thrown aside for a much hotter, more pressing one: Were he and his guys going to make it out alive? And temptations were negligible—even less than that, they were abstractions. Fellow servicemen had always been off-limits because they only compounded the risks. (A straight friend of his, trying to understand this dynamic, once offered this analogy: "So everybody there is basically like your best friend's wife—not just no touching, but no thinking about touching." That seemed about right to Damarkus.)

It wasn't difficult, in a combat zone, to transform yourself into a machine, to become not the human operator of your weapon but rather an extension of it, to see your own flesh as steel, your joints as welds. And in some ways, wholly unrelated to the tangential pangs of sexuality, you had to do that anyway. In order to kill a man you have to turn something off. It doesn't matter that he's trying to kill you—there's a lever inside and you've got to flip it off. And if you can pull one, you can easily pull another. You can turn off whatever needs turning off.

Until there comes a night, as the first snowfall begins dusting an isolated mountain outpost in Afghanistan, when you discover, with dizzyingly exultant horror, that one of those levers is broken.

IT WAS CAMERON who discovered the junked *Bronya*. Not that he was the first: What he found inside suggested that Afghans—one or more bored shepherds, probably—had been taking refuge inside it for decades. Littering the floor were ancient and thumbed-to-death magazines in Arabic: sports magazines with photos of cricket and soccer matches, ornamented brides staring proud-eyed from crinkled wedding magazines, raggedy celebrity tabloids with time-capsule shots of O. J. Simpson standing trial and Princess Diana cavorting in a swimsuit. Lumpy melted candles were everywhere like mushrooms. Someone had strung dyed feathers and beads and tinsel and lengths of painted chain around the dashboard, and thrown a small crimson rug across the thrashed troop seats, giving the space an eerie secret shrine vibe, eerie because all the powdery dust drifts and the slightly acrid funk betokened something lost and probably dead: whoever had made this sanctuary, plus whatever it was they'd dreamt here.

The first time Cameron showed it to Damarkus they sat beside one another in the drivers' chairs, admiring the archaeological coolness of the periscope and the analog gauges and toggle switches and red and green dash bulbs, Damarkus supplying his best guesses as to what each Cyrillic gauge indicated and how the Soviets had operated the thing. "This shit was heavy back in the day," he said, gripping the steering wheel like a kid playing make-believe in Dad's truck. A note of gloom began shadowing his voice as he said, "This was state of the art. These were their Strykers." Dots started connecting in his head, none he wanted to see. He expelled a long sigh. "That's the thing about fighting wars here. These people here . . . they don't gotta win. They only gotta stop us from winning. And that's a whole different thing."

"Damn," said Cameron, caught off-guard by the sudden bleak swerve. "You sounding like Beano now." The other PFC in the squad, Jason Beenora aka Beano, was always going on about Afghanistan being the graveyard of empires, arguing a case—founded mostly upon Reddit comments, apparently—that the Two-Forty-Four, like the rest of the U.S. military, had its ankle locked in a geopolitical bear trap.

"Don't be laying that shit on me now." Damarkus let out an uneasy laugh, fingers still curled around the steering wheel. As a squad leader, both here and in Iraq, he'd never once conceded doubts about the merit and sanctity of the greater mission—not even to himself, still-birthing such thoughts before they had the chance to develop in his mind. Something in the *Bronya*'s pinched, stirless atmosphere, however, was teasing out strange candor. He felt seduced by a sense that whatever was thought or said or enacted in that atmosphere wouldn't exist or even be remembered outside it, that perhaps emanating from all the dyed feathers and the tinsel was a kind of protective, short-radius magic. Talking to Cameron felt like talking to himself. "All I'm saying is that somewhere under this dirt there's probably a spear or a chariot from Alexander the Great's army, you feeling me. And somewhere down this valley there might be some British cannon. I'm saying the junk piles up, but nothing else looks like it changes. I'm saying this right here"—with a single sweep of his hand he took in the dashboard's quaint technology, the *Bronya* itself, the Soviet ghosts, the presence of every other invading force including their own— "might be all we really leave. That this is it, right here. This is it."

"This is it," Cameron repeated, like a quiet announcement. He brushed a feather with the back of his hand and then eagerly rolled a hanging string of beads between his fingers, slaking an abrupt need for touch.

The next time they went in together, just before Christmas, it was with a bottle of champagne that Damarkus had bought from a Slovakian heli-copter pilot who ferried supplies to the outpost. The military outsourced these supply runs to civilian contractors, nicknamed "Jingle Air." The Slo-vakian, named Janko, also had a nickname, Drunko, which he didn't seem to mind or was always too intoxicated to notice, and he openly advertised himself as a one-man bazaar for mildly illicit goods. (He was quick to al-literate his limits: "No pork, no pills, no pussy.") Damarkus scored three bottles from him: two to secretly share with the squad on Christmas, and one to share, far more secretly, with Cameron.

"Cambo does the honors," he said, passing the bottle onto Cameron's lap. It wasn't actually champagne—rather carbonated wine from China, with a snake on the label, but *grand cru* for a combat outpost.

Cameron stared at the bottle, blanching. "I don't know how."

"What you mean," Damarkus grunted, his voice a teasing towel-snap, "you don't know how?"

Cameron shrugged, embarrassed as before his mother's funeral when he had to confess to Jim that he didn't know how to tie a tie; his mother or Tanya had always done it for him. Defensively he sniffed, "Wasn't like there was a lot of champagne around my house growing up."

Damarkus's laugh came out soft and consoling. "I feel you. Mine was the same way. Chief, he still drinks that old nasty Colt Forty-Five. I'm always like, c'mon, Chief, you can't be serious drinking that shit. And he's always like, 'This here's what Billy Dee Williams drinks!'—Lando Calris-sian, you know, from the old *Star Wars* movies. I don't know if he read that somewhere or what. That's about as close to champagne as we got. But I had a b—" The candorous vapors of the tank came close to unloosening him, but Damarkus caught himself. "I had this friend back in Tacoma, worked at this high-end restaurant up on Pacific Ave. He was always drinking it. Guess he kinda got me hooked on the fizz."

Cameron gaped at the bottle. "What the hell do I do?"

"You take that foil off there first," Damarkus instructed him. The win-ter's first real snow was falling outside, and inside the *Bronya* their breath came out in puffs of steam just barely visible in the closed-in darkness. "Now you take that cage thingie off—yeah, just untwist that part. Now that sucker's weaponized, man. You shake it now and it's popping a hole through the roof. No—I'm joking, man, cut that shit out. All right now, this here's the finesse part. This is how you make it look smooth. Take your left hand now, put it 'round the cork—no, the other way, with your hand upside down. You got it. Now just work it on out of there."

Cameron's expression, with his face turned away from the bottle, suggested he was working with live ordnance, which Damarkus pointed out to him. "Shut up," Cameron bit back at him, with a grin. "Damn thing's stuck."

"Nah, just keep twisting it up. You're getting—"

The popping of the cork seemed thunderously loud inside the *Bronya,* and for a brief moment both men froze; then they looked at one another and broke into laughter.

Damarkus said, "See, ain't nothing to it. This is one of them skills your recruiter promised you'd learn in the Army." He pulled out the two canteen cups he'd brought along and held them steady while Cameron overpoured, froth rolling down the sides of the cups. "Whoa, easy now. This Chinese snake-fizz don't come cheap."

They clinked cups and took long, slow swigs.

"Man," Damarkus finally said, swirling his cup around. "This shit—it ain't that bad. I mean, for snake piss and pesticides."

"Ain't bad at all," Cameron said.

"You think so, huh? You on Team D with the fizz?"

"Honestly?" he said, going in for another swig. "Shit's amazing."

Damarkus parroted him, going in for another swig of his own. He held the wine in his mouth for a while, feeling the bubbles popping against his tongue and gums. Then softly he said, "Yeah," the word coming out heavy like a moan, Damarkus stricken with a sudden whirling dizziness and what felt like his insides tumbling downward, his heart sliding slick beside his mind as everything in him went gathering at his center—the sensation was of dropping, of being swallowed by a force as invincible as gravity, of rushing, ecstatic doom. A voice inside him was screaming but it was muffled and incoherent and while Damarkus knew what the screaming was for he pretended not to. "Yeah," he said again, and as though from afar he heard himself keep saying it, unable or unwilling to say anything else, not now, maybe not ever, *yeah.*

———

CHRISTMAS PASSED, AND come January snow began filling the Darah Khujz valley in such thick and recurrent layers as to obliterate it. The low winter clouds sagged into the mountains, concealing their peaks in dingy gray swathing, while the mountains' lower fissures and crevices turned to gently indented shadows, rendered toothless for the season. When the wind took a short cut through the valley, on its way to better places, it blew through with urgent contempt, whipping the outpost with an ice-white spray that felt laced with glass shards and cloaking its corners with glossy drifts that got shoveled into the Hescos. The light was mostly dismal but every once in a while the sun burned away the cloud deck and lit the valley with a vivid white that stabbed your eyes to look upon it during guard duty. The Darah Khujz dozed into hibernation: motionless, soundless, colorless, bloodless.

Potbellied stoves appeared in the barracks and the soldiers took turns stoking and replenishing them. The heat melted the big blankets of snow on the roofs, meltwater dripping down through cracks into buckets that the soldiers took turns emptying. Not frequently, but occasionally enough, someone in Cameron's squad would register his absence along with their staff sergeant's and ask where the hell they were. "Astronomy lessons," someone would jeer, though stars were rare in the winter-shrouded sky. "Smoking," someone else might say, though only Cameron smoked, not Lockwood. "Out fucking," someone else said more than once, though no one took this seriously. That some of their Afghan National Army counterparts smoked hashish was common knowledge; whiffs of hash smoke sometimes floated over from the huts, and Afghan soldiers often assembled for patrols with "eyes like the devil's ball sack," as one soldier put it, meaning veiny and red, their eyelids at half-mast. Lockwood and Harris were sometimes spotted heading together toward the Afghan huts back in the cleaver handle section, and a few soldiers wondered, whispered . . .

The snow made it difficult for Cameron and Damarkus to hide signs of their passage in and out of the *Bronya*, though because their route was always from the side of the junkyard facing the ANA huts, anyone who noticed would deduce the Afghans were using it for whatever Afghans used things for. This wasn't an unfair deduction, as the two of them were startled to learn one night: They lifted open the hatch to reveal a young Afghan soldier inside smoking hash. Caught by surprise, he blurted out a tench cloud, Cameron and Damarkus recoiling from the Cheech-and-Chong fumes that came billowing out. The Afghan cleared out in no hurry, stashing his homemade water-bottle bong under the steering wheel, and not just because he was stoned. With flamboyant gesturing of his arms he made to usher them inside, like a bellhop guiding honeymooners into their suite, his toothy leer signaling a trade of one secret for another.

"We can't do this no more," Damarkus told Cameron, not for the first time. But the gravitational pull was too great. The fresh reek of hash hung inside the *Bronya* like an exotic emotion, something else new to feel. Damarkus watched himself disappear into the hatch as through a distant camera lens, realizing, from that indefinite aerie, that he was sacrificing everything for this, that he was scratching out his own eyes so as not to glimpse the future, just as stupid and reckless as Cameron had been up in that exposed gun turret with bullets glancing off his helmet. He didn't know how, he didn't know when, but he was going to die from this. But he watched himself close the hatch behind him, he watched himself not care.

As for Cameron, the effects of that carbonated Chinese wine seemed yet to have ebbed, as though that half a bottle had rendered him permanently drunk and beyond all caring: Wherever Damarkus's hands were touching him was truth and wherever they weren't was a lie that he could no longer bear living.

ON THE MORNING of March 8, 2010, at oh nine hundred hours, Captain Gary Lindholm called Lockwood into the command center and shut the door behind them. Damarkus was hoping this was about the coming spring fighting season, some kind of squad-assessment rap, but the otherwise deserted room and the captain's noncommittal tone and averted eyes were signaling otherwise. Damarkus took a breath and flexed his fingers, steadying himself. Maps and memoranda were tacked to the plywood walls; fluorescent lights buzzed and flickered overhead; a radio squawked in the corner; and Damarkus took a seat, as directed, on a bench facing the captain's crowded plywood desk.

Lindholm was the same age as Lockwood but the similarities ended there. Two years earlier he'd graduated from West Point, but he didn't advertise it and rarely even acted like it. He led like a sponge, constantly seeking affirmation from his junior officers and NCOs as though consensus, not leadership, was what they'd taught him won wars back at West Point. He was also, to Damarkus's ear, too quick to remind everyone that this was his first deployment; maybe he was trying to project some humility, which was fine, *hoo-ah* for that, but the residual impression was of a commander salting excuses, advancing himself a defense against future bungles. That said, Lindholm was also quick—the higher brass would surely say too quick—to call in air support and indirects and reinforcements whenever Bravo Company was taking serious fire, to feed his men the maximum weaponry available then ask for more on top. He didn't fight lean, unlike other commanders Damarkus had served under who seemed capable of factoring in the $115,000 cost of a Hellfire missile while units were pinned down and bleeding—and this quality was cause for affection from Damarkus and most everyone else.

Lindholm began in a casual key, like he always did. The captain talked to everybody as though they were guests on his talk show. The question itself, however, wasn't casual at all—not to Damarkus: "You ever been inside that old Soviet ATC?"

"The *Bronya*?" He tried answering breezily, matching the captain's tone, as if the question were whether he'd ever seen the Grand Canyon or used a set of chopsticks. "Yessir I have."

Lindholm was staring at him with his elbows on his desk, wheezing through his nostrils. The captain wasn't actually fat but came across that way, with big squarish cheeks like Wonder Bread slices and a chin that appeared eager for the company of more chins. His eyes looked like they hadn't yet decided what color to be. Normally they were gentle eyes, belonging more to a chaplain than a company commander, but right now they weren't gentle.

"What for?" Lindholm asked.

"Curiosity," answered Lockwood, thinking: Here it comes. Here's how I die. Take away the ban on gays in the military and Damarkus was still sitting deep in court-martial territory for carrying on an intimate relationship with a subordinate. Except, no, you couldn't take that away, because one charge had to be proven and the other just had to be decreed. All Damarkus had to do was smell gay. "Propensity or intent": Those were the words in the statute, those were the words they could hang him from.

Another fear suddenly pierced him: Was Lieutenant Cantwell interrogating Cameron now? Exactly how much shit was hitting this fan? They'd gone over it all together, he and Cameron, during one of Damarkus's fits of what he'd hoped was paranoia: what to say, what not to. Captain Lindholm was blinking his eyes at him, cueing him to say something more. Damarkus fumbled out, "It's kind of interesting up in there."

"Interesting how?"

"Like an old Corvette'd be, I guess. Like, you know . . . like an antique. A classic car."

"A Corvette." Lindholm let this sit on his desk for a while, sizing it up like a profundity. "You into cars?"

"Little bit I am, yessir. I like wrenching on them some." Damarkus thinking, please don't ask me about my ride at home, don't make me admit a Subaru. "My grandad taught me how."

"Your grandad," the captain echoed, like here was an intriguing new wrinkle, as if Chief might be worth getting on the horn. "You been in that ATC"—Damarkus could see him tripping over something in his mind—"what'd you say it was called?"

"It's called a *Bronya,* sir."

"Brone-yah," the captain practiced, leaning forward with his lips circled like he was blowing out birthday candles. "Brone-yah. You been in it more than once?"

"More than once? Yessir."

"By yourself?"

"By myself?" Damarkus didn't know why he was repeating the captain's questions except to stall the inevitable. He felt like a beetle trapped in a chicken coop, getting scratched, pecked, scratched again: death coming slow but death surely coming. "Nossir, the times I've been in there it's been with another soldier."

"Different ones, or the same?"

"The same, sir."

Lindholm narrowed his eyes, drilling him again. "ANA?"

Damarkus's forehead squashed into a frown: Where'd *that* come from? "Nossir," he said, honest confusion muddying his face, "one of ours."

"And who's that?"

"Harris, PFC One," he said, Cameron's name feeling like a full confession rolling off his lips.

"Harris." Lindholm ingested the name without betraying any prior knowledge; Damarkus searched his face for a reaction but saw nothing. "He into cars too?"

It wasn't clear if he meant this sarcastically. Every word the captain said came out in identically uninflected pellets that took meaningful shape several beats later, like Sea-Monkeys in spoken form. Damarkus chose to ignore the question. "He's the one showed it to me, sir."

"What's he find interesting about it?" Fluttering his eyes, still the genial talk show host.

"Same things as me, I reckon. But you'd have to ask him that, sir."

Lindholm didn't seem to appreciate this redirect, grunting then pretending to study some paperwork on his desk, which Damarkus, quick-peeking, could see was an unrelated flow chart. When the captain raised his face again his expression was softer, doughier, his eyes less angry than mildly agonized.

"This is your fourth deployment, sergeant," he announced.

"Yessir it is."

"That's a lot of deployments."

Here, Damarkus knew, was the oddly placed fulcrum in the room, the source of its delicate imbalance. Lindholm had his captain's bars but the sergeant had the combat stripes. And while no one faulted the captain, and no one thought a lack of seasoning had anything to do with it, Bravo Company had lost two men and watched seven head home wounded during its first three months under Lindholm's virgin command. Damarkus had seen other officers rattled by less. They start fearing they're test takers, not combat leaders. They start deferring to whoever's got the most scars, mistaking experience for wisdom. "Deploying is what I trained for, sir," Damarkus said.

"But four?" Lindholm was trying to lead him somewhere. He clasped his hands together as though to pray. "Four's gotta take a toll, huh?"

What was the toll in Lindholm's head, Damarkus wondered: Loneliness? Horniness? "I like serving my country, sir," he replied, a blue steel rod in his voice. "It's what I live for."

Lindholm's clasped hands jerked forward, something blatantly prick-
ling him: impatience with Damarkus's boilerplate response, perhaps, or
a challenge to throw in his own steel rod. "Then you understand the incredibly high standards NCOs have to meet out here," he said, in a barked
recital, "to ensure a positive impact on discipline, authority, morale, and
the command's ability to accomplish the mission."

"Yessir I do. Absolutely."

Lindholm gave him a sharp and unexpectedly conclusive nod. The two
of them could've been reading aloud from an Army manual but the captain seemed strangely satisfied with the exchange, lifting his elbows off
the desk to slump back into his chair. He let some air through his nostrils
and picked at a loose layer of plywood at the corner of his desk. Damarkus
sat watching him, thinking: Get it out, dammit, just fire that gun you got
aimed at me. But the voice that emerged from the captain, seeming to slip
from the side of his mouth, was dreamy, scatty, solicitous, a therapist's
voice. "It's tough being out here in the middle of nowhere, isn't it?"

Impatiently, Damarkus said, "Not sure I follow, sir."

The captain shrugged, smirked. "Shoveling snow for the local nation-
als. You know."

Once again Damarkus felt the tug of an invisible leash. "It's been a
pretty quiet winter, sir, if that's what you mean. But quiet's got its own
challenges. And we all know it's fixing to end."

"Right," the captain said, like he'd heard the same rumor, his voice
trailing off. Then he bolted himself upright, sighed, and bent sideways to
pull something from a bag beside his desk. "Sergeant Lockwood," he said,
without looking at him, his eyes fixed on whatever he was hiding in his
lap, "you feel like telling me what the fuck this is?"

What popped onto the desk was a gnarly old twelve-ounce plastic
water bottle that looked plucked from a forgotten recycling bin. Except
it wasn't just a water bottle: The inside was smeared with a greasy gray
film and there was a hole carved into its bottom, roughly the diameter of
a cigarette. Damarkus's eyes went in and out of focus until, with a start,
he recognized it: the Afghan soldier's water bong, the thing he'd used to
smoke hash inside the *Bronya*. The one he'd ditched beneath the dash.

"Looks to be a water bottle, sir," he answered—too flippantly, for sure,
but his mind was cartwheeling: Was he being questioned on suspicions of

drug use? Or was drug use part of a larger pile that the captain was now starting to slowly peel away, in the same cruel way he was flaking the plywood from his desk? He was wishing Lindholm had introduced the bottle by saying, "Let's get to the point here," or, "Let me tell you why I called you in here this morning"—some kind of prompt that this was it, that he had just a single gun pointed Damarkus's way.

"Well, it *was* a water bottle, yeah," Lindholm said, with an unspoken *duh*. He unscrewed the cap to take a sniff then offered one to Damarkus, who didn't know how to acknowledge the stench: as familiar or unfamiliar, as innocent or guilty. He nodded ambiguously.

"We found this in the *Bronya*," Lindholm said, still getting the hang of the word. "You and Harris, what—you guys got a little hookah lounge going in there?"

"Negative, sir. Hundred percent."

The captain grunted, more of an oink. "You feel like telling me who does?"

"I don't want to point fingers, sir, but I don't think it's any secret that some of the ANAs have, uh . . ."

"Certain habits? Yeah, it's no secret." The captain rubbed the bottle as though to conjure from it a hashish genie that could clear everything up. Then he brought both hands to his face, his fingers splayed, and massaged a look of distress onto it. "You got anything you need to tell me, sergeant?"

About *what*, Damarkus was thinking: about that stenchy little bottle, or about the rest you ain't asked me about yet. "If what you're asking, sir, is whether that belongs to me, or whether I've smoked or been around someone smoking something illegal, the answer's no." He pounded it one more time: "The answer's no."

Damarkus had no clue whether the captain returning the bottle to the bag beside his desk was a good sign or a bad one: the end of this story or merely the transition to chapter two. Everything was up to Lindholm, he knew. The captain had a fondness for overwhelming force and, in this case, had the MPs at his disposal, the Uniform Code of Justice, fatal slips of paperwork. If he wanted to be a brick, rather than a sponge, it was nothing for him to crush Damarkus. But Damarkus also knew the ranks were thin, with his squad particularly shorthanded; getting more bodies in here before the Taliban launched its spring offensive wasn't likely to happen.

"You and Harris," the captain was saying, almost singing it, tracing a line across his desk with a fingertip, "just hanging out in the old Corvette."

"Ain't nothing more than that, sir," Damarkus said, a rising pitch in his voice. "We just kinda checked it out a few times, got to talking about what-all the Soviets had to fight with and some of the things we're doing different . . ."

"Well, it's padlocked now," the captain said, part of Damarkus wishing it always had been, another part of him feeling gaffed through the heart.

"Seems like a prudent action, sir," Damarkus said, jerking his chin toward the clouded water bottle now stashed behind the captain's desk. "Considering."

Lindholm let another sigh out of his nose. "You know I've got to ask you to pee in a cup," he said.

"Sir," Damarkus said, "I'd be grateful for the opportunity to clear any doubts."

"Yeah," the captain said, stretching the word too much for Damarkus's comfort, as if two more seconds of yeah would complete a bridge to other doubts, suspicions harder to express for a Minnesota Lutheran like Lindholm. The captain scribbled onto a piece of paper and handed it across the desk. "You're headed to the med tent directly from here, understand? Give them that."

Instantly sensing an opening, Damarkus stood up in one fast fluid motion, thinking: Don't ask me to sit back down. The captain looked slightly but not disagreeably surprised, like the guest on his show was vacating the chair before the commercial break kicked in, before the host was out of questions.

Which he wasn't. He was eyeing Damarkus head to toe, squinting at him like he was drawing a picture of him in his mind but not getting the lines quite right. "You married, sergeant?" he asked, but the genial tone was frayed now, a spear tip poking through.

"Married?" There he went again, echoing the question. "Nossir, not at this time, I am not."

"How come?"

"Four deployments haven't helped on that front, sir."

"I'll bet." Lindholm softened now, beaten back by Damarkus's grizzle. He tossed a life ring, asking, "Girlfriend, then?"

"If I say more than one," Damarkus said, the answer an old one, the roguish grin practiced, "can I trust you to keep it to yourself?"

The captain guffawed, enjoying this, his laughter untightening the room. But Damarkus felt himself more rigidly tensed than ever, so immobilized that he felt incapable even of blinking. The natural response, he knew, was to inquire why the captain was asking. But he knew why the captain was asking.

"The reason I ask," Lindholm said, taking care of it for him, "is you and Harris, you know . . . you guys playing peekaboo in that Bronya."

"Sir—" Damarkus began, not knowing what was coming next from his mouth and thankful for the captain cutting him off.

"Besides the fraternization, you know," Lindholm went on, swirling his head around as though to loosen his neck muscles, "people get funny ideas."

Damarkus sighed in an appalled sort of way, hoping that sent the right signal, whatever the right signal might be. "Yessir, I understand."

"Last thing you want out here is funny ideas," Lindholm said, letting it hang in the air.

Damarkus tried imagining what one of his fellow NCOs would say to this but everything he cued up felt like crotch-grab overcompensation, a pledge of allegiance to vaginas. What came out was merely, "Yessir, agreed," Damarkus cringing inside because it felt insufficient or, worse, like tacit confirmation of the allegation tucked inside Lindholm's questions. He feared the captain and possibly the entire valley could hear the clanging of his heart.

Lindholm opened his mouth to speak but, with a sharp little flurry of his head, stifled whatever he'd intended to say. Then, as though reading from a prepared script, or from a West Point class handout, he said, "You're a squad leader, sergeant." His posture matched his tone: stiff-backed, squared-off. "I'll ask you to keep that fact front and center in your mind with every action you take whether inside or outside the wire. And to consider the impressions your actions could have on the men you're leading. That clear?"

"Yessir." A long exhale.

"Med tent from here. Dismissed."

Damarkus had the doorknob in his hand when the captain said, "Lockwood, one more thing."

He wheeled around slowly.

"That piss of yours comes back positive, after this conversation? I'll fucking bury you."

Damarkus Lockwood had thrown himself to the ground in open fields while bullets streaked past him, he'd been flattened into a blackout by the concussive waves of an exploding RPG, he'd been hurled to the roof of a Humvee after it rolled onto an IED on Dead Girl Road in Baghdad and been one of just two soldiers to walk away unscathed. But in seven years in the Army he'd never been as scared as he was leaving that command center, because to die from a bullet was one thing but to die from shame another, because fearing an enemy was nothing compared to fearing yourself—so scared, in fact, that on his way to the medics' tent he retched into a trash barrel, the strain so visible on his face that upon entering the tent he was immediately guided to a bed.

Two days later, on a dingy, yellow-skied afternoon, the soldiers manning watch at Hila's Entry Control Point observed a lone figure climbing slowly toward the outpost, pausing at each turn in the switchbacks to peer backward before continuing upward. When he was eighty meters out they fired a warning shot and the man stopped and raised his hands and hollered up something in Pashto. A two-hour standoff ensued during which Lieutenant Cantwell, via Shpoon and a megaphone, ordered the man to disrobe to prove he wasn't a suicide bomber. A team of ANAs finally made its way out to the man, the American troops lining up their weapons on the Hescos in case he was a decoy for snipers, and then the ANAs returned with the story: The man knew the location of a cache of weapons, mortars and RPGs and other heavy fire, hidden in the valley. An American medic had saved his son's life during one of the autumn patrols and he'd hiked all this way because he didn't want the medic to be killed.

The decision to believe him or not fell to Captain Lindholm. Lieutenant Cantwell lobbied hard against it, pointing out what a perfect way this'd be for the Taliban to launch the spring fighting season: luring a winter-fattened squad out of the wire and into an ambush. Yet the worse scenario, to the captain's thinking, was the outpost coming under bombardment from a painstakingly accumulated trove of heavy weapons like the one the man was describing. And if the cache did exist, its location—as much as its contents—was high-value intel, because its existence would mean that one or more of the elders that Lindholm had been meeting for weekly *shuras* had been lying: not a surprise, not even really a disappointment, but an advantageous nugget of knowledge for the captain going forward. He brought out the medics to see if one could ID the man. Yeah, one of them said, peering through binoculars. I remember the guy's eye patch. His little kid fell off the back of his motorcycle and punctured a lung. We tubed the kid's chest.

Lindholm chose Cantwell to lead a squad out, the lieutenant drawing one concession out of the captain: If an ambush was in the works they'd be gearing for it tonight. Waiting twenty-four hours might throw them off. They sent food and water and a blanket out to the man with a warning that if he moved from that spot, even to pee or defecate, he'd be shot.

Due to patrol scheduling, the twenty-four-hour delay meant Cameron and Damarkus's squad would be the one going out.

Cameron had not, as Damarkus feared, been questioned about the *Bronya* by Cantwell or by anyone else. Damarkus didn't know much more than this because he'd kept as far away as possible from Cameron ever since leaving the med tent, at dinnertime joining a table of NCOs who didn't seem entirely receptive to his presence: Whatever hashish rumors had reached the captain, Damarkus figured, had also reached them. Damarkus picked at his food, radioactive from nonexistent hash fumes, furtively glancing at Cameron who was sitting with Beano listening blankfaced to a rant about why the Federal Reserve needed auditing. Cameron confronted him later, to ask what was wrong, but Damarkus froze him out. He was tense right now, he said, needed some space to focus. He dressed down the squad as a whole after a surprise weapons inspection, too, startling everyone. "Something sure crawled up his butt," Cameron overhead one soldier muttering afterward, another one saying, "Yeah, just not how he likes it," Cameron waiting for them to look his way—but they didn't, to Cameron's relief, Cameron deciding it was nothing but trash talk. Fact was, though, the entire outpost was tensing. Rumors of ominous enemy chatter seemed confirmed by the officers' renewed stiffness, and the local national lying in the dirt out front, whether a decoy or an informant, felt like a rebuke to the winter's lull: a human alarm clock blaring eighty meters from the front gate. Everything was tightening. Even the dogs outside the wire acted skittish, barking at the snow for melting.

Damarkus knew what he had to do the very moment he left the command center, that knowledge, he'd later think, supplying half the cause for his retching. The situation was clear, which meant the solution was too. He recognized it as a lose-lose scenario but told himself these were common in wartime. Captain Lindholm's newest predicament, for example: If he was wrongly trusting the guy out front, he was sending a squad into an ambush; if he decided not to trust him, and the guy was speaking truth, whatever was in that weapons cache was going to come raining down on them soon. Sometimes the choice was between loss and loss, and at times, when the losses were high enough, when the choice felt pitched between calamity and catastrophe, your mind could seize up, leave you feeling like you're choosing between going blind and going deaf: flipping a coin and suffering heads or tails. This was how Damarkus Lockwood felt. And this was why, in the eighty-four hours that elapsed between him retching outside the command center and suiting up for the patrol, he slept no more than an hour at a time.

They left the wire at twenty-three hundred hours, under a clear and guardian half-moon. The man they were already calling Gollum didn't know how to read a map and the route he intended to guide them sounded distressingly vague. This made it more difficult for the men back at Hila's command center to get an infrared-vision drone in proper place for surveilling the terrain ahead, since only Gollum knew where that was. And he didn't know too well, it seemed: The squad backtracked more than once, Gollum claiming the darkness was throwing off his sense of the landscape, Cantwell suspecting he'd found the ambush point vacant and now was either actively hunting the missing ambushers or just killing time, joyriding a U.S. Army squad. The soldiers hiked silent and nimble through a world rendered emerald in their night-vision goggles. Hours passed. Gollum grew more and more disoriented and Cantwell more and more wary. He decided to stagger the squad, assigning Cameron and Damarkus to take a more distant rear-watch position alongside two ANA soldiers.

Fifteen minutes later the ANAs just stopped and sat down, as though all these walking hours had been in search of an ideal picnic spot. Damarkus urged them forward but they shook their heads no and as one pulled something from his pocket the other raised a forefinger in that international code for break time. He radioed the news to the lieutenant. Cantwell cursed and told him to hold the position; the whole thing was a shit show and they'd circle back shortly.

Damarkus looked over at Cameron, propped against a boulder smoking a cigarette about thirty feet from the two Afghan soldiers who were likewise smoking and muttering languidly in Pashto. The timing, Damarkus decided, was unexpectedly perfect. The Afghans wouldn't understand what they were saying but their presence was a cushion against any dramatics.

He leaned beside Cameron against the boulder. "Look," he began. "This here's gotta be the deal going forward."

Cameron turned to him, nothing but curiosity on his face, a green ghost unaware that he was being vanquished into the past.

"None of it ever happened, okay?" Damarkus kept his voice to a clipped whisper. "Not the words, not the feelings, not one part of it. Everything that happened and everything got said in the *Bronya*—it's gone and it wasn't never there."

Even through night-vision goggles the confusion was blatant in Cameron's eyes. His chin came jutting forward, mock-bravely. "The hell you saying?"

"You heard me," Damarkus hissed, from the part of him wanting Cameron to say just yessir, the part of him holding the microphone right now. "It's gone outta my head and you're getting it out of yours. Nothing ever happened and from here on out we go about our business that way."

"Why you acting this way, D?" Cameron was facing him now, away from the boulder face. "What'd I do?"

"It ain't nothing no one did because nothing ever happened, you understand?"

"No, I don't." Cameron shook his head, dragging on his cigarette like it was an asthma inhaler. "Not even close."

"We ain't gonna be this way anymore, you hear me?"

"Why you doing this now?" His hushed voice full of pleading. "What happened?"

"It ain't *about* now," Damarkus said, alarmed by the rise in his own voice, wanting and not wanting to dull its serrated edge. He swung his head toward the Afghan soldiers as a funky smell reached his nose—the rumor must've reached them too, because the pair was openly smoking hash, passing a joint back and forth in the darkness. "I mean to say—yeah, it is about now," he said, as lost in his own incoherence as Gollum was lost in these lightless black mountains. "Because now's different than before. Because the only way out of this is if before didn't happen."

Cameron fell back against the boulder, crumpling. "You ain't making any sense, D," he whispered. The two ANAs were laughing now—maybe from the hash, maybe about the hash, maybe about something totally unrelated—and Damarkus could see the laughter rasping Cameron, could see him flinching at every acid chuckle. Whatever it was, it felt and sounded like ridicule, and Damarkus couldn't bear that for Cameron. He knew the Tommy Landry story—knew how laughter, real or perceived, was toxic to Cameron, was poisonously entangled in everything he knew about love. He glared at the ANAs but without goggles like his they didn't catch the glare. One was laughing at the other one's coughing. "Shit," Damarkus said. "Head over this way with me."

They didn't walk far. On the other side of the boulder from the trail was a wide and flat ledge with a spur of rock overhanging the cliff side, providing a natural lookout over the valley. Closer in were some bedraggled juniper and rosebay bushes eking a stunted living from the gravelly soil, the men's boots exacting further punishment on their forlorn branches. Down the valley in the east, a violet fuzz was outlining the lumpy horizon, dawn beginning to heave its way up.

Cameron was stumbling like a drunk, Damarkus suddenly fearing he might weave his way off the overhang. "Just stand still," he told him, Cameron stopping with his head dropped.

Damarkus's radio cracked, Cantwell saying, "Bloodhound Six, this is Echo One. You guys still parked? Over."

"Roger, Echo One, that's affirmative," Damarkus replied. "We're holding. Over."

"Headed back your way. Recontact in five mikes. Over."

Cameron had moved directly in front of him, not quite close enough to touch, pleading, "What are you saying, D?"

Damarkus inhaled, exhaled, trying to re-center himself with air. Lieu-

tenant Cantwell and the rest of the squad were five minutes out and after
that they'd need to fall back into the patrol line, thirty feet apart in forced
silence. *Walk it off,* Chief used to tell Damarkus when he was hurt. *You
can walk off most anything, boy.* Yet something in Cameron's voice—the
anguished warble, yes, but a heavier bass note of resistance—was telling
Damarkus he'd made a mistake here, the dimensions of which felt to be
telescoping by the second. He'd thought to avoid the danger of an ani-
mated conversation inside the wire, but he'd also thought his authority,
especially out here, would mute any protest. One other mistake he was
realizing: He hadn't understood, or he'd refused to understand, the intensity of Cameron's emotions.

"Look," he said, softer now, struggling to think over the thudding
of his heart, "the only thing that can come from me and you is—it ain't
nothing good, Cam. Don't matter how it felt last month or how it felt yesterday. There ain't nothing good at the end. We don't get to walk off into
that fucking sunrise over there. You feel me? This here ain't *life*, man. Me
and you got loose, I know we did—we got weak. But that weakness ain't
us. And best thing we can do is say that weakness never happened."

"I didn't get weak, D," Cameron said, his entire voice now drawn into
that bass note, solid, unbreakable, somehow dominant. "For the first time
in my life I got strong."

Damarkus reared back several steps, as from a sudden whoosh of
flames. "Naw, listen—you ain't getting me."

"I'll pretend whatever the fuck you want but you can't tell me I didn't
feel what I felt." Cameron banged a fist against his chest. "You ain't making me a liar."

Now it was Damarkus stumbling drunkenly, wheeling back in the
direction of the horizon's purple fringe. "Goddammit," he heard himself say, his breathing heavy as a runner's. Remember there's no choice
here, he tried reminding himself: just the incomplete line between *what
is* and *what has to be.* Yet another voice inside him, one he recognized
only dimly, maybe from the past and maybe from the future, was calling bullshit, spewing phrases that kept colliding and recolliding in the
raceway of Damarkus's mind: *what has to be; what can't be; what could be;
what should be—*

He was two separate men as he turned back toward Cameron. He was one man in love and the other man fleeing the very sound of the word, its lethal echoes. He was one man walking toward Cameron and the other walking away, conjoined twins being violently severed. He felt words filling his mouth but didn't know which man they belonged to. Before he could say anything, though, Cameron spun away from him, his fist still pressed to the front of his flak vest as though to restrain his very heart, and Damarkus, confused by how much Cameron hurting hurt him, and recognizing that this pain constituted love, felt himself take a lunging step forward—

Only his eyes had time to move once he registered the click beneath his heel. Cameron was turning back toward him. That's all he saw, in that final green landscape: a turn that could've meant nothing and could've meant everything. His lips cracked apart.

Boom.

after, pt. 5

neither will I hide my face any more from them;

for I have poured out my spirit

(saith the Lord)

twenty

D ID IT MATTER, AS AWARENESS OF CAMERON'S HOMOSEXUAL-
ity spread slowly and then fast, especially after the attorney for
Tommy Landry chose to leak it in a two-million-dollar civil lawsuit filed
against Cameron, Scott T. Griffin, Ain't No Picnic Productions, LLC
(Griffin's production company), Guidry's Lava Lounge, and various other
defendants? There's an answer to this question, but, as with so many of
those surrounding Cameron's recovery, not one that's easy to prove—not
with unequivocal data, anyway, not with resonance imaging of the mot-
ley and fluid national temper. But to many people of faith, particularly
those whose faith tilts more toward ideology than theology, both inside
and outside the Christ-haunted state of Mississippi: Yes, of course it did. It
mattered a great deal.

Plugging the words *miracle* and *Mississippi* into Google, in October
2014, yielded a raft of additional search term suggestions: *real; paralyzed;
amazing; veteran; true.* By late February 2015, Google's algorithm was
coughing up these: *gay; hoax; assault; debunked.* Most if not all legitimate
news outlets omitted Landry's allegation—in capsule form, that Cameron
had assaulted him to stop Landry from outing him—from their coverage of the lawsuit, filed January 12. The *Sun Herald*'s Jesse Castanedo,
for example, was leery of broadcasting an accusation that felt to him
like a venom-laced publicity gambit. (Plus, he says, "in half the fistfights
I've ever seen, from schoolyards to barrooms, someone gets called a fag
or some other gay slur. This just seemed like the same thing channeled
through a lawyer.") The gossip website Radar Online, however, gave it a
full-color splash ("Read the SHOCKING Police Report!"), and links to its

coverage went scattering swiftly and widely, like roaches fleeing a light. That Cameron refused to publicly confirm or even acknowledge any part of Landry's claims, and that Lifetime's Nicola Ash maintained a brusque no-comment regimen, mattered little. Because the revelation, oozing through the channels of social media, wasn't really about Cameron. His sexual orientation, cracked open for public examination, got appropriated into a much larger, older, and more bellicose dynamic—as a cudgel, not a complication.

This was particularly striking in the way hard-line atheist bloggers and webmasters took to trumpeting Cameron's outing: gleefully. They reveled in putting conservative Christians—Cameron's supposed fan base—into the pincers of an uneasy predicament: If God so abhorred homosexuality, why ever would he exert his miraculous grace on a homosexual? Their cackling was all but audible as they baited their trap: "Either God doesn't have such a big problem with hot man-on-man action," as one blogger, Chris Clairmont, writing as "The Fundy Unbeliever," wrote in late January, "or God didn't have anything to do with this man standing up and shouting hallelujah. Miracle or endorsement? Hmmm. Which one is it, all ye faithful? (Hint: It's a trick question. God doesn't exist.)"

A handful of Christian bloggers, including the thoughtful Catholic apologist Peter Heekin-Kaye, responded with the salient point that, scripturally speaking, God abhors the sin but loves the sinner, arguing that divine healing of a sinner—regardless of the sin—amounted to theological harmony, not dissonance. "These are political distinctions," he wrote, "not spiritual ones." Such political distinctions dominated, however, and began manifesting themselves in a curiously inverted way: Those who had initially promoted Cameron's recovery as a miracle, aligned generally with the Christian right, now clamored for a scientific explanation, while those on the more secular left who'd balked at and even ridiculed the idea of a miracle, and had sought its disproval, started cozying up to the notion, or at least to the theater of its implications. One faction appeared willing to suspend its belief while the other seemed inclined to suspend its disbelief. One flipped while the other flopped.

Yet Peter Heekin-Kaye's levelheaded middle ground—stripped of political cant, and open to the simultaneous possibilities that a genuine miracle could have occurred and that its recipient could be gay—attracted little support. Those who posited such a compromise found themselves shouted down on evangelical forums, no matter how often or how intently they quoted Mark 2:17 ("I came not to call the righteous, but the sinners"). No one would argue that the internet's atmosphere for meaningful discourse is anything but thin; still, this debate suffered a profoundly quick asphyxiation. Two competing conspiracy theories rose from the suffocating muck: that the revelations about Cameron being gay were false, planted by media supporters of a so-called "Rainbow Jihad" against Christians; or that Cameron's recovery itself was a hoax, either a television stunt or, more darkly, a trick by a flagrantly troubled (and gay) soldier to bilk four years of full disability from the government. (Links to the same coverage that Janice had mentioned to Euclide, about the not-quite-so-paralyzed Texas veteran caught grilling burgers, circulated widely.)

It didn't take long, then, for God to be shunted aside entirely, as seen in this Twitter post from late January, which provides a coarse if accurate distillation of the tenor of conservative Christians regarding Cameron's recovery:

Rob S. Stratton @Strattoncaster86
Glad for anyone, Sodomite or not, to recover from injury. But no one should pretend God had anything directly to do with it.
10:29 AM - 29 January 2015

BECAUSE CAMERON WAS NOT, in this constricted but widespread view, merely a sinner—a vessel for divine mercy whose worthiness was open to dispute. He was a bar brawler, sure, but not, to anyone's knowledge, a thief or a murderer or an adulterer; in fact he stood unaccused of breaking a single of the Ten Commandments.

No, Cameron was seen as something far more dangerous than that: a symbol. For God to raise a gay man from the sorrow of paralysis, in the polarized America of 2014, was for God to take a political stance—to divinely rebuke his own followers, betraying their adherence to what they took to be his everlasting word. And God, most of those followers said, wouldn't do that; ergo, Cameron's recovery couldn't be a miracle. It probably wasn't even a bona fide recovery, many people started saying—was probably just an act engineered for a TV show, or maybe, like others said, a long and unsavory con job, or maybe even, as a few others said, a flubbed diagnosis by the bureaucratic half-wits at the VA. But it wasn't a miracle—easy as that.

THE SHIFT WAS most readily apparent at the Biz-E-Bee. The large tour coaches disappeared almost at once, as if locked in place by a nation-wide recall, the last one rolling into the parking lot on January 28 to discharge a group of elderly Germans who seemed unaware not only of Cameron's new complexities but of Cameron and his recovery at all. They were tourists, not pilgrims, their driver-slash-guide shuttling them off the bus at various sites of interest between Houston and Miami.

Quỳnh stepped from the store to listen as their driver explained this stop's significance to them: The world-famous Biz-E-Bee, he told them, was the set of a major new American television show about an injured Iraq war veteran who had been working at the store when his injuries had suddenly and mysteriously been healed, the presentation failing to clarify whether the show was fact or fiction, never mind the underlying events. Ollie drifted beside Quỳnh and the two men stood listening together, Ollie throwing a querulous stare Quỳnh's way whenever the driver mangled another detail, Quỳnh just nodding back at Ollie with his lips pressed together, as if to say, I know and you know but it doesn't matter if they don't. This wasn't unlike the glances Quỳnh'd once traded with his brother-in-law Anh, Hat's sister's husband, as Anh's teenaged son went prattling on about a Vietnam War that he understood, or thought he did, exclusively from American movies. A bottle of entertainment, Quỳnh knew, will always outsell a bottle of history—and knowing this, he'd thought, had given him an advantage. What he hadn't known, however, was how volatile and perishable the contents of both bottles could be.

The Germans took hesitant, haphazard photos of the Biz-E-Bee, as though maybe their children or grandchildren back in Düsseldorf or Schweinfurt would recognize its elusive importance, but seemed otherwise unimpressed, a quarter of them retreating back to the bus the moment the driver finished. Inside the store the remaining Germans cleared out Quỳnh's inventory of orange soda but purchased only a few souvenirs—a rosary, a votive, one of Gil's funky snow globes that got shaken and re-shaken for guttural laughs. After ushering them back into the bus the driver broke for a cigarette, standing squarely and obliviously in the exact spot where Cameron had risen. Ollie had scrubbed the rectangle of paint from the parking lot weeks before, per Hat's command, but a dingy or-ange hint of it remained visible in the cracks, a ghost-like antumbra in the asphalt. "They saw alligators in Louisiana and now all they want to see is more alligators," the driver told Quỳnh, venting more than apologizing. Quỳnh shrugged and said he understood: Alligators were pretty amazing.

That Cameron was supposedly *bóng,* as gay men are derided in Viet-nam, had come to Quỳnh as little shock. One reason was because he didn't care. Why should he get an opinion on where someone else prefers to put his *cu*? Where Quỳnh enjoyed putting his, after all, was none of Cameron's business. It had long bewildered Quỳnh that America's loudest champions of liberty struck him as the quickest to erect a fence around the word—the same ones who, when Vietnamese immigrants like him began fishing the Gulf, strong-armed bait-shop owners into refusing to sell to Vietnamese fishermen, conspired to jack up boat prices, and lob-bied state legislatures to restrict the sale of new shrimping licenses, all in the name of protecting the "freedom" of the Gulf fishery from people like Quỳnh. He'd recognized their faces in the scowls aimed at him and Hat at Gil's funeral in little Chunchula, Alabama, from men irritated by the exotic mystery of their attendance as the Baptist preacher struggled to celebrate something of Gil's life beyond the penitence of its end, Gil's three ex-wives and six grown children sitting dry-eyed in the front pew as if watching justice being served.

But the other, deeper reason Quỳnh felt no shock was because Cam-eron being gay was simply the other shoe, the one whose drop he'd been inveterately awaiting. Exuberance had intoxicated him in November and December, had pried him from his fatalistic crouch, until news of Camer-on's fight had cold-splashed him. Not that he'd quite known what to make of the fight; he hadn't felt a fraction of Hat's alarm and disgust. Cameron beating someone up in a bar didn't seem like that other shoe. Quỳnh spent very little time in bars but his understanding, from the cops and from all the black-eyed, fist-bandaged drunks that came drifting through the Biz-E-Bee, was that people punched each other in bars all the time. But

Cameron being *bóng,* on the other hand—close to half a year of marketing to what he called "Bible beaters," and living with Gil, had equipped
Quỳnh with a fair sense of their quirks and limitations, and this development, if true, strayed far too afield for them. Poor old Gil, for one, couldn't
have stomached it; if the cancer hadn't killed him first this news would
surely have done him in. Owing to this Quỳnh foresaw the coaches disappearing even sooner than they did. He'd come out to see the Germans
only because, by his reckoning, they were already relics from a lost era—
stragglers arriving to the feast as the plates were being cleared.

For Hat, the revelation about Cameron threw her ever deeper into
spiritual vertigo. Like forty-two percent of her adopted countrymen (according to a 2015 Pew Research poll), Hat believes that homosexuals are
homosexual because they choose to be—that what constitutes homosexuality is not an inherent orientation but rather a selected set of actions.
Everyone, to her thinking, is susceptible; but strong moral fiber, and,
failing that, cultural proscription, keeps most people in check. Her dismay at Cameron's bar fight eventually waned—men were men, after all.
But countenancing Cameron as a gay man was something she didn't feel
equipped to do. If she no longer believed in God—not in the way she once
had, as a tender and careful overseer of human events—she still believed
in the need for him. She still believed in the bedrock moral code he represented, or was invented to represent. And she felt certain that Cameron
Harris, by choosing to be gay, violated that code.

Hat was alone in the store when Cameron came in—his first visit since
word reached her. If she hadn't been alone, she thought later, she might
not have said anything; Quỳnh, so generously accommodating of late,
would've likely tried shushing her. Cameron eased in mumbling his standard hello then asked for cigarettes. Hat slid two packs across the counter.

Quietly but sharply, as she rang him up, she said, "You shouldn't have
lied to us."

"Lied?" He stood there blinking. "About what?"

"You know what," grimacing.

Cameron blinked several more times before nodding, piecing it together from the way she was averting her eyes. "That wasn't no lie." He
rolled his shoulders in a pained shrug. "That just wasn't nobody's business."

Hat's mouth fell open. "Nobody's *business*?" She clawed toward the aisles of miracle merchandise behind him. "Look behind you, look at all that. It *is* our business. It's been most of our business for months."

Cameron did as instructed, pivoting to survey all the curios he'd inspired, that rainbow skyline of candles that his legs had made people want to light. He turned back to Hat. "I didn't ask," he said, "for it to happen here.

"Truth is," he added, more foggily, "I ain't even sure I ever asked for it to happen at all. Not the way it did."

Hat flattened her lips together as she uncreased the bills he'd passed her and added them to the cash drawer. "If you'd told us . . ." she began, flustered. "If you'd told us it would've been different."

She wasn't thinking about all the merchandise as she said this, her and Quỳnh's scuppered investment. Instead she was thinking about Gil. Because Cameron had betrayed Gil with his secret, she'd decided earlier: betrayed Gil by seeing him out there every day, by watching all that faith and devotion broiling on the asphalt, and doing nothing—when all he'd had to do, from the beginning, was take Gil aside, confide the truth to him, whisper how it was, so that Gil could understand that it hadn't been a miracle or at least not a miracle in the way Gil thought of miracles.

But then what? It suddenly occurred to her. She'd never played the scenario through to its end, always nipping it off at this point of principle. Shorn of his last hope, Gil would've almost surely limped back to Alabama, trailing a deflated, sagging cross, and died alone. Whereas in Biloxi his last months had been suffused with hope—so much hope, yes, and also food, laughter, Quỳnh's silly shoot-em-up movies, a three-year-old who never wearied of an old man's card tricks. And if loved ones hadn't ministered to Gil's final hours, the way it ought to be, then at least he'd died in the presence of someone who cared, who'd mourned. Which meant—and this was not just a thought, again, but a sensation that prickled her skin and dampened her eyes—that maybe God did exist, after all.

Cameron didn't acknowledge her hypothetical about outing himself to her and Quỳnh—it was too absurd to address. He dropped his gaze to where his cigarette packs were stacked on the counter. "It wasn't like I planned all this," he mumbled, part of him knowing he was taking more blame than he deserved but another part of him still oozing with guilt.

Then, less than firmly, he said, "I won't come around no more if there's hard feelings."

Hat let out a small, mewling sound, almost but not quite the word *no,* and for the first time so far raised her eyes to his. Regarding Cameron in the fluorescent store lights she found, with dizzying confusion, that she couldn't quite see him—not the way she could see other people, as contained and coherent. He was standing before her in triplicate or quadruplicate or even quintuplicate, each iteration—the one she knew, the one she thought she knew, the ones she didn't know at all—slightly different from the rest, one of them an affront to God but another of them his divine instrument. And yet the aggregate of all these Camerons—his sulky blue eyes, every set of them, dropping back to the counter—was somehow beyond her capture or comprehending, an unsolvable equation, not because he was gay and not because he'd risen in her parking lot but because he was at once so ordinarily and extraordinarily human. She released a long and lingering sigh. Here was yet another reason for God: He alone understood. "No," she finally said to him, slackening her voice with a gentler, maternal tone. "It's not like that. It's just . . ."

What was he to her, after all—or what did she need him to be—beyond a customer? She had no claim on his soul, nor he on hers. Except this wasn't true and she knew it. "It's just hard when you don't see what's coming," she said, recognizing as she spoke how insufficient this sounded but compelled to say something anyway, to lower her fists with words. She was fearing losing him. One iteration of him revolted her, it was true. But another iteration had proven to be her portal away from and now back to God. And yet another iteration seemed to her as frail and vulnerable as Little Kim had been in the neonatal ward and Gil had been on his deathbed, as though a part of him—his soul, maybe—was helplessly gasping.

Hat glanced down to where Cameron's hands were scooping the cigarettes and she plucked a dollar from the cash drawer. She slid it across to him and then, when he failed to react, tapped it twice.

"What's that?" he said, blinking again.

"I forgot your discount."

Cameron examined the dollar. "Quỳnh says it don't apply to smokes."

The way she swiveled her eyes made clear to him that Quỳnh wasn't there, and thus his rules weren't either. Confounded by these jumbled messages, Cameron pocketed the bill and nodded at her, wanting to apologize but not knowing what for and wanting to thank her but also not knowing what for: silenced by the anarchy of his own messaging. So he just nodded again, this time more deeply, and made for the door, over the jingle of the bell hearing her say, in that old familiar style, "See you next time, okay."

For a long while Hat sat motionless and blurry-headed behind the counter. When her concentration returned, focused by customers tramping in and then out, she found herself scanning the store with just one thing clear to her: They'd soon be broke again. Quỳnh had bet too many chips stocking souvenirs for the pilgrims. Those two full aisles of religious items in the Biz-E-Bee would be hogging that space for eternity if she and Quỳnh didn't start marking prices down, which is what they ultimately if reluctantly did: fifty percent off in February, then seventy-five percent off, for a loss, come March. They needed to recover that semi-sacred shelf space for products the neighborhood actually needed: Cat Chow and Lorna Doone cookies and Cheez Whiz and FastStart carburetor cleaner and New Orleans Saints logo'd automotive air fresheners. Perhaps somewhere else it might've been different, say in California where Hat's sister had recently moved. In Mississippi, however, they'd lost their license to sell faith and hope.

Yet something about this calamity didn't distress Quỳnh the way it formerly would've, and the way Hat feared it was going to. He didn't take to moping, or cursing, or fretting himself awake at three a.m. Like Gil, he'd gambled on a miracle and lost. But unlike Gil he'd only lost money.

And money, came a new thought, was like magic: It came and it went, and its value and meaning were for every man to decide for himself. Quỳnh consoled himself by thinking that life had thus far afforded him entry to two magical realms: his grandmother's farm at Vũng Tàu, with its talking geckos and twilit bat swarms and those low sorcerous gongs that'd lulled him to sleep; and the Biz-E-Bee in the autumn and early winter of 2014, when for a brief time he'd felt endowed with almost wizardly power, when for a fast and rollicking period people had looked to Quỳnh not for beer or cigarettes or diapers but for hope and for healing, when he'd been regarded, with reverence, as an emissary of something enchanted. But such realms were transitory, he decided, they were like gorgeously colored soap bubbles whose only destiny was to pop. And perhaps, he thought further, misfortune bore the same floaty impermanence. Only death was final. Everything else, like sunlight, like storms, moved in and moved out. What else was he to glean from Cameron's rising?

One unusually warm evening in late February Quỳnh was sitting out back with Steven Seagal, his pacifist fighting cock, and taking in nothing more than the funky salt breeze seeping through the trumpet vines and oleander and wax myrtle, when Little Kim slashed open the screen door and came waddling out to him. He scooped her in his arms and let her run her hands over his face as if she were blind and trying to identify him, the giggles he was charming out of her pitched lower than usual, issuing from someplace deep and nameless in her tiny chest. Jealous, Steven Seagal puffed and crowed and scrambled back when Little Kim probed a fingertip into his cage, and was soon scrambling in peckish circles as she did it again and then again, Quỳnh finding himself hypnotized by an old reflection he caught in her eyes. "Do you want to talk to Steven Seagal?" he asked her, and she laughed and said, "Chickens don't talk." But no they do, he told her, click-click-clicking his tongue so that the rooster cocked his head and waggled his big red comb and after a while emitted an intrigued few clucks. Little Kim's mouth dropped open and she clapped and called for more and Quỳnh asked her what she wanted him to say to the rooster. As she considered this, with her fist pressed to her chin, he glanced up to see Hat watching them through the screen door, a spatula hanging loose in her hand and her face soft with an expression Quỳnh first thought he hadn't seen in many years before realizing he'd never seen it at all. She smiled at Quỳnh, and as Little Kim told him to ask Steven Seagal his favorite color Quỳnh smiled back at her, thinking, Not two magical realms, no. Three.

A few days later a man showed up at the Biz-E-Bee wearing a rainbow sash. He was middle-aged, slender, tanned and sandy-haired like he'd been conceived on a surfboard, and spoke with a lispy New Orleans accent. He asked Quỳnh to direct him to where Cameron had risen, Quỳnh shaking his head no and telling the man that his wife didn't like them doing that anymore. The man smiled, said please, he was on his way back from a Mardi Gras event in Mobile and had stopped to say a quick prayer.

He wasn't the typical pilgrim, *bóng* for sure, so Quỳnh led him out to the parking lot and swirled a finger at the dim echo of paint on the asphalt.

Hat came around the corner at just that moment, walking back from having her hair done at the Snip 'n' Shear two blocks west. Quỳnh cringed at the sight of her, anticipating an angry scowl, but her expression was merely quizzical, her head mildly tilted. When she sidled up beside him she did so without a word.

The man stepped inside and lifting his hands brought both index fingers to his thumbs, as though measuring out an invisible length of string. Then he lowered his head and closed his eyes and silently mumbled for about half a minute while Quỳnh stood watching him with one hiked eyebrow. Afterward Quỳnh couldn't help asking, "What did you pray for?"

"Love and understanding," the man answered, so quickly and lightly as to suggest the answer was self-evident, like he was ordering dinner in a restaurant that offered a single dish.

Quỳnh pulled at his neck as he considered this, thinking the prayer was kind of fruity but at the same time remembering all the hundreds of people who'd hauled their private maladies into that same space seeking custom-tailored grace, begging God to focus his big lens exclusively on them, everyone, including him, hustling for a crumb of their own. "Yeah, okay," Quỳnh said gruffly, as if approval was his to dispense. He glanced at his wife beside him, but she didn't see him looking, her head bobbing softly in some intricately private way. "I like that," Quỳnh said. "That sound about right."

DID IT MATTER? Not in any official way, to the Lifetime Network, whose executives had already shelved *Miracle Man*, indefinitely, after the New Year's Eve brawl, and saw in the lawsuit reasonable grounds to cancel the show altogether, which they did on January 20, just prior to the Television Critics Association meeting that Cameron and Tanya had once been scheduled to attend. A complex and protracted bout of squabbling followed between Scott T. Griffin's agents and the network, mirroring the marriage separation proceedings that Griffin was also entering, but the arguing amounted, essentially, to a fight over money. Custody of the show—and of Cameron's story—didn't really factor; it was a foregone casualty, a failed draft consigned to a drawer.

Griffin, though, wasn't ready to be done with the story. He'd finally gotten Cameron on the phone, five days after the fight, Cameron showering him with apologies for, as he put it, losing his shit, but also exuding scarce signals that he wanted to continue with the show, which Griffin was still insisting was possible. Unable to get around the network's suspension, however, and bleeding money daily, Griffin cleared out of the Ocean Springs cottage and flew back to Los Angeles three days later. Honeybun, his valiant first mate, remained by his side until the end, with even Kaitlyn jumping ship before Griffin was conceding its sinking. Griffin understood that in the world of reality-television production he was a corpse: a guy who'd been crushed by a story too big and unruly for him to control. The allegations in the lawsuit—that he'd been inebriated during filming, that his reckless mismanagement had stoked a volatile situation—felt like gratuitous bullet holes, the shots movie hitmen fire at downed bodies to confirm a kill. He was dead and then he got deader.

Yet in the lawsuit's bigger allegation—that Cameron attacked Landry in order to keep his homosexuality a secret—Griffin was spying a diamond glint of opportunity. Not for television—screw television—but for a feature-length documentary, the kind of work he'd originally set out to do back when he was the golden boy of his MFA program, the real shit, the big screen, *art*. He wrote Cameron a long letter in early March, laying out his idea. The existing footage belonged to him, and if not he'd work out the clearances, which meant at least half the work was already in the can—it all just needed to be re-thought, re-framed, re-edited, re-lit with this bright new halogen beam of complexity. Alone in his bed, night after night, he watched the documentary-to-be in the multiplex of his imagination, brought to tears by Rufus Wainwright singing "The Battle Hymn of the Republic" over the closing credits, a nonexistent dream track that felt impossibly moving and unassailably vindicating.

"What else did I have to do?" Griffin says, that trademark laugh of his trailing into a weak, spumy cough. By February he was scrounging for advertising work, filming blue-vested actors watering plants and stacking lumber for stock ad footage for Lowe's while trying to juggle funereal phone calls from his agent and his divorce attorney and his personal attorney and his company attorney, half the conversations closing with them saying, "We'll get through this." Was there a word, Griffin wondered, for an anti-miracle? God healed and revived people, right, but did he also, you know, just zap others—bury them neck-deep in a divine dump of shit just to see if and how they'd wriggle free? As an adult he'd only ever been to church for weddings or funerals, so he didn't know; most of what he knew about God came from old Al Green albums. But a self-pitying part of him figured this might be his condition. Or maybe L.A.'s dippy namaste crowd—his yoga-pantsed, soon-to-be ex-wife among them—was actually onto something with their spacey talk about energy transfer and chi balance: Maybe Cameron, in the wake of that giant karmic explosion of his, had somehow vacuumed all the karma right out of Griffin, like some killer black hole, just hoovered him clean. Griffin didn't know. New Age philosophy wasn't his thing any more than Christianity or astrophysics was. All he knew was that his life started unraveling the moment Cameron Harris entered it, but that Cameron still seemed his best hope for stitching it back together.

Cameron never responded to his letter, which was, Griffin supposed, a kind of response in itself. But while he was still holding out hope he met Honeybun for drinks one evening over in Silver Lake. By this time Honeybun had landed a job on, to Griffin's astonishment, another Lifetime reality show, this one called *Little Women: L.A.* and about five women— "little people, not midgets," came Bun's admonition—living life below the four-foot mark. But it was an assistant camera gig, journeyman work. (Curiously, *Little Women: L.A.* would also suffer an on-camera bar-brawl incident, between cast members in January 2016, with Honeybun, groaning from déjà vu, operating the camera.)

Honeybun did what he always did lately: extracted grumbles of praise from Griffin for his majestic and unerring gaydar along with a formal admission of Griffin's error in having doubted him. Griffin submitted, having long since exhausted his excuses and by now embracing—relishing, even—the concept of a gay Cameron Harris.

Through the first round of drinks they bellyached about the torpid, glutted state of the reality-show industry, Griffin likening it to "end times of the traveling carnival era," before he started pitching his documentary idea. Honeybun sipped his drink through a straw and shrugged noncommittally as Griffin wound himself tighter and tighter into salesman mode. Honeybun sat listening to himself being inserted into the blueprint, Griffin charting the soulful new careers he was seeing for the two of them, a second vodka adding a rhapsodic note to Griffin's vision for the documentary. He talked as though he were reading from A. O. Scott's future *New York Times* review following the film's premiere at Sundance. Then Honeybun stopped him.

"Whoa, go back to what you just said," Honeybun told him. "About the metaphor . . ."

"Yeah, *yeah*," Griffin said, baring his teeth in a grin. He threw back some of his drink and wiped his lips with a forearm. "That's how you can frame this, right? Cameron rising out of his wheelchair—that was like him coming out of the closet, stepping into his true identity, unlocking his real self. That was him rising into, like, the full flower of his humanity. You following me?"

"Uh, no," Honeybun said flatly. He'd worked on and off with Griffin for ten years and had come to love him like a brother, but, like any brother, he sometimes longed to whack him with a bat. "You realize, right, that you're equating being gay with being paralyzed? That's just . . . stupid. And obnoxious."

"Not *gay*," Griffin said. He looked hurt. "Closeted."

"Dude." Honeybun shook his head. "You're just not getting it. Being paralyzed is being paralyzed. It's not a metaphor for anything. It's a neurological fucking *condition*."

Griffin frowned and shrugged, wary of tainting a rare night out with Bun but also too secure in his vision to engage the point any further. He started in on the potential for grant money, Honeybun stirring the dregs of his drink and looking away to scan the crowding rooftop bar and beyond it the sun setting over the Pacific, saying, "Uh-hunh," saying, "Sure," Griffin uncharacteristically oblivious to the fact that he was failing to close the sale—one more small thing, among so many larger others that year, that he'd find impossible to understand.

———

THE JANUARY 25 church bulletin at Our Lady Queen of Angels Catholic Church—which Cameron Harris, like most parishioners, skipped reading—included something odd. Inside a box claiming a sixth of a page, in an urgent-looking, bolded, italicized, fourteen-point font, was a passage from Saint Paul's First Epistle to the Corinthians, one of the later books of the New Testament:

> For as often as ye eat this bread, and drink this cup, ye do shew the Lord's death till he come. Therefore whosoever shall eat this bread and drink this cup of the Lord unworthily, shall be guilty of the body and blood of the Lord. But let a man examine himself, and then let him eat of that bread and drink of that cup. For he that eateth and drinketh unworthily, eateth and drinketh damnation to himself, not discerning the Lord's body.

A few parishioners, after reading this, found themselves glancing toward Cameron, who sat blankly in a pew, alone as always, in the same front-left area he commonly occupied, wearing the same basic uniform—khaki pants, white button-down shirt—in which his mother had always dressed him for Mass. They interpreted this, correctly, as a warning shot from Father Ace—a warning shot that Cameron, having folded the bulletin and tucked it behind one of the hymnal books, failed to see coming.

All Cameron knew of Father Ace's thinking came from a call the priest made to him after someone had alerted him to the contents of Landry's lawsuit. "People are talking about some very strange rumors and I will ask you to be straight with me," the priest said, the irony skating past Cameron until recounting the call later. Cameron paused for a swallow, then promised to oblige.

Father Ace asked, "Do you know what these rumors are?"

"I got some idea, yessir."

"And is there any truth to what they're saying—about your inclinations?"

"My inclinations?" He released a bubble of anxiety as a grunt. "I ain't sure what that means, Father."

"That you suffer from an attraction to men."

"Uh, I ain't sure about the suffer part, but, yeah . . ." Cameron fumbled a cigarette from his shirt pocket while holding the phone with his other hand. "This is kinda personal, and I ain't real comfortable talking about it, but . . . yeah, that's like the way I'm wired."

The priest sighed. "We are all 'wired,' as you say, for weakness. But what God asks of us is not only to resist sin, but to renounce it."

"Renounce it," Cameron repeated into the phone.

"The Lord delivered unto you an astonishing gift, Cameron Harris."

Cameron lit his cigarette, squinting. "He did, yessir."

"And what is that saying you have here? The horse that offers you a gift—you should never punch it in the mouth."

"It's something like that, yessir."

"This has not come up in your confessions," Father Ace said.

"Well, I ain't *done* anything to confess to you," said Cameron. "Not since, you know, everything happened."

A hopeful lilt entered the priest's voice, as if on top of one miracle he was finding layered another one. "You no longer suffer this attraction?"

Now it was Cameron's turn to sigh. "Father, I don't know how to confess to being what I am. That's kinda like asking you to hit me with ten Hail Marys for having blue eyes. It ain't like—ain't like I ever got a choice in the matter."

"Someone told you that," Father Ace said, "and that person is wrong."

"No one *told* me that, Father," he said, his mind reeling nine years back to when he opened himself to Jim Yarbrough, his mom's boyfriend, as if to fact-check his own statement; but no, what Jim told him was that a leopard had spots and a leopard couldn't choose not to. "I ain't talked to but like five people about this my whole life. Who you're attracted to—it ain't like choosing between Coke and Pepsi."

"Cameron—"

"I don't know how I'm supposed to confess to just—to being alive."

"You are alive," the priest came back, icily now, "because God created you. And you are walking, today, because God granted you an astonishing second chance. A *miracle*, Cameron."

"Then—but it's God who *made* me this way, Father." He was hating every second of this, feeling hurled backward in time to when he was fourteen and briefly believed, like Father Ace did now, that a choice was his to make—that willpower alone could relocate the true north of his desires. "Because I swear to you I sure didn't."

"You are very important to me, Cameron," Father Ace said, his voice coolly tightening. "Not just personally, though I care about you a great deal—but to our ministry in Christ. Do you understand that?"

"Yessir, Father, I do."

"You have been healed in one regard, but you must heal yourself further."

Cameron exhaled a long gray stream of smoke, shaking his head. "I can't change what I am, Father."

"This," the priest said, sighing, "is what a paralyzed man says."

Near the end of the eleven a.m. Mass on February 1, one week after the menacingly bolded passage from First Corinthians appeared in the church bulletin, Cameron stood up as usual and filed into line for Communion. While the Catholic liturgy's most revered sacrament, the routine is simple: The priest holds the Communion wafer aloft and declares, "The body of Christ"; the communicant cups his hands, and says, "Amen," to receive the wafer into his hands or else opens his mouth to receive it upon his tongue.

Only this time it didn't go that way. Cameron stepped forward with his hands cupped, as usual, but Father Ace shook his head twice before jerking it sideways, to move Cameron along. Confused, Cameron said again, "Amen," this time as a question, but Father Ace stood motionless and waxy-eyed, refusing him the sacrament. Cameron dropped his head, his face flushing hot as he made his way back to the pew, feeling the eyes of the church tracking him like those upon a convict shuffling toward the gallows.

He remained in the pew, his own gaze fixed upon his shoelaces, as the church emptied. Alone, lit by the polychrome shafts of Sunday light slanting through the stained-glass windows, he found himself staring at the mahogany crucifix behind the altar with its sculpted Jesus nailed to the cross. Cameron's focus narrowed to the expression on Jesus's face: serene and assured and fulfilled, unlike that of any dead man Cameron had ever seen. That was the point, Cameron supposed—that Jesus transcended all sorrow and agony. But didn't it also deny, he found himself wondering, an equally essential point: that Jesus was one of us, extraordinarily but ordinarily human, built from flesh and bones and nerve fibers to which he, too, had to answer—master but also servant to all the pain and privations of bodily existence? Who Cameron was, inside, had never been any secret to Jesus, whether God had designed him that way or whether, as Father Ace implied, Cameron had somehow, with no memory to affirm it, redesigned himself. And yet Jesus had hoisted him to his feet anyway, reconnected his nerves, awarded him back the disorienting mess of his former life. He peered raptly and steadily at Jesus's expression. It wasn't the face of a deal maker, a man who'd trade mercy for acquiescence. It was the face, if he stared long and hard enough at it, of a man who might understand.

Father Ace, when he returned to the sanctuary, wore a different expression—that of a man scalded by betrayal. And from a distant, empathetic angle Cameron gathered why: For six months now Father Ace had been extolling Cameron from the altar, pointing to him as a model of God's infinite power and love; he'd pushed his skeptical bishop into green-lighting the miracle investigation and had devoted hours and days to Cameron's case, hours and days that he could've otherwise bestowed on his parishioners with their rehab stints and restraining orders and dying parents and spiritual skidding. He'd staked his entire ministry, in some sense, upon Cameron, who now sat blinking at him, dejected and confused. Father Ace had brought him back into the church, and now he was kicking him out.

"Do you wish to make a confession?" Father Ace asked, less an invitation than a challenge. It struck Cameron as such a small question, with Jesus hanging from the cross behind and above the priest, his benevolent-looking presence looming large as the sky.

Weakly, Cameron said, "For being me?"

The priest shut his eyes and very slowly shook his head, as though counting something off. "This cannot be the way," he finally said, "that you repay his incredible mercy."

"Father," Cameron pleaded, "I don't feel, not in here, like who I am is *wrong.*"

"Until you renounce your sins, and deliver your weakness unto the Lord," Father Ace said, backing away to punctuate this as his final statement, the folds of his cassock seething in retreat, "you cannot be said to be living in a state of *grace*. And therefore I cannot and will not grant you the Sacrament of the Holy Eucharist." He paused inside a ribbon of color-stained sunlight. "With great tenderness in my heart, I leave this choice to you."

It wasn't until Cameron was outside, descending the steps of the church, that it struck him. He noticed his legs carrying him down the concrete stairs, as only he could notice them, watched them flexing and tautening and flexing again beneath his khaki pants as they conveyed him to the base of the steps. He wheeled around and faced the open church door, the flooded veins of his neck surging. "I'm not living in a state of grace?" he said aloud, unconsciously shifting from foot to foot in a defiant shuffle-step, every one of his lower body's nerves thrumming and twitching, his voice climbing from a choke to a shout. "*I'm* not? *I'm* not?"

THE TRUCKING MAGNATE Norton Skag's response to Cameron's homosexuality, delicately disclosed to him from Rome by Dr. Antonio Liuni, after Euclide Abbascia's report from Georgia, was all of two words: "Who cares?"

This took Dr. Liuni by surprise, partly because it echoed Euclide's nonplussed reaction. Dr. Liuni had been ascribing the latter, however, to his investigator's youth and loose cosmopolitan leanings as well as to his over-lawyerly way of interpreting the gospels. (Of the 2,026 words attributed to Jesus in the four gospels, Euclide exasperated him by pointing out, not a single one addresses homosexuality.) But Skag? Dr. Liuni had been girding himself for smoking brimstone to come spraying from his phone. Dr. Liuni is of an older generation of Catholics, less apt to view church doctrine as something malleable and elastic, and his impression of Skag was of a man even farther to his right, a paleo-conservative in matters theological. Skag was known, in the United States, to be a significant donor to socially conservative politicians, a cash machine for the nation's culture warriors, particularly generous to antiabortion activists.

On the phone with Dr. Liuni, however, Skag wasn't interested in theology or politics or even morality; he was only interested in a miracle for the Reverend Fahey. "The recipient doesn't matter," Skag growled. "You explained that to me yourself twenty years ago. Doesn't matter if he's a fairy.

The *miracle* is what matters." This was true, Dr. Liuni was forced to agree, but only in a legalistic sense. And after nearly half a century as a lawyer Dr. Liuni understood the wide gulf between the theory of the law—canon law especially—and its practice. Still, he did as his client demanded: He proceeded forward with the claim.

He didn't have far to proceed. On March 16, the head of the Biloxi Diocese, Bishop Xavier R. Coburn, retracted diocesan support for the miracle inquiry, due to "irredeemable inconsistencies in testimony," and disbanded the four-man board he'd appointed to oversee it—effectively blocking Fahey's route to sainthood as it wound through Cameron Harris.

Skag was incensed. This time sparks did fly from Dr. Liuni's phone, Skag breathing fire all the way from Detroit. It was a conference call, Euclide patched in from Washington. "What do these sons of bitches want down there?" he asked, suggesting Euclide tender some kind of offer. "A new church? Fine. A rec center? A seminary? My checkbook's right in front of me. They can have all the zeros they want on it. I mean, for God's sake, all we're asking them for is a stamp so the case can move on up to the *Consulta*."

Cautiously, Dr. Liuni said, "It's not exactly how these things are done."

"But it's ridiculous," Skag fumed. "This is a slam dunk case. Archbishop Fahey healed this boy, clear as day, and they're brushing it aside. Why? I'd like one of these sons of bitches to tell me why."

Euclide cleared his throat. "Because they're scared," he said.

"Scared of what?"

"The resonance," Euclide said.

"I don't even know what that means," Skag grumbled. "All I know is that mercy's not to be feared. Mercy's to be celebrated."

This happened to align with Euclide's view, but he took it one step further than Skag might have: love, in whatever form it took, wasn't to be feared either. And this was why, in early April, while Euclide was in Tallahassee, Florida, looking into a cancer-remission case that had barely a tenth of the miracle potential of Cameron's case, he found himself using a free day to drive four hours to Biloxi.

When no one answered the door at the house on Reconfort Avenue, Euclide called Janice, by now aware that Father Ace had washed his hands of Cameron. Janice seemed weirdly protective of Cameron. Though she and Euclide had spoken on the phone since their interview, to jointly clear their suspicions about him, this still felt like a shift. After Euclide explained his purpose, though, she texted him Cameron's number with a message saying he was full of surprises.

Cameron, more so than Janice, also sounded wary on the phone— Euclide promised him he was paying an unofficial call, unrelated to church business—but said he was working a slip shift at work and would be headed home shortly for a couple hours. He'd meet him there.

With time to kill Euclide wandered down to the Biz-E-Bee, exchanging pleasantries along the way with an old woman on her porch who noting his accent hollered out, "Where *you* from, child?" The MIRACULOUS DISCOUNTS sign was still hanging across the front of the store, and inside were printouts of the news coverage taped haphazardly to the walls, but there was little, otherwise, to denote what'd happened there: a far cry from Euclide's last visit. From the man behind the counter whom he took to be Quỳnh, Lê Thị Hạt's husband, Euclide purchased the single worst cup of coffee he'd ever tasted and carried it outside. He stood near the door for awhile, watching a man sweep the parking lot, the man uttering strange bleating sounds with every third push of his broom. The man paid extra attention, Euclide noticed, to the section of the asphalt where Cameron had risen, still faintly marked. When he was done sweeping the man rested awhile in that very spot, leaning on his broom, slightly swaying, his eyelids fluttering and his lips softly trembling, Euclide observing him over the rim of his paper coffee cup. Yes, Euclide thought, his lips bending into a slow smile. God is there, friend. Don't let anyone tell you he's not.

He arrived back at the house just as Cameron was pulling into the driveway. Cameron climbed out of the car in a uniform: shiny black pants and a bright blue shirt onto which a gold badge was pinned. Shaking hands and leading Euclide inside, Cameron told him that he was a month into his new job at the airport, working for the Transportation Security Administration, the TSA, or as Cameron wryly put it, "America's varsity squad." Polyester uniform aside, Euclide was struck, after all this time spent circling him, by how unremarkable Cameron seemed, by the folksy Huckleberry Finn-ness of him: the accommodating grin, the gleaming blue boyishness in his eyes, his mussed, sticky-looking hair, the clumsy cowboy drawl, the unkempt way he chugged half a quart of

Gatorade standing in front of the open refrigerator. He seemed both familiar and exotic to Euclide, irregularly regular, an everyman who from various angles resembled and evoked no one else.

Euclide didn't stay long. His mission was a narrow and very precise one, and on one basic level unlike most of his others—he was there not to receive information but to dispense it. But he began with a question anyway: "Have you spoken with Sergeant Lockwood since your recovery?"

Cameron's face paled, a range of expressions swirling across it. He reached for a cigarette, Euclide saw, in much the same way Dr. Liuni reached for an aspirin when his chest began stinging. "D?" Cameron said. "Nossir I ain't."

"I have," Euclide announced.

Cameron nodded, Euclide inventorying what he saw flickering through Cameron's eyes: resurrected pain, maybe; guilt; an old and persistent confusion; and something brighter, too, the thing Euclide'd hoped to see.

"I am very certain he would welcome hearing from you," Euclide told him, from his vest pocket fishing a folded piece of paper, with Damarkus's cellphone number on it, and passing it to Cameron. Cameron unfolded the paper and stared at it as though reading a long and emphatic letter. "That's really all I came this long way to say," Euclide said, adding, "I thought I should do it in person."

Cameron's mouth opened to speak, but nothing but air came out.

"You and he, it seems clear," Euclide said, "have some unfinished business," tapping his chest. Cameron sat motionless for a while, not even blinking, Euclide continuing to tap at his chest until he was certain Cameron was registering his meaning, until Cameron's eyes were blooming as wide as they could bloom, his unlit cigarette poised motionless between his fingers.

Before leaving Biloxi Euclide stopped by Mary Mahoney's Old French House, idly recalling the young waitress—lovely in his memory—who'd flirted him that second Negroni several months before. But she was off that day, the bartender told Euclide. He sighed and sipped his drink, watching the bartender wiping glassware in the window light, thinking maybe it was just as well: He'd had enough romance for one day.

———

By DINT OF COINCIDENCE, or maybe owing to the crisscrossing spokes of small-town life, Nap Cuevas was the first lawyer Tommy Landry contacted seeking representation a few days after the fight, Nap having represented Landry's uncle three years before in one of the myriad cases arising from the BP oil spill. Nap let Landry talk for about ten minutes until his response felt fully formulated. Then he stopped him. "Mr. Landry, I've never said to this to a prospective client before, and it's hard for me to imagine I'm ever going to say it to another one," he said. "But based upon some knowledge of this case that I happen to have, and on what you've told me so far, I'd like to invite you to go fuck yourself."

And that, minus a few more turns of the screw, was how Nap Cuevas became Cameron Harris's attorney.

This story—exaggerated hardly at all—was soon being told and retold at dinner parties and in beachfront bars, with proud whiskeyed zest, by an unexpected and unannounced visitor to the Mississippi Coast: Janice's father, Winston Lorimar. He arrived at his daughter's house one night in early March, trailing a pair of disturbingly large suitcases along with Zeno, his fragrant Plott Hound, for what he described, blithely and benevolently, as an "open-ended stay." He admitted he was rather early to greet the birth of his first grandchild, six months or so, but said the thought of Janny's belly blossoming so distant and unseen had been ripping him into confetti. Plus, he announced, he wanted to deliver Janice her old crib from the attic. It wasn't actually Janice's old crib, rather her little brother Johnny's, because her old crib had been put to use as a brooder for ducklings, but it was a sweet gesture anyway and Janice decided that, with a coat of paint, the crib could be adorable—and a tactile link, as well, to her mother, who was supposed to be here for this.

Nap, to Janice's surprise, seemed entirely—even irritatingly—unruffled by her father's invasion. His presence gave Nap an excuse to mix his Sazeracs and provided him a partner for watching basketball, which Lorimar didn't particularly enjoy but found pleasant enough to stare at so long as the volume stayed low ("Just can't take all them *shoes* squeakin'").

Janice, in contrast, found herself recurrently galled, though after a while more by the dog, which climbed daily onto the sun-drenched kitchen table to doze, than by her father, who seemed uncharacteristically inclined to help out around the house: He took over mowing the lawn, for instance, which was obliging of him though she wished he wouldn't pilot the riding mower shirtless wearing a scarf and goggles like Snoopy atop his Sopwith Camel, to the neighborhood's gawky delight. From embarrassment, Janice sometimes found her hands covering her face, as they'd so regularly done during her teens, but she also began noticing a curious shift in her view of her father, a softer, more forgiving focus, which she was crediting to being pregnant. She realized, as a mother-to-be, that she was locked into her lineage; she was an individual, of course, but also a kind of middleman passing something more than mitochondrial DNA down the line, something deeper and less obvious than eye color and height and susceptibility to cancer. The differences, for the first time, felt less important than the similarities. Her father was crazy, yes, a yowling, sixty-seven-year-old dervish, and his response to life had always been to flail at its mysteries and discordances with fabulist stories—but then she too, as evidenced by the last few months, wasn't immune to that.

Winston liked hearing about Cameron. He liked bringing the case up in bars in the late afternoons, squinting at locals claiming to have known it was a hoax all along. He liked visiting the Biz-E-Bee and standing in that faded rectangle, chewing gum with his hands in his pockets. He liked ogling people in the Biloxi casinos and, whether they were impaired in any visible way or not, trying to determine why God might've opted to pass them over for a miracle. As a fiction writer, he sometimes invented backstories for them when the reason—someone snapping at a cocktail waitress, cussing a slot machine, general inertness—wasn't obvious to him.

The reasoning he devised for Cameron's selection, on that note, went like this: "One by one God took away the boy's daddy, his dog, his mama, his first true love, then his legs. After a while God felt bad about all that so he gave back the legs."

His daughter didn't mind this interest—in fact she rather enjoyed it, as her father had never before paid much attention to her work—but she did find herself trying to steer him away from the metaphysical toward the physical, from the invisible to the visible. Winston Lorimar isn't religious, but he is fond, in his words, of "the hoodoo in life": the cracks in our knowledge and perceptions, the existential equivalent of the unplayable tones lurking between the black and white keys of a piano.

Janice did have to concede to him that what was visible about Cameron's case was limited and ambiguous, that the only conclusion the data and imaging could muster was a shrug. She was still doing what she could to investigate the case, feeling obligated to redouble her efforts after having steered herself into a ditch with her hoax theory. She'd experienced no eureka moments, not yet, and her progress felt measured in inches, but she had, nevertheless, arrived at a few conclusions.

One was that whatever neuroregenerative process occurred had happened slowly, not instantly, so that Cameron's rise from his wheelchair marked not the moment of his recovery but rather his realization of it. His lack of sensory response, until then, was likely psychological—a kind of reverse placebo effect, Cameron failing to notice the changes because his mind kept invalidating them. Her second conclusion was that his ability to stand and hobble a few steps, despite his atrophied leg muscles, was more than likely an adrenaline response. Cameron's combat history, which she heard about from Euclide and verified with Cameron, suggested a man unusually reactive to the effects of adrenaline, able to channel those effects into very specific physical actions. And the third was that some anomaly in the glial scar environment—and that was as precise as she could get, some anomaly—had allowed neuroregeneration to transpire where medical science says it can't, akin to a flower blooming in the absence of light.

"So that's the story you're telling," her father said one night, after she'd laid it all out for him. They were sitting on the screened-in patio, Janice chiding her father for smoking and her father pretending not to hear. He had a tall glass of bourbon in front of him, her a steaming cup of Healthy Mama herbal tea. Zeno was snoring by his feet, having exhausted himself chasing moths, and the backyard was clamorous with cicadas, a thousand miniature tambourines being shaken in the dark.

"It's not a *story,* Daddy," she said. "Come on. It's a hypothesis. It's as empirical as I can get right now."

"Naw," he said, pursing his lips and shaking his head a shade too smugly for Janice, like someone holding the answer to a guessing game. "A hypothesis, that's just a story told a different way. It's a summary of observations, right? This led to that. When this happens, this other thing here does."

"That," she said, shooing smoke away, "is a seriously simple way of looking at it."

"Simple? Here's simple." He stubbed out his cigarette and took a bracing sip-and-a-half of bourbon, grimacing happily. Winston Lorimar no longer resembles David Levine's illustration of him in the *New York Review of Books* circa 1979, when *Lieutenant Lucius & the Tristate Crematory Band* was the passing rage. His face has widened and gone pouchy and the wild-man shock of hair that Levine accentuated went swirling down the bathtub drain decades ago. But the jungly eyebrows and over-plump lips that dominated Levine's rendering still dominate Winston Lorimar's face, imbuing his expressions with something of an epic quality. When he draws a cigarette to his lips it might as well be a roasted turkey leg. When he laughs it feels on behalf of an entire realm or at least a pub. He exudes a largeness of spirit, something overcrowded within.

"Tolstoy said there's only two stories in all of literature," he began. "Fella goes on a journey, that's one. Stranger comes to town, that's the other. Or in this case here I reckon we'd say, anomaly comes to town." His face glowed puckishly. "Sounds a little Greek, doesn't it? Hail ye Anomaly, scion of Medicina . . ."

"Science isn't stories, Daddy," Janice said flatly, reminded anew why she'd relished living in Pittsburgh during med school. No one ever seemed to sit on porches making up stories.

"Oh, of course it's just stories," he said. "Fella goes on a journey, that's Darwin's plot, that's evolution. This fish, see, he's bored, wants to check out what's beyond the water, so he jumps out onto the land, gives it a quick look-see, says I'm going to need me some lungs and some feets. But he don't got them. So he tells his fish kids and they tell their fish kids until one of them grows some lungs and some feet and next thing you know they're living in trees gnawing bananas until one of them says, y'all watch this, I'm fixing to blow some minds by walking on two feets. And so on and so forth. Different fellas but they're on the same journey."

Janice sipped her tea, hearing the cicada music recede and then crest behind her father's voice, finding herself both irritated and enchanted to feel seven years old again.

"And stranger comes to town, Tolstoy's other one," her father went on, darkness creasing his face as some of the playfulness ebbed from his tone. "Well, that's the Earth itself coming into existence, isn't it? That whole ball of wax. Or pan out wider and it's the origins of matter, of the universe. The story of a fella named Something arriving at a place called Nothing."

Janice laughed. "All you're demonstrating," she said, adding some girlish velvet to her tone in order to blunt any sting, "is that if you make the box big enough you can fit anything inside it."

He grunted softly, more stimulated than stung.

"But you're also missing a crucial difference," she continued. "Science doesn't *tell*. It asks."

He shrugged. "Same way stories do."

"That so?" she said, the arch of her eyebrow signaling more amusement than she was actually feeling.

"Oh indeed. Indeed." His big lips glistened from a fresh sip of bourbon. "Stories, made-up ones anyway, they always begin with a tacit question: *What if?*"

"What if," Janice echoed.

"That's right, what *if*," he said. "What if a woman named Anna married a mouse named Karenin but fell dumbly in love with a louse named Vronsky? What if a little-bitty redneck boy named Thomas Sutpen never got over a slave making him use the back door of a plantation house? What if biting a single cookie could crack open the essence of time itself, every one of the little-bitty crumbs like atoms bursting with experience? Stories, see, they ask *what if* the same way experiments do. They both start from the same place."

"And where's that?"

He mulled this for a while, stretching his neck and surveying the backyard, before announcing, "Leflore County, Mississippi."

"Oh, Daddy . . ."

"Now hear me out, Janny. Follow this old white rabbit for just a minute." Janice waited while he dropped his gaze and cocked his head, as though struggling to hear something. He rubbed a fingertip against his glass. "I could tell you two stories right now. One involves ol' Snuffy Covington, who was before your time. He was the county agent back in the fifties, real peculiar fellow, and he figured out how to control the boll weevil one night after listening to the Rocky Marciano–Jersey Joe Walcott fight on the radio." He paused to regard Janice's blank expression, then said, "The other one's about your mama dying."

She nodded her selection at him, steeling herself, and he began with a question: "You ever hear about the Heider-Simmel experiment?"

Janice frowned at this starting-line digression, tightening her jaw and shaking her head no.

"A famous psychological study from back in the forties," he explained. "Heider and Simmel, they showed people a short film with nothing but a few geometric shapes moving along the screen then asked those people what-all they'd seen. Just like that: What'd you see? And all but one of them people come back with a story. The big triangle was trying to help the circle, they said. The little triangle was trying to get the circle away from the big one. The rectangle that didn't move was apathetic to the drama. That sort of thing. Only one of them, out of dozens, said he'd just seen some moving shapes. Just one of them."

Janice vented an impatient sigh. "I thought this was about Mom . . ."

"Those shapes," he shot back, "were your mama's cancer."

He studied the table for a while, his daughter studying him, the cicadas hushing themselves as though respecting the moment.

"Those shapes came to take her away and every night the universe asked me what I was seeing," he went on. "And every night I tried telling myself and her and y'all a new story that wasn't just these meaningless shapes of cancer erasing her from our lives. Every night I wrote and revised those stories in my head because I refused—and to this goddamn day I still refuse—to accept her cancer as some movement of random shapes, as a purely biological concern. Because to accept that I'd have to accept her as a random shape, too, as one more meaningless fragment in a meaningless mosaic. And she wasn't."

"No," Janice heard herself whisper.

"No she wasn't." His hand gripped his glass as though to lift it for a sip but all he did was squeeze it. "She was extraordinary in every sense but also in the sense that we're all extraordinary, that human life is extraordinary, that we're all somehow endowed with a consciousness allowing us to see with our eyes closed, to conjure what's not there and sometimes what never could be there, and with lips and hands, too, that allow us to convey that vision to the consciousness of others, to transmit not only information but *meaning* as well. Meaning and joy and heartbreak and whatever the invisible molecules are that constitute love."

The cicadas crested again and for a few speechless moments it appeared that father and daughter were doing nothing more than listening to them.

"So I told stories," he said. "Some of them were sad and some funny and some were ridiculous and some were just me spinning whatever I had to keep spinning to keep from crying. Maybe they weren't the best stories and if I could do it all over again I might've kept back a few of them from you and your brothers because the trust of a child is infinite but so easily breakable too. But I couldn't be like that single cold bastard from Heider and Simmel's experiment. I couldn't accept her dying as just her dying. If there were laws to the universe then those laws had to be just ones, and I felt it was mine to prove that somehow—to myself if no one else. Otherwise what cause did I have to put you and the boys on the school bus every morning, make y'all finish your greens every supper? What was to stop me," he said, lifting his glass and shaking the ice as though brandishing a pistol, "from doing anything but this all day?"

Janice hadn't registered much after his reference to the cold bastard, which she'd felt to be a drive-by slight aimed at or at least near her—a half-concealed critique of her own clinical dispassion, her capacity for describing without ascribing, despite knowing that her hoax theory had shown these qualities to be more aspirational than inherent. Her mind swirled. The way her father had reckoned with her mother's illness and death had been an open wound for twenty-three years, but this fresh sting, a pinprick in comparison, was now eclipsing it. Did the deficit of imagination her father seemed to see in her bespeak a corresponding deficit of love?

"But there's a *true* story, Daddy," she protested. "And what's true doesn't need to be imagined. You can see it right in front of you. It wasn't shapes that took her, it was brainstem glioma. And that doesn't mean Mama died without—without meaning."

The way he smiled at her, like his heart was bunched in his throat, felt like a correction. It told her she'd misunderstood him—had substituted herself for her father's strawman, had *imagined* the slight. She'd always been too sensitive to his disapproval, she knew, even back when it'd conversely validated her. She softened, watching her father's face twitch with thought or emotion—it was never clear, with him, where one stopped and the other started.

"Imagination," he said to her, "isn't just seeing what's not there." His voice was gentle, a barrel-aged murmur. "Imagination is also what we use to figure out why what's there is the way it is."

She said nothing as he lit another cigarette, so forcefully shaking the match as to also shake off the old grief he'd summoned.

"Let's throw William Blake's notion onto the table," he said, as Janice waved smoke from the actual table, "that between what's known in the universe and what's unknown there are doors. Imagination is the only thing that opens those doors."

Janice sighed. "Imagination is also the quickest path down rabbit holes," she said, thinking of her own.

"That's surely true." Her father let out a smoky grunt. "I reckon history would show rabbit holes outnumbering Blake's doors by about a hundred thousand to one."

"But the questions I'm asking about what happened to Cameron," she said, circling the conversation back to where it'd begun. "They're *questions,* Daddy, they're not parts of any story, and they're not imagined. I feel like you're lumping me in with all the miracle thumpers. I don't have something to prove."

"Of course you do," he said. "What you aim to prove is that the body, like the universe, works according to static laws. That what applies to one set of nerves applies to all sets of nerves. That the story, once identified, resolves the same way every time. The miracle thumpers—I like that phrase—their desire is for the opposite. Isn't that right? That those laws can be suspended by a higher power. That your biological fate is not necessarily mine. But it's too easy, now, to overstate these as competing aims. It's a common and rather toxic form of glibness. Because what they are, see, they're just parallel routes to the same place."

"And that's what?"

"Consolation," he said.

"Not understanding?"

"Understanding's just a form of consolation. Understanding something means trusting that it's true. Doesn't mean it is true. Just that you believe it is."

Janice smiled, wagging her head and emitting a low, exasperated moan. "If we were on the phone," she said, a dimple dotting her cheek, "I'd be saying, sorry, Daddy, you're breaking up on me."

"Well, that's why this here's better," he said, matching her dimple for dimple as he ashed his cigarette. He leaned forward. "All I'm saying to you is that what happened with this boy was more than mechanical. I don't mean the actual mechanism, the anomaly. Thing is, you imagined him staying in that chair and he somehow imagined himself out of it. You wrote one story—and by you I mean everyone relying upon our agreed-upon ideas of the known world—and his body wrote another. And all these people heard that story of his and every one of them tried and failed to understand it so they rewrote it in whatever way made sense to them, whatever way consoled them, until it didn't make sense to them anymore so they had to write it another way. And maybe one of those stories was true and maybe none of them were. Maybe the true story is the one you'll tell when you figure out the anomaly. But it won't really matter, not in what we call the grand scheme."

"And why is that?" she said, feeling a faint twinge in her middle: the regular smoosh of digestion, probably, but—possibly?—the baby's first tentative, exploratory kick, another set of legs sparking with life deep inside her.

"Because it's like what Muriel Rukeyser wrote," her father was saying, dreamily now, and peering out into the yard as if reciting lines printed upon the night sky. "'The universe is made of stories, not of atoms.'" He turned to her with a grin, lush crinkles framing his eyes, and reaching not for his glass but for his daughter's hand he asked, "And isn't that, doctor . . . why, isn't that just about as beautiful as it gets?"

epilogue

THE PLAYLIST FOR THE TRIP WAS CAMERON'S: PATSY AND Willie and Dolly and Tammy, all the old warbly-voiced, pedal steel–smeared standbys, one twangy heartache after another. The route plugged into the GPS was likewise of Cameron's design: east to Mobile, up through the piney woods to Montgomery, then over to Macon for a wide northbound swoop around Atlanta toward the mountains and into White County, Georgia. The blue car, too, belonged to Cameron, though not in any technical sense: Three months after the still-birthed cancellation of *Miracle Man,* no one from the production company or the network or from Ford had come to reclaim the twin sedans granted to its stars. Yet the driver, as always, was Tanya, a Bonus Value Light smoldering idly between her fingers on the steering wheel, like a stick of incense, her other hand pressing her phone to her ear.

"Aw, girl, you know," she was saying to a friend. "Regular old Saturday. Just driving to Georgia to meet my brother's gay black lover."

She flashed a wide and wicked grin her brother's way, silently cackling at her own teasing, and Cameron responded with a tolerant roll of his eyes before returning his attention to the landscape clicking past: billboards for lawyers and preachers, tattered roadside memorial wreaths, homemade signs for deer processing with arrows pointing every direction, the earth painted a single mutt color of green and beige save for the early pastel wild-flowers bending in the spring breeze. Feeling his stomach knotting again Cameron cracked the window and lit a cigarette, listening to Tanya going on about her new job at their mama's old hospital and the night classes she was taking to become a nurse. The job had her working with the elderly—

"I'm getting so damn good at wiping butts," she was saying—but she was gunning for a slot in the pediatric ward. What she wanted was to work with kids. She was good at that, she thought. Her brother might be proof.

Finishing the call, she announced, "Cheryl says hey."

"Hey," he said back, to the window.

"Says she still thinks she can turn you."

"Reckon I been turned enough," he said.

Tanya dunked her cigarette into a coffee cup in the console and then took in the passing scenery, humming vacantly along with a pedal-steel solo. She blinked at the windshield, her eyes narrowing. "You remember riding up this way to see Aunt Bylinda and them?" As Cameron shook his head no she said, "Yeah, might be you were too little to remember."

He shrugged. "Must've been."

"Yeah, you were back in your car seat singing 'Barney' songs. Mama singing along. Y'all bout to killed me with that. Guess you don't remember the bull neither."

He swung his head. "What bull?"

"Uncle Bill's. Thing was huge, with these big old horns. Like those Texas cattle or something. You and me rode out with Uncle Bill to feed the hogs one night. You was in the bed of his truck when that bull come up and sticks his head right in there, snorting at you like this." She flared her nostrils and grunted. "Then you got to screaming and kinda curled yourself into a ball which just gets the bull more curious or something so he's rocking the whole truck sticking his head in there and snorting. You about peed your pants."

Cameron couldn't tell whether Tanya meant this as a funny story or not. It didn't sound funny to him. "What'd Uncle Bill do?"

"Aw, you know him. He was off feeding the pigs and shouting at you not to worry. Saying the bull was friendly. You wasn't buying it."

After a few beats of silence Cameron stared at her and asked, "What were you doing?"

"Me?" Tanya frowned as if her own role in the incident hadn't occurred to her. "I was back there with you. Trying to keep that bull off you. I starting shoving his head away and shit. Pushing on its nose."

"Telling me it was all okay," Cameron said.

She brightened. "You remember now?"

"Naw." His voice was quiet, pensive, but assured. "I just figured."

He took a drag from his cigarette, exhaling the smoke sideways out the cracked window.

"You always been protecting me, ain't you?" he said.

Tanya swallowed, eyes fixed upon the highway. "Not always," she said.

"It's sure felt like always to me."

What to say to this—Tanya didn't know. A FreightConnex tractor-trailer hurtled past in the left lane, Reverend Fahey's quotation on its backside passing unnoticed. Kitty Wells was singing a duet with Red Foley, sounding to Tanya like some archaeological recording engineered with tin cans and fence wire. Cracker Barrel, two miles ahead. A boarded-up church off the frontage road, its sign reading, THE BIBLE PREVENTS TRUTH DECAY. Finally she said, "That wasn't me back at the Biz-E-Bee."

"Wasn't me neither," said Cameron.

For a long while thereafter they rode through Alabama in silence, the mystery riding with them as it probably always will, its presence disturbing and comforting in shifting but ultimately equal measures, undeniable yet unfathomable: a ghost of wonder that may never cease to haunt them and those close to them, untethering them from the world's known limits. Perhaps this will always be their routine: a reminder, a thick and ponderous silence, and then an unsettling sense of strange liberty and stranger privilege.

Tanya lit another cigarette as Cameron was absently doodling the window with a fingertip, as though tracing the contours of the highwayside.

"You nervous?" she said.

"Little bit," he admitted.

"I mean, *shit*," she said, squinting less from the sun than from the thoughts in her head. "All these years gone by and y'all ain't been nowhere together except Afghanistan." She paused, wagging her head as she absorbed her own words, ingesting the dilemmas of her brother's nearing future. "What the hell do you even do?"

"I don't know," said Cameron, still tracing something onto the window, the glass cold against his wandering fingertip. Yet his voice, moving seventy miles an hour in the open right lane, was without shakes and quivers, that vein in his neck pulsing gently and unseen. "I guess it's like everything else. You just hope it was real."

afterword

I N NOVEMBER 2015, AS PART OF A RESEARCH INITIATIVE OR-
chestrated by Janice Lorimar-Cuevas, MD, Cameron Harris flew to
New Haven, Connecticut, to undergo a five-day battery of tests, including
a spinal tap for evaluation of his cerebrospinal fluid, at the Yale School of
Medicine's Center for Neuroscience and Regeneration Research. His case
is also under investigation by Stephen Levitan, PhD, professor in the de-
partments of neurology and neurobiology at the University of California,
Berkeley, a senior Veterans Administration medical research scientist, and
one of the nation's foremost authorities in the field of axonal regeneration
and remyelination. At the time of this book's publication, however, the
research has yet to yield any conclusive determinations about Cameron's
recovery except—per Dr. Levitan's terse formulation—that, somehow, "it
happened."

acknowledgments

THE LARGEST SHAREHOLDER IN MY GRATITUDE IS, OF COURSE, Cameron Harris, who entrusted me with his story and then maintained his trust as that story, and his life, grew ever more unruly and complex. I've tried to merit that trust with empathy and accuracy.

Tanya Harris's stricken reaction, when I introduced this book project to her and Cameron back in September 2014, went like this: "A whole book? About Cam?" I wish to thank her, very fondly, for all the tolerance and openness she provided me during my half-year stay on the Coast, as the idea of a whole book kept getting wholer and wholer. Her apprehensions about the project, as the story zigzagged forward, were to be expected. Less expected—extraordinary, even—was her refusal to go back on her word.

I cannot fathom how Janice Lorimar-Cuevas, MD, could have been more generous with her time or more open about her life and work. My initial presumption was that Janice, being the daughter of a novelist, was merely sympathetic to the weird delicacies of a writer's craft; but I soon enough came to see that Janice extends her sympathies to everyone and everything. She showed infinite patience with reconstructing events and conversations and recollecting subtle (and sometimes regretted) thoughts and impressions. I am especially grateful for her willingness to share her notes, files, recordings, emails, and, most of all, the personal diary she kept during the events described herein. I'd be remiss not to extend thanks as well to Nap Cuevas, her husband, who could've rightfully grumbled about my constant intrusions into their lives but instead mixed up Sazeracs and cooked us all killer meals and more than once took it upon himself to soothe and quiet their daughter, Lacey, when Lacey longed to add some baby yowls to the conversation.

Quỳnh and Hat Lê were likewise gracious, their door ever open even as confusions and disappointments curdled their story. A soft pleasure of mine was babysitting Little Kim so that the Lês could enjoy a rare night out together; it helped ease some of the homesickness I was feeling for my own children back up north. Euclide Abbascia was reluctant to speak with me at first, but I pray—and I use that verb deliberately—that the affectionate care I tried according his story leaves him with no regrets about participating. I'll say the same about Scott T. Griffin, who recognized the dark crannies in his role in the story the moment we first sat down in his office, but agreed that the story of Cameron Harris warranted a full and open airing, even if it was someone else doing the airing. The benevolence he showed by sharing hundreds upon hundreds of hours of footage with me, along with all his notes and recollections from the *Miracle Man* production, proved crucial to the writing of this book.

I also want to express deep and very real gratitude to the following advisors, guides, and sources who aided me in my research and reporting: Michael Stillman, MD; Steven Williams, MD; Tricia H. Kroth, DO; Bill Saxon, my Rome counsel; Mary Kay Gominger; Doug Stanton; C. Russell Muth; Angie Galle Ladner; Fred Lusk, Esq.; Julie Holder; Jay Carmean, Esq.; and dear Rayya Elias. And to gratefully acknowledge, as well, the information and/or inspiration provided by the following works: *The Book of Miracles* by Kenneth L. Woodward; *The Last Deployment* by Bronson Lemer; *Outlaw Platoon* by Sean Parnell; *The Good Soldiers* by David Finkel; *The Viet Kieu in America*, edited by Nghia M. Vo; *Soldier of Change* by Stephen Snyder-Hill; *The Outpost* by Jake Tapper; *The Vatican Prophecies* by John Thavis; and *Medical Miracles* by Jacalyn Duffin.

Tula, Mississippi, Dec. 2016

about the author

JONATHAN MILES is the author of the novels *Dear American Airlines* and *Want Not,* both *New York Times* Notable Books. He is a former columnist for the *New York Times,* has served as a contributing editor to magazines ranging from *Details* to *Field & Stream,* and his journalism has been frequently anthologized in *Best American Sports Writing* and *Best American Crime Writing.* He is also the author of a book on fish and game cookery, *The Wild Chef,* and competed in the Dakar Rally, an off-road race through Africa. Formerly of Oxford, Mississippi, he lives with his family in rural New Jersey.

ANATOMY
OF A MIRACLE

ESSAYS,
READER'S GUIDES,
AND MORE

A Reader's Guide

In order to provide reading groups with the most informed and thought-provoking questions possible, it is necessary to reveal certain aspects of the plot of this novel. If you have not finished reading *Anatomy of a Miracle*, we respectfully suggest that you do so before reviewing this guide.

Questions and Topics for Discussion

1. *Anatomy of a Miracle* opens as Tanya wheels her brother, Cameron, to their local convenience store, the Biz-E-Bee. This site is important to much of the novel's action, being the scene of the seemingly miraculous moment when Cameron, formerly paralyzed from the waist down, steps out of his wheelchair and onto the asphalt of the store's parking lot. What kind of atmosphere does this scene evoke? How does the routine of Tanya and Cameron's daily errands speak to the circumstances of their lives? Is it indicative of small-town life in the Deep South?

2. Jonathan Miles's novel is set years after Hurricane Katrina, though Biloxi, Mississippi, is still defined by the storm. Where do you see Katrina's lasting effects on the town?

3. What were your first impressions of Cameron and Tanya and of their brother/sister relationship? Early on, their home in Biloxi is described as "starkly devoid of family history," swept away with their possessions by the hurricane. Did your opinion of the characters develop as you gained insight to their backstories?

4. What do you make of the internet and social media's role in the novel? Does it reflect things that you see on Facebook and Twitter?

5. What do you think of Cameron's doctor, Janice? Is her confidence in science similar or different from the faith that other characters have in religion?

6. In the story, there is controversy about what constitutes a miracle. How would you define a miracle? Can one at once believe in miracles and doubt the existence of God?

7. Cameron struggles with feelings of guilt and unworthiness. Why do you think he feels this way?

8. How did you feel about the way people tried

to capitalize on Cameron's recovery? Think of the Biz-E-Bee's conversion to a site of public pilgrimage with its own line of spiritual novelties for sale or the reality television show *Miracle Man*. Do you agree or disagree with attempts to make money off of Cameron's life?

9. How do Cameron and Damarkus react to postwar life and adapt to their injured bodies? Cameron agonizes over life's *what-ifs* while Damarkus settles for *what is*. Does Damarkus exhibit acceptance for what happened? Does Cameron?

10. Tanya believes that a cocktail of antidepressants, sleeping aids, and anti-anxiety medications saved her brother's life following his return from Afghanistan. How does this compare to Cameron's self-medication with alcohol and nonprescription drugs? Why are Tanya and Janice concerned when Cameron stops taking his medications?

11. What do you think of the reported style of the novel? How do you think the blend of fact and fiction reflects current cultural preoccupations with the truth?

12. Honeybun chastises Griffin for wanting to represent Cameron's recovery as a metaphor for self-acceptance. Did you read the "miracle" as a metaphor?

13. The last figure that we witness visiting the Biz-E-Bee tells Quỳnh that he prays for "love and understanding." How do you think this message applies to the story overall?

14. Toward the novel's end, Janice's father, Winston Lorimar, discusses science and religion with his daughter, arguing that storytelling is a way of understanding the world whether or not you believe in God. Do you agree with him?

15. Having finished reading the novel, do you think it "really matters" whether or not Cameron's recovery was a miracle?

A Conversation with Jonathan Miles

Q. You spent many years in Oxford, Mississippi. Why did you decide to return to that state as the setting for *Anatomy of a Miracle*?

A. The story led me there rather than vice versa. My vision of the novel's central event arrived fully formed, as in a dream, and an essential component of that vision was a tumbledown Mississippi convenience store in the withering August heat. But in stepping back from that vision, squinting at it, the setting made some sense to me: Mississippi is arguably the most haunted sector of what Flannery O'Connor called the "Christ-haunted" South, and therefore (I thought) an ideal setting for a Christ-haunted event. That said, writing about Mississippi—not my native or current state but the state I will always consider home—was both comfort and challenge. Comfort because it's intimately familiar and challenge because Mississippi has hosted more great novels by more great novelists than probably any other state. You have to find new rocks to turn over.

Q. *Anatomy of a Miracle* is written as an ostensibly nonfiction reported piece. How did you think of using that method to tell the story, and what do you think it accomplishes that a more traditional method would not? Did you find your own background in journalism helpful to this approach?

A. Narrative calculus played into this. I wanted to show the broad effects of a purported miracle, the ripples in the pond, so a first-person narrative struck me as too limiting. Third-person omniscient narrators are by nature rather God-like, all-seeing and all-knowing, and that seemed a little wonky for a novel in which the characters are grappling with the existence or nonexistence of divinity. ("Hey, look up here!" I imagined that narrator hollering in such moments.) So I worked out this unusual device: presenting the story as reportage, which dovetailed with the characters' quests to ferret out the truth about what happened. Twenty years of newspapering and magazine reporting made the voice of that offstage narrator fairly easy to conjure.

Q. There's an incredible level of detail to the parts of the book that deal with medicine and war (and reality television). Did you have to do a lot of research to write those sections?

A. For me, anyway, that's always one of the pleasures. I don't write autobiographically. For me the fictional process is less upload than download. I approached the research for this novel as a reporting assignment, but instead of asking "How did x happen?" I was asking people "How *could* x happen?" On occasion I gathered physician friends and traded them wine for counsel. These conversations often leapt from the practice of medicine to the limits of medicine, from what's known to what's unknown, and in those moments I felt the novel's nerves twitching, felt it coming more and more alive as it found mystery to feed upon.

Q. You've mentioned before that *Anatomy of a Miracle* deals with the malleable nature of truth—or, as we might say now, "fake news." Have current events changed the way you view that aspect of the book?

A. When I began this novel, in 2014, the phrase "fake news" had yet to enter the national lexicon. But I sensed that part of the fictional reaction to the event I was chronicling would hinge upon how people assimilated information about it—that how people apprehended it, whether as a miracle or a medical riddle or a suspected hoax, et cetera, would in great measure depend upon their source of information about it, be it Facebook or internet forums or general or niche media or reality television or firsthand encounters with my protagonist. And then I wanted to track how those reactions might contort as new and more complicated facts emerged, and how some of these details might be dismissed, in Kellyanne Conway's memorable formulation, as "alternative facts." In my original conception, my reporter-narrator would be an authoritative sifter of these facts, but as the culture shifted around me, especially in 2016, I realized that the ostensibly reliable narrator I'd created might be the most unreliable narrator of our times. In many ways this novel is explicitly about "fake news," or the perceptions thereof: about how people react to information that rebukes their worldviews. And in another sense the novel itself is, by definition, "fake news": it's fiction disguised as nonfiction.

Q. Much of the book concerns the ways different people relate to or express their faith, and how they cling to or reject an ideology. How did you approach that element of the story?

A. By setting up intentional clashes between characters and their worldviews: between the physician and her atheism, between the convenience-store owner and her Catholic faith, between Cameron and his agnostic sense that nothing is really explicable. The concussions of the miraculous-seeming event forces these and other characters to confront, sometimes painfully, their belief systems—what they believe and why they believe it.

Q. Did Cameron's story change as you wrote the novel? Did anything end up surprising you?

A. This novel surprised me on a weekly basis. Characters are in some ways like children: you create them with vague expectations or at least hopes about how they'll act, what principles they'll possess, and how you'll be able to direct them, and then under your care they transform into complex, headstrong creatures who can be influenced but never quite managed, whose passions are their own, who will eat only the cookies from their school lunch no matter what else you pack them. It's confounding and magical. The Vatican investigator, Euclide, might be the character who surprised me the most. He entered the novel with an almost malevolent *whoosh* but soon charmed me as much as he was charming the rest of the cast. Put another way: writing a novel is essentially performing improv routines with imaginary friends.

Q. What writers, fiction and/or nonfiction, do you find yourself returning to? Which inspire you?

A. The ghost of Walker Percy probably hovers somewhere over this novel. I consider rereading Katherine Anne Porter akin to popping vitamin supplements. Every time I reread Thomas McGuane I'm reminded that reading should be line-by-line pleasure, and that the difference between tragedy and comedy can often hinge on nothing more than an adjective. Same goes for rereading Updike and Nabokov, though on a more aesthetic level, like watching a classical guitarist's fingers. There's almost always a Faulkner book on the bedside table, some of them half-memorized by this point. I reread *Anna Karenina* every couple years, when I have too much breath and need it taken away.

Q. In the novel, the character Janice has a fundamental disagreement with her father over the tensions between storytelling and science. What's your opinion about their debate?

A. I was a mere fly on the wall for that debate. But as a novelist I can't help but adore the Muriel Rukeyser line that Janice's father quotes: "The universe is made of stories, not of atoms."

"How I Got This Story"
by Jonathan Miles

Novelists lie for a living—what is a novel, after all, but an assembly of fibs paradoxically meant to illustrate something true?—but generally see a distinction between lying on the page and lying off it. If Winston Lorimar, the once-celebrated author of *Lieutenant Lucius & the Tristate Crematory Band*, is aware of this distinction, he doesn't show it, which makes Lorimar either the purest novelist alive—a 24/7 fount of fiction, his life and his work indivisibly fused—or, as some in his homctown of Greenwood, Mississippi, would have it, just a lying sumbitch. The truth, as ever, probably lies somewhere in bctween.

Lorimar is sixty-nine, and forty years removed from the publication of his one and only book, but to know Lorimar—as I have since 1995—is to experience, woozily, the fictive limbo at the heart of any novel. I was twenty-four when I met him, assigned to write a profile for a Southern literary magazine in which I deemed him a "trippier version of Harper Lee": a one-book *wunderkind* gone silent ever since.

(The comparison seemed fair at the time, but, alas, *Lieutenant Lucius* has weathered poorly over the years, dropping out of print eight years ago.) I didn't realize what I was up against until the magazine's fact-checker vetted Lorimar's quoted stories, slicing my article's word count by more than half. He'd lied to me, effusively, but for some reason I never took offense. As alternate universes go, his was enjoyable—its colors a bit brighter, its moral architecture a little sturdier.

It's not quite sufficient to call him the unreliable narrator of his own existence, as a mutual friend once did; we are all of us, every one, unreliable narrators of our existences. The angle we give the bathroom mirror is always meant to flatter. No, Lorimar views his life as a story in progress, as one long and ever-malleable narrative, and as the author of that story he engages in a revising process so constant and fine-grained that it might well be pathological. Here's how I described his dissembling in my most recent book, *Anatomy of a Miracle: The True* Story of a Paralyzed Veteran, a Mississippi Convenience Store, a Vatican Investigation, and the Spectacular Perils of Grace*, in which he makes a cameo appearance:

> The sign at the entrance to the family home reads LORIMAR PLANTATION, CIRCA 1848, which is about as bald as a lie can be shaved: Donovan Lorimar, Winston's grandfather, arrived in the Delta from Ireland in 1907 to work on the railroad, and the farm itself dates back only to the Great Depression. (A clue to Lorimar's career withdrawal might lurk inside a comment

he once made to a friend in Greenwood: "As an Irishman and a Southerner, I ravenously suckle defeat.") The farm's history, much like his daily life appears to be, is an act of imagination. After writing a novel, he began living one. His fictions can be small ("If you see him at the diner," says one local, "he'll tell you how fine the chicken that he just ate was, with a big steak bone sitting right there on the plate") or large (to get out of a dinner engagement, he once left a friend a voicemail saying he'd been stabbed in the neck by an intruder).

This is not meant to expose or indict Lorimar, whom I've long admired and have come to consider a friend. He owns up to his fictive impulses, albeit evasively, and with a wink, by saying, "He who dies with the best stories wins." This is rather to contextualize my reaction when Lorimar told me, in September 2014, that one of his daughter's paralyzed patients—his daughter Janice is a VA physician on the Mississippi Gulf Coast—had spontaneously and inexplicably risen from his wheelchair outside a Biloxi convenience store. (That reaction, unspoken, was all of one word: *bullshit*.)

I was passing through Greenwood on a month-long magazine assignment chronicling the 1,500-mile record tour-by-bicycle of a Minnesota singer/songwriter named Ben Weaver. (My account of that tour, if you're interested, is at www.bicycling.com.) Lorimar had always known me as an unrepentant smoker and more general body-wrecker, like himself, so he assessed this new smoke-free iteration of me, straddling a bicycle on which I'd already clocked a thousand miles, with acid bemusement. (But not disapproval; Lorimar, after all, can begrudge no one his or her revisions in life.) As our host for the evening, before we continued our pedal-push toward New Orleans, Lorimar laid out a buffet of fried food and whiskey and was soon regaling us with stories that Weaver, of course, had no cause to disbelieve. I did not have the heart to later correct Lorimar's assertion that his late wife, Jacqueline, had been crowned Miss America, which caused Weaver's eyes to pop a little. In Lorimar's view, she'd been so beautiful that she should've or could've been crowned Miss America, or at least, in the pageant of his mind, actually *was* Miss America—to him, if not to the world. As Ken Kesey once wrote: "It's the truth even if it didn't happen."

The night's offhand story of the miraculous patient, then, seemed just another Lorimarism: a spectacle from his imagination, told with sufficient zest and detail to be convincingly entertaining if not entirely convincing. (Having years ago met his daughter Janice, who is her father's antithesis in almost every way, I knew how she'd cringe at playing a starring role in one of her father's fabulisms.) The conversation moved on and went careening late into the night. One does not retire early with Winston Lorimar, nor does one wish to—not even when facing a ninety-mile ride the next morning, in the rain, through a stretch of country where cyclists are so few that dogs feel a mighty urge to try to taste them.

It would be better, I suppose, to say the story of

the unparalyzed man started haunting or at least itching me. But it didn't. As anyone who's done a long-distance cycling trip will attest, your mind goes mostly blank; it often feels like just a switch for turning on and off your legs. Eventually we made it to New Orleans, where Weaver played the tour's last gig and where we scarfed down an obscene number of oysters at Felix's and where, having slept the last thirty nights on couches and at Catholic worker farms plus the occasional roadside motel, I let the magazine splurge for a swanky downtown hotel room for us. You know what feels good after a 1,500-mile bike ride? (No, not a cigarette, though I briefly considered it.) Spending an afternoon lying on a baroquely fluffy bed flipping through TV channels. It feels like majesty. For most of those thirty days on the road I'd been devoid of news—that ticker of headlines and breaking reports that underlies most of my desk days—so I pleasurably started catching up.

And then I saw it. Or rather *her*—Janice Lorimar!—on a brief segment on the local news. Channel 4, I believe, WWL. I bolted upright from my wallow of luxe throw pillows, the remote frozen in my hand. There she was, fleetingly refraining from comment, in a segment about a paralyzed Biloxi man who'd, yes, somehow walked right out of his wheelchair after four years. (Winston Lorimar said five years, but that, astonishingly, was his sole inaccuracy.) The man himself—Cameron Harris— was interviewed, too, and seemed genuinely thunderstruck, his wide eyes looking like they'd failed to blink since his rise. Appearing also was his older sister, who'd witnessed his out-of-nowhere rising and who happened to be wearing on television, I couldn't help noticing, a T-shirt reading COWBOY BUTTS DRIVE ME NUTS.

"So was this a true miracle?" I remember the reporter concluding, as she threw back to the anchor desk. "That answer to that question, Leslie, might depend on what your definition of a miracle might be, and just what makes it true." My forehead knotted. Here was a television reporter pondering the truth of a story that just days ago I'd casually dismissed, because of the source, as untrue. It was a turducken of truthiness.

Naturally I called Lorimar. "You didn't tell me that story was *true*," I said, all but scolding him.

"Everything's true," he replied, in that breezy way of his, by which he might've meant the details of the story or his daily verbal output or even the holes in the epistemological fabric of human consciousness. With Lorimar, it's anyone's guess. "You should cut out that damn exercise and call Janice, write it up."

Which I did. Was I skeptical? Deeply. Here was an unfathomable, biblical-level event in which Winston Lorimar's DNA played a role. I recalled my shrinking shame from almost twenty years before, as the fact-checker read me the inventory of Lorimar's embellishments and outright fabrications. But Janice was skeptical, too—not of what'd happened to Cameron Harris, but how and why it'd happened—and this, coupled with her probing scientific approach (she really is her father's obverse), felt reassuring. I ditched the bicycle and rented a car for the hour and a half trip to Biloxi.

I ended up staying six months, feverishly working to separate the true from the untrue, the possible from the impossible, the fact from the fiction. There were twists, there were secrets, and in time there came a reality-television crew, an investigator from Rome paralleling my own investigation, a dying drifter shouldering a huge inflatable cross, a bizarre court case arising from a barroom brawl that was itself an extension of a terrible teenage cruelty, and hiding in plain sight one of the more beautiful love stories I've ever encountered.

At some point, dizzied by the circus atmosphere hanging over what was seeming more and more to me to be a mystery with profound, even shattering implications, and feeling thwarted by the metaphysical knot at the mystery's center, I called up Winston Lorimar. In the course of my late-night bellyaching, I fell to citing Lord Byron's overused-to-death maxim about truth being stranger than fiction.

"Well of course it is" came Lorimar's reply. "See now, fiction has to make sense. That's why we cling to it. It cooks existence into something digestible. But truth—you start gnawing on that and your damn teeth'll break. Because all truth has to be is true."

Originally published on Powells.com on March 21, 2018.
http://www.powells.com/post/original-essays/
how-i-got-this-story